I0629472

Powders To BandAids

The Guardian of Bird Island, Volume 3

Wallace Berry

Published by Wallace Berry, 2024.

This is a work of fiction. Similarities to real people, places, or events are entirely coincidental.

POWDERS TO BANDAIDS

First edition. August 12, 2024.

Copyright © 2024 Wallace Berry.

ISBN: 979-8990123663

Written by Wallace Berry.

Table of Contents

Prologue

As Wally, Elena, and Robert stand united on Bird Island, their eyes scan the thriving living fortress around them, and a sense of awe fills the air. Their extraordinary journey has led them to this moment, where innovation, courage, and an unyielding pursuit of knowledge converge—a tale birthed from a simple yet revolutionary discovery hidden deep within the island's unique ecosystem.

In the beginning, Wally Eastwood, a brilliant young scientist, stumbled upon a groundbreaking find: microorganisms with unparalleled potential, capable of enhancing human abilities in ways never before imagined. Accompanied by his childhood friends, Pug and Richie, Wally embarked on a quest to unravel the secrets of these microscopic wonders that lurked within the island's soil.

Their adventures unfurled into the pages of their first tale, titled "Powders to Microorganisms," where the trio faced challenges that tested their resolve and deepened their friendship. This pursuit of knowledge set the stage for their next adventure in "Powders to FlexiCommander," during which Wally's ingenuity gave birth to the revolutionary FlexiCommander Suit. This cutting-edge armor, powered by the island's microorganisms, became a symbol of their commitment to harnessing innovation for the greater good.

Now, as the saga continues into "Powders to BandAids," the seeds of discovery sown in the island's fertile ground have blossomed into a medical revolution. The microorganisms, once offering enhanced cognitive abilities, are now being adapted to heal the wounded, to mend what was broken, and to restore hope to those who have lost it.

A new chapter beckons: "Powders to ShadowGhost," will take their journey to new depths with the development of the ShadowGhost—a state-of-the-art submarine crafted to protect Bird Island and its invaluable resources. Side by side, Wally and Dr. Elena Sanchez bring their combined brilliance and unwavering dedication to the forefront, fostering both a partnership in science and a profound bond in life. Together with Robert, the enigmatic hermit whose wisdom has illuminated their path, they are transforming Bird Island into a bastion of knowledge—a testament to the power of human ingenuity intertwined with nature.

Yet, even as they stand on the precipice of this new era, a shadow looms over their triumphs. The origins of the powders and microorganisms still shroud themselves in mystery—a puzzle yearning to be solved. And as dark forces seek to exploit the island's treasures for their own gain, Wally, Elena, and Robert know their roles as guardians have only just begun.

Armed with their unbreakable bond, groundbreaking inventions, and an unwavering commitment to both science and nature, they are prepared to face whatever challenges may arise. Together, they stand as pioneers at nature's frontier, ready to embark on yet another thrilling adventure.

Chapter 1

Securing his seaplane, he glanced over his shoulder at the low-lying shape of Bird Island, blurred in the late afternoon humidity. Pelicans circled lazily overhead as Wally gathered his pack and supplies, mind already racing ahead to the task at hand in his hidden island laboratory.

The winding trail through stands of cordgrass and live oak soon opened up, revealing the inconspicuous concrete mound marking one of the island's World War II bunkers. Wally pulled aside a tangle of vines, exposing a rusted iron hatch, bunker entrance E3. The heavy door creaked open, stale air rushing out to greet him. Descending the steps, Wally made his way through the dark passageways from memory alone, having traversed the same path countless times before.

At last, he reached the cleverly disguised entrance to his lab. With a sequence of coded knocks, the false wall released and swung inward. Stepping inside, Wally set his bag on the workbench among an orderly array of glassware, notebooks, and scientific equipment. Here, in the quiet isolation of this abandoned bunker, Wally pursued his research undisturbed.

Opening his bag, Wally carefully removed a rack of test tubes, each one containing a faintly glowing, engineered microorganism sample suspended in nutrient broth. Over the past weeks, he had meticulously cultured and combined genetic material from the original microbes discovered on Bird Island, searching for the perfect sequence to heal his friend Ronnie's wounded leg.

Wally recorded the sample details in his notebook, then carried the rack over to a large aquarium tank. Inside, a redfish with a ragged dorsal fin drifted listlessly, wounded by a boat propeller. Wally administered one of the experimental microbes into the tank's intake valve, watching as the solution diffused through the water. Now it was time to observe, record, and wait.

Working late into the night, Wally monitored the redfish, tracking its response to the microbe's regenerative effects. The results were incremental, but promising. Before retiring to the simple cot in the corner, Wally injected samples from the newest batch of cultures into sterile vials for transport back to his home laboratory. There, further trials on cell cultures could commence in tandem with the redfish observations.

Wally awoke before dawn, eager to collect more data before returning home. As the first light filtered in through the bunker's slit-like windows, he noted accelerated healing in the redfish's torn flesh. The microbe was clearly interacting with the fish's cells, stimulating tissue regeneration beyond anything Wally had previously observed. He would have to parse the sample's genetic sequence to isolate the specific peptides responsible when he returned to his fully equipped lab.

Packing up the remaining test tubes, notebooks, and monitoring equipment, Wally ensured the hidden door to his bunker lab was securely fastened. He navigated the dim passages with swift familiarity, hatching a plan to synthesize a derivative of the lead microbe compound back home. If he could decode the mechanisms of tissue regeneration at the genetic level, the applications for Ronnie and others were boundless.

Wally blinked against the dawn light as he emerged from the bunker's shadowy depths. The new day held promise; he was certain this microbe would prove more successful than any before it. The data thus far indicated curative properties beyond even Wally's optimistic hypotheses. As Seawings lifted off from the glassy bay surface, Wally took one last look at Bird Island's receding outline. Somewhere within its tangled interior, a tiny microorganism held the key to healing wounds both old and new. Wally just needed to tease out its secrets. With a mix of focus, intellect, and luck, he would unravel this mystery as he had done many times before, guided as always by the island's enduring mysteries.

WITH THE HIGH HEAT and humidity, Seawings felt heavy as Wally lifted off of the water. The young pilot could feel the density in the air as he guided the amphibious aircraft into the late afternoon sky, the Rotax engine whining against the thick coastal air.

Wally leveled out at 500 feet, skimming above the shimmering waters of East Matagorda Bay as he set course for home. The aviator's t-shirt clung to his back, damp with sweat from the subtropical heat. He glanced down at the small cooler secured in the passenger seat, contemplating the precious cargo within. The experimental microbes, their regenerative potential now proven through the rapid healing of the wounded redfish, represented a vital key to unlocking a cure for his friend Ronnie's disability.

Wally thought back to his time spent in the hidden laboratory on Bird Island. Hours of trial and error, analyzing genetic sequences under the microscope, all driven by his fierce determination to find an elusive treatment for the lingering effects of Ronnie's leg injury. For the first time, Wally felt hopeful that the solution was finally within reach.

90 minutes later he was approaching his local hometown airport, he was almost back home. The sun hovered just above the horizon as Seawings descended towards the small airfield. Wally expertly flared

the aircraft, touching down smoothly on the runway. He taxied toward the row of hangars, easing the seaplane into its space.

Wally carefully placed the cooler containing the microbe samples into his SUV, securing it on the passenger seat for the drive back to his house on the outskirts of town.

He pulled into the driveway of his modest single-story home just as dusk settled across the landscape. Grabbing the cooler, he made his way to the small shed behind the house which served as his personal laboratory. This is where Wally would analyze the microbes to decode their genetic sequence.

Stepping into the cramped space illuminated by a single overhead bulb, Wally set the cooler on the workbench alongside an array of glass beakers, vials, and microscopes. He gingerly removed one of the petri dishes containing the experimental microbes, marveling at the tiny organisms with such immense healing potential.

Wally prepared a slide and placed it under his most powerful microscope. Peering through the eyepiece, he could see the microbes clearly - their tiny flagella still propelling them through the viscous solution. Now it was time to sequence their DNA and unravel the genetic code responsible for their incredible restorative properties.

He begin to work, extracting a sample of the microbes' DNA, his mind wandered back to Ronnie Ray Polk, the retired marine and family friend who had sacrificed so much serving his country. The gruff farmer-turned-soldier had lost some mobility in his leg during combat, but never lost his fighting spirit. Wally was determined to find a way to help restore Ronnie's strength and independence.

If he could decode the microbe's DNA, he might just discover the secret to regenerating muscle and nerve tissue. But it would be a painstaking process requiring weeks of scrupulous examination and testing. Wally gazed at the microbes through the microscope and smiled. The answers were there in front of him, he just had to put the pieces together. For Ronnie's sake, he would solve this confounding genetic puzzle - no matter how long it took.

Wally worked late into the night, absorbed in the complex challenge. As he worked he remembered back to when he, Pug, and Richie were exploring Bird Island and along the shoreline at the high tide mark, found a half-buried chest. Inside, it houses Dr. Sinclair's personal journals filled with detailed observations, complex diagrams, and notations on esoteric wartime projects. It is within these pages that references to vials of curious microorganisms are found—specialized strains with potent and unconventional effects that challenge the boundaries of biology and genetics. Wally realizing the dangers of this discovery has keep it hidden, unknow to Pug and Richie to this day. It is from this discovery that Wally can exhibit superhuman abilities and has become the Guardian of Bird Island.

WALLY LEANED BACK IN his desk chair, rubbing his temples as he pondered the implications of his recent experiments with the regenerative microbes. The original DNX-109 compound had exhibited remarkable healing effects when tested on his friend Jimmy's nerve damage. However, it did not seem to have the same efficacy when administered to the injured redfish in his hidden island laboratory.

His modified version, on the other hand, had clearly accelerated the fish's recovery, mending its damaged fins and scales at an astonishing rate. This divergence suggested the modified DNX-109 was somehow better suited to aquatic, cold-blooded organisms. But would it retain its potency in warm-blooded creatures like humans and birds?

Wally thought back to an incident a few weeks prior when he had discovered an injured seagull with a badly broken wing near his seaside cottage. Feeling empathy for the struggling bird, he had carefully splinted its wing and then decided to test the modified microbes. To his amazement, the seagull's fractured bones had knitted back together within days, allowing it to take flight again much sooner than expected.

That result seemed promising, implying the tweaked microorganism could facilitate rapid healing in both fish and avian species. Perhaps his modifications had broadened its therapeutic range beyond just humans. If true, this could have profound implications for veterinary medicine.

But before getting ahead of himself, Wally knew he needed to validate the microbe's effects across a range of warm-blooded animals. He contemplated testing it on some of the rodents housed in the small animal facility connected to his home laboratory. Mice would make ideal test subjects due to their genetic similarities to humans.

First, though, Wally needed to fully sequence the modified microorganism's DNA to identify the specific alterations responsible for its enhanced potency. Its complex genome was likely still holding some secrets that, if unlocked, could provide valuable insights into precisely how it stimulated regenerative pathways.

Wally powered up the gene sequencer and prepared a sample, eager to finally solve the genetic puzzle. As the machine began its high-speed analysis, base by base, he turned his attention to preparing cages and supplies for the upcoming rodent trials.

He started assembling everything he would need - glass aquariums with wire lids, aspen bedding, food pellets, and water bottles. His mind wandered as he worked, musing about the microbe's origins and mechanism. Where had this unusual organism come from? Some exotic thermal vent deep in the ocean? What biochemical triggers were initiating the tissue repair?

Once the sequencer had finished its read, Wally eagerly inspected the cryptic lines of code on his computer screen, looking for any subtle differences that could explain the modified microbe's enhanced effects. To his surprise, one sequence stood out immediately. The original DNX-109 contained a short transcription factor region that regulated gene expression. But in the modified version, this entire region was duplicated.

His pulse quickened as he realized the significance of this discovery. The duplicate segment must be enhancing the microbe's ability to activate regenerative pathways in its host. This accidental modification had essentially supercharged its therapeutic potential!

WALLY WINCED AS THE sharp tip of the protruding wood screw sliced across the back of his hand, leaving a two-inch laceration in its wake. Blood began to well up from the wound almost immediately.

"Damn it," Wally muttered, quickly grabbing a rag to apply pressure to the cut. This was just the sort of nuisance injury he didn't need right now, not when he was in the midst of carefully packing up his infrequently used lab equipment.

As he elevated his hand and continued to apply pressure, Wally's thoughts turned to the vial of modified DNX-109 sitting on the other side of the lab. He had successfully decoded the microbe's genetic sequence and introduced a few key alterations that seemed to amplify its regenerative effects significantly. Though he had observed promising results in fish and birds, Wally had yet to test the modified microbe on any warm-blooded animals.

Perhaps this minor injury could provide the perfect opportunity for an initial trial with a mammal. The laceration wasn't serious, but it would take a week or two to fully mend on its own. With the help of the genetically enhanced microbe, the healing process could potentially be accelerated to just a day or two.

Wally wavered, uncertain whether he should risk being the first guinea pig for an untested microorganism modification. But his scientific curiosity eventually won out. This could be a major breakthrough, and the wound was superficial enough that any potential side effects were unlikely to be dangerous.

Decision made, Wally grabbed the vial of modified DNX-109 and a sterile syringe. With the rag still pressed to his hand, he awkwardly drew a small sample of the chartreuse liquid into the syringe. Going over to the sink, he rinsed the cut until it was clean and the bleeding had mostly stopped. Then, wincing slightly, he injected the microbe directly into the wound site.

He bandaged his hand securely and then went about his day, trying not to obsess over the altered genetics now coursing through his body. That evening before bed, he carefully unwrapped the bandage to examine the wound. To his astonishment, the once angry, two-inch laceration now appeared to be a mildly irritated scratch less than half an inch long. The microbe was clearly accelerating healing just as intended.

Over the next 36 hours, Wally monitored the cut closely. Each time he checked, it looked significantly better than before. By the morning of the third day post-injection, the wound was completely sealed with fresh pink skin—healed perfectly without even the slightest scar.

Elated, Wally immediately started planning the next phase of trials with the modified microbe. Clearly it was safe and effective in mammals like himself. The logical next step would be testing it on his friend Ronnie's slow-to-heal leg wound. But Wally knew he would need proper dosage guidance and monitoring protocols in place first.

He decided to order some lab rats to determine ideal dosage ranges. But he also realized that the microbe's effects could vary in different mammalian species. To get data from an animal closer to humans, he would try to locate a rescue dog or cat that happened to have a superficial wound or injury. A shelter vet could assist with oversight and documentation of the microbe's impact.

Wally's mind raced with ideas as he prepared for these pivotal trials. The potential to help Ronnie walk again kept him determined and focused. The modified DNX-109 could very well lead to a revolutionary treatment for all manner of injuries and chronic wounds. But Wally also remained cognizant of the need for rigorous testing - he would not rush this to humans prematurely.

After cleaning the lab and safely securing all his supplies and equipment, Wally decided to unwind with a celebratory flight over the marshlands in his seaplane. As he soared over the island where this research had all started, he gazed down at the vibrant green landscape below. He said a silent thank you to that special place and made a mental vow to return soon. Wally knew there were more secrets still to uncover out there, more microbes waiting to be found. But today, he just felt grateful for the progress made and hopeful for Ronnie's future. Banking the plane gently northeast, Wally turned towards home.

AS WALLY WALKED BACK into his home, he wondered if DNX-190 would still work as an infused cookie and not injected, all of the others he tried did, so would the modified one work. Wally began to set up a jar of dough infused with DNX-190 following the grow instructions. If it activates then there is hope, he will know in a few days if the dough is alive and growing.

Stepping into his modest kitchen, Wally set his satchel containing the vials of DNX-190 and his lab notes on the counter. He opened the refrigerator and gathered eggs, butter, flour, and the other necessary ingredients to make a basic sugar cookie dough.

While mixing the dough, Wally's mind wandered back to the first time he had attempted to culture one of the microbes in food. It had started with a simple loaf of bread, inoculated with a pinch of microbe VAM-345. To his surprise, the bread had risen just as normal yeast would cause it to. More unexpected was when he took a bite and suddenly demonstrated enhanced hearing abilities.

That serendipitous discovery had opened up a new avenue of experimentation for Wally, finding that many of the microbes could indeed be cultured in food and retain their unique effects. He hypothesized that the microorganisms were able to influence the digestive system and bloodstream when consumed, much like a medication or supplement.

Now he hoped to replicate that success with the modified DNX-190. He carefully measured out a portion of the grayish powder containing the dormant microbes and kneaded it thoroughly into the cookie dough. If the microbes were viable, they would feed on the flour and sugars, multiplying and producing metabolic byproducts that caused the dough to rise, just as standard yeasts did.

Wally lightly oiled a glass jar and spooned the inoculated dough inside. After fastening a loose metal lid, he placed the jar on a shelf in the corner of the kitchen, where the ambient warmth from the oven should create an ideal activation environment.

"If this works, it could make dosing so much easier," Wally muttered to himself. Rather than needing to isolate the microbes and prepare injections, he could simply bake them into treats. It would be far more practical for frequent applications, and the effects seemed less jarring when consumed with food rather than injected.

Over the next 48 hours, Wally periodically checked on the dough's progress. On the second day, he noticed the first promising signs - a few small bubbles dotting the surface of the dough. By the third day, the bubbles had multiplied and the dough had expanded by nearly 25%, pressing lightly against the glass sides of the jar.

"Jackpot," Wally said with a grin. The microbes were active and metabolizing the dough. Now it was time to test if their unique properties had survived the culturing process.

Donning a kitchen apron, Wally got to work baking a test batch of cookies, using a scoop to form small mounds on a sheet pan. The aroma of fresh baked goods soon filled his kitchen. Once cooled, he selected one of the cookies and took a small nibble. Nothing seemed out of the ordinary at first. Then about 10 minutes later, Wally noticed a strange tingling feeling along his forearm. Rolling up his sleeve, he revealed a nearly-healed scar from a laceration he had gotten while renovating part of his home. The scar looked noticeably diminished, with the tissue appearing fresh and new.

"Well how about that," Wally chuckled. It seemed the microbes were just as potent baked into cookies as when cultured and injected in the lab. This opened up an incredibly convenient dosing method, avoiding the need for injections using isolated microbe cultures. He could now test the effects on Ronnie and other mammals using simple cookies as the delivery mechanism.

Wally's jubilation was tempered with a pang of sorrow as his thoughts circled back to Ronnie. His dear friend had suffered extensive nerve damage, little to no feeling in his left leg from the thigh down, and conventional medicine provided little hope for a full recovery. Ronnie would likely never walk again unaided. But with the remarkable tissue regenerative properties of DNX-190, perhaps there was a chance. Maybe, just maybe, Ronnie could be made whole again.

After carefully packing a supply of the special cookies for travel, Wally headed out to his seaplane. Tomorrow he would pay Ronnie a visit at the FFOne plant. If these cookies worked as well in humans as they had in Wally's preliminary trials, it could change the trajectory of Ronnie's life forever. For the first time in months, Wally allowed a sense of genuine optimism to wash over him. There was hope.

WALLY SAT IN HIS OFFICE going over the latest test results on DNX-190. The data showed tremendous promise for cell regeneration in animal trials. This breakthrough microbe could be the answer to restoring feeling in Ronnie's left leg.

Glancing at the clock, Wally saw it was nearly 7 AM. Ronnie would be arriving any minute to start his shift overseeing operations at FFOne. Wally straightened the pages on his desk and walked briskly to the entrance to greet Ronnie.

Right on time, Ronnie's black pickup truck rolled into the parking lot. Wally waved as Ronnie parked in his designated spot.

"Morning Ronnie!" Wally called out as Ronnie stepped down from the truck.

"Hey Wally, beautiful day isn't it?" Ronnie replied, gazing up at the clear blue sky. A gentle breeze ruffled his closely cropped salt and pepper hair.

Wally fell in step beside Ronnie as they entered the building. Though Ronnie wore a leg brace and walked with a slight limp, he moved with purpose. Wally knew Ronnie's disability never defined him. He was as strong and determined as ever.

They made their way to Ronnie's office to go over the day's schedule. After reviewing some paperwork, Ronnie leaned back in his chair.

"You seem eager about something," Ronnie said, studying Wally over tented hands. "I can see those wheels turning in that head of yours."

Wally smiled. Ronnie could always read him like a book.

"I've been waiting for the right time to tell you..." Wally began. He went on to explain the experiments with DNX-190, its incredible effects on tissue regeneration, and his hopes it could restore feeling and mobility in Ronnie's leg.

Ronnie listened intently, his sharp green eyes fixed on Wally. When Wally finished, Ronnie stroked his chin thoughtfully.

"I won't deny it would be incredible to have my leg back to normal after all these years," he said. "But I don't want you putting yourself at risk on my behalf."

Wally shook his head. "After all you've done for me, consider this me trying to return the favor."

He told Ronnie about the modified cookies, leaving out their true origin. If Ronnie was willing, this could be a major breakthrough.

Ronnie considered for a long moment before giving a nod. "Alright, let's give it a shot. I appreciate you looking out for me."

Wally felt a swell of gratitude. He retrieved the container of cookies from his office and offered one to Ronnie along with a glass of milk. Ronnie bit into the cookie, savoring the taste.

"Not bad," he mused. "Could use a few more chocolate chips though."

They both chuckled at that. Now came the waiting game to allow the microbes time to work. Ronnie finished his cookie and milk then headed out to walk the production floor.

Wally busied himself with paperwork, periodically checking in on Ronnie's progress. Around noon, he found Ronnie inspecting one of the new filtration systems.

"How's the leg feeling?" Wally asked hopefully.

Ronnie paused, considering the question. "You know, it does feel a little different - kind of tingly below the knee. Can't say for sure though."

Wally's excitement grew. Tingling could mean the nerves were reactivating. Only time would tell if the microbes performed their magic.

At the end of the day, Wally met Ronnie by his truck. "Any more progress with the leg?"

"The tingling's definitely stronger now," Ronnie said. "Feels like my foot's fallen asleep - pins and needles."

"That's an amazing sign after just one dose!" Wally said. "Here, take a few more cookies to have over the weekend. Call me if you notice any major changes."

Ronnie accepted the cookies appreciatively. As he drove off, Wally felt a growing sense of hope. DNX-190 could truly change everything for his friend.

Over the weekend, Wally anxiously awaited Ronnie's call. By Sunday evening, he could wait no longer and phoned Ronnie himself.

"Wally! I was just about to call you," Ronnie answered excitedly. "The feeling is coming back more and more. I can move my toes now and feel pressure on my foot when I walk."

Wally was elated. "Ronnie, that's incredible!"

They agreed Ronnie would come to the lab first thing Monday morning for more thorough sensory tests. Wally eagerly anticipated the results. This was the breakthrough they had been waiting for.

Early Monday, Wally prepared the lab equipment to assess Ronnie's nerve conduction and reflexes. Hearing the door, he looked up to see Ronnie enter, a renewed spring in his step.

"I can feel the floor with each step now," Ronnie said with amazement. "Never thought I'd have that sensation again."

Wally blinked back tears of joy. "I'm so glad to see the regeneration working."

He ran Ronnie through a battery of tests, monitoring tactile responses and reflex reactions. The results astounded him - nearly full restoration of sensory function and reflexes in just a few days.

When they finished, Ronnie turned to Wally with gratitude. "I'll never be able to repay you for this miracle."

Wally waved it off. "Seeing you get your mobility back is payment enough."

There was still much research ahead, but this momentous breakthrough gave Wally hope that DNX-190 could transform countless lives. The microbe's incredible power could restore health and quality of life to people across the globe.

Wally knew his work at Bird Island would continue in secrecy, but outcomes like Ronnie's recovery made the sacrifices worthwhile. He felt honored to follow in Dr. Sinclair's footsteps, ushering in a new era of healing through nature's mysterious microworld.

WALLY AWOKE FRIDAY morning to the songs of cardinals filtering in through his open bedroom window, their melodies drifting in on the soft breeze. As he rubbed the sleep from his eyes and sat up in bed, his thoughts immediately turned to the events of the past week. The breakthrough with the regenerative DNX-190 microbes represented a monumental moment—one that he knew would reshape the course of his research and could change countless lives, including Ronnie's.

Yet as exhilarating as this discovery was, Wally also felt the weight of responsibility settling upon his shoulders. This microorganism's capabilities exceeded anything he could have imagined when he first stumbled upon it years ago on Bird Island. Its power to heal and restore was profound. But in the wrong hands, Wally realized, it could also be extremely dangerous.

If knowledge of DNX-190's regenerative properties got out, there was no telling who might try to exploit it for their own benefit. Wally thought of the government, the military, pharmaceutical companies - what wouldn't they do to harness the microbe's power? Even the world's most ethical medical researchers could be corrupted by the temptation to play God in selecting who gets access to the microbe.

Wally shook his head. No, the only way forward was to keep this strictly between himself and Ronnie. He would share the microbe's healing effects with those who truly needed it, but the actual formula could never be disclosed. The risk was simply too great.

After showering and dressing, Wally headed downstairs to his basement lab. Passing his silver Hyundai Santa Fe parked in the driveway, he made a mental note to take it in soon for an oil change. Entering the lab, he paused to look proudly at his state-of-the-art equipment—test tube racks, microscopes, a lyophilizer for freeze-drying bacterial samples. His parents had always encouraged his scientific interests, even helping him convert part of their home into a fully functional lab.

Wally's thoughts turned to his mom and dad. He realized with a pang that if knowledge of DNX-190 did get out, it could put them in danger too. Simply being associated with Wally would make them potential targets. It hurt Wally to think he might be putting his own parents at risk, but he also knew they would support his decision to pursue this, just as they always had supported his unconventional path through life.

Shaking off those worries, Wally got to work preparing slides of the DNX-190 bacteria, gazing at their microscopic forms through the lens of his microscope. He would run tests today analyzing any changes to the microbe's genetic structure after interacting with mammalian digestive systems. Meticulously labeling each slide, he documented his observations in a leather-bound journal, occasionally brushing back his light brown hair where it fell across his forehead.

After losing himself in work for several hours, Wally decided to take a break. He headed outside to where his sleek white-and-blue ICON A5 amphibious seaplane was parked on a trailer hitched to his silver pickup truck. Wally had always loved aviation and earned his pilot's license at 16. The agile seaplane was ideal for quick trips between home and his family's fishing cabin near the coast.

Giving the aircraft a pre-flight inspection, Wally made sure it was fueled up and ready to go. He would head to the coast later today - it was just the sort of distraction he needed after such an intense week of experimentation. And being back at the remote cabin where he first discovered the regenerative microbes years ago would provide ideal contemplative setting to reflect on their implications.

Wally returned inside and glanced at the clock—11:30am. Ronnie would be arriving soon. Wally had invited him over to share the results of the latest experiments. He was excited to hear about Ronnie's continued improvement after consuming the special cookies Wally had baked with the DNX-190 infusion. But he also needed to have a serious discussion about keeping all of this under wraps, at least for now. The stakes were simply too high.

Right on time, Wally heard Ronnie's old Ford pickup crunching across the driveway. He walked outside to greet his friend as Ronnie swung open the truck's creaky door and climbed out, moving stiffly but without the aid of a cane.

"Wally my boy, you wouldn't believe the change these last few days! I swear I've got more spring in my step now than I've had in years," Ronnie exclaimed, clapping a hand on Wally's shoulder.

"That's amazing news," Wally replied, unable to keep the huge grin off his face. "C'mon inside, let me get you some coffee and we'll catch up."

The two men headed into Wally's kitchen, where he poured two mugs of black coffee. Taking a seat at the table, Ronnie launched eagerly into recounting his renewed mobility and lessened nerve pain after eating Wally's special cookies earlier in the week.

Wally listened intently, continuing to feel awed by the microbes' restorative power. At the same time, an internal debate raged inside him. He wanted nothing more than to share news of this discovery with the world. But the risks were simply too catastrophic if DNX-190 fell into the wrong hands. Wally knew the only course was to keep this strictly need-to-know.

Taking a deep breath, Wally met Ronnie's expectant gaze. "Before we go any further, there's something important I need you to understand..."

SUNLIGHT DAPPLED THROUGH the kitchen window, casting warm patterns across the worn oak table where Wally and Ronnie sat, each nursing a mug of black coffee. The scent of pine and earth mingled with the rich aroma of the brew. Ronnie's presence filled the room, not just in stature but in the air of newfound vitality that surrounded him.

Wally's fingers traced the rim of his cup, eyes fixated on the liquid's dark surface. "Ronnie," he began, his voice steady despite the gravity of their conversation, "we've stumbled upon something incredible, but with it comes a weight we must both bear."

Ronnie nodded, the tingling in his leg a constant reminder of the miracle he had experienced. He set his mug down, his gaze meeting Wally's. "I know where you're headed with this," he replied, "and you're right. We're treading on thin ice here."

Wally leaned forward, his earnestness evident. "If word gets out about DNX-190... about what it can do... we'll have more than just the FDA knocking at our door. It could be anyone—corporations wanting to exploit it, governments seeking to weaponize it."

Ronnie's jaw tightened at the thought. "Not to mention every Tom, Dick, and Harry looking for a miracle cure," he added. The room grew silent but for the ticking of an old clock on the wall and the distant call of a mourning dove.

"The cookies," Wally continued, breaking the silence, "they're just the beginning. I've seen what DNX-190 can do for plants and animals. But humans? We're opening Pandora's Box."

Ronnie leaned back in his chair, rubbing his chin thoughtfully. "I reckon we need a plan," he said after a moment. "We can't just sit on this. But we've got to be smart about who we trust."

"Exactly," Wally replied with a nod. "The fewer people who know about this, the better." He paused, considering his next words carefully. "And we need to protect ourselves too—legally and physically."

Ronnie's eyes hardened with resolve. "I didn't fight through hell and back to watch something good turn sour because we weren't careful." He took a deep breath before continuing. "We'll keep this between us until we figure out our next move."

Wally felt a surge of gratitude for Ronnie's loyalty and shared sense of responsibility. They both understood that their discovery was more than scientific—it was deeply personal.

"We'll continue testing," Wally said thoughtfully. "Small scale, controlled environments only." He glanced up at Ronnie, seeking affirmation.

"Agreed," Ronnie responded firmly. "And if there's any sign of trouble... if it looks like this might get out... we destroy everything."

The two men exchanged a solemn look; their pact was sealed without another word.

A red cardinal landed on the windowsill outside, tilting its head as if eavesdropping on their heavy conversation before flitting away into the brightness of day.

Wally watched its departure before turning back to Ronnie with renewed focus. "For now, let's keep our ears to the ground and stay alert."

Ronnie nodded in agreement as they both rose from their chairs.

"We're dealing with something that could change lives or destroy them," Wally stated as he walked Ronnie to the door.

"And it's up to us to steer that course," Ronnie finished for him.

With a firm handshake that sealed their understanding, Ronnie stepped out into the fresh morning air.

Wally watched him go before turning back inside, feeling both empowered and burdened by the secret they carried.

WALLY SAT AT HIS DESK, contemplating the immense potential and peril of his recent discovery. The regenerative properties of DNX-190 held such promise, yet also danger if misused or exploited. Glancing out his window at the vibrant cardinal perched on a branch, Wally knew secrecy was paramount.

His mind turned to the remote Bird Island bunker. With its seclusion and existing security measures, it could serve as the ideal off-site location for discreet experimentation. Wally picked up his phone and called his trusted friend Ronnie Ray to discuss the idea.

"I've been thinking more about DNX-190," Wally said. "We need an ultra-secure spot for further testing."

Ronnie listened intently as Wally described the abandoned bunker on Bird Island. Its isolation and overgrown surroundings meant little risk of being observed. Ronnie agreed it was perfect for their covert research.

The two men hashed out the specifics - they would expand part of the existing bunker to house a concealed laboratory. Wally proposed bringing in their friend Richie to assist. His meticulous nature would prove useful in constructing and disguising the lab area.

Ronnie nodded approvingly. "Good call. We'll need Richie's sharp eye for detail."

Wally punches in Richie's number on the phone. "Richie, it's me, Wally. There's something we need to discuss right away, it's urgent." Richie says, "Urgent huh? No problem, I'll come over to your place within half an hour, see you soon." Richie ends the call.

The air was heavy, and the drone of cicadas in the distance seemed almost rhythmic in the stillness of their conversation. Wally's gaze was locked on the horizon, but his mind was decidedly elsewhere—on the weighty revelation he was about to unload.

"Richie," Wally began, a slight tremor detectable in his voice. "There's something I've been carrying for a long time. Something I think you need to know now."

Richie nodded, attention focused on Wally, registering the gravity of his tone.

"Remember when we found Dr. Sinclair's trunk?" Wally waited for Richie's nod. "Well, there was more to it than just old papers and maps. There were microorganisms, Richie. Potent ones with capabilities... capabilities that could change everything."

Richie's brows drew together, a look of concern etching his features. He had always known there was an undercurrent of mystery lingering around Wally but hearing it laid bare was another thing entirely.

"Wally, what are you saying?" Richie asked, his voice low and steady. "Are you in some sort of trouble?"

Wally shook his head and attempted a reassuring half-smile, which didn't quite reach his eyes. "No, not trouble as such. But danger? Perhaps. That's why I kept it to myself all these years. The fewer people who knew, the less risk of... unintended consequences."

The weight of Wally's choice to shoulder this burden alone wasn't lost on Richie. He realized the depths of their friend's protective instincts and the years of silent vigilance he must have endured.

"So, why now, Wally? Why bring this up after all this time?"

"Because I need help," Wally answered honestly. "I need you, Richie. But I need you to know the stakes before you agree to anything. This isn't going to be a regular gig. There'll be no contracts, no payroll records. What we're doing—it's off the grid. The kind of work where our handshake is the only thing holding us to each other and the project. Can you handle that?"

Richie's eyes held Wally's, the weight of their shared history and innate trust acting as the silent bond between them. It wasn't the allure of adventure that coaxed Richie's consent, nor was it the intrigue surrounding the clandestine nature of what lay ahead. It was the unspoken bond of brotherhood and the tacit assurance that, come what may, they had each other's backs.

"I'm in," Richie said simply, picturing the winding path they'd traverse with their eyes wide open to the seriousness of the journey.

Wally expelled a breath he didn't know he'd been holding, the tension in his shoulders easing at Richie's quiet affirmation. They clasped hands, their grip a testament to their resolve. They understood that this was the beginning of something fraught with as much potential as peril. But as the evening grew dim and the first stars began to peep through the slowly darkening sky, one thing was clear—whatever lay ahead, they'd face it together.

The three began work, taking a small skiff loaded with building materials across East Matagorda Bay under the cover of night. Dressed in dark clothing, they navigated the coastal waters with ease. Upon reaching Bird Island, they followed overgrown trails to the WWII-era bunker.

Inside the dank concrete structure, Wally showed Ronnie and Richie the way to the hidden passage leading to the observation deck. Halfway down the passage, they began work transforming a small alcove into an expanded, clandestine laboratory.

Richie proved indispensable. He cleverly disguised the lab's entrance behind a false wall that perfectly blended with the existing bunker architecture. His carpentry skills created concealed storage cabinets and a ventilation system employing the bunker's original materials. Wally and Ronnie handled the technical installation - electricity, plumbing, and lab equipment.

Within a week, the covert lab was complete. Wally stood back, marveling at their work. No one would suspect a state-of-the-art biotech facility lay hidden in this decrepit old bunker. It was the perfect off-grid site for advancing his microbe research.

Wally's thoughts turned to their next phase - testing DNX-190's regenerative effects on warm-blooded animals. He and Ronnie had agreed to start small, using whatever mammals they could catch around Live Oak Bayou. Wally grabbed his wildlife trapping gear and headed for the boat shed.

As his jon boat motored down the bayou, Wally reviewed the testing protocols in his mind. They would trap small rodents, carefully administer doses of DNX-190, then closely observe the effects. All findings would be documented in secrecy. He and Ronnie had sworn an oath to immediately terminate everything if any testing ever breached ethical lines.

Dropping a wire mesh trap baited with peanut butter near a tangle of brush, Wally surveyed the landscape. The bayou's isolation made it an ideal spot for their confidential tests. Still, Wally's eyes probed his surroundings, alert for any signs of surveillance. With a discovery like DNX-190, the threat of a biotech company trying to steal their research was all too real. Satisfied he was alone, Wally headed upstream to set more traps.

That night at the bunker, Wally and Ronnie donned lab coats and prepared their first trial with a brown rat specimen. They carefully measured a precise dose of DNX-190, administered it, then placed the test subject into a controlled enclosure. Methodically, they began documenting any observable effects, watching for signs of enhanced tissue regeneration.

Hours passed with no noticeable changes. Wally frowned, feeling discouraged. Then suddenly, before their eyes, the rat's injured hind leg began exhibiting rapid cellular restoration. The men watched, stunned, as the creature's wound regenerated fully in a matter of minutes. Their experiment was an astonishing success.

Over the coming weeks, their covert testing yielded similarly astounding results across multiple small mammal species. The regenerative potential of DNX-190 continued to amaze and inspire Wally. He began contemplating larger trials on animals like pigs or goats. But a voice inside gave him pause - was he moving too fast? Wally resolved to stay the course, advancing his research one step at a time with the utmost caution. There was too much at stake to let ambition outpace ethics.

For now, he and Ronnie would continue their confidential tests, remaining vigilant for any outside surveillance. Wally stared out the bunker's slit window at the moonlit bayou beyond. Somewhere in DNX-190's unique genetic code lay incredible healing properties.

Unlocking its secrets would take time, care, and above all, secrecy. Wally's path forward seemed clear, if narrow - progress slowly in obscurity. With prudence and patience, this extraordinary microbe could change everything. But such power, Wally knew, must be harnessed carefully.

WITH THE SUN SINKING into the western horizon, casting long shadows over the sprawling marshland of Bird Island, Wally guided the ICON A5 aircraft into a gentle ascent. Below them, the lush cordgrass of the island began to fade into a twilight haze, their hidden sanctuary disappearing from view. The flight back home was always bittersweet, their secluded paradise replaced by the reality of mainland life.

In the rear of the plane, Ronnie sat with a satisfied grin on his face. His fingers gingerly traced over his thigh, still marveling at the sensation that had been absent for so long. He had a renewed sense of purpose now, an inner drive reignited by the promise of DNX-190 and the incredible potential it held. Despite his age and his leg injury, he was once again on active duty - not in a battlefield overseas, but on a secret mission that could change countless lives.

Next to Ronnie, Richie found himself torn between two worlds. His adventurous spirit reveled in the excitement of their covert operations on Bird Island, yet he yearned for the familiar comfort of home and his wife's tender touch. As they soared above East Matagorda Bay, Richie couldn't help but feel a twinge of anxiety for having left her worried.

Their island bunker was secure now, thanks to Wally's technological expertise and Ronnie's military acumen. They had meticulously installed sensors on every door and trail, ensuring that if anyone dared to set foot on Bird Island without their knowledge, they would be detected in an instant. The bunker was more than just a hidden lab—it was their fortress, a stronghold protecting their precious secret.

But as they flew over Texas's sprawling landscape, another reality was waiting for them. Back in Houston, Wally's other life as a software developer demanded his attention. His company Flex-Code Software had begun to accumulate a backlog of work during their time away.

A call from Jeff, their liaison with Dr. Sanchez, had confirmed it. Another order for 500 FlexiCommander Suits had come in from the military R&D facility. Wally felt a surge of pride at the news—his creation was proving its worth. But with that pride came the daunting realization of the task that lay ahead.

Despite the rush of adrenaline at the thought of returning to work, Wally knew he needed to tread carefully. He held a secret that could revolutionize medicine, but it also carried a dangerous potential if it fell into the wrong hands. As he steered the plane towards Houston, he vowed to maintain their pact of secrecy.

Leaving Bird Island behind didn't mean abandoning their cause—it simply meant fighting their battle from another front. As they descended towards Houston, Ronnie, Richie, and Wally were not just returning home; they were gearing up for the next phase of their mission. Their secret was safe for now on Bird Island, guarded by nature's embrace and their advanced security system. It was time to tackle what awaited them back home—a world oblivious to the groundbreaking discovery nestled in an unassuming bunker on a remote island.

For Ronnie, Richie, and Wally, the flight home was not just a journey across Texas—it was a bridge between two worlds: one defined by scientific discovery and secrecy, and another marked by everyday responsibilities and relationships. And as they each prepared to step back into their regular lives, they carried with them a shared resolve to protect their groundbreaking discovery at all costs.

Wally piloted the Icon A5 low over the bay, skimming just above the glassy surface with the expertise of an avid seaplane enthusiast. The glow of the setting sun glinted off the aircraft's wings and cast elongated shadows across the rippling water. Beside him in the cockpit, Richie took in the panoramic view, marveling at the changing hues streaking the evening sky.

In the back seat, Ronnie leaned forward, gesturing at something in the distance. "Hey, look over there," he called out over the engine noise, pointing toward a flock of birds flying in formation near the shoreline.

Wally banked the seaplane gently, altering course to bypass the birds' path. "Looks like white pelicans," he commented, identifying the large-billed waterfowl. Their bright white plumage shone in the waning daylight.

The trio watched as the pelicans landed on the glassy surface, bobbing atop the water as they grouped together, their throat pouches contracting as they vocalized to each other.

"Hard to believe DNX-190 could help injured birds like those heal," Richie remarked, glancing back at the receding flock.

Wally nodded, contemplative. "It's got so much potential, but we have to be incredibly careful." He checked the instruments on the dash, mindful of their fuel levels for the flight home.

"Don't worry, our secret's safe," Ronnie assured, leaning back in his seat again. "We'll keep testing small-scale, no risks."

The seaplane droned onward, coursing above the intricate network of bays and inlets, bound for home under the darkening sky.

Chapter 2

After three days of almost non-stop research, the morning light came sooner than Wally hoped for. Maybe coffee could get him to focus.

Forging through his backpack, Wally pulled out a blue cookie and washed it down with his first cup of brew. Soon his attention span improved, it improved immensely. The regenerative properties of the modified BRV-076 microbes worked their magic, sharpening his mental clarity and allowing him to power through the complex tasks at hand.

By mid-afternoon, Wally had finished work on all of Bake-Ritez's change orders and was looking over RiverRock's notes. RiverRock wanted to update its encryption method for credit card retention, and then reload all archived records where cards were involved, providing improved protection against theft.

For this update, changing the code would take less time than rewriting all of the data. Wally dove into the challenge, his enhanced mental faculties making quick work of assessing the current encryption schema. He began drafting an improved algorithm, optimizing it for speed and security.

As evening approached, Wally had crafted an elegant new encryption method. He started running test batches, encrypting sample data with his revised technique. The results were astonishing - encryption speeds increased five-fold without compromising security. RiverRock would be thrilled.

Wally leaned back in his chair, stretching his tired limbs. He was amazed at what he had accomplished in a single day, thanks to

BRV-076. The microbes' benefits were incredible, but Wally knew he needed to be careful. With great power came great responsibility. He would move slowly, and cautiously, guided by ethics rather than ego.

Wally closed his eyes, listening to the crickets chirping outside. Despite everything, he still found peace in simple things. He was grateful for this moment, this capacity to create and help others. But he remained wary of the shadows that lurked around every great light. Wally sighed and opened his eyes. There was more work to be done.

FILLING A HEFTY CUP of coffee, Wally ambled to the patio seats beside his garden shed. What might be the greatest medical breakthrough ever could also be a catastrophic occurrence in terms of unemployment. DNX-190 harbored the potential for massive fortune, but also the chance of being regarded as the most detested individual on the planet.

Wally could not see a way around this, the effects of DNX-190 would be far-reaching with huge unintended consequences.

Sitting down on the worn wooden bench, Wally took a long sip of the steaming coffee. The warm liquid helped ground him amidst the swirling thoughts in his mind. He stared out across the backyard, taking in the dim moon light filtering through the old pecan trees.

This breakthrough was supposed to be a good thing. Wally had started his work on regenerative microbes with the sole intention of helping his friend Ronnie regain mobility after his devastating injury. And they had succeeded beyond his wildest dreams - the microbes had restored nearly full function to Ronnie's leg in a matter of days. It was incredible. Miraculous even. But therein lay the problem.

Wally took another sip of coffee, leaning forward with his elbows on his knees. If DNX-190 could truly heal any injury or ailment with such astonishing speed and efficacy, it would upend the entire healthcare industry. Everything from pharmaceuticals to hospitals to medical device manufacturers would become obsolete almost overnight. Millions of jobs would vanish. Stock markets would crash as investors frantically dumped healthcare stocks. Chaos would ensue.

And that was just the beginning. If people no longer feared debilitating injuries or illnesses, extreme sports would explode in popularity. Warfare would become even more horrific as soldiers were repeatedly healed from gruesome wounds and sent back into battle. And what of the implications for life expectancy? Humanity was nowhere near equipped to deal with a potential tripling or quadrupling of the average lifespan. Resources would be strained to the breaking point.

Wally furrowed his brow, staring blankly into his now tepid coffee. He had created a miracle that could easily become a curse upon the world. Part of him wished he could just destroy all traces of DNX-190 and forget this had ever happened. But he knew that was impossible. Too many others were now involved. And if he didn't continue to refine DNX-190, someone else eventually would. That genie could not be put back in the bottle.

No, ceasing his research was not the answer. But extreme caution was warranted. Wally resolved to limit testing to small mammals for now. And all samples and research would remain under his strict control, shared only with Ronnie and Richie under a blood pact of secrecy. They would take things slowly, methodically, watching for any dangerous repercussions of wider DNX-190 use.

Wally stood up from the bench, joints creaking. He stretched his lanky frame before gathering up his empty coffee cup. His path forward was clear, if not easy. Tread with great care. Do no harm. Remain vigilant for signs of calamity. He would become the Guardian of DNX-190, protecting the world from his own discovery if needed. Wally felt the weight of this monumental responsibility settle upon his shoulders as he turned and headed back inside, ready to call it a day.

AS WALLY SIPPED HIS coffee, his thoughts turned to the countless lives that could be transformed by his creation. Soldiers returning home from war with devastating injuries, children suffering from rare genetic diseases, burn victims bearing emotional and physical scars - what if DNX-190 could restore their health and hope? The possibilities seemed endless.

Yet Wally knew such power could also be dangerously misused. Rogue governments weaponizing DNX-190, terrorists manipulating cells to create new bioweapons, even well-intentioned doctors accidentally causing cellular mutations with unpredictable effects. Hard lessons from history warned that any scientific breakthrough held equal capacity for good or evil.

Wally realized this discovery needed guidance from an ethical mind and expert oversight. Someone intimately familiar with battlefield trauma who could advise how DNX-190 might first be applied to help, not harm.

By mid-morning, Wally had an idea. He needed some key questions answered, like: What are the most common combat injuries? Which battlefield wounds are the most difficult to treat? What types of lasting damage weigh most heavily on returning soldiers?

Wally knew the perfect person to consult - his old friend Dr. Elena Sanchez, the distinguished military research scientist. During his Navy SEAL days, she had valued his on-the-ground insights while developing new protective equipment. He trusted both her knowledge and integrity.

Wally located the number for Dr. Sanchez's laboratory. After a brief exchange with her assistant, he had the doctor herself on the line.

"Elena, it's Wally. Got a minute? I know it's been a while, but I could really use your expertise for a sensitive project I'm working on. Any chance we could meet up sometime soon? Say over lunch, my treat?"

WALLY SAT ACROSS FROM Dr. Elena Sanchez in a quiet booth at the back of the Ausair Sandwich shop. The popular airport restaurant was conveniently located at the Austin Executive Airport, not far from Elena's military research facility. Though it was mid-afternoon, the lunch rush had passed, leaving only a few patrons scattered among the tables. This afforded Wally and Elena the privacy they needed for their clandestine meeting.

"So tell me more about your friend's injury," Elena said, her voice low as she leaned forward.

Wally stirred sweetener into his iced tea, choosing his words carefully. "Well, it was a bad fall that caused some spinal damage. Lost feeling and mobility below the waist."

Elena's expression was sympathetic. "I'm very sorry. That must be devastating for someone so young. I imagine he's been through multiple surgeries and therapies?"

"Some, but nothing has helped so far. It's been about two years now." Wally kept his tone even.

"And you mentioned a potential treatment that could restore neurological function?" Elena raised an eyebrow.

Wally nodded. "I've been researching certain...substances. Their effects are unlike anything I've seen before."

He went on to give a vague overview of DNX-190, being intentionally obscure about its origins. Elena listened intently, asking pointed questions. It was clear her scientific curiosity was piqued, even as her expression remained neutral.

"This all sounds highly unusual, I must say. And you've seen tangible results so far?"

"Yes, in both animals and my friend. His sensory abilities started returning within days."

Elena sat back, eyebrows knitted in thought. "Well, I can understand you not wanting to provide specifics. But the regeneration of that magnitude...it warrants further exploration. What is it you need from me?"

Wally lowered his voice further. "Guidance. These substances are powerful. I want to help people, but I'm aware of how easily things could spiral out of control." He held Elena's gaze. "You understand the realities of these situations better than anyone. So I'd value your perspective on how to proceed in an ethical, controlled manner."

Elena nodded slowly, seeing the weight on Wally's shoulders. She chose her next words carefully. "Well, you're right to be cautious. Situations like these require the utmost discretion." She paused. "If the results are legitimate, I may be able to conduct small-scale trials through discreet channels. But we're talking years of careful testing before even considering wide release."

Wally nodded along, relieved to hear her prudent approach.

"You also must consider security," Elena continued. "Limit the substance's availability to prevent misuse. And have measures in place to destroy it if necessary." Her tone was grave.

"I understand completely," Wally said. "I want to make sure this helps people, not harms them."

"Of course. You seem to have a good head on your shoulders." Elena gave an encouraging smile. "Why don't you tell me more details, and we'll take the next steps..."

Over the next hour, Wally opened up about his experiments, with Elena asking thoughtful questions and providing sage advice. By the end, he felt assured that he had an ethical partner who shared his caution and conscience. They left the restaurant with a plan to reconvene at Elena's facility, eager to carefully explore the incredible potential sitting before them. But both carried the weight of guardians entrusted with a discovery that could alter the course of human health - for good or ill.

WALLY LEANED BACK IN his desk chair, reflecting on the conversation he'd had with Dr. Elena Sanchez yesterday. Her insights into combat injuries were enlightening, yet also sobering. Wally's mind turned over her answers to his questions, imagining the suffering endured by soldiers and realizing the gravity of this undertaking.

The most common injury sustained by returning combat troops was traumatic brain injury, Elena had explained. The percussive waves from explosions exacted a devastating toll, often leaving veterans with lifelong cognitive and psychological challenges. Wally pondered the complexity of the human brain, appreciating how even the remarkable regenerative properties of DNX-190 could only go so far in repairing such intricate damage.

Elena was unequivocal that spinal cord injuries remained impossible to fully cure. The intricate network of neurons in the spinal cord, once severed, could not be restored with even the most advanced medical technology and regenerative therapies. Wally grasped the permanence of paralysis for many wounded veterans and was humbled by the limits of his discovery in the face of such catastrophic harm.

Burn injuries emerged as the most financially burdensome wound to treat, particularly severe third-degree burns. The extensive care and skin grafts required put treatment costs into the millions for a single patient. Wally considered the toll taken not just on the veterans themselves, but also on the healthcare system struggling to provide such intricate long-term care. It gave him pause as he contemplated the wide-ranging impacts of wartime injuries.

Yet burns seemed an area where DNX-190 could make a major difference. By accelerating skin regeneration, Wally thought his microbes might reduce dependence on painful skin grafts and save enormous healthcare expenditures. But he also knew that radical new treatments often faced resistance. The complex web of implications left him pensive.

Elena had underscored how multi-organ trauma from IED blasts created some of the most devastating wounds. The intense pressure changes ruptured delicate internal structures like the lungs, liver, and intestines. Survival was a precarious emergency surgery marathon just to stabilize the veteran. Wally imagined the despair of families sitting in waiting rooms, the fate of their loved one uncertain. He thought of Ronnie and his own friends, reminded of the very human toll.

A troubling category Elena had highlighted was combat stress and PTSD. The emotional wounds might not be visible, but they extracted their own lingering toll on veterans' lives. Wally pondered the inner turmoil boiling beneath the surface for those haunted by trauma, and the struggles faced in trying to return to civilian life. He wished he could heal the nightmares, anxiety, and depression as readily as physical injury.

The most heart-wrenching were amputations, usually from IED blasts. Elena explained how the damage was often so severe that saving the patient's life required immediate field amputations. Wally envisioned the stumps and prosthetics, considering the sacrifices made by those who survived. He thought of children who would ask about their parent's missing limb, casualties of a faraway war. It made him reflect on how easily he had taken his own body for granted.

Elena emphasized how most injuries were polymorbid, with multiple interconnected traumas complicating treatment and recovery. Wally grasped the medical complexity of combat wounds, humbled by how much care and rehabilitation was needed to enable veterans to regain functioning in their daily lives. It required a major effort from medical teams, families, communities and the veterans themselves.

In closing, Elena had underscored that any innovation in treating combat injuries had to keep the whole patient in mind. Beyond physical recovery, their mental health, self-identity and social integration mattered enormously. Wally took this to heart, realizing any solution had to account for the human being behind the injury.

As Wally emerged from his reflections, the weight of responsibility rested heavily on his shoulders. DNX-190's regenerative capacity seemed almost miraculous. But healing trauma, whether physical or emotional, was never straightforward. Wally would need to proceed with the utmost care, beginning with small trials under Elena's guidance. Their work demanded patience and diligence.

Swiveling his chair to face the window, Wally watched a cardinal land gracefully on a branch outside. Its song provided a sense of hope, reminding him that even humble actions could make a difference. He was grateful that Elena would help steer his efforts in an ethical direction. With her partnership, and wisdom greater than his own, perhaps DNX-190 could change lives for the better. There were no easy answers, but Wally felt committed to trying.

The cardinal took flight once more, its crimson form bright against the sky. Wally tracked it until it disappeared into the distance. Wherever this endeavor led, he knew he wouldn't face it alone.

Rising from his chair, he prepared himself for the challenging but rewarding path ahead.

WALLY LEANED BACK IN his desk chair, staring up at the ceiling as he contemplated the potential applications of DNX-109. His recent experiments had shown remarkable regenerative effects when the microbe was applied to damaged tissue, but finding the right delivery method was proving to be a challenge.

Burn treatments seemed like one of the more straightforward applications. Bandages or adhesive strips infused with DNX-109 could provide targeted delivery right to the site of the burn while keeping systemic absorption low. The microbe would enhance the body's natural healing response, repairing the damaged dermal layers.

But Wally knew that the regenerative properties of DNX-109 would make it a target for replication or misuse if it fell into the wrong hands. He needed to find a way to utilize the microbe while preventing it from being recovered and analyzed after application.

What if there was a way to program an extremely short active lifespan into the microbes on the bandages? Just long enough to spur regeneration when applied to the wound site, but short enough that the microbes would essentially self-destruct before the bandage was removed. It seemed theoretically possible to engineer DNX-109 to be potent yet ephemeral.

Wally's mind raced as he envisioned a specially coated wound dressing infused with micro-encapsulated DNX-109, programmed to become inert within hours of application. The microbe would penetrate the damaged tissue when the dressing was applied, initiating rapid healing. But by the time the dressing was removed a day later, the microbes would have degraded to the point of being undetectable. It would be nearly impossible to recover viable DNX-109 samples from the used dressing.

This approach could work for more than just burns, Wally realized. Bandages, sutures, implantable sponges - all could be loaded with DNX-109 configured for short-term activity. As long as the lifespan was tightly controlled, the microbe's remarkable effects could be harnessed without risk of it being misused or reverse engineered.

Wally smiled, invigorated by the challenge of this formulation problem. He had his work cut out for him designing a tightly controlled delivery system, but the potential benefits were immense. If he could unlock the regenerative power of DNX-109 while safeguarding it from abuse, the medical applications could be groundbreaking. Wally felt the weight of this discovery settling on his shoulders, but his optimism and determination buoyed him. He knew he would need to proceed with the utmost care and wisdom, but the possibilities seemed endless.

WALLY WALKED OUT OF Sammy's Roadhouse Grill, stomach full and spirits high after his meeting with Dr. Sanchez. He strolled past the classic cars gleaming in the parking lot and slid into the driver's seat of his Hyundai Santa Fe. As he cruised down Airport Boulevard, Wally contemplated the immense potential and responsibility of his recent medical breakthrough.

Wally's mind drifted to more immediate matters as he passed the retro-style burger joint situated between FFOne and the local airport that housed his seaplane, Seawings. He had eaten there often, drawn to its charm and familiarity when dining alone. Wally decided to make a quick stop for an afternoon pick-me-up.

Inside, Wally ordered his usual - a double bacon cheeseburger, fries, and a chocolate malt. He savored the meal, letting his mind empty of all pressing thoughts. After finishing the last salty fry, Wally headed out the door, refreshed.

As he walked across the parking lot, his phone rang. Glancing at the screen, he saw it was Dr. Sanchez. Wally answered promptly, "Hello Dr. Sanchez, it's Wally."

"Wally, glad I caught you," Dr. Sanchez responded. "I wanted to give you an update on the last shipment of FlexiCommander suits we received."

Wally listened intently as he unlocked his car. He started the engine but remained parked, focused on the call.

Dr. Sanchez continued, "The latest batch is performing even better than our initial trials. The team is reporting increased maneuverability and durability across field tests."

"That's great to hear," Wally replied, picturing the suits in action. He felt a swell of pride, knowing it was his technical expertise at FFOne that had brought these innovative protective suits to life.

"Yes, your modifications to the flexi-weave material really paid off," Dr. Sanchez remarked. "I'll send over the full analysis later today. Also, command is eager to get the next delivery ahead of schedule. Think your team can ramp up production?"

Wally contemplated the request for a moment. "We should be able to meet an accelerated timeline," he responded with confidence. "I'll verify supply chain status and get back to you with an updated production and delivery plan."

"Perfect. Knew I could count on you," Dr. Sanchez said approvingly. "Speak soon."

"Will do, have a good one," Wally replied before ending the call. He placed the phone in its dashboard mount and pulled out of the parking lot, wheels turning with ideas on how to meet the new production needs. His route took him past FFOne, its exterior modest despite the groundbreaking innovations happening inside. Wally's mind churned with plans, feeling the gravity of his responsibilities as both Guardian and innovator.

THE FAMILIAR HUM OF Wally's SUV faded into the mid-afternoon hush as he left Sammy's Roadhouse Grill. As the distance between him and the bustling eatery grew, an unexpected symphony began to play from his pocket. His phone, nestled among loose change and a set of keys, emitted a series of beeps in a coded rhythm. It was an alert from Bird Island; one of the motion sensors he'd installed had been activated.

A prickling sense of unease tingled at the back of his neck. The Island was supposed to be vacant, a haven only for him and his friends. The intrusion sent his thoughts spinning into overdrive. He glanced at his rearview mirror, where his trusty backpack lay in the back seat, packed with essential tools and supplies for any unforeseen situation.

With a determined set to his jaw, Wally swung the steering wheel, changing course from the suburban landscape to the private airfield where Seawings rested. He accelerated, pressing down on the gas pedal as if it could hasten time itself. The road stretched out before him, unfurling like a ribbon towards the waiting aircraft.

Less than an hour later, Wally sat in the cockpit of Seawings, guiding her towards Bird Island. The familiar drone of the Rotax 912 engine filled his ears as he charted a direct course for their sanctuary. His eyes were trained on the horizon where Bird Island rose like a green jewel from the sapphire expanse of water.

He descended towards Southeast Bunker Entrance "E3," their favored access point due to its natural concealment. It was nestled amid dense foliage, a silent testament to its forgotten military past now repurposed for their clandestine activities.

Seawings skimmed over the water with practiced ease as Wally guided her to land along the southeastern tip of Bird Island. Once settled, he secured her to a sturdy live oak tree that had become their customary anchor. The tree's gnarled roots provided a firm grip, its wide canopy a natural shield against the elements.

With Seawings safely moored, Wally reached for his backpack. He unzipped a side pocket and extracted a small pouch, the crinkling sound of the plastic wrapping in sharp contrast to the soothing symphony of the island's wildlife.

He withdrew four cookies, each distinct in color: red, violet, blue, and orange. They were no ordinary treats; each was infused with a specific strain of microorganisms. He took a bite of the red one first, relishing the sweet taste that belied its powerful influence. As he chewed, he felt a surge of energy coursing through his veins.

Next came the violet cookie, its effects as remarkable as its hue. His ears pricked up at the distant sounds of nature that suddenly seemed much closer. The chirping of birds and rustling of leaves were now crystal clear, his auditory perception amplified to an extraordinary level.

He followed it with the blue cookie. Almost instantly, his mind sharpened, becoming more receptive and retaining every minute detail around him with photographic precision.

Finally, he bit into the orange cookie. As he chewed and swallowed, his vision brightened and clarified until it was as if he was seeing through a high-definition lens. Every color seemed more vibrant; every detail stood out with startling clarity.

Now prepared for whatever awaited him on Bird Island, Wally shouldered his backpack and set off towards Entrance E3. His senses were heightened, ready to face any challenge that dared cross his path on this afternoon adventure.

A LIGHT BREEZE SWEPT over the island, rustling the tall cordgrass and whispering secrets in the foliage. The sporadic cawing of birds and the rustle of small creatures in the underbrush formed a symphony that only Wally could decipher with his enhanced auditory perception. But he wasn't listening to nature's music. His ears strained for something unnatural, an anomaly in the island's soundscape - human voices, shuffling footsteps, anything that suggested unwanted company.

Approaching the bunker entrance labeled E3, Wally scrutinized his surroundings with hawk-like precision. His pulse quickened as he noticed something offbeat – a disruption in the usual pattern of leaves and dirt scattered haphazardly across the bunker's threshold. A series of footprints, freshly imprinted on the earth and untouched by wind or wildlife, led into the heart of the bunker.

A cold shiver snaked down Wally's spine as he examined them. They were unmistakably human, a far cry from the paw prints or feather marks he was accustomed to spotting on his solitary island. Two distinct sets were visible, their outlines sharp and crisp against the dull concrete floor. The memories of two men previously found lurking within these depths bubbled to the surface of Wally's mind.

He remembered their desperate faces and hardened eyes, their fingers stained with the remnants of a mysterious substance that had sparked this whole chain of events. They had been intruders then; could they be intruders now? Or were these footprints a calling card from different uninvited guests? Either way, they represented a threat to the secrets nestled within the bunker.

Moving stealthily, Wally followed the trail deeper into the bunker, his senses stretched to their limits. His eyes scanned the dark corners and crevices, while his ears picked up the faintest echoes bouncing off the cold, concrete walls. He could hear his own heartbeat thumping in his chest, a rhythmic reminder of the high stakes at hand.

With each step deeper into the bunker's belly, Wally's apprehension mounted. His enhanced eyesight painted a vivid picture of recent activity. Disturbed dust, shuffled items, and a faint odor of sweat hung in the stale air - silent witnesses to the trespassers' intrusion.

His fingers brushed against the cold steel door leading to one of the storage rooms. A smudge of dirt on its surface suggested recent use. The room beyond held countless relics from Bird Island's past and served as a crucial hub for his ongoing research. Whoever these intruders were, they had breached far too close to secrets that were not meant for prying eyes.

WALLY SLOWED HIS STEPS as the muffled voices grew louder, echoing through the concrete corridors. He strained to listen, picking up snippets of rapid Spanish from two men up ahead.

"...este lugar es perfecto, ¿no crees, Marco?" said one voice excitedly.

Wally crept forward and peered around the corner. In the bunker's command center stood two men in dark clothing, surveying the space. The shorter man, who had just been addressed as Marco, nodded.

"Sí, es aislado y difícil de encontrar. El escondite perfecto," Marco replied. His sharp eyes scanned the room methodically.

Wally studied the men warily, puzzled by their presence. Marco moved with purpose, checking the room's perimeter and testing the locking mechanisms on a large cabinet along the far wall. The other man fidgeted impatiently, eager to explore further.

"¿Qué crees que guardaban aquí?" the tall one asked Marco.

Marco didn't answer right away, focused on examining the contents of the cabinet he had unlocked. He pulled out a folder stuffed with yellowed papers and rifled through them.

"No estoy seguro, Javier," he finally said. "Parece que este lugar fue algún tipo de centro de operaciones militar, hace mucho tiempo."

Javier nodded, only half-listening as his gaze wandered around the room. He paused at a heavy door on the opposite wall, emblazoned with a sign reading "Acceso Restringido."

"¿A dónde llevará esta puerta?" Javier wondered aloud. Before Marco could stop him, Javier grasped the handle and shoved hard, forcing the rusted door open. It led to a dark passageway sloping downward.

"¡Javier, ten cuidado!" Marco hissed. But Javier had already flicked on a flashlight and started down the passageway. Marco cursed under his breath. He quickly stowed the folder into his pack and followed Javier into the tunnel.

Wally shadowed the two men at a distance, silent as a specter. He felt increasingly uneasy about their presence on the island. Who were they, and what were they looking for in the long-abandoned bunker? Wally intended to find out.

The passageway ended at another heavy door marked "Entrada E4." Javier tried the handle and huffed with annoyance when it didn't budge.

"Está cerrada con llave," he muttered.

Marco studied the lock, then pulled a small leather case from his pocket. He selected two slender metal tools and went to work picking the lock. After a few moments of maneuvering the picks, the lock clicked open.

Javier grinned. "Bien hecho," he said, pulling the door open. A rush of stale air escaped the chamber beyond. The men coughed and waved away the dust. As it settled, the beam of Javier's flashlight revealed a cavernous room filled with crates. The men glanced at each other, eyes glinting. This was exactly what they had hoped to find.

They moved cautiously into the room, prying open one of the smaller crates. It was filled with canvas bags sealed shut. Marco took out his pocketknife and slit one open, peering at the contents.

"¿Qué demonios es esto?" he muttered. He dipped his fingers into the bag and pulled out a pinch of fine, powdery grains.

Javier opened another bag, shaking his head in disappointment. "No sirve para nada."

"Llevémoslo afuera para examinarlo mejor," Marco suggested, resealing the bag.

Together, the men lugged several bags out of the storage room and down the corridor. Wally followed noiselessly, unsure of their intentions. Soon the men emerged topside, squinting in the late afternoon sun. They carried the bags toward the edge of the clearing. Wally took cover behind a twisted live oak to continue his surveillance.

Marco took out his knife again and opened the bags one by one, dumping the powdery contents onto the scrubby earth. His lips curled in frustration.

"Basura inútil," he growled, tossing the empty bags aside. He turned to Javier.

"Vámonos. No hay nada de valor aquí."

The men headed back to the bunker entrance, empty-handed. Wally remained hidden until their voices had faded entirely. He let out a breath he didn't realize he had been holding. There were trespassers on his island, and they had discovered things that should remain secret. Wally's role as guardian just became much more complicated.

MARCO PAUSED, SURVEYING the secluded Bird Island with its dense vegetation and strategic location, nodded his agreement to Javier. His dark eyes scanned the horizon, the cogs in his mind already turning with plans and contingencies. "Si, es ideal," he conceded with a measured tone, "it's isolated, easy to defend, and off the radar of the Coast Guard." His assertive demeanor left no room for doubt—they would set up their operation here. Marco's life began in a small town near the Texas-Mexico border, where he quickly realized that the local economy was entangled with illicit activities. As a teenager, he dipped his toes in the waters of smuggling, keeping watch for a local gang. His competence and calm demeanor during tense situations led him to climb the ranks, and he eventually honed his expertise in planning smuggling routes and evading law enforcement.

Javier's muscular frame relaxed slightly, a smile creasing his rugged features as he envisioned their future successes on this hidden gem of an island. "Then it's settled," he said, clapping Marco on the back with a heavy hand, "we make our move here." Javier's story began in the tough neighborhoods of Houston, where he learned that strength could be his greatest ally. He first worked as a bouncer, impressing local criminals with his formidable physique and lack of fear, which landed him a position alongside Marco, who shaped him into his most trusted enforcer.

As the two began to discuss logistics, the air around them teemed with the implicit understanding that Bird Island would soon become the lynchpin in their smuggling empire, a secret haven known only to those loyal to Alvarez and his Brotherhood.

WALLY RECALLED THE last time he encountered Marco and Javier on Bird Island. Several years back, the two men had stumbled upon the hidden bunker entrance and gained access. As guardian of the island's secrets, Wally knew he had to take action. Rather than directly engage the intruders, he opted for a more subtle approach to deter their return.

After the men left the island that first day, Wally ground up leaves and vines from the abundant poison ivy plants into a viscous green paste. Donning gloves and long sleeves for protection, he returned to the bunker and liberally applied the toxic mixture onto all surfaces the men had touched - the metal door handles, the aged control panels, the dusty storage containers.

Wally had laid low and kept watch for the smugglers' return. Sure enough, Marco and Javier were back, continuing their explorations of the bunker's hidden chambers. Wally observed them from a distance, noting their reactions. Within an hour, both men were scratching incessantly, their exposed skin blotchy and inflamed from contact with the poison ivy residue. Cursing their misfortune, they cut their visit short, but not before Wally overheard angry threats about making whoever was responsible pay. Wally remained out of sight, satisfied that the irritating sabotage had achieved its purpose. The men had not returned since.

IN THE SOLITUDE OF his clandestine bunker, Wally's mind raced. He had been blindsided by the intrusion of Marco and Javier, but he was not defeated. His gaze drifted over the hodgepodge of antiquated military tech and cutting-edge lab equipment. His mind latched onto a memory, a half-forgotten detail from his extensive exploration of the bunker. There was something he could use.

He moved through the labyrinthine corridors of the bunker with an air of quiet determination, each step echoing in the damp stillness. A dimly lit sign reading "Storage Room CHEM-4" signaled his destination. He pushed open the door, revealing rows of metal shelves laden with relics from a bygone era—tools, clothing, documents, and containers. One container in particular drew his attention: a hefty canister labeled "Magnesium Citrate."

His fingers traced over the familiar words, etched into the canister in stark black letters. The contents of this canister were far from sinister—a laxative, used in small doses to alleviate constipation. However, in large quantities, it could cause a nasty case of diarrhea.

A wry smile played on Wally's lips as he lifted the canister off the shelf. This was no high-tech weapon or sophisticated defense system; it was a humble compound used for medicinal purposes. But in this scenario, it might be just as effective.

After securing the canister under his arm, Wally moved back through the winding corridors towards the exit. He emerged from Entrance E3 and into the dusky twilight enveloping Bird Island.

He spotted Marco's skiff nestled among the reeds along the shoreline—a stealthy shadow against an indigo backdrop. He approached with measured steps, mindful not to leave any traces behind.

In the skiff, a single 20 liter container caught his eye—the only source of fresh water aboard that he could see. His heart pounded in his chest as he unscrewed the cap, his movements deliberate and precise.

He opened the canister, revealing a fine, white powder that glistened under the pale moonlight. Carefully, he poured a generous amount of the magnesium citrate into the canteen, watching as it disappeared into the water. He gave the canteen a gentle shake, ensuring the compound was thoroughly mixed.

Replacing the cap and returning the container to its original position, Wally retreated from the skiff. His heart still thumped wildly in his chest as he walked away from the shoreline and back towards Entrance E3.

As he disappeared back into the bunker, Wally couldn't help but imagine Marco and Javier's reaction when they discovered their unexpected ailment. He didn't relish in their discomfort, but this was about more than just payback. It was about safeguarding Bird Island—the secrets it held, the life it nurtured, and the sanctuary it provided.

Wally had no illusions about what he was doing; this was an act of sabotage. But it was a necessary one. The intruders had to be deterred from returning to Bird Island. They were a threat not only to Wally's work but also to the delicate ecosystem of Bird Island itself.

As he reentered his bunker, his heart rate finally began to slow. The deed was done. Now, all he could do was wait and hope that his plan would be enough to protect Bird Island from those who sought to exploit it.

The island's nocturnal inhabitants resumed their chorus as Wally disappeared into Entrance E3, leaving behind a seemingly untouched landscape under a velvet sky. Unseen by any human eye, nature reclaimed its dominion over Bird Island for another night.

Marco and Javier's skiff bobbed gently among the reeds on the shoreline—a silent testament to the confrontation that had occurred and the confrontation yet to come. The magnesium citrate, a subtle weapon in the fight for Bird Island's future, waited patiently within the confines of the water source. Its effects would soon manifest, tipping the balance of power back towards Bird Island's rightful guardian.

As Wally returned to his work in the hidden depths of his bunker, a quiet resolve filled him. He was the Guardian of Bird

Island, and he would do whatever it took to keep it safe from harm. The stage was set, and now all he could do was wait for Marco and Javier's inevitable departure from Bird Island.

MARCO AND JAVIER CONTINUED their meticulous exploration of the labyrinthine bunker, their flashlights casting long shadows on the walls as they moved through the cold, underground corridors. Although the search was tedious and their progress slow, Marco's strategic mind remained focused, intently searching for anything that could be leveraged for their smuggling operations.

Periodically, Javier would voice his impatience, scarcely concealed behind a thin veil of respect for Marco's leadership. However, even his deep-set frustration couldn't overshadow the seriousness with which he took their mission. To keep their energy levels up and quench a growing thirst from the dusty air, they would occasionally halt their search to take sips of water from the 20-liter container in their skiff. Little did they know that the water they depended on for relief was now laced with magnesium citrate, thanks to Wally's clandestine intervention.

With each room they cleared, the substance in the water was slowly taking effect. Initially unknowing, they continued to peer into decrepit storage rooms, checking behind rusted filing cabinets and under decaying cloth tarps. As they worked, pointlessly scrutinizing outdated navigation gear and electrical components stripped of any value, they hydrated from the contaminated canteen, unknowingly exacerbating their impending predicament.

While Marco methodically catalogued the contents of each chamber, Javier used his sheer physical strength to dislodge the heavy, rust-coated doors of storage lockers and dusty wooden crates, some of which had not been opened in decades. Their process was one of repeated patterns: search, document, hydrate, and move on. Each drink they took hastened their descent into discomfort.

Hours into their exhaustive search, a subtle shift began to take place. Javier complained of stomach cramps and a growing need to relieve himself, trying to brush it off as a minor inconvenience. Marco, ever reserved and cautious, also felt an unusual rumble in his gut but said nothing, choosing instead to press on with tightened lips.

The men were diligent, but the mounting effects of the magnesium citrate were becoming harder to ignore. They took more frequent and increasingly desperate sips, hoping to alleviate their dry throats, only to rouse the quiet chemical chaos brewing within them.

By the time they reached a secluded section that may have been an officers' quarters – furnished with little more than a table and some vandalized lockers – the discomfort was unavoidable. They were forced to alternate between the search and hurried trips to find a suitable corner of the bunker to act as a makeshift latrine.

The duo became less concerned with uncovering lucrative secrets and more preoccupied with the growing urgency in their bowels. As time passed, what began as an operation marked by precision and hopes of wealth deteriorated into an embarrassing and uncomfortable ordeal, driven by the deceptive contents of a seemingly innocuous water container.

WALLY WENT BACK TO Marco and Javier's skiff, his footsteps light and careful across the muddy shore. As he reached the small motorboat, he scanned the area, ensuring its owners were still occupied within the bunker's depths. Satisfied he was alone, Wally crouched by the outboard motor and stealthily removed the transom drain plug, concealing it under the rear bench seat.

Next, he scooped up a large handful of mud mixed with cordgrass, compacting it into a ball. Wally firmly packed the mud and grass mixture into the open drain hole, lodging it deep into place. He knew the makeshift plug would hold initially but slowly dissolve once the men got underway, transforming into a troublesome leak.

Wally rose and briskly walked away from the compromised skiff, putting distance between himself and the site of interference. He found a concealed vantage point in the reeds near the shoreline, providing a clear view of the boat while shielding him from detection. Now came the waiting game. Wally settled in, prepared to monitor the smugglers' return and subsequent struggles with their sabotaged vessel.

An hour passed before Marco and Javier emerged from the bunker's entrance, squinting against the harsh midday light. Wally observed silently as the men trudged to their boat, grumbling about the lack of valuables and setbacks they had endured. Marco yanked the starter cord and brought the engine sputtering to life. He steered the skiff away from shore, cutting across the bay's choppy waters.

At first, their passage appeared normal, the skiff bouncing across the waves with Javier perched up front. But ten minutes into the journey, the stern began riding lower in the water. Javier shouted something back to Marco, gesturing emphatically at the worsening leak. Even from a distance, Wally could see Marco's frustration as he alternated between vainly trying to bail water and coaxing more speed from the struggling engine.

The swamped skiff limped along, taking on water at an alarming rate. It was clear the men would not make it back to their intended destination. Javier pointed off to the south, likely indicating a closer shore where they could ground the sinking boat. With a resigned nod, Marco turned the skiff toward land.

Wally watched the scene unfold with stoic satisfaction, knowing he had succeeded in protecting Bird Island without directly confronting the intruders. There would be no evidence of tampering, only the misfortune of an untimely leak. The island's isolation and bounty of life remained preserved for another day. Wally gathered his pack and slipped back into the brush, his presence on the island still undetected.

Chapter 3

The warm autumn sun beat down on Wally as he stood outside the entrance to the hidden bunker, labeled E3 above the steel door. He surveyed the area, taking note of the trampled grass and vegetation stripped away from the concrete, leaving the portal exposed. This was the work of the two intruders he had covertly observed earlier that day.

Wally's face was etched with determination as he began the work of meticulously restoring the surroundings to their natural state. He grasped the cordgrass, branches, and vines that had been carelessly tossed aside by the men and replanted each one, taking care to mimic the original placement. As he worked, Wally's thoughts drifted to the storeroom the men had discovered, filled with mysterious bags whose contents they ultimately discarded as worthless. He wondered what secrets had lain inside those vessels, secrets he was now sworn to protect.

When the last vine was secured in place, Wally stepped back, scrutinizing his work. The entrance was once again obscured by the thickets and greenery that had reclaimed the concrete edifice. Satisfied with the camouflage, he turned and headed into the bunker's depths.

Down below, he entered his hidden workshop, glancing at the lab equipment and research notes on regeneration he had been studying. From a shelf, Wally retrieved a mason jar labeled ESP-628. He had discovered this microorganism during his initial explorations on Bird Island. It possessed the unexpected ability to stimulate rapid plant growth.

Wally ascended the steps back up to the E3 entrance. After double-checking that he was alone, he carefully twisted open the lid of the jar. Reaching inside, he grasped a handful of the rich brown powder contained within and began sprinkling it liberally around the entrance and down the first few stairs. As he dispensed the microorganism, Wally pictured the accelerated plant growth he hoped to achieve, once again concealing any trace of the bunker entrance.

His work complete, Wally returned to the hidden lab and gathered his belongings. He took one last look around, ensuring no evidence of his presence remained. Ascending the stairs, Wally secured the secret door behind him and blinked as his eyes adjusted to the late afternoon sunlight. He glanced around, satisfied that the entrance was again obscured by the rampant coastal foliage. Now it was time to head home.

Wally trekked across the island and soon reached the clearing where his seaplane, SeaWings, awaited. He swiftly prepped the aircraft, loading his gear and supplies. Moments later he was airborne, gaining altitude before circling back over the island. Wally gazed down, scrutinizing the landscape for any remaining signs of human interference but found none.

As Seawings reached the open water of the bay, Wally banked right, beginning a wide-sweeping patrol pattern. He peered intently at the glimmering waters below, searching for the intruders' boat, eager to confirm their departure. Wally maintained his focus for several minutes before a small craft came into view. He circled above it briefly - a fishing boat with two occupants. Neither individual resembled the men he had observed at the bunker.

Wally continued his patrol. The late afternoon sun dipped lower on the horizon as he flew further out over the bay. He found no signs of other watercraft. Satisfied that the two men had left, Wally pointed Seawings northwest, towards home. Within minutes, the island was out of sight, obscured by distance and the bird's eye view from the cockpit.

Wally settled in for the remainder of the flight, occasionally scanning the open waters around him. He let his mind wander, reflecting on recent events on the island. The intrusion had been unsettling, but Wally took comfort knowing that, at least for now, Bird Island's secrets remained protected. He had taken the necessary steps to conceal any evidence of his or the men's presence.

The sun hung low over the airport as Seawings gracefully touched down on the surface near Wally's private hanger. He secured the aircraft and grabbed his belongings, eager to be back in the comfort of his home. Wally took one last look around as he walked to his SUV in the fading light.

WALLY SET HIS PHONE down on the table, letting out a long exhale. His call to Dr. Sanchez had gone smoothly - no questions asked about his need for the aerosol grenades. He was grateful for her discretion.

Staring out the window of his hidden lab on Bird Island, Wally watched the sun dip lower in the sky, casting long shadows over the salt marsh. It would be dark soon. Time to head home.

After one last check of the lab equipment and a fresh coat of plant growth formula scattered around the cleverly concealed bunker entrance, Wally grabbed his backpack and locked up.

The short hike through the brush to the small inlet where Seawings was moored gave Wally time to reflect. So much had changed since he first discovered this island, back when he was just a teenager. Now in his mid-twenties, he felt the weight of responsibility as the Guardian of Bird Island.

Wally arrived at the secluded inlet as the last sliver of sun disappeared below the horizon. The familiar sight of the white and blue seaplane filled him with both comfort and purpose. After stowing his gear and completing the preflight checklist, Wally started the engine. The propeller spun to life, and Seawings began gracefully taxiing across the smooth water.

Moments later, they were airborne, gaining altitude over the island. Wally banked the plane to the northeast, towards home. He would arrive back under cover of darkness.

As Seawings cruised at 2,700 feet over the bay, Wally's thoughts returned to the impending delivery from Dr. Sanchez. The aerosol grenades would prove useful if he had to deal with any more intruders on the island. A non-lethal way to incapacitate them without resorting to violence. Wally disliked confrontation, but he would do whatever it took to protect Bird Island.

The lights of Houston soon came into view. Wally radioed the private airfield, announcing his arrival. He touched down smoothly and taxied the seaplane into its hangar.

After securing Seawings for the night, Wally loaded his backpack into the Santa Fe and headed home. He was looking forward to a hot shower and a good night's sleep in his own bed.

The next morning, Wally stopped by the private airfield on his way to FFOne. Sure enough, a package from Dr. Sanchez awaited him. He stowed the discreetly packaged grenades in the hidden compartment of Seawings before continuing to the office.

Wally had a busy day ahead at FFOne, but the impending delivery of aerosol grenades lingered in the back of his mind. He was grateful to Dr. Sanchez for acquiring them without any difficult questions. Her assistance would prove invaluable for protecting Bird Island and its secrets.

DAYLIGHT WAS JUST MAKING its way over the earth's curvature when Wally spotted Bird Island emerging from the morning mist. He gently banked Seawings to the right, lining up for his approach. As the small island grew nearer, he scanned the bay below but saw no signs of boats or activity. It seemed Marco and Javier had not yet returned.

Wally set the seaplane down in the glassy water near the southeastern tip of the island. After securing Seawings to a small live oak tree, he grabbed his backpack and the aerosol grenades he had received from Dr. Sanchez, then headed inland. He moved with purpose through the dense brush, munching on cookies specially formulated with microbes as he went. With determination, Wally made his way through the thick foliage, consuming specially crafted cookies laced with microorganisms. The red cookie transformed his muscle fibers, significantly boosting his stamina. Meanwhile, the blue cookie sharpened his cognitive focus. The violet and orange cookies enhanced his auditory and visual senses. Feeling a surge of energy, Wally was well-prepared to tackle the challenge that lay ahead.

Reaching the first hidden entrance to the underground bunker, labeled E3, Wally set down the grenades and got to work. He intended to rig tripwires that would set off the non-lethal but highly disorienting vapor when triggered. Marco and Javier had proven too persistent to be deterred by Wally's previous efforts. He needed to take more serious action if he wanted to protect the secrets hidden below.

Wally set the thin, nearly invisible wires at shin height across each entrance just inside the bunker and in the main corridors, anchoring them securely. One by one, he connected them to the grenade pins. Now even a slight disturbance of the wires would pull the pins, unleashing an intense burst of debilitating vapor. Satisfied with his work, Wally did a final check before gathering his supplies and slipping back out of the bunker.

After re-securing the hidden entrance, Wally headed to the shoreline. He pulled a small vial from his backpack and tipped its contents onto the ground near where he had docked Seawings. The microbes would quickly stimulate dense plant growth, further concealing any signs of recent activity.

Wally took one last look around, ensuring he had left no trace of his presence. Seeing nothing amiss, he boarded his seaplane and took off, staying low over the water to avoid detection. As he gained altitude, he did a quick patrol around the island. There was still no sign of Marco and Javier's boat, bringing Wally some relief.

Satisfied that he had done all he could for now, Wally set a course for home, reflecting on his role as guardian of Bird Island's secrets. He knew he was taking a calculated risk by escalating his deterrent methods, but the safety of the island had to come first. Wally could only hope he had found the right balance between protection and restraint.

The sun rose higher as Wally flew over the bay, the light glinting off the water in brilliant shades of gold and orange. In the distance, he could make out the shoreline of mainland Texas. Wally smiled, happy to be going home after ensuring the security of the hidden treasures that awaited his return to Bird Island.

SUNSET DRAPED ITS GOLDEN shroud over the FFOne Plant Facility as Wally navigated his Hyundai Santa Fe down the stretch of Airport Blvd. His mind, a tumultuous sea of thoughts, churned relentlessly. He had just left the Bird Island, and the wheels of innovation were already spinning at a feverish pace.

Wally's gaze, locked onto the road ahead, belied the cerebral spectacle unfolding within him. Micro-encapsulated DNX-109 — it was more than a scientific breakthrough; it was a marvel of nature he had stumbled upon and nurtured in his labs, both on Bird Island and here at Home.

The microbe had already proven its extraordinary potential for regeneration, breathing new life into damaged tissue. But to make it a viable medical solution, Wally needed to engineer a method of delivery that was not only effective but also safe. His mind raced as he mulled over the challenge.

He visualized a wound dressing — not an ordinary one but a specially coated fabric infused with micro-encapsulated DNX-109. As the dressing made contact with the damaged tissue, the microbe would penetrate deep within, initiating rapid healing. However, unlike traditional treatments that left traces behind, DNX-109 would self-destruct within hours of application.

By the time the dressing was removed — Wally figured about 24 hours later — any remaining microbes would have degraded to the point of being undetectable. The beauty of this approach was its impermanence; recovering viable DNX-109 samples from used dressings would be nearly impossible. This safeguard would prevent misuse and protect his groundbreaking discovery from falling into the wrong hands.

But as he pulled into his driveway and parked beside his Shed, his private sanctuary of research and innovation, he realized that burns were just the tip of the iceberg. The possibilities were boundless. Bandages for cuts and abrasions, sutures for surgical incisions, even implantable sponges for internal wounds — all could be loaded with DNX-109.

And it wasn't just about wound care. If the microbe's lifespan was tightly controlled, its regenerative effects could be harnessed for a myriad of medical applications. Wally's mind whirled with the possibilities: targeted joint injections for osteoarthritis, controlled-release capsules for gastrointestinal conditions, resorbable stitches for surgical recovery. The list went on.

He stepped out of his car, the evening air cooling his flushed face. The thrill of discovery pulsed through him, but so did the weight of responsibility. With every step toward Wally's Shed, he felt the magnitude of his undertaking.

As he unlocked the door to his lab, Wally knew that the work ahead was colossal. It would require precision, patience, and a level of discretion he had never exercised before. But as daunting as the task was, Wally was undeterred. He was on the brink of a revolution in medical science — a revolution that had started in a hidden lab on Bird Island and was now unfolding in the heart of FFOne Plant Facility.

Inside his back yard lab, Wally rolled up his sleeves and began prepping his workspace. Tonight marked the beginning of a new chapter in his journey as a scientist and guardian of DNX-109. The road ahead was uncertain and fraught with challenges. But if there was one thing Wally had learned from his adventures on Bird Island, it was that no challenge was insurmountable when met with determination and ingenuity.

As night descended upon Wally's home, a light burned bright within Wally's Shed — a beacon of innovation amid the sprawling industrial complex. Unseen by the world outside, Wally delved into his work, spurred on by the promise of what lay ahead: a future where the miracle of healing was not just a possibility, but a reality.

WALLY STOOD MOTIONLESS in his lab as the morning sun shone through the windows, its silent scrutiny matching the conflict raging within him. He wrestled with the implications of patenting his remarkable creation, DNX-109. To patent would mean disclosure - a broadcast of his life's work available for anyone to see. He knew that could open the door to unimaginable progress, with researchers across the globe collaborating to unlock the microbe's full potential. But it could also expose DNX-109 to those with far more nefarious aims.

Wally sighed, the weight of this decision sitting heavily on his shoulders. The duality of sharing his work for the betterment of mankind while risking the inherent danger of abuse continued to torment him. Today, he resolved, he would not take that risk. He would follow a different course, one less illuminated by the glare of praise but blessed with the stern safety of obscurity.

The afternoon hours found Wally ensconced in study, the air around him alive with possibility and caution in equal measure. He worked with meticulous precision, refining DNX-109's delivery system without divulging a sliver of its true nature. Like a cryptographer wielding the most valuable secrets, he encrypted his techniques with a proprietary sequence only he could unravel. The strands of innovation were woven deep, shrouded from view.

Wally begins by rigorously testing the micro-encapsulated DNX-109 wound dressing. Unexpectedly, he discovers that different fabric materials can affect the release rate of the microorganisms, leading to different healing times. This eureka moment inspires him to patent a range of dressings tailored to specific injuries.

He refines the composition of the microbe's encapsulation, enhancing its stability and ensuring its controlled degradation. He successfully demonstrates this property in his laboratory, which, after extensive documentation, moves him closer to securing a design for his innovative dressing.

As evening descended, Wally fortified his lab, conceiving it as a vault harboring invaluable treasures. He knew breaches could come from any corner, any entity lured by the scent of his work. But now his research existed in a vault not of steel or stone, but of cutting-edge digital locks under his sole control.

When dawn broke the next day, Wally immersed himself in contemplation of the ethical quandaries shadowing his every move. The waltz of potential criticism and praise from the medical community danced at the edge of his thoughts. He scribbled furiously, outlining protocols and guidelines forming the bastion of future clandestine trials. With each scribble, a question arose - a specter of moral conundrum demanding contemplation.

The afternoon followed as Wally traced potential trajectories, sketching plans and stratagems that might never leave this room. How could he test DNX-109 without the world discovering Bird Island? Each scenario demanded different precautions, but Wally's resolve remained steadfast as he plotted every course with a cartographer's detail.

As twilight descended, Wally faced the fears of DNX-109's long-term legacy. He chewed on stark thoughts of the tremendous impact and grave threat it could present. His contemplations carried him to forgotten times when scientists also held the power to heal or harm. It was a roll of the dice, yet his hands steadied by the gravity of his discoveries.

IT WAS VERY EARLY MORNING when Wally's phone reported an intruder on Bird Island. His heart raced as he sprang out of bed, his mind instantly racing to the possibilities. Could it be Marco and Javier, those two men who had dared to intrude upon his sanctuary before? Wally thought so, and the idea filled him with a sense of unease.

Hurriedly, Wally dressed in his usual attire, he grabbed his backpack, making sure to include essentials like a cookie strip, first aid kit, and a small supply of food and water. With everything in order, Wally was on his way to his hanger.

Seawings awaited him there, its sleek form gleaming in the dim light of the early morning. Wally climbed aboard and started the engine with practiced ease. The sound of the engine roared to life as he taxied down the runway and took off into the sky.

It must have been around 3:30 AM when Wally was pulled from a deep sleep by the sudden jolt of Seawings hitting turbulence. The plane shook violently as it navigated through thick clouds that seemed to appear out of nowhere. Wally gripped the controls tightly, his eyes scanning the instruments as he tried to make sense of what was happening.

As suddenly as it had begun, the turbulence subsided, leaving Seawings rocking gently in the calm air once more. Wally let out a sigh of relief as he steered the plane towards Bird Island. He knew that whatever was happening on the island needed his attention now more than ever before.

Soon Bird Island was in sight, its familiar contours looming large against the backdrop of darkness that still clung to the sky. Wally slowly circled the island, scanning every inch of its perimeter for any sign of life or movement. His heart sank as he spotted a boat moored near Entrance E3 - it could only belong to Marco and Javier!

Wally descended towards the island's surface, landing smoothly on its grassy expanse despite the darkness that shrouded everything around him. He quickly disembarked from Seawings and grabbed his backpack once more before setting off towards Entrance E3 at a brisk pace. His heart pounded in his chest as he approached - would Marco and Javier still be there? And if so, what would he do?

As he drew closer to Entrance E3, Wally could hear voices echoing through the darkness - it was definitely Marco and Javier! With stealthy precision, Wally crept closer until he could see them clearly - they were searching through one of his hidden bunkers! What were they doing here? And how had they found it?

Wally's mind raced as he tried to come up with a plan - he couldn't let these men get their hands on whatever secrets lay within those bunkers! With quick thinking and deft movements, Wally managed to sneak up behind them without being detected. As they continued their search oblivious to his presence nearby, Wally began plotting his next move...

WALLY STOOD MOTIONLESS in the shadows, observing Marco and Javier as they rummaged through the contents of his hidden bunker. He slowly reached into his backpack and retrieved one of the microbe-infused cookies he had brought, taking a small bite as he continued surveilling the scene.

The cookies were a recent creation, one of Wally's many experiments with the regenerative microbes he had discovered on this very island. Infusing the dough with a refined version of the microbes, which he had labeled by color, which enabled an accelerated boost to his physical and mental faculties for a short time after consumption.

As Wally chewed, he could feel the now familiar tingling sensation spreading through his body as the microbes took effect. His senses became heightened - small sounds from outside the bunker reached his ears with clarity, and his vision sharpened enabling him to see even the smallest details within the dimly lit space. He knew his strength and reflexes were also being enhanced to their peak potential, readying him for confrontation if needed.

The two men were now examining the torn open bags they had discovered within the storage room, their voices echoing off the concrete walls. Wally strained to listen to their conversation, picking up mentions of "smuggling routes" and "law enforcement evasion." It was clear they had nefarious plans for exploiting the isolation and obscurity of the island bunker. Wally would not let that happen.

As the first rays of dawn began streaming into the small windows near the bunker ceiling, Wally contemplated his next actions. The men had somehow bypassed the non-lethal booby trap he had set up at Entrance E3. He needed to escalate his efforts to remove this threat, while still adhering to his oath to never grievously harm another living being.

Glancing down at his backpack, inspiration struck. He carefully opened the bag and retrieved one of the non-lethal aerosol grenades that Dr. Sanchez had provided him. They would incapacitate the men long enough for Wally to remove them from the island.

Wally silently positioned himself just inside the bunker entrance, his back against the cold concrete wall. In one smooth motion, he pulled the grenade's pin, allowing the handle to snap free. He took two long strides forward and lobbed the hissing canister into the room just as Marco and Javier turned toward the sound.

The grenade landed at Javier's feet. He stared down at it in confusion which quickly shifted to panic as a thick vapor began spewing from the device. The men's shouts echoed through the chamber as the incapacitating effects took hold.

Wally watched impassively as they collapsed to the floor, the vapor dissipating as quickly as it had appeared. His expression was grim yet resolute. The island's secrets would remain protected.

MARCO AND JAVIER EMERGED from the bunker's entrance coughing and wheezing, their faces flushed and eyes watering.

"What the hell was that?" Javier choked out between ragged breaths. He leaned against the concrete wall of the entrance, beads of sweat forming on his brow.

Marco rubbed his eyes vigorously, as if trying to physically wipe away the irritation. "No idea, but let's get the hell out of here. Something's not right."

Javier spat on the ground. "No kidding. We need to regroup and figure this out. I've never felt anything like that before." He took a few more deep breaths, the fresh air helping to clear his lungs.

Marco nodded, equally mystified. "It was like the air itself turned against us. Like some kind of invisible poison." He looked back into the dimly lit depths of the bunker uneasily.

Javier pushed himself off the wall, still shaky. "Well whatever it was, we ain't going back in there until we know what we're dealing with."

The two men moved away from the entrance and back towards the cover of the trees, the effects of the strange occurrence slowly subsiding. Marco pulled a water bottle from his pack and took a long drink, hoping to wash the acrid taste from his mouth.

"We need to tell the boss about this," Javier said grimly. "Could be some kind of old war gas or something. This place might not be as abandoned as we thought."

Marco's face clouded with frustration. This island bunker was supposed to be their ticket to expanding operations. Now it seemed more trouble than it was worth. "Let's get back to the boat. We'll figure this out later."

Javier readily agreed, more than happy to leave the island behind for the time being. As they hurried towards the hidden cove where their boat was moored, neither man noticed Wally trailing silently behind them, ensuring their hasty departure.

WALLY REENTERS THE bunker at the E3 entrance. He is trying to understand why the bunker door grenade did not trip when the 2 men entered the bunker.

There, lay on the floor the grenade protecting the door, the trip wire unbroken, somehow the grenade had pulled loose, the pin had not been extracted for what ever reason. Wally repositioned the grenade and restrung the trip wire.

He examined the pin and lever closely. Both seemed to be intact and functional. The pin was firmly lodged in place, requiring a good amount of force to extract it. The lever was also rigidly attached. There was no sign of damage or malfunction that would have allowed the grenade to come free of the tripwire prematurely.

Wally traced the nearly invisible fishing line he had used as the tripwire. It remained tautly strung across the doorway, approximately shin height. The line showed no indication of having been disturbed or tripped. He methodically followed its path, verifying that both ends were securely fastened out of sight around the door frame.

Everything appeared to be in working order. Wally was baffled as to how the intruders had managed to enter without springing the trap. He considered the possibility that they had somehow detected the tripwire and disarmed it. But the lack of any cuts or slack in the line seemed to rule that out.

Wally replayed the intruders' conversation in his mind, searching for clues. They had made no mention of encountering any security measures before entering the bunker. Their dialogue indicated a straightforward entry, with no need to bypass or disable any traps.

Perhaps the grenade had simply come loose on its own, Wally theorized. The constant humidity inside the bunker may have affected the adhesive he used. He made a mental note to switch to a more heavy-duty epoxy that could withstand the environmental conditions.

Wally also considered adjusting the sensitivity of the tripwire. The current tension required a pretty forceful impact to pull the pin. Maybe something more delicate would be more easily triggered by an inadvertent leg or boot brushing past it.

After verifying that the tripwire was re-secured and functional, Wally did a final sweep of the entrance. He found no other indications of what could have allowed the undetected entry. For now, the reason remained a mystery. But Wally was determined not to let it happen again. He would continue monitoring and reinforcing the bunker's defenses.

Satisfied with the repairs for the moment, Wally headed deeper into the complex to inspect the rest of the facility. He moved swiftly and silently through the corridors, senses heightened for any signs of disturbance. The familiar twists and turns of the passageways showed no obvious indications of intrusion.

Wally cautiously approached the heavy vault door protecting the main storage room. He inspected the door and surrounding walls closely but found no breaches. The vault appeared untouched since his last visit. Wally entered the lengthy combination on the aged keypad, hearing the solid thunk of the locking bolts retracting.

The thick door swung open with a creak, revealing rows of shelves filled with innocuous-looking containers. Wally scanned the interior, verifying that nothing seemed disturbed or missing. He felt a simultaneous sense of relief and unease. So far there was no evidence that the intruders had accessed this room. But their presence and interest in the bunker still posed a threat that Wally would need to neutralize.

After ensuring the vault was still secure, Wally locked it up and moved on. He had one more area of the bunker to check before feeling confident that its most critical secrets remained protected.

Wally approached the hidden entrance concealed behind a rusted electrical panel. He entered another code into the keypad, causing the false panel to swing outward. The revealed passageway led to Wally's covert underground laboratory.

Wally felt his pulse quicken as he descended the short staircase into the lab. This contained some of the bunker's most sensitive contents related to Wally's scientific research. If the intruders had managed to find it, the implications could be disastrous.

But as Wally scanned the small lab space, everything initially looked untouched. The key equipment, notebooks, and stored samples all seemed undisturbed. He allowed himself to breathe a small sigh of relief even as he remained alert for any sign of entry.

After a thorough sweep of the lab, Wally could find no definite indication that the intruders had accessed this space. As far as he could tell, its existence still remained a closely guarded secret. He felt cautiously optimistic that the bunker's most critical secrets had avoided exposure.

Wally exited the concealed lab, ensuring the entrance was securely closed behind him. As he retraced his steps through the maze of corridors, he contemplated his next moves. He needed to reinforce the bunker's defenses and surveillance to prevent any further incursions. Wally's mind turned over various options as he approached the exit and the sunlight beyond. He had work to do, spurred on by the day's close call. But Wally was confident in his abilities to protect the secrets of this island, whatever it took. For now, the bunker's contents were still safe under his vigilant watch.

WALLY HAD A THOUGHT, he reentered the bunker. He moved with purpose through the dimly lit corridors, his footsteps echoing off the cold concrete walls. Though he had just scared off the intruders Marco and Javier, Wally knew they would likely be back - and he had to be prepared.

Wally entered the main storage room, scanning the space intently. His eyes settled on a tall metal cabinet in the back corner. He remembered stumbling upon this very cabinet years ago, discovering the hidden entrance to the secret underground laboratory behind it. Wally crossed the room and examined the cabinet closely. It was the perfect place to set a trap for any intruders who managed to break in.

Reaching into his backpack, Wally pulled out a grenade canister labeled "Vapor Aerosol Grenade." It was non-lethal but would effectively incapacitate anyone in the vicinity for up to 15 minutes - plenty of time for Wally to intervene. He inspected the sturdy cabinet doors, determining the best way to rig the grenade.

After a few moments, Wally sprang into action. He used a small drill to create holes near the cabinet handles. He threaded strong fishing line through the holes and attached each end to the grenade's pull ring. Wally carefully arranged the line so that opening either cabinet door would yank the ring and activate the grenade inside.

Satisfied with his work, Wally closed the cabinet doors. Anyone who opened them would get a nasty surprise. This would deter Marco and Javier from further snooping around the bunker's secrets.

Wally paused, considering the hidden laboratory entrance behind the cabinet. An idea struck him. He pulled out a second vapor grenade and rigged it to the secret door as well, concealing it expertly. Now both cabinet doors were armed with non-lethal traps. Unauthorized access to the bunker or lab would prove very unpleasant.

Wally stepped back and observed his handiwork. Thanks to the grenades, the bunker's secrets would remain protected even in his absence. Marco and Javier wouldn't know what hit them if they dared to return. Pleased with his preparations, Wally headed out of the bunker under cover of night. He would return soon to check on things. For now, the island's mysteries were secure.

Chapter 4

Wally leaned back in his desk chair, rubbing his eyes after hours of intense focus on the computer screen. His lab was dimly lit except for the halo of light around his workstation, where he had been utterly absorbed in researching combat injuries. Strewn across the desk were opened medical journals, their pages marked with colorful sticky notes and highlights. Wally's fingers trailed over an article as he muttered to himself, "Shrapnel...burns...blunt force trauma..."

The young scientist was driven by a solemn purpose - to adapt the incredible regenerative capacities of DNX-109 to heal the horrific wounds inflicted by war. He had delved into case studies of injuries sustained in the field, from deep lacerations by shrapnel to third-degree burns. His expression was grave as he studied diagrams of damaged tissue and bone, envisioning how DNX-109 could knit together ruptured organs or regenerate skin seared by flames.

Wally crossed the room to his whiteboard, uncapping a marker. In a neat column he wrote: shrapnel, burns, blunt force. His mind churned with ideas on optimizing DNX-109. For shrapnel wounds, a timed release capsule matched to average extraction time could minimize scarring. Burns needed a dressing that stabilized skin growth. Blunt force trauma was trickier - perhaps a two-stage delivery to stop internal bleeding then regenerate tissue.

He stared at the whiteboard, feeling the weight of his undertaking. So many variables, so much potential. But he couldn't lose sight of the end goal - to alleviate suffering on an unimaginable scale.

Wally's phone buzzed with a text. It was his research partner, Dr. Elena Sanchez from the military lab. "Case studies secured. Ready to synergize approaches at 0900 tomorrow." Just the confirmation he had been waiting for. With a tired but satisfied smile, Wally texted back his thanks. He was grateful to have such a brilliant mind as an ally.

At his computer again, Wally pulled up files sent by Dr. Sanchez. His quick eyes scanned through combat reports, analyzing patterns of injury. Here a soldier was blinded by an IED, there another lost two limbs to a landmine. Wally's expression clouded at the senseless destruction. But he could do something, he told himself. He could make a difference.

Opening a program on his computer, Wally began modeling the interaction of DNX-109 with different wound types. Adjusting for shrapnel velocity, thermal intensity, and impact force, he simulated the microbe's effects. Hour after hour he tweaked parameters, seeking to optimize regenerative time while minimizing scarring across the widest range of injuries. It was a monumental task, but Wally was fueled by purpose.

Outside, the night deepened as Wally worked tirelessly on adapting DNX-109. He ignored his growling stomach and dry eyes. He was close, so close to a breakthrough. The simulator results looked promising, but still needed refinement. Wally gulped down some cold coffee, wincing at the bitter taste. He had to keep going. Soldiers were depending on him, even if they didn't know it yet.

Finally, as dawn's light peeked through the blinds, Wally sat back with a look of triumph. There, on his screen, was the key - a controlled release capsule that could be adapted to injury type while guarding against over-replication. Paired with Dr. Sanchez's medicinal expertise, this could be the revolutionary combat treatment he had sought.

Wally allowed himself a moment to take it all in. He thought of the countless lives that could be saved, the suffering that could be avoided. It was a staggering realization, and sobering responsibility. But Wally had never backed down from doing what was right. He would proceed with the utmost care and discretion. The road ahead would not be easy, but with this breakthrough, he was one step closer to achieving something incredible. For now, there was hope.

DR. SANCHEZ SAT IN her office, phone pressed to her ear as she made her final plea to General Matthews' assistant. "I understand the general is a busy man, but this technology could truly be a game-changer for our troops in the field. All I'm asking for is 15 minutes of his time."

She held her breath, listening intently to the voice on the other end of the line. Finally, the assistant relented. "Alright Dr. Sanchez, I'll see what I can do. But no guarantees."

A rush of relief washed over her. This meeting could open the door to getting the regenerative technology she had seen in action into the hands of military medical teams. "Thank you! I truly appreciate you going to bat for me on this."

Two weeks later, Dr. Sanchez straightened her blazer as she strode purposefully into the Pentagon. After passing through rigorous security clearances, she was escorted to a nondescript conference room deep within the bowels of the building. Waiting inside were General Matthews, Colonel Rogers from Army Medical Command, and Captain Sosa, a renowned battlefield surgeon.

Dr. Sanchez shook each of their hands firmly before taking her seat at the head of the table. She opened her briefcase and removed a thin folder containing only a few sheets of paper.

"Thank you all for taking the time to meet with me today," she began, interlacing her fingers on the table. "What I'm about to share with you is highly confidential. It represents a potential breakthrough in treating combat injuries that could change the game for frontline medicine."

The officers exchanged glances but remained silent, waiting for her to continue.

"In my role researching advanced materials, I've recently become aware of an innovative technology that allows for rapid and comprehensive healing of wounds - both internal and external." She paused, letting her words sink in. "I've seen it work first-hand. The implications are nothing short of extraordinary."

Colonel Rogers leaned forward, his interest piqued. "Are we talking about some kind of regenerative medicine?"

Dr. Sanchez nodded. "Essentially, yes. But the key is how rapidly it works. We're talking recovery times up to ten times faster than anything currently available."

"That does sound promising," Captain Sosa replied. "But surely there are limitations?"

"Of course, it's still in the early phases. But even in its current form, it could save countless lives on the battlefield. The difference between a soldier bleeding out from an abdominal wound versus being back on their feet in hours is incalculable."

General Matthews furrowed his brow. "And what exactly is this miracle treatment, Doctor?"

"The details are highly proprietary for now. But I assure you, I've seen it work with my own eyes. On a gunshot wound, recovery was near instantaneous."

The officers murmured between themselves. Dr. Sanchez could tell their curiosity was piqued, but she also sensed their hesitation.

"With all due respect, these kinds of claims require extraordinary evidence," General Matthews said frankly. "Do you have any data to back this up?"

Dr. Sanchez nodded. She removed two photos from her folder and slid them across the table. "As you can see, this is the 'before' and 'after' of a trial done on a mammal. The results were achieved in under 20 minutes."

The officers examined the photos closely, shaking their heads in disbelief. It was clear they found it hard to fathom.

"I understand your skepticism, believe me," Dr. Sanchez continued. "I felt the same way when I first learned of this technology. But I vowed that if it proved out, I would do everything in my power to get it into the hands of our military medical teams. It could save countless lives."

She let that sink in for a moment before continuing. "What I'm asking for today is your support to pursue controlled, sanctioned trials with your medical staff. If the results live up to the potential, I'm confident we can work together to expedite deployment."

General Matthews leaned back in his chair, rubbing his chin thoughtfully. "Well Doctor, you've certainly piqued our interest, I'll give you that. But as I'm sure you know, we can't move forward based on photos alone. We'll need to see thorough trial data and have our own people analyze it."

Dr. Sanchez nodded. "I understand completely. And I'm fully prepared to conduct sanctioned trials under whatever protocols you deem necessary."

Captain Sosa spoke up. "I must say, I've seen a lot of experimental treatments come and go. But if this technology works even half as well as you say, it could radically change how we treat battlefield injuries."

"I agree," Colonel Rogers chimed in. "We owe it to our men and women in uniform to fully investigate anything with this kind of potential."

General Matthews turned to Dr. Sanchez. "Very well then. Draw up a trial protocol for our review. If it meets our standards, we'll greenlight a small-scale trial with select Army medical staff. Consider this an invitation to make your case, Doctor."

Dr. Sanchez felt a thrill of victory, but kept her demeanor professional. "Thank you, General. I assure you, we'll make it a top priority."

The officers rose, shaking her hand again before departing. Alone in the conference room, Dr. Sanchez allowed herself a moment to savor her success. The first critical hurdle was cleared. But she knew the real work was still ahead - proving without a doubt that the technology worked as promised. The battle had just begun.

DR. SANCHEZ WALKED briskly down the pristine white hallway of the military medical research facility, her heels clicking on the polished floor. Trailing slightly behind her was Wally, carrying a large metal case containing the precious DNX-109 bandages and data samples. Despite having been through extensive security checks, Wally still felt on edge in the unfamiliar environment. He knew they were about to demonstrate something unprecedented to an audience of skeptical experts.

As they approached the auditorium, Dr. Sanchez turned and gave Wally a reassuring smile. "Don't worry, we've got this," she said, placing a hand on his shoulder. "Just follow my lead and let the results speak for themselves."

Wally nodded, steeling his nerves as Dr. Sanchez pushed open the doors to reveal a spacious auditorium filled with military medical personnel. They walked onto the stage, where a patient table and medical supplies were set up for the demonstration. In the front row, Wally recognized General Matthews flanked by two stern-looking colonels he presumed were doctors. The audience watched them intently, some with interest, others with undisguised suspicion.

"Good morning, I'm Dr. Elena Sanchez and this is my research assistant, Walter Eastwood," Dr. Sanchez began confidently. "Today we will be demonstrating a groundbreaking new treatment for severe burn injuries using these prototype bandages." She opened the case and held up one of the nondescript bandages infused with DNX-109.

"As many of you know, serious burns often lead to excruciating pain, disfigurement, and long recovery times," she continued. "The dressings we will demonstrate today utilize a compound that has shown unprecedented healing capabilities in trials."

Dr. Sanchez nodded to Wally, who began preparing the simulation. He started by creating two identical artificial burn injuries on the patient - one on each arm. The wounds looked gruesomely real. He then applied a normal burn dressing to one arm while discreetly applying the DNX-109 bandage to the other.

"Over the next two hours, we will be comparing the healing process of these identical burns, one treated with a standard dressing, the other with the prototype," Dr. Sanchez explained. "We will be documenting the process comprehensively."

As the demonstration progressed, audible murmurs began rippling through the audience. The DNX-109 treated wound was visibly improving by the minute, while the control wound remained severe. After just 30 minutes, the prototype-treated injury already looked days ahead in healing.

Dr. Sanchez highlighted key metrics - reduced inflammation, accelerated skin regeneration, decreased pain signals. Wally provided supporting data from trials and real case studies. Some audience members leaned forward with intense interest while others exchanged skeptical glances.

At the 90 minute mark, the difference was undeniable. The prototype-treated wound looked nearly healed, a stark contrast to the angry, blistered control wound. Dr. Sanchez invited the senior medical staff to examine the injuries up close. General Matthews and the colonels approached, inspecting the wounds thoroughly. Their eyes widened as they processed the dramatic divergence.

"As you can see, after only 90 minutes, the wound treated with the prototype dressing exhibits healing equivalent to weeks of natural recovery," Dr. Sanchez summarized confidently. "We have robust data from clinical trials that support these results."

Wally held his breath as the doctors exchanged hushed words with General Matthews. He could see their skepticism gradually giving way to guarded optimism. One colonel turned back to address Dr. Sanchez.

"Your data is quite remarkable. However, we need to validate it independently through more extensive trials before even considering adoption," he said. Murmurs of agreement rippled through the audience.

Dr. Sanchez nodded. "Of course. We welcome rigorous validation and are happy to provide details on our trial protocols."

The demonstration continued to the two hour mark, by which point the difference between the wounds was akin to years of healing. With the stunning visual evidence before them, Wally could see the last vestiges of doubt dissipating from the audience. Quiet discussions gave way to eager questions and requests to examine samples.

As the doctors left the stage, Wally saw General Matthews in close conversation with the colonels. Though not fully convinced, their body language signaled that a wall of skepticism had developed cracks. Thanks to Dr. Sanchez's masterful demonstration, the door was now open for more extensive trials.

Wally felt a swell of hope. Though the path forward would be long, this first step felt pivotal. For the first time, he allowed himself to truly envision DNX-109's healing potential blossoming to help countless wounded soldiers. There was much work left to be done, but Dr. Sanchez had been right - the results spoke volumes.

DR. ELENA SANCHEZ AND William "Will" James stood in the sterile confines of the testing room. The air was thick with anticipation as they prepared for the next phase of their revolutionary regenerative technology, DNX-109.

The demonstration had been a resounding success, with the bandages' remarkable healing abilities leaving the senior medical staff in awe. Yet, despite this initial enthusiasm, the officers remained cautious, eager to proceed with caution and strict guidelines in place.

General Matthews, a seasoned veteran with a stern countenance, addressed the room. "Dr. Sanchez, Mr. James, your work is impressive, but we must proceed with caution. We propose a small-scale, field distribution of these bandages to special units." His eyes scanned the room, his gaze steady and unyielding.

"Understood, General," Dr. Sanchez replied, her voice steady and assured. "We have taken every precaution to ensure the safety and efficacy of our product. However, we recognize that moving beyond the lab's controlled environment will be the true test of its potential."

Will nodded in agreement, his hands clasped behind his back. "Absolutely, General. We're prepared to do whatever it takes to make sure this technology is deployed safely and effectively." His voice carried a note of determination, a testament to his years of service and dedication to protecting those on the front lines.

General Matthews acknowledged their responses with a nod before continuing. "In light of this, we've laid out strict guidelines for reporting and surveillance. We must be vigilant and prepared for any unforeseen consequences that may arise from this new technology."

Dr. Sanchez's eyes narrowed slightly as she considered the gravity of the situation. "Of course, General. We understand the responsibility that comes with this groundbreaking innovation. We will adhere to all protocols and remain vigilant in our pursuit of further advancements in combat wound care."

Will interjected, his voice firm and resolute. "Rest assured, General. We're committed to ensuring that this technology not only enhances the lives of our soldiers but also remains within our control at all times." His words were a promise, a vow to protect the integrity of their creation and safeguard its potential benefits for those who needed it most.

The room fell into a somber silence as they contemplated the weight of their collective decisions. The officers exchanged glances, acknowledging the complexity of the situation and the potential risks involved in bringing such a groundbreaking technology to the battlefield.

General Matthews broke the silence, his voice echoing with authority and conviction. "Very well. We'll proceed with a small-scale field distribution to select units under strict guidelines and monitoring. Dr. Sanchez, Mr. James, I expect you to remain available for consultation and collaboration throughout this process."

Dr. Sanchez nodded in agreement, her expression serious and focused. "We'll be ready to assist in any way we can, General. We understand the importance of this collaboration and are eager to see our work make a difference in the lives of our soldiers."

Will echoed her sentiments, his voice carrying a note of pride and honor. "Yes, General. We'll do everything in our power to ensure that this technology is deployed safely and effectively for those who need it most." His words were a commitment to his former comrades-in-arms and a testament to his unwavering dedication to protecting those on the front lines.

As the meeting concluded and the officers dispersed to discuss their next steps, Dr. Sanchez and Will exchanged a knowing glance. They were acutely aware of the challenges that lay ahead as they prepared to bring their revolutionary technology to the battlefield, where it could potentially save countless lives but also expose them to an entirely new set of dangers and unknowns.

With a sense of cautious optimism and unwavering determination, they knew that their journey was far from over – but they were ready to face whatever lay ahead with grace, grit, and an unyielding commitment to making a difference in the world they had dedicated their lives to serving.

THE FIRST REPORTS TRICKLED in slowly, almost hesitantly. A platoon medic noted a soldier's minor shrapnel wound closing rapidly after application of the Sanchez bandages, as if the ragged edges were knitting themselves back together. In another unit, a sergeant remarked on a teammate making a swift recovery from a leg laceration that previously would have taken weeks to heal.

Gradually, the stories accumulated, spreading in hushed voices through the barracks and mess halls. Soldiers began to speak of wounds mending in days instead of weeks under the new bandages, with some not even leaving a scar. Cases of stubborn infections drying up and fading away after starting a course of treatment with the novel dressings.

Then came the photos, clandestinely snapped with contraband phones and shared through back channels. A jagged incision on a soldier's arm, captured in a series of images over several days. The angry red edges smoothing, the wound closing, nothing but a faint white line remaining. A swollen, discolored calf wound with damaged muscle and tendons rapidly regaining normal contours after Sanchez bandage application.

The photographic evidence was stark, even shocking in its implications. Soldiers who previously faced months of rehabilitation or even medical discharge after severe injuries were recovering full mobility in a fraction of the anticipated time. The Sanchez bandages were demonstrating results beyond what anyone had thought possible.

Within the barracks, talk of the new technology reached a fever pitch. Soldiers on light duty swapped stories of their own rapid recoveries thanks to the Sanchez treatments. Others asked about getting their hands on some, hoping to accelerate their healing and return to full duty. The reputation of the bandages spread by word of mouth, taking on an almost mythic status among the troops.

"You hear about what happened to Martinez? Took a piece of shrapnel to the gut, we all thought he was done for. Doc slapped some of those Sanchez bandages on him, next day he's up walking around eating chow with the rest of us," said one soldier.

His buddy shook his head in disbelief. "I saw Rivers take a bullet straight through his shoulder, shredded that joint to hell. One week with the Sanchez wraps, he's already got full motion back. It's unreal."

When Sergeant Evans' squad was pinned down by enemy fire, he took a round to the thigh that blew out a chunk of muscle. The medics applied a Sanchez dressing and within 72 hours, he was not only walking normally but led his squad on a 10-click hike through the Hindu Kush.

"I've never seen anything like it," Evans told his platoon. "That bandage juice healed me up faster than seemed humanly possible. I went from being laid up in the aid station to being back on patrol in less than a week."

Stories like Evans' fueled demand for the novel bandages. Troops started specifically asking corpsmen for "some of those Sanchez bandages" when they got injured. Soldiers on patrol would check their first aid kits to ensure they were carrying a supply of the coveted dressings. For severe trauma cases, the first words out of a soldier's mouth in the field hospital were often, "Do you have the Sanchez bandages?"

Through back channels and off-the-record conversations, word of the bandages' capabilities reached the upper echelons. Generals and colonels who had written off injured soldiers as permanently disabled were stunned to see them return to duty in a fraction of the expected recovery time. Entire units crippled by combat wounds were restored to battle readiness almost overnight thanks to the Sanchez treatments.

In mess halls and barracks across every branch of the military, the Sanchez bandages were becoming the stuff of legend. Troops lucky enough to receive the novel dressings recovered miraculously fast. Soldiers without access lamented not having their hands on some of these "miracle bandages."

Medics and corpsmen quickly learned to use their limited supplies of Sanchez bandages only for the most severe and infected wounds. Soldiers began bargaining and bartering to get their hands on some of the coveted dressings, knowing they could mean the difference between being evacuated versus staying with their units.

On bases and aboard ships, service members swapped reports of the Sanchez bandages' capabilities like sports fans comparing stats. They spoke in hushed, reverent tones about wounds healing seamlessly, infections disappearing practically overnight, mobility and sensation returning unexpectedly fast. The dressings were becoming prized and coveted commodities across every branch.

Among the rank and file, grumblings began. Why were the miraculous Sanchez bandages only selectively available? How come some units had ample supplies while others had none? Troops wondered why the military wasn't mass producing the novel dressings to get them in the hands of every soldier, sailor, airman and Marine.

Conspiracy theories took root in the speculation. Secret stockpiles of Sanchez bandages reserved only for elite units. Generals hoarding supplies to curry favor. Pharma lobbyists suppressing full production to protect profits. Some began to accuse their superiors of rationing the life-saving technology, refusing to provide it to the troops who needed it most.

As the stories of cures and rapid recoveries reached a crescendo, so too did pressure within the ranks. The troops had gotten a glimpse of a medical technology that could change the face of warfare. No longer did injury inevitably mean a long and painful road to recovery. This revolutionary advancement was proving it could get them quickly back to duty, back to their units, back to the fight.

Now the service members were asking, even outright demanding: Why is this miraculous technology being rationed? How come every soldier doesn't have access to the Sanchez bandages? They had seen the results firsthand, seen gaping wounds heal seamlessly under the novel dressings. They knew this invention could save lives and careers - so why, they asked, was the military holding it back?

The swell of chatter and speculation in mess halls led to pointed questions in briefings. Troops pressed their commanders: When will we get more of the Sanchez bandages? How come other units have it but we don't? The brass deflected, urging patience and citing production limits - but their answers did not satisfy the rank and file.

In barracks and aboard ships, one phrase was on the lips of every soldier, sailor and Marine fortunate enough to have used the Sanchez bandages: "Game changer." They had witnessed this technology swiftly heal grievous wounds that should have permanently disabled them. It was a breakthrough they knew could alter the face of warfare and save countless lives - if only it were put fully into the hands of those who needed it most.

So the troops continued to press their superiors, the support swelling into a chorus. "More Sanchez bandages!" became a rallying cry. Service members from every branch, having witnessed the life-saving results firsthand, joined in demanding the military provide this revolutionary technology to all of its personnel. They knew its implications - and they knew the difference it could make on the battlefield, if only given the chance.

WALLY LEANED BACK IN his desk chair, rubbing his eyes after another long night in the lab. The successful small-scale trials of the Micro-encapsulated DNX-109 bandages had yielded overwhelmingly positive results, but he knew the real challenge still lay ahead. Scaling up production while maintaining complete secrecy and control would require meticulous planning and execution.

His phone rang, jolting him alert. It was Dr. Sanchez.

"Elena, I was just thinking about you," Wally said. "Have you had a chance to review the trial data?"

"I have, and it's remarkable, Wally," she replied, the excitement clear in her voice. "I know we need to proceed cautiously, but this technology could change everything. We should discuss next steps."

Wally leaned forward, intrigued. "I agree. Why don't we meet at our usual spot tomorrow evening to talk it through?"

The next day, Wally arrived at Sammy's Roadhouse Grill and slid into the corner booth where Elena was already waiting. After placing their orders, Elena withdrew a stack of papers from her briefcase along with two sleek, secure laptops.

"I took the liberty of drafting a production scaling plan," she said, her eyes glinting behind her glasses. "If we're going to do this, we need to build our own dedicated facility and control every aspect of the process."

Wally nodded, impressed by her foresight. "That makes complete sense. We can't risk exposing our methods to anyone else. What are you thinking in terms of size and location?"

"Small and discreet, at least to start," Elena replied, opening her laptop to display architectural plans for a modest facility. "I have just the spot in mind near the base. The paperwork trails back to a shell company, nothing traceable to us."

They dove into the details, hashing out production batch sizes, security protocols, and contingency plans. Wally's apprehension gave way to growing excitement as their vision took shape.

After hours of discussion, Elena closed her laptop decisively. "I think we're ready for the next phase. My team can start procuring equipment and materials through secure channels. We'll keep each batch small, no more than 50 vials of DNX-109 at a time."

Wally nodded in agreement. "Start with 20. We'll document the process thoroughly before increasing. Each vial will have a coded serial number for tracking."

"Precisely. And I'll personally oversee the first production runs," Elena said. She extended her hand across the table. "To a new chapter?"

Wally shook it firmly. "To changing lives."

Over the next two months, Elena's team quietly constructed and outfitted the production facility while Wally perfected the Micro-encapsulated DNX-109 formula and protocols. Soon, they were ready for their first test batch.

The day arrived, and Wally could feel the tension and excitement hanging thick in the sterile air. Every precaution had been taken, every variable controlled. He nodded to Elena; it was time to begin.

They worked in perfect sync, two scientists at the top of their game. Each step was executed flawlessly, every measurement precise. As the final vial rolled off the production line, Wally and Elena shared an exhausted but triumphant smile.

Later, in the secured lab room, Wally held up the first coded vial. Micro-encapsulated DNX-109-B001. It represented years of research and a medical breakthrough like no other. But it also carried the weight of lives and futures they aimed to restore.

"Only 19 more to go for this batch," Elena said, placing the vial gently into a storage case. "Then we document, analyze, and decide if we're ready to increase to 50."

Wally agreed, acutely aware they were venturing into uncharted territory. Success would require constant vigilance, controlling every minuscule factor without cutting corners or compromising their ethics.

But as he looked around the state-of-the-art facility, he felt confident in what they had built together. This unassuming space, hidden away from prying eyes, could become the birthplace of a revolution in medicine.

After locking down the lab, Elena and Wally walked out together into the night. They had taken the first step, the beginning of a marathon journey. But with meticulous care and patience, each small batch would pave the way forward.

MAJOR HELEN MIRA STEPPED out of the rental car, smoothed her impeccable uniform, and surveyed the unassuming warehouse that served as the clandestine production facility for the revolutionary Micro-encapsulated DNX-109 bandages. As the military liaison for this highly sensitive project, she understood both the gravity of its implications and the critical importance of maintaining utmost discretion.

Approaching the entrance, Helen pressed her thumb to the biometric reader and entered a complex access code. The heavy steel door slid open, granting her access to the sterile interior workspace. Her polished boots clicked decisively on the concrete floor as she made her way to the main production area.

Wally looked up from a computer terminal as Helen entered, immediately straightening his posture almost instinctively in the presence of the imposing officer. "Major Mira, welcome back," he said. "Production is right on schedule for this week's shipment."

Helen nodded, her keen gaze sweeping over the machinery fabricating the remarkable bandages - each infused with Wally's ingenious healing microbes. "Very good, Mr. Eastwood. I trust all protocols are being strictly followed?"

"To the letter," Wally affirmed. "Dr. Sanchez oversees every aspect of the process personally."

Right on cue, Dr. Elena Sanchez emerged from the laboratory area, pulling off her gloves as she approached. "Major, good to see you. I assure you, quality control remains our top priority."

"It has to be," Helen responded solemnly. "You both understand how much is at stake here. These bandages will save lives, but in the wrong hands..." Her voice trailed off, the unspoken implications clear.

Wally and Elena exchanged a look. They knew Helen spoke from experience. Her role went far beyond oversight - she had seen firsthand the toll of combat injuries. This project was personal for her.

"Believe me, we understand," Wally said gravely. "That's why we're taking every precaution. Our distribution is limited strictly to Army medical staff, starting with frontline trauma centers."

Helen nodded. "Good. We proceed cautiously. Expand the trials incrementally. I'll navigate the bureaucracy on my end." Though reserved professionally, her passion shone through.

Elena smiled warmly. "Your guidance has been invaluable, Major. Your background in medical logistics has made this possible." Helen's stoic demeanor softened slightly at the praise.

"I'm just doing my duty," she replied simply. After a thoughtful pause, she continued, "When I lost my brother David in Afghanistan, he bled out from an injury that could have been treated if the right supplies had reached his unit. I won't let that happen to others if I can help it. Even a single life saved means..." Her voice caught briefly before she regained composure. "Well, you know why this matters."

"We do," Wally said. Moved by her candor, he added, "Your brother would be proud of what you've accomplished here."

Helen blinked back a sheen of tears, touched by the sentiment. With a polite nod, she said, "Thank you, Mr. Eastwood. Now if you'll excuse me, I should review the latest production numbers."

As the major walked away, Elena let out a slow exhale. "What a tremendous weight she carries," she reflected somberly.

Wally nodded. "She's been through a lot. But she knows we share the same goal - saving lives. That's what drives us all."

They stood a moment in thoughtful silence. Then it was back to work - there were shipments to prepare, rigorous procedures to follow. Neither took this responsibility lightly.

When Helen returned, her professional demeanor was firmly back in place. "Gentlemen, everything looks in order. You run a tight operation here. Let's keep it that way."

"We will," Wally assured her. Their eyes met in a look of mutual understanding and respect.

With a crisp nod, Helen took her leave, the echoes of her precise footsteps fading as she exited the warehouse. The weight of the past and future rode heavily on her shoulders. But she allowed herself the rarest of smiles, feeling, perhaps for the first time, a sense of hope.

DR. SANCHEZ SAT ACROSS from General Matthews in a small, windowless conference room deep within the Pentagon. She had prepared meticulously for this meeting, poring over military manuals and regulations late into the night. Now, seeing the general's furrowed brow and tightly clasped hands resting on a thick folder, she knew her work was cut out for her.

"Let's get right to it, Doctor," General Matthews said gruffly. "I've reviewed your proposal, and frankly, I have some concerns."

Dr. Sanchez nodded. She had expected resistance. "Of course, General. I'm happy to address any issues you see."

Matthews flipped open the folder, scanning a document within. "First off, your plan lacks sufficient security protocols. These bandages utilize proprietary technology developed outside the military. We can't have soldiers walking around with classified healing abilities."

"You're absolutely right," Dr. Sanchez replied smoothly. "I've already devised extensive security measures to conceal the technology's origins. The bandages will be indistinguishable from standard-issue medical supplies."

The general grunted in reply, turning a page. "Okay, fair enough. But I also see problems with your proposed distribution scheme. Giving these bandages to special ops teams first raises too many questions."

Dr. Sanchez had prepared for this too. "Of course, we want to avoid any appearance of favoritism. I suggest an incremental rollout, starting with rapid deployment units across branches, then expanding from there once we have proven success."

General Matthews studied her, then gave a grudging nod. They continued reviewing the proposal line-by-line, clause-by-clause. The meeting stretched on for over two hours, but Dr. Sanchez held her ground, justifying every detail with military precision.

Finally, Matthews closed the folder and sat back with a sigh. "Well Doctor, I've got to hand it to you. I expected to shoot this down quick, but you've addressed every concern thoroughly. I'm tentatively approving a small-scale trial run."

Dr. Sanchez exhaled in relief. "Thank you, General. I assure you, we will proceed cautiously and keep you appraised of all developments."

They stood and shook hands firmly. As she left the Pentagon, Dr. Sanchez allowed herself a small smile. She had won this battle - but the war was just beginning.

Meanwhile, at his private lab facility, Wally input a complex 64-character password to access the hermetically sealed clean room where the miracle Micro-encapsulated DNX-109 bandages were produced. Once inside, he inspected the biometric security system he had installed to restrict access. Only his and Dr. Sanchez's handprints could open the final door to the manufacturing apparatus.

Satisfied with the physical security, Wally moved on to inspecting the closed-circuit camera system he had rigged throughout the facility. High-resolution, infrared cameras tracked every inch of the lab, monitored 24/7 from an encrypted offsite location. Motion sensors would detect any unauthorized access, triggering lockdown procedures and alerting Wally instantly.

Despite the exhaustive security measures, Wally knew the bandages themselves remained vulnerable outside the lab. He retreated to his workstation to continue developing a self-destruct mechanism for the dressings. Once peeled from the wound after use, the bandage would break down at the molecular level, preventing tissue samples or trace elements from remaining.

It was a challenge engineering the timed destruction sequence, but after weeks of experimentation Wally had a working prototype. He carefully packaged samples of the self-destructing bandages, triple-sealing and encrypting the case. These would go to Dr. Sanchez for final validation before being incorporated into production.

Wally took one last walkthrough, verifying every security camera and biometric lock. Though exhausted, he felt confident the lab's secrets were protected. The bandages could save countless lives on the battlefield - but only if their existence remained undisclosed.

After locking down the facility for the night, Wally returned home. He fixed a simple meal and ate slowly, considering the day's events. Though he and Dr. Sanchez had made great strides, danger lurked around every corner. Human nature could not be underestimated.

Wally cleaned up and headed to bed, resolving to redouble his vigilance. The bandages were only the beginning. There were so many more discoveries to be made, so many more lives to save - but only if the work continued in utmost secrecy. As he drifted off, Wally's mind churned with ideas for how to conceal the next phases of their revolutionary research from prying eyes. The mission was just beginning.

Chapter 5

Wally leaned back in his desk chair, rubbing his eyes after hours of poring over data and reports. The latest results from the field trials of the regenerative bandages were nothing short of astounding. Every quantitative metric showed massive improvements in healing outcomes - decreased recovery time, lower rates of infection, accelerated wound closure. The numbers and graphs on his computer screen told an incredible story of scientific triumph.

But even more profound was the qualitative data he had started receiving in the form of firsthand accounts from soldiers treated with the bandages. Their stories of survival and renewed hope brought the significance of his work into sharp focus. This was no longer just an intellectual exercise with data points and statistics. Real lives were being saved and changed.

Wally clicked open a video file sent over by Dr. Sanchez. It showed a soldier named Private Miller describing how he had suffered a grievous shrapnel leg wound that should have taken over a year to recover from. But after being treated with the regenerative bandage, he was back on his feet in a matter of weeks. "This bandage saved my leg - saved my career," Miller said, his voice brimming with gratitude. "I'd be maimed or worse without it. Hell, I was halfway to planning my medical discharge before they wrapped me up with that miracle dressing."

Another file contained a letter from a Sergeant Hopkins recounting how she had been certain she would lose her hand after a bomb blast tore through her left arm. Infection had set in by the time she was evacuated from the field. But within days of getting the Sanchez treatment, the redness and swelling had receded. She regained full use of her fingers soon after. "You gave me back my career, doc," her letter read. "Can't thank you enough."

With each account, Wally felt the weight and significance of his work sink in. This was the culmination of years of research, a seemingly impossible scientific quest. And it was paying off in the form of lives changed, injuries healed, hope and purpose restored. Soldiers who should have been confined to wheelchairs were walking again. Careers cut short were given new life. For the first time, the fruits of his labor were rippling out into the real world.

Wally thought of his friend Ronnie, whose own injury had been the genesis of this journey. Ronnie too had benefited enormously from the regenerative effects of DNX-109. But this was so much bigger than just one person now. Soldiers across the globe were reaping the rewards. It was humbling and deeply gratifying.

Of course, Wally knew he could not rest on his laurels. The trials still had months to go, and scaling up production of the bandages remained a massive challenge. General Matthews continued to express concerns about leaks and security breaches if too many people became aware of the secretive project. Wally would need to solve the engineering problems required to ramp up manufacturing without compromising discretion and safety protocols. No easy task.

For today though, Wally allowed himself a brief moment of reflection on what had been achieved. So much meticulous research and testing had led to this point. Late nights puzzling over genetic sequences, poring over electron micrographs, and observing countless trials in his hidden island laboratory. It had been a long, winding road to get here. But the payoff had been monumental.

Wally powered down his computer, tidied up his lab notes, and locked up his home office. Stepping outside into the twilight, he decided to clear his head with one of his favorite activities - a bike ride along the bayou. As he pedaled, fireflies flickered among the rushes lining the path. A horned owl called out from the darkness. Wally let his mind empty, focusing only on the gentle motion of the pedals and the night sounds of the wetlands.

By the time he arrived back home, Wally felt rejuvenated. He settled down on the back patio with a glass of iced tea and watched the moon rise over the silvery waters of the bayou. A deep sense of fulfillment washed over him. He was struck by how far he had come from his humble beginnings tinkering with model airplanes as a boy. Back then he could scarcely imagine contributing something meaningful to the world. Now here he was, on the cusp of a discovery that could alter the course of modern medicine.

Of course, Wally knew the road ahead remained long. This was only the beginning. Rigorous trials still lay ahead. Challenges of manufacturing and distribution had to be solved. Not to mention navigating the complex ethics of whether and how to eventually make the technology available beyond the military. Wally carried the weight of these dilemmas lightly but seriously.

For tonight though, he let those concerns fade into the background. Tonight was for appreciating how far his work had already come. Somewhere out there, soldiers were recovering from grievous wounds, their bodies knitting themselves back together at extraordinary speed thanks to the bandages' regenerative microbes. Careers were being saved. Families reunited.

Wally raised his glass in a silent toast to those whose lives had been transformed. And to those who would be touched in the future if he could continue to develop the technology responsibly. He knew the road ahead would be long and difficult. But the rewards were already crystal clear. Wally drifted off to sleep that night with a profound sense of purpose, ready to continue his vital work.

WALLY PULLED HIS TRUCK into the driveway, the crunch of gravel under the tires a familiar sound after another long day. As he walked up to the front door, fishing his keys out of his pocket, a prickling sense of unease washed over him. He paused, keys hovering over the lock, and scanned the front of the house. Nothing seemed amiss, but the feeling persisted. Wally stepped back and slowly circled the perimeter, searching for any sign of an intruder.

Rounding the far corner, he spotted it - a tiny camera lens protruding from a gap in the siding near the ground. Wally's breath caught in his throat as he crouched down to examine the device. This was no amateur operation; the camera was cleverly concealed in weatherproof housing painted to match the wood siding. A chill ran down Wally's spine as the implications sank in. Someone had found him, had been spying on his home, and possibly his lab.

Wally hastily disabled the camera and pocketed it, hands shaking slightly despite his attempt at calm. Safely inside, he did a thorough sweep for bugs or any other monitoring devices, but found nothing. Whoever placed the camera hadn't made it inside - yet.

Wally's mind raced, questions swirling. How long had the camera been there? What exactly had it captured? Was he being watched now? He tried to quiet the building panic as he sat heavily on the couch. He knew he needed to get rid of the camera and cover his tracks.

Grabbing a hammer, Wally smashed the device and disposed of the pieces in various dumpsters around town. He then purchased new siding at the hardware store to patch the gap left by the removed camera. Wally worked quickly, nerves on edge as he covered any trace of the monitoring.

Exhausted but wired, Wally debated his next steps. He couldn't ignore what had happened, but he also couldn't be sure of the threat level. Had he slipped up somehow, exposed his research? Or was it just an opportunistic criminal looking for a remote home to target?

Wally decided his lab needed checking as well. If someone had found this house, they may have discovered the lab's location too. He headed out to the hidden bunker, taking a meandering route in case he was being followed. Upon arrival, he inspected every inch but found no signs of intrusion. He replaced the keypad lock with a newer system just to be safe.

Over the next week, Wally withdrew from his normal routines. He varied his driving routes, kept odd hours, and made unexplained trips out of town. He needed to know if he was still being watched. Nothing seemed out of the ordinary, but Wally's unease lingered.

Nearly a month later, Wally was working late in his home office when he noticed a nondescript van slowly pass by. Something about it rang a bell - hadn't he seen it earlier that week? He watched the van reach the end of the road, turn around, and drive by again in the opposite direction. Wally's pulse quickened. He was still being watched.

Wally immediately called Ronnie and Richie for an emergency meeting at a secure location. Catching them up on the camera and the surveillance van, Wally saw his own anxiety reflected in their tense expressions. Ronnie proposed they sweep the lab again and move any sensitive materials to a more secure location, just to be safe. Richie suggested going on the offensive to gather information, but Wally vetoed anything risky for now. They agreed to meet again soon to reassess the situation.

In the following days, Wally withdrew even further from public life. He relentlessly analyzed each encounter for anything suspicious, seeing threats in every unfamiliar face. He knew he was spiraling, paranoia threatening to overwhelm reason, but the invasion of his privacy had shattered his sense of security.

DR. SANCHEZ SAT ACROSS from General Matthews in the Pentagon, sensing the growing pressure emanating from the esteemed officer. "The reports on your regenerative bandages have been remarkable," Matthews said, shuffling through a stack of files on his desk. "Injuries that would normally take weeks or months to heal have been resolving in days with your technology. You've made a groundbreaking advancement for our troops."

Sanchez nodded politely. "Thank you, sir. My team has worked diligently to refine the bandage prototypes into a viable product."

"And now we need to get them to more units on the frontlines," Matthews continued, his tone sharpening. "The success of the small-scale deployment has been proven. It's time to expand distribution."

The scientist hesitated, choosing her next words carefully. "Of course, sir. We are prepared to gradually scale up production and access. However, each stage requires meticulous oversight to ensure..."

Matthews held up his hand, cutting her off. "You've made your position clear, Doctor. And I understand the need for discretion. But we're facing mounting pressure from all branches to make these bandages universally available. The reports of rapid healing have fueled intense demand."

He rose from his seat and paced behind the desk. "We have a duty to provide every advantage possible to our men and women in combat. Your technology could be the difference between life and death for many." Turning, he fixed Sanchez with a piercing look. "Can I count on your cooperation?"

Sanchez stood her ground. "You have my full commitment to serving our troops, General. My colleague, Mr. Eastwood, and I will initiate the next phase of controlled distribution. However, this will be a gradual process requiring the utmost care."

Matthews studied her silently before giving a curt nod. "Very well. Draft a distribution plan and we'll review it next week." As Sanchez turned to leave, he added, "And Doctor, time is of the essence. I trust I've made that clear."

The flight back to Houston was filled with contemplation as Sanchez considered the immense responsibility before her. Eastwood had proven a trusted ally, his discretion and technical expertise assuaging her doubts about expanding access to their creation. And yet, the risk of exposure grew with each passing day.

She arrived at the discreet production facility, where Eastwood was inspecting a batch of freshly produced bandages. "How did it go?" he asked without glancing up.

"As expected," Sanchez replied. "The reports of success have placed us under intense pressure to increase distribution."

Eastwood nodded, his expression unsurprised yet grim. "I figured that call was coming. But we both know the dangers of moving too quickly. One breach of security and this whole operation could come crashing down."

"Precisely. I was able to secure more time to plan our next steps." Sanchez moved to examine the bandages. "For now, we focus on production. The first expanded rollout will be limited to five hundred units. Specific combat divisions are still to be determined."

The pair worked late into the night, meticulously accounting for every bandage and triple-checking security protocols. The weight of their work lingered in the air - the knowledge that each bandage produced could save lives on the battlefield. And yet, any mistake could spell disaster instead.

At dawn, Sanchez met Eastwood on the tarmac at a private airfield outside Houston. A small jet awaited them, cleared for travel to the Army's Medical Research Institute of Infectious Diseases in Maryland. There, they would present their distribution plan to General Matthews and the Officer's Council.

"Are you ready for this?" Eastwood asked as they boarded the plane. "Today decides the fate of everything we've worked toward."

Sanchez gazed at the rising sun, steeling her nerves. "As ready as I'll ever be. We both know what's at stake here - for our troops and for the future of medicine. It's time to change the world, my friend."

The flight was smooth but tense. Upon landing, a military escort drove them to the secure facility. They were ushered into a conference room where General Matthews and five senior officers awaited them.

"Thank you for coming," Matthews greeted them. "I trust you've prepared a wise plan?"

Sanchez stepped forward. "Yes, General. Based on successful small-scale deployment, we propose distributing five hundred bandage units to select Special Operations units. This will allow us to closely monitor results while limiting exposure."

She proceeded to outline their exhaustive security protocols for inventory, delivery, and use. The officers listened intently, periodically interjecting with sharp questions which Sanchez handled deftly.

After an hour, Matthews leaned back in his seat. "You've been quite thorough. And discretion remains paramount. Very well, you may proceed with your plan." Rising, he extended his hand. "You have our gratitude, Doctor. Your technology will save many lives."

The flight home was filled with optimism tempered by a solemn understanding of their duty. Upon returning to the facility, Sanchez and Eastwood supervised the preparation of the five hundred bandages, each marked with a hidden tracking code. They worked late into the night, driven by their commitment to the troops who would soon benefit.

As Sanchez finally departed near midnight, the first small shipment already en route to its destination, she allowed herself a moment of reflection. Gazing up at the stars, she whispered a silent prayer - for the soldiers, for the future, and for the strength to walk the difficult road ahead. The path was long, but she took comfort knowing she did not walk it alone.

WALLY SAT IN HIS HOME office, staring blankly at the screen. The latest batch of regenerative bandages had shipped that morning, marking a major milestone in getting his creation into the hands of those who needed it most. But instead of feeling proud, Wally was gripped by an unshakable sense of unease.

His phone rang, jolting him from his thoughts. It was Dr. Sanchez. Wally took a deep breath before answering.

"Wally, I wanted to check in after today's shipment went out," she said, her voice wavering slightly. "I know it's a big step."

Wally rubbed his temples. "It is. And if I'm being honest, I'm not sure it was the right one."

"I've had the same doubts," Dr. Sanchez admitted. "We're venturing into uncharted territory here."

They were both quiet for a moment, the weight of their shared burden hanging heavily between them.

"When we started this project, it was so straightforward - we just wanted to help people heal," Wally said. "Now it feels like we've opened Pandora's box. The potential for misuse is terrifying."

Dr. Sanchez sighed. "I know. Believe me, I've lain awake at night thinking through every possible scenario. Rogue nations weaponizing the technology, terrorists holding civilians hostage..." Her voice trailed off.

"Exactly," Wally said grimly. "And that's just the start. What if the regeneration process gets out of control and causes tumors or mutations?"

"A valid concern. We've run so many tests, but there are always unknowns," Dr. Sanchez conceded.

Wally stood and paced his office. "I keep asking myself - have we gone too far? Should we have destroyed the research, ended this before it began?"

"Part of me wishes we had," Dr. Sanchez admitted. "But there's no going back now. Pandora doesn't return to her box once opened."

They sat in solemn silence again. Wally knew she was right. The genie was out of the bottle now, for better or worse.

"So where does that leave us?" Wally finally asked. "We have a responsibility here - to use this technology ethically and minimize harm. But how?"

"By staying vigilant," Dr. Sanchez said firmly. "Closely tracking every bandage, auditing distribution and being ready to intervene if anything seems amiss."

Wally nodded slowly. "Alright. We'll watch things like hawks. And at the first sign of trouble, we shut it down."

"Agreed. This will take constant diligence on both our parts," Dr. Sanchez said. "Are you prepared for that burden?"

"I have to be," Wally said gravely. "Like you said, there's no going back now."

They discussed logistics and protocols for keeping close tabs on the bandages. Wally felt fractionally relieved having a concrete plan, but his underlying anxiety remained.

After they hung up, Wally stood at his window overlooking the moonlit valley below. Somewhere out there, his creation was already changing lives. He desperately hoped it was for the better. But only time would tell.

Wally arrived at Dr. Sanchez's office first thing Monday morning. She ushered him inside, her expression grim.

"What's happened?" Wally asked, his pulse quickening.

"Two of our test bandages have gone missing," Dr. Sanchez said. "They were signed out for a training exercise but never returned."

Wally felt his stomach drop. "Any indication where they went?"

Dr. Sanchez shook her head. "I've already spoken to everyone involved. As far as they know, the bandages were lost in the field."

"Do you believe them?" Wally asked pointedly.

"I'm not sure," Dr. Sanchez admitted. "It seems plausible, but..."

"But we can't afford to assume anything," Wally finished. He began to pace. "If those bandages fell into the wrong hands..."

Dr. Sanchez nodded gravely. "I know. We need to consider all possibilities here."

Wally's mind raced with terrifying scenarios - rogue agents, enemy operatives, profiteering smugglers. Anyone could be behind this.

Dr. Sanchez placed a hand on his shoulder. "Wally, try to stay calm. We'll handle this methodically."

He took a deep breath. "You're right. Sorry, it's just my worst fear come to life."

"Mine too," Dr. Sanchez said. "But we planned for this. We'll track those bandages down and get to the bottom of what happened."

Wally felt marginally relieved. If anyone could find the missing bandages, it was Dr. Sanchez.

Over the next few weeks, they discreetly investigated, following every lead and thread. But the bandages had vanished without a trace.

Wally grew more anxious by the day. Someone out there had a piece of dangerous technology that he was responsible for creating. And he had no idea what they planned to do with it.

WALLY STRAIGHTENED his tie and took a deep breath as he entered the conference room, Dr. Sanchez close behind him. Before them sat a panel of stern-looking military officials, their faces betraying no hint of favor. At the center of the long table was General Matthews, his salt and pepper hair neatly combed. To his right sat Major Helen Mira, her gaze sharp and assessing.

"Let's begin," General Matthews said, his voice crisp and authoritative. "You claim these bandages represent a revolutionary advancement in wound treatment. Make your case clearly and concisely."

Wally stepped forward, speaking evenly. "General, esteemed officers - what we've developed is no mere incremental improvement. The regenerative microbes in our bandages accelerate healing on the cellular level at an unprecedented rate. As evidenced by our trial data, they can fully mend lacerations and burns in a fraction of the normal time, often with no scarring."

Major Mira leaned forward, her expression skeptical. "Yet you wish to restrict access. If this technology is so miraculous, why such secrecy?"

Dr. Sanchez responded calmly and precisely. "The regenerative microbes are extremely potent. While safe when properly handled, they could have dangerous unintended consequences if misused. We aim to prevent any potential abuse."

"So you expect us to entrust our soldiers' lives to a substance you deem too hazardous to share freely?" a colonel challenged.

"With respect, the hazards pertain to replication, not topical use," Dr. Sanchez countered. "The bandages are designed to deliver a precise dose in a controlled manner. We have safety protocols in place."

The officers whispered among themselves as Wally and Dr. Sanchez waited tensely. After a few moments, General Matthews cleared his throat. "Your trial results do seem remarkable. Very well, outline the security precautions you propose."

Wally stepped forward again. "First, the production facility location will remain undisclosed, known only to myself, Dr. Sanchez, and now your panel. The regenerative microbes cannot self-replicate alone - they require a proprietary nutrient solution we control."

He continued explaining their redundant security plan, emphasizing the tracking measures built into every bandage. The officers listened, faces unreadable.

After Wally finished, Major Mira spoke up. "You make a reasonable case for control. But our priority is saving soldiers' lives - are these restrictions truly necessary?"

Dr. Sanchez's voice was earnest. "We understand your conviction, Major, and share it. But consider the risk if our formula fell into the wrong hands. The damage could be incalculable. Precautions are essential."

Major Mira pondered her words silently. General Matthews leaned forward, hands clasped on the table. "You raise fair concerns. We'll need time to deliberate the merits and risks you've presented. Unless there are further points to raise, we'll adjourn and reconvene tomorrow."

Wally and Dr. Sanchez exchanged a look and a subtle nod. Their presentation was complete. The officers filed out, faces pensive. Alone in the room, Wally and Dr. Sanchez allowed themselves a measured sigh of relief. The hardest part was done - now they could only wait and hope.

The next day, Wally paced the hallway outside the conference room, awaiting the judgment on their proprietary technology. Dr. Sanchez sat serenely, the picture of poise, yet her fingers working a pen betrayed her own anxiety.

At last they were summoned back to the room. The officers were already seated, General Matthews at the head of the table. "After careful evaluation, we've reached a decision regarding your regenerative bandages," he announced. "While impressed with the results, we have concerns about long-term impacts and security risks."

Wally felt his heart sink, but the general continued. "However, the potential benefits are significant enough that we will approve an initial limited deployment under your proposed protocols. 500 units, tracked and monitored. We expect detailed data reports."

Relief surged through Wally. They had done it - the chance to save lives and prove their invention's worth. Beside him, Dr. Sanchez nodded gratefully. "Thank you, General. We pledge to proceed with the utmost care and responsibility."

Major Mira spoke up, her tone serious. "I carried men back from war with horrific wounds. If your invention can spare others such pain, it is worth the trial. But heed this - if we discover any breach or misuse, the program will be shut down immediately."

"Of course, Major," Wally responded sincerely. "You have our word - we will safeguard our technology closely."

General Matthews stood, signaling the meeting's conclusion. "Very well. We will be watching closely. Dismissed."

Wally and Dr. Sanchez walked out, exhilaration mingling with the weight of their new accountability. The first crucial hurdle was cleared, but the real trial still lay ahead. Wordlessly, they each understood they were on the cusp of a monumental moment in medical history. But success would require constant vigilance - one misstep could jeopardize everything.

Squaring their shoulders, they headed down the hallway together. The future awaited.

A TENSE WAIT PRECEDES the final verdict: a conditional green light that authorizes the distribution of 'Sanchez Bandages' on a larger scale within the armed forces.

Wally sat motionless in the small conference room at the military research facility, his gaze fixed on the polished oak table. Across from him, Dr. Sanchez reviewed her presentation notes, making small adjustments here and there. The only sounds were the shuffling of papers and the ticking of the clock on the wall, counting down the minutes until their meeting with the joint chiefs.

After weeks of proposals, demonstrations, and negotiations, it had all come down to this final decision point. The data and test results had been thorough and unambiguous - their regenerative wound dressings represented a revolutionary advancement in battlefield medicine. But introducing any new technology into the complex machinery of the military required overcoming immense inertia.

A soft knock at the door pulled Wally from his thoughts. Dr. Sanchez looked up from her notes, her expression morphing from concentration to cautious optimism.

"Here we go," she said under her breath.

Wally straightened in his seat as a uniformed officer stepped into the room. "They're ready for you now. Follow me."

The walk down the hallway felt interminable. Wally could hear the pounding of his heart competing with their footsteps on the polished floor. At the large oak door of the meeting room, the officer held up his hand for them to pause.

"I'll let them know you've arrived. Wait here."

Wally looked over at Dr. Sanchez. Her face was a mask of calm professionalism, but he noticed she was gripping her tablet tightly to keep her hands from shaking. In this high stakes moment, they were united by a nervous energy - and a hope that their work could shape the future.

After what seemed an eternity, the door opened, and the officer waved them into the room. Inside, five officers in decorated uniforms sat around a large table, their expressions unreadable. At the head of the table was General Matthews, his salt and pepper hair neatly trimmed and his piercing blue eyes peering over tented hands.

"Dr. Sanchez, Mr. Eastwood. Thank you for being here today." His voice was steady and measured. "Please, have a seat."

Wally and Dr. Sanchez settled into the chairs facing the officers. She placed her tablet on the table, ready to begin her presentation.

General Matthews templed his fingers, his gaze moving between them. "I'll get right to it then. We've reviewed your data, deliberated extensively, and discussed this technology at the highest levels. Our decision comes down to this: we are granting conditional approval for wider deployment of your regenerative wound dressings within the United States military."

Wally felt a simultaneous rush of excitement and trepidation. Glancing at Dr. Sanchez, he could see the gravity of the moment etched on her face even as her eyes shone with satisfaction.

"However," the General continued, "this authorization comes with strict oversight protocols and limitations on distribution. We cannot risk uncontrolled proliferation of devices with such...disruptive potential."

The other officers nodded in agreement.

"You will provide us with detailed tracking of all materials and finished dressings. Their use will be restricted to select special operations units for now. And your team," his gaze bored into them, "will be directly responsible for ensuring proper control and security throughout the supply chain. No exceptions. Is that clear?"

"Yes, sir," Dr. Sanchez affirmed without hesitation. "You have my word that we will follow protocols to the letter. Our team is prepared to do whatever is necessary to facilitate the controlled introduction of this technology."

Wally nodded, echoing her assurances. Inside, his thoughts swirled with the intricacies of the task now before them. But he pushed down the doubts and focused on the opportunity they had been given.

"Very well," General Matthews said. "We are placing significant trust in your judgement here. Do not let us down."

His tone made it clear just how heavy the burden of that trust truly was. The dressings represented a watershed innovation - one that could alter the course of conflicts and change lives. But revolutionary advances often brought unforeseen consequences. They would need to tread carefully.

"Now, let's discuss the details of the distribution plan..." The General opened the discussion to the group.

As they delved into the specifics, Wally felt the nervous energy settle into a quiet determination. This conditional approval was just the first step, one pebble cast into the vast waters. The ripples it produced would depend on their vigilance and discretion going forward. He glanced at Dr. Sanchez, seeing his own steely resolve mirrored in her eyes.

They had arrived at this point through long days and sleepless nights - all leading up to this pivotal moment. Now their real work would begin. The gravity of what they had set in motion was not lost on either of them. As Wally considered the road ahead, he knew with certainty that they would proceed with the utmost care. The Sanchez bandages would remain firmly in their guardian hands.

Chapter 6

As dusk fell on Bird Island, Marco "The Planner" Alvarez huddled with Javier "The Muscle" Rodriguez to finalize the details of a smuggling operation they believed would set them up for months to come.

Unbeknownst to them, word of their plans and sightings of unusual boat traffic had already reached Wally Eastwood, who was no stranger to the signs of covert activities near the island.

Marco and Javier sat hunched over a map illuminated by a battery-powered lantern, their voices barely above whispers. Around them, the night sounds of insects and frogs filled the humid air, punctuated by the occasional splash of fish jumping.

"This channel here will be perfect for moving the shipments," Marco said, tracing a winding route along the island's eastern shore. "It's too shallow for the Coast Guard cutters to navigate."

Javier grunted in agreement, his muscular frame tense with anticipation. As Marco continued going over the details - scheduled meetups, contingency plans, equipment needs - Javier's mind wandered to the payoff this job would bring. Enough cash to get that tricked-out truck he'd been eyeing. Maybe even that luxury condo in Galveston.

"You got all that?" Marco's sharp voice cut through Javier's daydreaming.

"Yeah, yeah," Javier mumbled. "I got it."

"This ain't amateur hour," Marco scolded. "One screw-up and we're fish food. Feds don't play down here."

Chastised, Javier sat up straight and met Marco's steely gaze. "I'm good. We're good. Just ready to get this thing going."

Seemingly satisfied, Marco folded up the map and switched off the lantern, plunging them into inky darkness broken only by shards of moonlight reflecting off the water. He unzipped a weathered duffel bag and produced two night vision goggles.

"Let's do one last sweep, make sure we're alone out here." Marco's tone made it clear this was not a suggestion.

They slipped on the goggles and scanned the island, the landscape now bathed in an eerie green glow. Nothing seemed amiss. Just thickets of cordgrass rippling in the breeze and stands of live oaks cloaked in Spanish moss.

The men crept through the underbrush, years of smuggling experience allowing them to move swiftly and soundlessly. As they neared the crumbling remains of a WWII-era bunker, Marco froze. He held up a clenched fist, signaling Javier to stop.

Javier's senses went on high alert. He strained to detect any sign of danger but heard only ordinary night noises.

"Thought I saw movement near that old bunker," Marco whispered. "Like a shadow shifting."

Javier scrutinized the area. "Don't see anything now. Probably just a raccoon."

Marco remained motionless, considering. Finally he nodded and gestured forward. They continued their patrol, discovering no further anomalies.

Satisfied that the island was secure, they returned to their skiff just as the first tinges of dawn lightened the eastern sky. As Marco steered them away from shore, Javier took one last look at Bird Island. He felt certain that soon it would be their smuggling empire's crown jewel. Their ticket to bigger and better paydays.

Little did Javier and Marco know, but at that very moment Wally Eastwood was observing them through high-powered binoculars from his hiding place atop the old bunker. He had tracked their movements for weeks as they scouted the island, and he knew exactly what they had planned.

Wally waited until their boat disappeared over the horizon before emerging from the bunker's shadowy entrance. He had a lot of work to do before they returned. The island held secrets that only he was entrusted to protect, and he would do whatever it took to keep interlopers like Marco and Javier from exploiting its hidden treasures.

After concealing his own skiff in the bunker's boathouse, Wally began meticulously covering any traces of his presence. He used a small spray bottle to mist the surrounding area with a special concoction of his own making. The solution contained microorganisms that would stimulate rapid plant growth, concealing the entrance within hours.

Wally then deployed a series of motion sensors both onshore and in the waters around the island. Linked to his smartphone, these sensors would alert him immediately if anyone set foot on Bird Island. Marco and Javier's return was imminent, and Wally vowed to be ready for them.

Satisfied with his preparations, Wally made one last sweep of the island under the cover of darkness. Detecting nothing out of the ordinary, he boarded his skiff and headed for home as the first pink rays of dawn crested over the horizon.

The trip back to the mainland gave him time to ponder his next moves. Marco and Javier were just the latest in a string of smugglers and thieves lured to the island by legends of hidden riches. But Wally alone knew the island's true secrets, and he had sworn to protect them at any cost.

This was not a responsibility he took lightly. Bird Island had been a sanctuary for his family for generations. It was a place of both natural wonder and hidden history. As a teenager, Wally, Richie, and

Pug had discovered an underground bunker filled with artifacts that defied explanation. On that day, his grandfather revealed that their family had long served as the island's silent guardians.

Now, years later, it fell to Wally to continue that legacy. Marco and Javier would not find easy pickings on Bird Island. Wally's knowledge of its twisting subterranean passages and hidden security measures would ensure that. This was only the latest in a long line of threats he had thwarted, though he took no pleasure in the task.

As Wally's skiff neared the weathered dock of his boathouse, he set his jaw in determination. Marco and Javier had no idea who they were up against. But soon enough, they would realize that Bird Island was not unprotected. Its secrets would remain safe under Wally's watchful eye.

Wally secured his boat and headed up to the house. He had just enough time to shower, change, and grab a quick breakfast before heading into the office. But his mind was already churning, contemplating his next moves in the unfolding situation on Bird Island. For now, Marco and Javier believed they held the element of surprise. Wally smiled wryly. He looked forward to disabusing them of that notion.

This was shaping up to be far more than just another day at the office.

WALLY WAS NO STRANGER to the rough undercurrents of confrontation — his time spent keeping an eye on the island had taught him to anticipate trouble before it reared its head. Understanding that Javier and Marco's return to Bird Island was not a question of if but when, he set about crafting a defense rooted in the very environment he sought to protect. The island was his home, his place of solace, and he took any impending encroachment personally.

The air seemed to vibrate with an unspoken warning, each gust carrying the weight of impending conflict. In the dimming light of dusk, the cordgrass whispered secrets of survival as Wally maneuvered through the landscape with the stealth and purpose of a natural predator. There was resolve in his movements and an acute attentiveness mirroring the wildlife that inhabited this secluded haven.

Wally's plan didn't rely on brute strength or firepower; instead, it hinged on his deep knowledge of the island's topography and the subtle art of misdirection. He dug pits near areas he surmised smugglers would traverse, covering them with a mix of branches and foliage that blended seamlessly with the ground cover. Along the paths most traveled, Wally constructed spring-loaded snares from vine and wire, which could entangle an unsuspecting intruder just long enough for him to assess and react accordingly.

He strategically placed noise-making items — tin cans with a few pebbles inside — suspended from low branches, creating a primitive but effective early warning system. His makeshift alarms were scattered, ensuring no corner of Bird Island remained unchecked. At the shoreline, he utilized streaks of chalky clay and minor rock formations to obscure any signs of his traps, maintaining the untouched facade of the natural landscape.

In the seclusion of an old WWII bunker, his sanctuary within the sanctuary, Wally reviewed maps of the island. He plotted points of vulnerability and advantage with meticulous precision, underpinning his strategy with a blend of cunning and the guerrilla tactics he'd read about in the annals of history. This wasn't merely a skirmish of wit and muscle; it was a quest to maintain the sanctity of a place that to him was far more than a mere geographic location.

As night fell, the initial stillness of Bird Island gave way to the nocturnal symphony of its unseen inhabitants. Wally took a moment to let the songs of the night wash over him, finding resolve in the constancy of nature's cadence. He knew the next time Javier and Marco's boots crunched on the Bird Island sands, the island would be ready — alive with the traps and diversions of its silently vigilant guardian.

ON THEIR APPROACH, the crew of eight smugglers, led by Marco and Javier, were confident in the operation's success. Their skiff cut smoothly through the dark waters of the bay, the moonlight glinting off the gentle ripples in its wake. Marco stood at the helm, one hand resting casually on the throttle as he guided them toward the hulking shadow of Bird Island looming ever closer.

Javier paced the deck behind him, his muscular frame silhouetted by the moon as he inspected their equipment for the tenth time. The rest of the crew busied themselves with final preparations, checking their supplies and gear in anticipation of what lay ahead. An undercurrent of tense excitement charged the night air.

Yet, they were not prepared for what awaited them. Hidden in the island's dense foliage, Wally watched the skiff's progress through high-powered binoculars. He noted their direction and estimated time of arrival. Satisfied with their trajectory, he slipped the binoculars back into his pack and pulled out a small tin.

Wally carefully opened it, the pungent, earthy aroma of freshly baked cookies wafting up. He selected one of the crumbling discs, noting the bits of dark berries studded throughout. Taking a small bite, he closed his eyes as the flavors bloomed on his tongue, rich and chocolatey with a hint of spice. Swallowing, he felt the now familiar tingle spreading through his body as the unique ingredients took effect.

These were no ordinary cookies. Wally had baked them that very afternoon, carefully following the recipe he had perfected over many trials. But the key ingredient was not something found in any conventional pantry. Into the cookie dough, Wally had gently folded a powdered form of the microorganism AXI-218.

At normal doses, AXI-218 granted the consumer enhanced auditory capabilities. But Wally had found that when baked into cookies, the effects were amplified tenfold. After consuming just one, his hearing became superhuman. Wally could perceive even the subtlest of sounds from astonishing distances. His ears became attuned to frequencies beyond normal human range. Tonight, those cookies would be his secret weapon.

As the skiff neared the rocky shore, its engine lowered to a deep throbbing purr. Wally pressed himself back into the dense foliage, the leaves and branches folding around him with barely a rustle. He took slow, measured breaths, willing his heartbeat steady as he strained his enhanced hearing toward the approaching boat.

The slap of water against the hull was crisp and clear, the creak of shifting weight on the deck boards rang out like gunshots. He could perfectly track each crew member's movements, picturing their positions based on the location and quality of every footfall, cough, and murmur. Marco's baritone murmur came from the stern, rattling off commands. Javier's bass grunts of assent placed him toward the bow.

The skiff eased up against an outcropping of rock. Footsteps thumped onto stone. A rope zipped and caught against itself as it was looped around a boulder. Metal clinked and grated against the rocks—oxygen tanks, scuba gear. The men were suited up and ready to begin their dive.

Now came the riskiest part of Wally's plan. As Marco called out final directions, Wally reached into his pack and retrieved a small cylinder, specially fitted with a compressed air nozzle. He had spent hours harvesting the rare purple flowers that grew in clustered vines throughout the island's interior.

Now, their delicate petals and leaves were ground into an ultra-fine powder contained within the canister. Wally took another cookie bite, steeling himself before taking careful aim at the gathered crew. He pressed the trigger, launching a concentrated cloud of glittering dust. It swirled and expanded as it drifted on the ocean breeze, descending over the smugglers on the rocks below.

The powder was absorbed into their clothes and skin on contact. Soon, the effects of the rare flower took hold. Marco stumbled mid-sentence, overcome by powerful yawns. Javier rubbed aggressively at his eyes, which suddenly felt gritty and dry. The crew shifted restlessly, mouths gaping in uncontrolled yawns, eyes watering from an overwhelming urge to sleep.

Marco tried to shake himself alert, blinking rapidly and massaging his temples. "What...what's happening?" he slurred. "Feel...so strange suddenly..." But his own remedies were useless against the rare flower's potency. Within minutes, the entire crew was slumped unconscious on the rocks, their scuba gear forgotten.

Wally waited, listening intently for any signs that his sleep-inducing powder hadn't fully incapacitated them. But he heard only slow steady breathing and the occasional snore echoing up from the shoreline. When enough time had passed, he slipped from his hiding place and approached the sleeping smugglers.

He gathered up their scuba tanks and remaining gear, concealing them in the forest. The men would awake cold, confused, and stranded on the island's rocky shore.

AS THE SMUGGLERS REGAINED their senses, they found themselves facing a labyrinth of non-lethal but highly effective traps. Ropes snatched at feet, causing men to trip and cargo to scatter, while eerie lights darted amongst the trees, crafted by mirrors and clever lighting to confound and frighten.

Marco surveyed the scene with growing unease, his usual calm demeanor shaken by the strange occurrences. He barked orders to his men, directing them to gather the dropped parcels and crates haphazardly strewn along the sandy shoreline. Javier set to work assisting the crew, cursing under his breath as he untangled ropes from around ankles and shins. The burly enforcer scanned the tree line, searching for any sign of what had triggered their troubles.

Finding no obvious cause, Javier stomped over to Marco. "This place is cursed," he grumbled, keeping his voice low so the rest of the men wouldn't overhear. "We should get what we came for and get out of here."

Marco nodded slowly, still deep in thought. This island was supposed to be an untouched paradise, secluded and forgotten. Yet everything about their landing felt calculated, orchestrated with purpose. The Planner wondered if they had stumbled onto something beyond their experience, forces on this island that did not take kindly to their presence.

He weighed their options carefully. Retreating now would mean abandoning this smuggling route, one that had taken months to establish and had the potential to greatly expand their operations. Marco was not one to scare easily or walk away at the first sign of trouble. And yet...something about this place unnerved him in a way he couldn't quite explain.

As the last of the cargo was collected, Marco addressed his men. "Fan out and secure a perimeter. We need to inspect the island before proceeding." The crew complied, moving cautiously with weapons drawn as they established a defensive ring around the landing area.

Marco nodded to Javier, and together they began combing the tree line, searching for any sign of inhabitants or activity.

They discovered nothing but the normal sounds of wildlife and vegetation. Javier shook his head, confused. "There's no one here, boss. Must have just been some kinda freak accident with the landing." Marco remained silent, still not fully convinced. His senses told him someone, or something, was watching them.

A faint rustling sound from deeper in the forest snapped Marco's focus. He drew his pistol and gestured for Javier to follow. Moving stealthily between the trees and underbrush, they tracked the source of the noise. As Marco peered into a small clearing, his eyes widened.

WALLY, ENERGIZED AND focused, utilized the Stealth Navigation System housed within the old military bunker to keep a silent vigil over the island's unwelcome guests. His movements were a shadow in the night, tracing the smugglers' steps, ensuring he was never seen nor heard.

The antiquated system was Wally's ace in the hole, allowing him to monitor the movements of Marco, Javier and their crew from the safety of his hidden control room. Though decades old, the technology was advanced for its time - using electromagnetic fields to render ships undetectable by radar.

Now, Wally had ingeniously repurposed it. Powered by an independent generator, the stealth system created pockets of interference that obscured his presence as he stalked his quarry under the cover of darkness. To the smugglers, the island appeared deserted, unaware of the unseen eyes tracking them.

Wally moved swiftly and soundlessly, relying on his intimate knowledge of the terrain. He traversed hidden paths through the brush, circumventing the smugglers' position. Utilizing the cover of night, he was virtually invisible. Wally felt a swell of satisfaction, knowing the tables had turned. Marco and Javier had breached his sanctuary - now he would gain the upper hand.

Approaching the shoreline, Wally took position behind a rocky outcropping. He observed the anchored smuggling vessel, laden with cargo yet to be unloaded. Wally's mind raced, calculating how to neutralize the threat. As he surveyed the scene, he reached into his pack and produced a cookie laced with AXI-218 - the auditory-enhancing organism.

The cookie's effect was immediate, allowing Wally to overhear the smugglers discussing their plans. They were on high alert after encountering Wally's deterrents, yet remained determined to establish a foothold. Wally would not allow it. He had to disable their operation before it gained momentum.

As he monitored the smugglers, Wally devised a strategy. He would create a diversion to draw them away from their vessel, then sabotage it to prevent their escape. Timing was critical - he had to act swiftly once they took the bait. Wally steeled himself, then launched the next phase of his plan.

From his hidden vantage point, Wally deployed a sound-generating device into the water. It emitted a distress signal used by boats in danger, amplified by the cookie's effect on Wally's hearing. To the smugglers, it sounded like a cry for help somewhere offshore. They scrambled to investigate, boarding two smaller boats to search the bay.

This was his chance. Wally emerged from the shadows and stealthily boarded the main smuggling vessel. He descended into the hold, using his enhanced vision from the cookies to locate the engine room in the dark. Wally quickly disabled the motor, irreparably damaging its internal workings before slipping away unseen.

By the time the smugglers realized the distress call was a decoy, it was too late. Their ship was dead in the water, its engine beyond repair. Consternation ensued as Marco and Javier argued over their next move. Little did they know, Wally was already one step ahead.

Under the cover of the stealth system, Wally returned to the shore to continue his sabotage efforts. He located the smugglers' cache of supplies and contaminated their fresh water with a powerful laxative. Wally then deployed remote-triggered noisemakers around their camp designed to deprive them of sleep.

Soon the smugglers were in disarray, beset by equipment failures, gastrointestinal distress, and inability to rest. Marco and Javier descended into bickering, blaming each other for their reversed fortunes. The crew's morale plummeted as conditions worsened.

Wally observed it all, an invisible puppet master subtly pulling strings. His unconventional tactics were achieving results without violence. He took no pleasure in their suffering, only resolve to protect that which he held dear - Bird Island and its secrets.

As dawn broke, Wally executed the final blow - remotely activating the noisemakers surrounding the smugglers' camp for a maddening dawn chorus. Bleary-eyed and increasingly paranoid, Marco finally conceded defeat. This place was inhospitable at best, cursed at worst. He ordered an immediate evacuation.

Wally watched, hidden and satisfied, as the remaining functional boats were loaded with disgruntled, exhausted men. Marco vowed never to return as they retreated across the bay. Javier made a protective gesture to ward off evil spirits as the island shrank from view.

Soon Wally stood alone on the shore as the last vestiges of the smuggling operation disappeared over the horizon. Thanks to the stealth system, his presence had gone completely undetected. Bird Island's secrets remained protected and secure.

Though he had succeeded, Wally felt no elation, only solemn duty and caution. Marco and Javier's tenacity made them dangerous foes. This was merely one skirmish in the greater campaign to safeguard Bird Island. Wally would remain vigilant.

As the sun rose higher in the sky, Wally began meticulously erasing all evidence of the smugglers' presence. He scoured the island for any traces they may have left behind, retrieving his surveillance equipment and removing all traces of his own activity. Wally was always careful to cover his tracks.

By mid-morning, it was as if no one had ever set foot on the island. Wally took one final survey of the pristine shoreline before retiring to the bunker's hidden entrance. He secured the entrance then descended to the control room, ready to resume his silent watch.

The antiquated system hummed, cloaking Wally once again in its electromagnetic shadow. He placed a marker on the navigational display, vowing to increase patrols around this sector. Though exhausted, Wally felt renewed purpose. He was the island's guardian, and he had prevailed.

With the immediate threat neutralized, Wally's mind turned to the next phase - fortifying Bird Island's defenses. The smugglers' infiltration proved the existing security measures were insufficient. He contemplated his next steps...

THE ANXIETY AMONG THE smugglers grew as bizarre, unexplainable events occurred one after another. Marco and Javier had assembled a crew of six men to help establish their smuggling operation on the secluded Bird Island. But from the moment they arrived, things had gone awry.

First, their boat's engine failed just as they were approaching the island's shore, forcing them to row the last hundred yards. Once they dragged the vessel onto land, three of the men immediately came down with severe rashes after trekking into the woods to scout the terrain. The men scratched and complained, their skin inflamed by some unknown toxin.

Then at night, eerie noises echoed through the trees - strange moans and screeches that put everyone on edge. And when Marco inspected their supplies the next morning, he found that someone had clearly rummaged through their provisions, with cans opened and packets torn.

Their conversations, ripe with paranoid theories, were easily intercepted by Wally thanks to his keen auditory enhancements. He listened from his hidden observation point as the men sat around a smoldering fire, glancing nervously over their shoulders.

"I'm telling you, this place is haunted," said one of the men, tossing a stick into the flames. "We've woken some old island spirit and it's messing with us."

Javier scoffed. "Don't be ridiculous. Next you'll say there's buried treasure here."

"Hey, you never know on an old military base," another man offered. "Maybe we stumbled onto something big."

Marco shook his head. "Let's stick to facts. We need to get the boat fixed and scout the bunkers. That's our mission."

Privately though, even Marco had a growing sense of unease. Their misfortunes seemed more than just coincidence. And the island, shrouded in fog, felt watchful, as if hidden eyes tracked their every move.

Wally smiled to himself as he listened to their hushed conversations. His plan was working perfectly. A few more well-placed disruptions and he could drive them from the island for good.

When a thick mist rolled in that evening, Wally made his move. Under cover of the fog, he slipped into the smugglers' camp, moving silently as a specter. At their radio, he adjusted the frequency ever so slightly, then tweaked the volume.

Later, when Marco attempted to hail their mainland contact, all he heard was garbled static in response. "Something's wrong with the damn radio," he grumbled. "All we're getting is white noise."

"Told you this place is haunted," one of the men whispered. "We've stirred up some bad mojo here."

Wally also began subtly moving their supplies around the camp and untying knots on their tents, sowing confusion. As the men became more and more on edge, Wally ramped up his efforts.

When a heavy rain fell overnight, he snuck to their boat and loosened the mooring lines just enough for the vessel to break free. The men awoke to find their boat adrift in the bay, requiring hours of work to recover it.

"This is getting ridiculous," Javier fumed, as they hauled the waterlogged vessel back onto shore. "It's like the island is working against us."

At this point, Marco could no longer dismiss the men's concerns. But he wasn't ready to give up yet. "Let's do one more scout of the bunkers," he suggested. "If we still come up empty, we move the operation."

The bedraggled men agreed, their enthusiasm for this cursed island quickly waning.

As the group hiked inland, Wally utilized the auditory enhancements of AXI-218, gifted to him by Dr. Sinclair, to listen in from a distance. He tracked their footsteps crunching over twigs, gauging their position.

Up ahead, he knew the trail split. To steer the men away from his hidden coastal laboratory, he made a split-second decision.

Cupping his hands, Wally emitted an eerie moan that carried through the trees ahead of the smugglers. The men froze, their heads swiveling toward the sound.

"You hear that?" Marco said.

Wally moaned again, the haunting sound echoing down the left fork of the trail.

"It's coming from that way," Marco pointed.

"I ain't going down there," one man protested. "We should head right."

The other men murmured in agreement. With some urging from Marco, the group proceeded down the right-hand path, unwittingly moving away from Wally's secret bunker lab near the coastline.

After letting the men wander a bit longer, Wally decided it was time to end this charade. He stealthily made his way back to the smuggler's camp ahead of them.

In their absence, he had set up a small speaker, hooked to an MP3 player. Hidden in the bushes, Wally now pressed play on a pre-recorded track: A cacophony of shrieks and unearthly screams, guaranteed to scare off even the most resolute intruder.

The men came thrashing back into camp moments later, their faces drained of color.

THROUGHOUT THAT LONG night, the rustle of gulf cordgrass and the distant calls of blue-winged teal seemed to conspire against the trespassers. Wally moved like the wind, bending nature to his will, using environment-driven tactics that whispered of the island's wrath.

Crouched low, he crept through the swaying cordgrass, the crescent moon casting just enough light for his enhanced vision to discern the smugglers' camp ahead. Marco and Javier huddled near a small fire, their conversation muted by the steady breeze. Wally circled wide, coming up behind their beached skiff. The hull rose out of the water, laden with contraband cargo.

Wally slipped a small bottle from his pack and knelt beside the boat. With an expert hand, he drizzled the clear liquid along the seam between hull and deck. The solution, invisible but pungent to wildlife, would soon attract the attention of hungry critters from both land and sea.

Satisfied, Wally melted back into the grass, making his way towards the men. He passed the spot where they'd carelessly strewn trash from their meal. Wally scooped up a discarded water bottle and slipped it into his bag before continuing on.

As he neared the camp, Javier's voice carried on the wind. "I'm telling you, something ain't right here. This place gives me the creeps."

"Don't be stupid," Marco snorted. "It's just an old bunker on a deserted island. There's no one here but us."

Wally's lip curled. Just an old bunker? If only they knew the secrets it contained. Moving silently as a specter, he circled around the camp's perimeter, sprinkling a fine white powder onto the men's packs and supplies. By morning, the powder would seep into the fabric and induce a relentless, burning itch.

That should encourage them to head home early. Wally glanced at the sky, gauging the remaining hours of darkness. Time to move these rats along.

He reached into his pack and pulled out a small recording device. With a tap of his finger, an eerie sound emanated out across the island - a low moan that seemed to come from everywhere and nowhere.

Javier jolted, eyes wide. "What the hell was that?"

"Relax, it's just the wind." But Marco didn't sound convinced.

Wally crept a safe distance away and triggered another sound, a shrill, unearthly cry that echoed over the bay.

The men scrambled to their feet, back to back, searching the darkness. Javier's hand went to the revolver at his hip.

"This place is freakin' haunted, man. Let's grab the cargo and get out of here."

Marco hesitated, reluctance clear on his face.

Time for the final touch. Wally circled wide around the trembling cordgrass until he reached the shoreline. He dropped to his belly and slithered forward on his elbows, stopping just shy of the lapping waves.

With a tap on his device, an eerie blue glow appeared in the water, drifting closer with the tide. Wally suppressed a smile at the power of bioluminescent microorganisms. As the glowing apparition neared, he let out a low, rumbling groan, like a beast from the deep.

Javier stumbled back, cursing loudly. Before Marco could react, he turned and sprinted away from the shoreline.

"Forget this! I ain't dying out here over some lousy cargo." His voice faded as he disappeared into the darkness.

Marco watched him go, realization dawning on his face. Their plan was falling apart. With a last look at the glowing waves, he turned and followed Javier away from the beach.

Wally listened as their footsteps retreated through the grass. He allowed himself a small smile of satisfaction before slithering backwards into the darkness.

The sounds of their terror faded away as Wally reached the tree line. He rose and brushed the sand from his clothes, then headed inland towards the hidden bunker. The intruders' tracks were easy to follow.

Wally approached the concealed entrance with care, wary of tampering. But the surrounding brush showed no signs of disturbance. He let out a breath, allowing his shoulders to relax. Tonight had been a success.

Wally lifted the hidden hatch and descended into the bunker. He went immediately to the corner cabinet, inspecting its contents. The microbe cultures, log books, and data chips were all undisturbed. He breathed a sigh of relief. The bunker's secrets remained safe.

After a final check of the space, Wally secured the hatch and worked quickly to conceal all evidence of his presence. He used a small spray bottle to mist the surrounding shrubs with a potent plant growth formula. By morning, any signs of disturbance would be erased.

BY DAWN, MARCO AND Javier were at each other's throats, their once foolproof plan unraveling in the face of an invisible adversary. The two leaders stood at the edge of the smuggler's makeshift camp, gesturing angrily as they debated their next move. Around them, the rest of the crew hurriedly packed up supplies, eager to flee the island and its escalating strange occurrences.

"This place is cursed, I'm telling you," Javier insisted, his voice tinged with uncharacteristic panic. "We need to get off this island now before something worse happens."

Marco rubbed his temples, struggling to rein in his own unease. Things had gone wrong from the start - engine troubles delayed their arrival, campsites were ransacked overnight, and just yesterday a shrieking apparition had emerged from the trees, sending the crew running in terror.

"Someone's messing with us," Marco countered, though even he was beginning to doubt his usual logic. "We can't abandon the operation just because of a few setbacks."

Javier threw up his hands in exasperation. "A few setbacks? The boat's nearly sunk, half our supplies are gone, and the men are ready to mutiny! Face it, your perfect plan failed."

Their disagreement peaked when a close encounter with an alligator, its eyes gleaming in the moonlight, pushed the crew toward a unanimous and superstitious conclusion: Bird Island was cursed.

The immense reptile had crawled right into the heart of the camp, sending smugglers scrambling onto boxes and chairs in fear. It circled menacingly before disappearing back into the marsh, as if summoned from the depths by an unseen force.

To Marco's frustration, this final omen cemented the crew's refusal to remain another night. As the sky lightened, the camp was hastily dismantled, with smugglers tossing gear into the damaged boat in their rush to escape.

"We're leaving, and there's nothing you can do to stop it," Javier declared. "Your grand plans failed, just admit it."

Marco's eyes flashed with anger and humiliation. He had staked his reputation on this operation. To leave empty-handed was unacceptable.

"You expect me to tuck my tail between my legs and slink off like a coward?" he spat. "I didn't get where I am by running from a few bumps in the road."

"This is more than a bump, and you know it," Javier retorted. "Sometimes you have to cut your losses. We'll figure out another way."

The crew watched the standoff nervously, divided between their loyalty to Marco and their desire to flee. Marco noted their skittishness with disgust. He expected more backbone from his men.

"Fine, you lily-livered rats," he snarled. "Hightail it back to shore if you're so afraid of the dark. But I'm staying - this island is the perfect base, and I won't be scared off that easily."

A ripple of unease passed through the group. No one felt comfortable abandoning Marco alone.

"Don't be stupid," Javier said. "You really think you can handle this by yourself? We need to stick together."

Marco crossed his arms stubbornly. "I'm not leaving. The rest of you can do what you want."

The two men locked eyes, at an impasse. Around them, the wind picked up as if fueled by their standoff.

In the distance, a strange wailing cry echoed over the marsh. The crew shifted nervously, exchanging glances. Marco set his jaw, refusing to show fear.

"Let's go, now!" one smuggler finally shouted. Others began scrambling to the boat, eager to escape the island's oppressive aura.

Javier grabbed Marco's arm in a final effort to persuade him. "Don't do this," he urged. "We'll find another way, but right now we need to leave."

Marco wrenched his arm away, pride wounded.

"I don't run from anything," he growled. "You'll crawl back here eventually, after you realize there's no better option. I'll be waiting."

With those defiant words, he turned and stalked away from the camp toward the island's forested interior.

Javier watched him go with a mix of frustration and concern. He considered chasing after Marco but knew his friend's stubbornness when challenged.

With the crew waiting anxiously, he had no choice but to abandon Marco on the island for now. But Javier silently vowed to return once the men's panic had subsided.

As the skiff disappeared across the bay, Marco stood at the tree line, peering into the marshy forest. The island was still now, no sign of the sinister forces that had driven his men away.

"You don't scare me!" Marco shouted into the silence. "I'm not leaving."

A bird cried out, making Marco flinch involuntarily. Angry at this reaction, he steeled himself and strode into the trees. He would explore every inch of this island until he uncovered the source of the disturbances.

Marco was confident he could handle any human adversary. And despite the crew's wild claims, he refused to believe an island could be supernaturally cursed. Someone was sabotaging his operation, and he would discover who.

By midday, however, Marco's bravado had eroded. The forest was eerily still, with no sounds of animals or insects. Even the wind had died down, leaving an oppressive silence hanging over the island. Marco rationed sips from his canteen as he walked, already feeling the effects of dehydration.

When he emerged from the trees into a small clearing, Marco froze. In the center lay a makeshift camp, with familiar boxes and supplies scattered around a burned out fire pit. Uneasy, Marco realized this had been their crew's campsite just last night. But there was no sign of recent activity or departure now.

A prickling feeling crept up Marco's neck. He spun around, scouring the tree line for any sign of life. Nothing moved except a lone heron passing overhead.

"Who's there?" Marco called out, one hand hovering near his holstered gun. "Show yourself!"

The only reply was the heron's cry fading into the distance. Marco retreated from the abandoned campsite, nerves on edge. With each step, the feeling intensified that unseen eyes were tracking his every move.

When a screech erupted from the marsh behind him, Marco whipped around, gun drawn. Had the menacing alligator returned? Peering into the reeds, he saw nothing but still water.

Wary, Marco continued on, senses hyperalert. Strange animal sounds and cries followed him, seeming to come from all directions. Marco stumbled on in growing exhaustion, refusing to acknowledge the fear creeping through his veins.

As the sun dipped low, painting the sky blood red, Marco knew he had to find shelter for the night. The marshy terrain offered little cover, but finally he spotted a rocky outcrop that could provide refuge.

Too tired to be cautious, Marco crawled into the cave-like opening. He would rest here briefly, then continue his exploration at dawn. Within moments, Marco fell into a fitful sleep, gun gripped tightly in his hand.

COME MORNING, IN A hasty decision under the effects of the laxative spiked water, Marco made for his boat. Wally, from his hidden observation point, nodded solemnly. It was time for Marco to leave, but not without a parting gift.

Marco stumbled through the dense foliage, cursing under his breath as thorns and branches clawed at his clothes and skin. The events of the past day weighed heavily on his mind - the strange occurrences, Javier's desertion, the unnerving noises in the night. Now his insides churned and cramped, thanks to tainted water. He needed to get off this cursed island.

Emerging from the trees, Marco spotted his boat, still secured to the makeshift dock. At least Javier and the others hadn't completely abandoned him, though he figured they were halfway back to shore by now. Grimacing, Marco hurried down the rocky shoreline.

Just as he stepped onto the dock, a sharp snap sounded from the tree line. Marco froze, peering into the shadows between the trunks. Nothing moved except the ferns stirring gently in the sea breeze. After a tense moment, he continued toward the boat. Probably just some animal, he told himself. Still, he couldn't shake the prickling sense of being watched.

As Marco boarded and prepped for departure, the boat's engines roared to life with ease. In his haste, he didn't question the stroke of luck. He just wanted off this island as fast as possible. Casting off,

Marco pointed the bow toward open water and shoved the throttle forward. The boat leapt eagerly over the waves.

On shore, Wally stepped out from the trees as the boat shrank into the distance. Everything had gone according to plan. Marco's departure ensured the island's secrets would remain protected a little longer. Yet Wally knew the smugglers would likely be back - and in greater numbers next time.

Reaching into his pack, he produced a small waterproof case. Inside nestled a tracking device, no bigger than a matchbox. Earlier, Wally had covertly attached the tracker to Marco's boat while it was unattended. Now he could monitor the vessel's movements and coordinate his next steps. Wherever Marco went, Wally would maintain vigilance.

Satisfied with Marco's unknowing assistance, Wally headed inland, following a nearly invisible trail back through the trees. There was much to do in preparation for the smugglers' inevitable return. His work had only just begun.

Wally arrived at a cleverly concealed bunker entrance along a rocky ridge. Checking that the coast remained clear, he slipped inside the hidden door and secured it behind him.

Descending a winding passageway, Wally entered a sprawling underground complex. This was the nerve center of his operation, filled with equipment and resources to protect the island. He moved swiftly through the corridors, inspecting traps and security systems. Everything seemed in order.

In one section, Wally inspected a collection of non-lethal countermeasures. Smoke bombs, flash grenades, sound emitters - all designed to confuse and disorient threats without causing permanent harm. Wally refused to take a life if it could be avoided. Still, he needed to be prepared for confrontation.

Deeper inside the bunker, Wally entered a sterile laboratory space. Here he cultivated and studied obscure flora found only on the island. Many specimens exhibited unique medicinal properties, which Wally researched in hopes of harnessing their healing potential. This precious ecosystem drove his steadfast protection of the land.

Adjacent to the lab stood a heavy vault door securing Wally's most sensitive project. A cutting-edge navigation suit designed to blend seamlessly with the surrounding environment. Using a network of sensors and adaptive camouflage, the suit rendered the wearer nearly invisible. Wally relied on this stealth technology to observe and maneuver undetected around the island.

After inspecting the suit's power supply and calibration, Wally turned his focus to the tracking monitor. Marco's boat appeared as a blinking dot on the screen, well on its way across open water. Wally zoomed the map out, watching the dot's trajectory. It appeared Marco was heading south, likely back to a smuggling outpost Wally had been monitoring.

"Just where I wanted you to go," Wally muttered. This presented the perfect opportunity to infiltrate the smugglers' operation from the inside. With the suit and other gear, Wally could follow Marco right to the source. There he could gather intelligence and formulate a plan to dismantle their smuggling ring for good. It would be risky, but worth it to protect his haven.

Wally checked his watch, then headed toward the exit to grab supplies from his seaplane. He had eight hours before Marco reached the smuggling outpost - plenty of time to prepare. As Wally secured the bunker and trekked back through the cordgrass, his mind turned with thoughts of the mission ahead. And somewhere, on a boat slicing through open sea, Marco remained unaware of the stowaway beacon ensuring he would lead Wally right to the heart of the smugglers' lair. The game was on.

THE FIRST TENDRILS of dawn stretched out over Bird Island, the warm glow seeping into every crevice and casting long shadows on the sandy beaches. It was a sight that never failed to captivate Wally, even amidst the tension of his recent endeavors.

Around him, the island was waking up. Seagulls cawed as they performed their morning acrobatics in the sky, their white bodies stark against the clear azure expanse. In the dense foliage, critters rustled and chattered, emerging from their nighttime hideouts. The air hummed with life, with vitality.

The island was untouched by human greed once more, its serenity undisturbed. Yet as Wally stood there in silent contemplation, he felt an undercurrent of disquiet run through him. He had won this battle but knew that peace might be fleeting. The thought left a bitter taste in his mouth.

Turning his back to the sea, Wally began his descent towards his hidden bunker. His footsteps were quiet against the backdrop of nature's orchestra, and his movements were precise, leaving no trace behind. As he reached the entrance hidden beneath an overhang of tangled vines and weather-beaten rock, he cast a final glance towards the retreating boat.

In his pocket, a tracking device hummed softly, its small screen blinking with coordinates. The smuggler's boat had been tagged during their hasty departure, and now Wally held in his hands the key to dismantling their operations once and for all.

Inside his bunker, he unfurled a large map spread across a wooden table. It was a detailed topography of the Texas Gulf Coast – every bayou bend, every waterway etched with meticulous precision. He traced the smuggler's route with a practiced finger, marking the probable location of their home base, East Matagorda Bay Paddlesports Park?

A new day was dawning, not just on Bird Island but in his quest for justice. His heart pounded in his chest, a drumbeat of resolve.

The solitude of his island fortress echoed around him, a stark reminder of the burden he bore. This was his mission, his alone.

Chapter 7

Dr. Sanchez leaned back in her office chair, gazing thoughtfully out the window. The sprawling military research campus spread out before her, cutting edge facilities filled with the brightest minds developing innovative technologies to support the troops. Yet her thoughts kept returning to a conversation from earlier that day.

She had been consulting with Dr. Alden, a pediatric surgeon and trusted colleague, about recent burn cases he had treated. Though survival rates had improved over the decades, the treatments remained grueling for tiny patients to endure. Dr. Alden spoke passionately about the need for new solutions that could drastically improve quality of life for these children.

In that moment, Dr. Sanchez glimpsed the potential of her regenerative technology in a bold new light. She saw a chance to not just incrementally advance burn treatment, but to completely transform it. A chance to eliminate the repeated, excruciating cycles of debridement that young patients faced. A chance to restore healthy, flexible skin and prevent disfiguring contractures. A chance to let children heal and live joyfully as children should.

Her mind buzzed with new possibilities. What if the regenerative microbes could be specifically tailored to pediatric patients? Tweaked at the genetic level to optimize regeneration for a child's delicate skin? Her team could investigate pediatric stem cell lines and signaling factors to enhance the microbes' therapeutic effects.

And the delivery mechanism - that could be the real game changer. Her standard wound dressings had proven effective for battlefield injuries, but children required special care. Nanoencapsulation could allow gradual microbe release over time matched to the healing needs of a child's burn. Combine that with a flexible, wearable bandage matrix ideal for a small body in motion. The microbes would build new skin layer by layer, all while avoiding the need for painful debridement sessions.

The more Dr. Sanchez envisioned this new application, the more compelled she felt to pursue it. The squeak of her office door opening drew her from her thoughts. Her trusted assistant, Lieutenant Evans, entered with a thick folder of lab reports.

"The latest tissue sample analysis you requested, Doctor," Evans said, placing the folder on her desk. "The cellular regeneration rates from the new microbe strain show a 13% improvement over the previous generation."

"Excellent work," Dr. Sanchez said, opening the file. "This microbe iteration paired with the bandage delivery method is getting us close to the next level of healing ability."

She paused, debating whether to disclose her new idea. Evans had proven himself trustworthy, and she valued his perspective.

"Lieutenant, what would you think about investigating pediatric applications for this technology? Specifically for burn treatment?"

Evans' eyes widened slightly in surprise, then his expression turned thoughtful. "That's an interesting concept, ma'am. The potential to reduce suffering for seriously injured children would be profound."

Dr. Sanchez nodded. "Yes, exactly. The standard procedures are extremely difficult on small children. We may be able to completely change the paradigm."

She outlined her vision - the tailored microbes, nanoencapsulation, matrix bandages. With each new detail, Evans grew more engaged, asking insightful questions about research approaches and obstacles they may face. His measured input was reassuring.

"You raise excellent points, Lieutenant. I believe pursuing this project would be high risk, high reward. It will require the utmost discretion and care." She met his eyes. "But I am convinced that, if successful, we could give hope to many who desperately need it. What are your thoughts if we proceed?"

Evans took a slow breath. "I think you may be right about the potential impact, Doctor," he finally said. "And that, if anyone can navigate the risks to achieve it, it's you and your team."

Dr. Sanchez smiled slightly. "Thank you for the vote of confidence. I'll submit a formal proposal for you to review. Your discretion remains crucial."

"Of course, ma'am. My role is to support you however I can."

They discussed logistics until Evans was called away for a security briefing. Alone again, Dr. Sanchez gathered her things to head home for the evening. She felt the weight of responsibility at exploring such a sensitive new application of the technology. But deeper still pulsed a growing sense of hope and purpose. If they could translate this vision into reality, they could transform young lives for the better.

WALLY SMILED AS HE read Dr. Sanchez's email detailing her idea for using their regenerative technology to help pediatric burn victims. Though they had made great strides with the military applications, he was excited by the potential to bring comfort and healing to children enduring painful procedures and long recoveries.

Inspired, Wally decided to devote his efforts to creating a special line of DNX-109 bandages just for kids - the 'FlexiBandies'. He wanted to make the bandage experience less clinical and more fun for children.

Wally started brainstorming ways to transform the sterile white bandages into something inviting and comforting for kids. He sketched out ideas for bright, cheerful colors and patterns featuring fun characters. Wally's mind raced with possibilities - bandages shaped like animals, vehicles, flowers, sports equipment. The variations were endless.

Most importantly, Wally wanted to create a mascot - a brave, comforting character that would become the face of FlexiBandies and bring smiles to children during their treatment. After filling pages with doodles and notes, he finally conceived the perfect mascot: Bandie the Brave.

Bandie would be a friendly bear wearing a bandage cape, representing bravery, protection and healing. Wally refined the character, giving him a cute smile and kind eyes. He imagined stuffed animals and toys in Bandie's likeness that could keep kids company as they recovered.

Wally worked tirelessly over the next few weeks to bring the FlexiBandies vision to life. He developed child-friendly packaging decorated with Bandie the Brave. The boxes and wrappers were brightly colored with fun fonts and playful designs.

Most importantly, he perfected the DNX-109 infusion process to work with the new materials while retaining the bandages' incredible healing properties. He rigorously tested each new iteration until they performed flawlessly.

Soon Wally had produced prototype FlexiBandies in a variety of shapes and patterns - circles, stars, hearts, flowers, superhero logos, and more. He packaged them in boxes with Bandie cheering the children on.

When Dr. Sanchez visited his lab, her eyes lit up as Wally revealed the finished FlexiBandie packages. She was thrilled by the transformation of her idea into a product that would truly uplift kids' spirits while healing their wounds.

They decided to give the FlexiBandies a trial run by donating packages to a local children's hospital. Wally felt nervous but excited as they arrived with boxes of the bandages in tow.

The staff was delighted by the bright, playful designs. One nurse remarked, "These will definitely boost our patients' moods during treatment!"

Wally and Dr. Sanchez had the honor of distributing the first FlexiBandies to a few of the patients. Seven-year-old Sophie grinned ear to ear when Wally handed her a box decorated with rainbows and unicorns. "These are so cool!" she exclaimed.

Next was Tyler, a ten-year-old boy who had been glum about upcoming bandage changes for his burns. But when Wally gave him a package with a race car theme, Tyler's face lit up. "Awesome, thanks!" he said, immediately opening the box to check out the contents.

The last patient they saw was Sarah, a shy six-year-old still adjusting to the hospital. Wally gently offered her the Hello Kitty FlexiBandie box. Sarah carefully took it, gave a small smile, and hugged the package as she examined the pictures of Bandie.

Over the next few days, Wally and Dr. Sanchez received extremely positive feedback on the FlexiBandies from the hospital staff. The kids were responding wonderfully to the new bandages, which not only healed their injuries but also brought fun and comfort to their treatment.

Observing the joy and smiles firsthand was incredibly rewarding for Wally. He felt that same sense of fulfillment he experienced when his inventions helped others. It reaffirmed his commitment to using his work for good.

Wally returned to his lab eager to expand the FlexiBandies line with more options. He would continue improving the designs to help as many kids as possible.

Dr. Sanchez also left the hospital visit feeling inspired. Her vision had become a reality, and she looked forward to supplying FlexiBandies to more pediatric facilities. She hoped their work might reach children facing medical challenges across the country.

In a world of clinical white bandages, the FlexiBandies brought a dose of optimism. Their mission was not just to heal wounds but also heal hearts. As he refined ideas for new themes, Wally was already imagining the next smile that a FlexiBandie package would bring to a child's face. That alone made all the late nights in the lab worthwhile.

WALLY STARED PENSIVELY out the window of his home office, watching the first rays of dawn peek over the horizon. The stillness of the morning usually brought him a sense of peace, but today, a feeling of unease lingered. His breakthrough discovery with the regenerative microbes had the potential to change countless lives, especially for injured children. However, with such great power came immense responsibility.

Lost in thought, Wally was startled when his phone buzzed with an incoming call from Dr. Sanchez. They exchanged greetings, and she got straight to business, telling him that she had spent the past several days reaching out to various children's charities and foundations focused on assisting youth who had suffered severe injuries. She proposed that they could provide the regenerative bandages discreetly through these organizations without revealing the true source of the groundbreaking treatment. Wally agreed it was a prudent approach and a promising avenue to help those in need.

Over the next week, Wally and Dr. Sanchez had extensive discussions with the leadership of several nonprofits, including the Children's Burn Foundation, the Pediatric Injury Association, and Hope for Hurting Kids. They were transparent about the incredible healing effects of the bandages while being intentionally vague regarding their origin. Given the dramatic results, most organizations were eager to distribute the bandages to children under their care, even with the limited information provided.

Strict protocols were put in place, requiring the nonprofits to keep usage statistics confidential and prohibiting any attempt to reverse engineer the bandages. Dr. Sanchez personally trained select medical staff from each organization on proper application and the bandages' unique properties. Despite their excitement over the medical miracle, all parties acknowledged the importance of discretion in rolling out this powerful new treatment option.

Soon, special shipments labeled as "experimental wound dressings" began arriving at children's hospitals across the country. The materials appeared ordinary from the outside, simply white boxes with basic medical packaging. But inside, each box contained a supply of the life-changing FlexiBandies. Doctors were briefed on their rapid healing effects for severe burns, lacerations, abrasions, and other traumatic injuries.

Yvette, a 7-year-old girl who had suffered third-degree burns over 30% of her body from a house fire, was one of the first to receive the FlexiBandies. The pediatric specialists at her burn center were amazed to see her wounds heal in a fraction of the normal time, with significantly reduced scarring. The pain she endured with daily dressing changes and debridements was also remarkably decreased thanks to the pain-reducing properties of the bandages. Yvette's successful treatment was mirrored in dozens of other early cases.

As youth returned home from their hospital stays days or weeks ahead of expectations, glowing testimonials began trickling into the children's charities from parents. They spoke of the rapid healing, reduced suffering, and hope restored to their children after receiving the "special bandages." It was affirmed that for these families, the treatment was nothing short of miraculous.

Seeing the dramatic impact firsthand, the nonprofits quickly requested additional supplies to meet the growing need. Wally and Dr. Sanchez were cautious about scaling up production too rapidly and potentially garnering unwanted attention. But they diligently worked to increase their capacity, continuing to funnel the bandages exclusively through select children's organizations.

One morning, nearly a month after the initial rollout, Wally received a call from Amelia, the executive director of the Children's Burn Foundation. Between sobs, she explained that a young boy named Caleb who had been treated with the bandages was featured in a local news story hailing his remarkable recovery. The dressing was never mentioned, but the medical staff had been so astonished that someone apparently reported the case.

Wally felt his chest tighten, knowing this was precisely the scenario he had hoped to avoid. He thanked Amelia for the alert and quickly contacted Dr. Sanchez. She agreed they needed to be proactive, so they immediately called the other nonprofits to reiterate the critical importance of confidentiality regarding the bandage distribution program.

Fortunately, the news story about Caleb gained little traction beyond the initial local coverage. But it was an urgent reminder that even one slip could unravel everything. Wally doubled down on enhancing security protocols around the production process. He also began developing a contingency plan with Dr. Sanchez and the nonprofits in case a need arose for them to swiftly cut ties and disappear.

As a precaution, Dr. Sanchez recommended halting any increase in bandage dissemination until they were confident all risks had been addressed. Wally concurred, and they instructed their partners to continue serving existing patients while suspending any expansion.

Despite this sobering setback, as Wally watched the sun rising fully into the clear morning sky, he felt hope. They had successfully gotten the regenerative treatment into the hands of children who needed it most, changing lives. Though the future was uncertain, Wally was committed to pushing forward responsibly, staying true to his mission of harnessing innovation for good.

WORD GRADUALLY SPREAD throughout the pediatric burn care community about the seemingly miraculous recoveries of several young patients who had been treated with the new DNX-109 bandages. While the regenerative technology behind the bandages was still highly confidential, guarded closely by Dr. Elena Sanchez and her trusted partner Wally Eastwood, the visible results spoke for themselves.

Tales circulated among nurses and doctors of children with severe burns, the kind that would typically require painful daily scrubbing and dressing changes, healing remarkably fast with minimal scarring after application of the brightly colored FlexiBandies. Some wrote it off as exaggeration or random chance, but others were intrigued enough to dig deeper, requesting information on accessing these special bandages for their own patients.

Dr. Sanchez and Wally exchanged knowing glances when asked about the FlexiBandies, neither confirming nor denying anything. "We're just glad to see these brave kids recovering so well," Dr. Sanchez would say diplomatically. Still, it was clear this was no ordinary product.

When young Megan Pierce was rushed into the emergency room at St. Mary's Children's Hospital with second and third degree burns over 12% of her body from an accidental scalding, the outlook was bleak. As the staff debrided the wounds and prepared for what would be a long and painful recovery, Megan's mother Susan Pierce overheard a couple of nurses mentioning the 'miracle bandages' they had heard about. Susan immediately asked them to tell her more, desperate to ease her daughter's suffering.

Unsure whether she could access the rumored bandages, Susan still pleaded with the doctor to try them for Megan. After much persistence, a box of FlexiBandies was retrieved from a locked storeroom and applied to Megan's wounds. The nurses showed Susan how to gently clean and re-apply them daily.

Within three days, Megan's wounds already showed signs of dramatic improvement, the angry redness fading as healthy skin regenerated at an astonishing pace. A week later, new epithelium had covered the deepest burns. Susan took pictures to document the changes, shocked at her daughter's rapid turnaround.

Megan's story spread quickly on social media, the images of her injuries hard to look at initially but then incredibly heartwarming as the wounds closed. Comments flooded in, with many asking where they could get these special bandages. Susan simply said they were a gift when her daughter needed them most.

Similar scenarios played out across Texas as Dr. Sanchez and Wally quietly distributed small batches of FlexiBandies to various facilities. Eight-year-old Tyler, burned on his leg and hand from a backyard bonfire, was running and playing again in days. Little Sophia, scalded when she pulled a pot of boiling water off the stove, healed without the anticipated skin grafts. The DNX-109 worked its magic time and again, restoring fragile skin and bringing relief.

Of course, such remarkable outcomes soon attracted attention from the media. Reporters caught wind of the sensational stories and pressed the hospitals for interviews. Employees were instructed to defer all questions to the communications department, who provided only vague, generic details about innovative treatments, careful not to reveal the true source.

Still, journalists and medical professionals pursued the trail, intrigued by whispers of these miracle bandages. Some attempted to reverse engineer the FlexiBandies, analyzing their materials and properties. But the microencapsulated DNX-109 remained inscrutable, its regenerative mechanism hidden. Wally's ingenious delivery system ensured the bandages yielded no secrets.

With public awareness growing, Dr. Sanchez kept a low profile, avoiding conferences or events where she might be pressed for information. Wally doubled down on security at his lab, knowing their work was protected by anonymity. They continued to quietly channel the bandages only to select pediatric units, providing just enough supplies to help the neediest patients without arousing too much suspicion.

Despite their caution, passion around the bandages kept building. The families of burned children shared their experiences through social media, posting updates and images of the bandages' effects. A grassroots movement emerged, with parents connecting to demand access to this treatment.

Online groups like "Healing Hugs for Burned Kids" and "FlexiBandies for Families" brought together community members to share knowledge and resources related to obtaining the bandages. Their numbers swelled as more families witnessed their benefits firsthand. Heartfelt testimonials fueled public interest and sentiment.

This groundswell caught the attention of political leaders and advocates, who called for investigations into this seemingly miraculous technology. They lobbied for its wider distribution to help more of the thousands of children suffering devastating burns each year.

Dr. Sanchez and Wally now faced a dilemma - proceed slowly and judiciously as planned, or accelerate access to meet the growing public pressure and need. They agonized over the decision, balancing their caution with the pull to help more young lives. Whatever they chose, one thing was clear: their regenerative technology had sparked a movement, and its ripples were just beginning to be felt.

Wally landed Seawings on the southern tip of Bird Island, the plane's pontoons skidding to a stop along the shallow inlet. He had opted for this discreet approach, keeping the aircraft far from Marco's expected location on the northern half of the island. As the propeller spun down, the sudden silence felt heavy, broken only by the screech of a lone gull. Wally sat motionless, peering out the bubble canopy and listening intently. No sign of the smugglers yet. He reached under his seat, verifying the aerosol grenades were still secured in their case, then pulled out his binoculars and scanned the tree line. Nothing. For now.

Wally opened the cockpit and climbed out, boots sinking into the muddy bank. The air was thick and humid, hinting at distant storms. He wore his FlexiCommander suit, the stealthy matte material absorbing the faint light. Marco would not see him coming. Wally moved with purpose through the cordgrass, making a beeline for the interior game trail that led to his hidden bunker entrance. He slipped inside, securing the portal behind him. Down the metal steps, past the cold concrete walls, and into the command center he went, movements quick and precise. At the surveillance station, he pulled up the tracker program, studying the screen closely. There it was - Marco's boat, a blip slowly moving along the island's northern edge.

Wally's pulse quickened, but his mind remained focused. He opened a locker, reviewing its contents: smoke bombs, flash grenades, tear gas. Non-lethal deterrents. Running scenarios in his head, Wally grabbed a selection and placed them in his trench coat pockets. He then powered up the Stealth Navigation System, securing the lightweight headset over his balaclava. The shielded goggles gave him a live overhead view of the island, along with infrared vision. Marco's boat appeared on the display, two small heat signatures aboard. Wally was ready.

He climbed back out of the bunker, tapping on his goggles to verify the feed and GPS marker. Then he moved silently into the trees, weaving between palm trunks with agility afforded by the FlexiCommander suit. The goggles tracked Marco's location, his boat having come ashore further inland now. Wally's ears strained, picking up muffled voices ahead. He slowed his pace, careful to avoid snapping twigs or rustling leaves. As he drew closer, the words became clear:

"I'm telling you, this place is trouble," came Javier's nervous whisper. "We never should've come back."

"Don't be a coward," Marco hissed in reply. "I'm not leaving empty handed again."

Wally crept nearer until he had a visual. The two men stood with their backs turned, Marco scanning the treeline while Javier fidgeted anxiously. Wally's hand went to his coat pocket, feeling the smooth metal sphere inside. Just a little closer...

Marco cocked his head suddenly, holding up a hand to silence his partner. He turned, squinting in Wally's direction. Watching through the goggles, Wally froze. Had they heard him? A tense moment passed. Then Marco shook his head and continued onward, Javier following reluctantly behind.

Wally exhaled slowly before shadowing their path. Soon the dense forest opened up into a small clearing surrounding the concealed bunker entrance. This was it. Wally took cover behind a large oak, watching as Marco began examining the steep embankment. Time to act.

Wally pulled the smoke bomb from his pocket, twisting the top to arm it. He rolled it silently across the leafy ground until it came to rest just behind the men. Marco's head snapped around at the sound, but too late. The bomb erupted in a cloud of pale smoke, enveloping the smugglers instantly. They coughed and stumbled back, shielding their faces.

"What the hell?" Marco shouted, eyes watering. But Wally was already on the move.

He closed the gap in seconds, bursting through the smoke and sweeping Marco's legs out from under him. The man crashed hard on his back with a grunt. Before Javier could react, Wally delivered a swift chop to his neck followed by a knee to the stomach, dropping the muscular enforcer to his knees. Wally then twisted Javier's arm behind his back, applying pressure.

"Don't move," he commanded, his voice a low growl. Marco started to push himself up, but froze at the sight of the goggles trained on him. He raised his hands in submission.

Wally kept Javier pinned. "You've come here for the last time," he stated coldly. "This island is off limits, understand?"

Javier nodded, grimacing against the restraint. Marco sat motionless, eyes burning with anger even as he complied.

Satisfied they got the message, Wally released his hold on Javier and stepped back, ready to defend himself if needed. But the men stayed down, slowly getting to their feet with cautious glances at the ominous figure before them.

Wally pointed back toward the shore. "Take your boat and go," he commanded. "If I see you here again, you won't get another warning."

The smugglers exchanged a look, then turned and pushed through the dissipating smoke without a word. Wally watched until they disappeared from view, then pulled up the tracker on his goggles. Sure enough, moments later the dots indicating Marco's boat were moving rapidly away from the island. It was over.

Wally let out a long breath, allowing his heart rate to settle. He had avoided violence, but made it clear this sanctuary would not be violated. Marco and Javier now understood the risks. Wally gazed around at the quiet forest. Once again, Bird Island's secrets were safe.

MOVING QUICKLY, WALLY policed up the bunker making sure the entrances were concealed. He gathered his supplies and ensured no traces remained of his presence before departing the subterranean hideaway. Making his way through the dense island foliage, he arrived at the clearing where his seaplane awaited. Wally stowed his gear and started the engine, the propeller soon slicing through the humid air. He taxied across the water and lifted off, leaving behind the verdant paradise that harbored so many secrets.

As the island faded from view, Wally's thoughts turned to recent events. His role as guardian and protector of Bird Island had led him down an unexpected path, one fraught with difficult choices. And yet, he mused, the island's isolation and obscurity were what made it ideal for his work. The regenerative microbes he had discovered in that ancient bunker held such monumental potential, for good or evil. Wally was profoundly aware of the immense responsibility that came with this knowledge.

The drone of the engine and the endless expanse of water below set Wally's mind at ease. He had taken every precaution to conceal his activities and throw off any potential interlopers. Marco and Javier's smugglers would not find it easy to return; Wally had seen to that. Now it was time to head home and drop the FlexiCommander suit off at the FFOne facility.

Wally checked his coordinates as the shoreline came into view. Before long, he was flying low over the coast, weaving between tall buildings. The white tilt walls of the FFOne facility stood out among the warehouses and factories. Wally circled overhead before touching down on the adjoining landing pad.

After securing the seaplane, Wally retrieved the FlexiCommander suit from the cargo hold. He ran his fingers over the material—his own ingenious creation, yet the result of wisdom passed down through centuries. The suit embodied his life's work and aspirations.

Wally entered FFOne and was greeted by his trusted friend and colleague Ronnie. "Right on schedule," Ronnie said. "Let's get this stowed away." Together they carried the suit to a secure storage room. Ronnie input a complex passcode and placed his hand on a biometric scanner to gain access.

Inside the pristine room, Ronnie hung the suit on a mannequin form. He stepped back and let out a low whistle. "A sight to behold. You've outdone yourself, Wally." Pride swelled within Wally as he gazed at the suit, though he remained humble. "All in service of the greater good," Wally replied.

After ensuring the suit was properly secured, the two men made their way to the facility's central hub. FFOne was abuzz with activity, teams of workers assembling medical devices and equipment. Ronnie gave Wally a pat on the back. "Because of you, we're on track for record production this quarter. Couldn't do it without you, boss."

Wally smiled, taking in the fruits of their labor. He and Ronnie had built this operation from the ground up. Their innovations were helping save lives, even if the source of Wally's ideas remained undisclosed. Some secrets were best kept that way.

Bidding Ronnie farewell, Wally departed FFOne invigorated. But there were still pressing matters requiring his attention. He drove the 20 minutes to his secluded home laboratory, anticipation building. It was time to analyze the data from the latest trial.

Meanwhile, across town at Houston Medical Center, Dr. Elena Sanchez walked purposefully through the bustling hospital halls. She was laser-focused on the clinical trial underway evaluating her regenerative wound dressings. The first phase had yielded remarkable results, with injuries healing rapidly. But Dr. Sanchez knew that rigorous, replicated testing was imperative. This technology was far too powerful to be rushed to market.

Approaching the secure treatment room, Dr. Sanchez input her credentials. The heavy door slid open, and she stepped inside. Before her lay a soldier, sedated for a procedure to analyze the effects of the bandage on a traumatic leg wound. Dr. Sanchez reviewed the chart and vitals, then addressed the team of doctors and nurses present.

"Let's begin. You all know the protocol." The team nodded solemnly and took their positions. Dr. Sanchez proceeded with meticulous precision, step-by-step, to remove the bandage and examine the wound. She documented her observations, then applied a fresh bandage and wrapped the leg securely.

Afterward, she oversaw the transfer of the soldier to recovery and scrubbed out. Only then did Dr. Sanchez allow herself to process the results. The wound had healed at an astonishing rate, with minimal scarring. It was better than she could have imagined, yet she tempered her excitement. Rigorous testing was still needed.

Dr. Sanchez stopped by each patient room, speaking warmly with the recovering soldiers. Their spirits were high, and some were on their feet again after injuries that should have taken months to mend. It was humbling and deeply motivating.

Before leaving for the day, Dr. Sanchez checked on the next trial phase. Her team updated her on their progress preparing for expanded trials. She reminded them to take care and follow each protocol exactly. Lives depended on it.

Departing the hospital, Dr. Sanchez contemplated the future. What had started as a glimmer of hope had grown into a remarkable reality. There were many challenges ahead, but she had faith in the process. Progress required prudence. If they stayed the course, Dr. Sanchez knew they could change medicine forever.

Chapter 8

Wally smiled warmly as he walked through the bright, cheery halls of Houston Children's Hospital, nodding in greeting at the staff he passed along the way. Though he had only been visiting for a few weeks now, he was already on a first name basis with many of the nurses, doctors, and support staff. His easygoing charm and genuine interest in the patients had quickly endeared him to the hospital personnel.

Wally made his way to the pediatric burn unit, where colorful drawings decorated the walls in an effort to brighten the difficult healing journey of the young patients there. He stopped by the nurses station, where Clara was just starting her morning shift.

"Good morning, Clara!" Wally said cheerfully. "How's everything looking today?"

"So far, so good," Clara replied with a smile. She appreciated Wally's consistent concern for the children under their care. In the short time she had known him, he had demonstrated more compassion than some doctors she had worked with for years. "We've got a new patient coming in later - a 6 year old boy who was burned when some fireworks went off too close. But this morning has been pretty smooth."

"Well I'm glad to hear it's been an easy one so far," Wally said. He glanced down the hall where laughter floated out from one of the rooms. "Sounds like Jayda is having a good morning?"

Clara nodded, "Dr. Morris is in there now for her dressing change. She's been trying to distract her with some jokes. Jayda's burns were looking much better when I checked on her earlier."

"That's wonderful to hear," Wally said, clearly delighted by the news. Since bringing his experimental bandages to the hospital, he had seen remarkable improvements in the recovery of several young patients' severe burns, including little Jayda's. However, Wally was careful not to reveal to the staff that the rapid healing came from anything other than standard burn dressings. Only Dr. Morris knew the full truth about the bandages' regenerative powers, though she had no knowledge of their highly confidential origins.

"Well, I'll get out of your way and let you focus on your patients," Wally told Clara warmly. "Don't hesitate to page me if I can help with anything."

Clara nodded in appreciation as Wally continued down the hall, peeking into rooms to greet the children inside. He stopped to chat with a shy 7 year old named Michael who eagerly showed Wally his drawing of a dragon.

"Wow, that is one fierce dragon!" Wally said enthusiastically. "I especially like the spikes on his tail. I bet he uses that to defend himself from knights trying to attack him."

Michael nodded, grinning. He pointed to the bandages covering burns on his arm. "When my burns get better, I'm going to draw more dragons and knights."

"That sounds like an awesome idea," Wally agreed. "And it looks like your burns are healing up great. I bet those bandages will be off before you know it."

Wally gave the boy a high-five before continuing on down the hall. He waved through the window of another room at a girl playing a game on a tablet.

Popping his head into an empty room being prepped for the incoming patient, Wally asked the nurse, "Hey Frank, how's your day going so far?"

"Oh, hey Wally," Frank replied, glancing up from the supplies he was organizing. "It's going well. Just getting things ready here for our burn patient coming from the ER later."

"Great. Let me know if you need anything," Wally offered. He was always looking for ways to assist the hospital staff and make their difficult jobs a little easier.

Wally headed down to the playroom at the end of the hall, where an art therapy class was underway. He took a seat at one of the tables beside a 10 year old girl named Sophia who was painstakingly painting a puppy.

"Well, that's turning out great!" Wally praised. "I especially like the spots you gave him."

Sophia grinned shyly. "Yeah, he's gonna be a Dalmatian when I'm done. That's my favorite kind of dog."

"I can see why, they're so unique looking with those spots," Wally agreed. "What are you going to name him?"

As Sophia contemplated names, Wally continued chatting with her and some of the other children, offering encouragement on their artwork and making them laugh with funny voices as he examined their creations.

After staying for a bit, Wally gave a friendly wave and headed out of the playroom. He went to find Dr. Morris, who was just finishing up with Jayda's dressing change.

"Hey there, how did it go today?" Wally asked.

Dr. Morris gave him a subtle nod. "Really well. The new dressing held up perfectly and the wound is improving remarkably." She lowered her voice slightly. "I really can't thank you enough for providing these. They've made a huge difference in recovery time for my patients."

"I'm just glad to see them helping these kids heal quickly and comfortably," Wally replied sincerely. "Please let me know if you need any more. I should have additional shipments soon."

"Will do," Dr. Morris agreed. She was still curious about the bandages' origins, but Wally remained vague on details. He had simply said a colleague of his developed them, but offered no specifics. Regardless, she was thankful for the incredible results they produced.

Wally bid Dr. Morris farewell and glanced at his watch, realizing it was nearly lunch time. He headed down to the cafeteria, hoping his daily meal visits might provide the overworked cafeteria staff a brief bright spot in their busy shifts.

Grabbing a tray, Wally got in line behind two nurses. "Hey Rose, hey Aisha, how are you ladies doing today?" he asked.

The nurses greeted Wally warmly, already accustomed to his friendly presence. "We're hanging in there," Rose replied. "Looking forward to sitting down for a few minutes to eat."

"I hear you there," Wally agreed. "Well, lunch is on me today, order whatever you'd like."

"Oh Wally, you don't have to do that," Aisha protested with an appreciative smile. But Wally insisted, and the nurses thanked him as he paid for their food.

Wally got his own lunch and joined the nurses at a table, chatting lightly and bringing a smile to their faces with a silly story about his dog. After a while, he bid them farewell with a promise to catch up again tomorrow.

As Wally left the hospital, he felt glad to have brightened the days of some of the staff, even in small ways. He knew the long hours and stressful work took a toll, especially in the burn unit. By building rapport and trust with the personnel, he hoped to ensure the continued success of the bandages for the patients who so desperately needed them. And so far, his relationships at the hospital were not only helping the children, but providing Wally with a sense of purpose unlike anything he had known before.

WALLY WALKED DOWN THE bright pediatric ward of Houston Children's Hospital, glancing into rooms as he passed. Some held sleeping patients while others hosted families laughing and playing games together. Despite the heaviness that hung in the air of the burn unit, it was not devoid of joy.

Coming upon room 218, Wally paused in the doorway. Inside, a young boy no older than four sat propped up in his hospital bed, focused intently on a coloring book in his lap. Bandages covered the child's arms and parts of his face, a solemn reminder of the painful injuries that had brought him here.

Wally rapped gently on the doorframe. "Hey there, buddy. Whatcha working on?"

The boy glanced up, breaking into a grin when he saw Wally. "Hi! I'm coloring a picture for my mom. Wanna see?" He held up his coloring book, proudly displaying a partially finished image of a house and family.

"That looks awesome!" Wally stepped farther into the room. "I'll bet your mom is going to love it."

"Yeah, I'm gonna give it to her when she visits tonight." The boy resumed coloring enthusiastically.

Wally pulled up a chair beside the bed. "My name's Wally. What's yours?"

"I'm Jacob." The child kept his focus on the coloring book. After a moment, he asked quietly, "Have you ever gotten burned bad?"

Wally nodded, a solemn understanding passing between them. "Yeah, I have. When I was a little older than you."

Jacob set down his crayon and looked at Wally with curiosity. "Did it hurt a lot?"

"It did at first. But the doctors and nurses helped me, just like they're helping you." Wally gave him a reassuring smile. "And now I'm all better. Just like you're going to be."

The boy glanced down at the bandages on his arms. "Yeah. The doctor said I can go home soon. I miss my house and my toys and my dog Rufus."

"I'll bet Rufus misses you too. But it sounds like you get to see him again real soon."

Jacob nodded, picking up a blue crayon. "Yeah. I can't wait. Hey Wally, what's your favorite color? I'll color part of my house that color."

"Hmm, tough choice." Wally pretended to think hard. "I'm gonna have to go with green."

"Green's a good one," Jacob agreed. Switching to a green crayon, he began filling in part of the house's roof.

Wally watched the child color, a mix of emotions welling up inside. Seeing Jacob's resilience and optimism despite his injuries only strengthened Wally's resolve to keep developing the special bandages. The DNX-109 prototypes currently on Jacob's arms were clearly accelerating his recovery. Wally hoped that one day, no child would have to suffer through the pain and challenges of severe burns.

After a few peaceful minutes, Jacob broke the silence. "Wally, will you draw something on my picture too?"

"Sure, I can try. I'm not the best artist though," Wally chuckled.

Jacob passed him the coloring book and a black crayon. Tongue between his teeth, Wally carefully sketched a lopsided dog beside the house. "There you go, a dog for you to play with when you get home."

"Thanks! That's perfect." Jacob took back the book, beaming at Wally's contribution.

Just then, a nurse entered carrying a tray of food. "Alright Jacob, lunchtime! Your favorite, grilled cheese and tomato soup."

Jacob's face lit up. As the nurse situated his tray, he turned to Wally. "Wanna stay and eat with me?"

Wally smiled, touched by the invitation. "Thanks, but I should probably let you eat. I'll come back and visit again though, okay?"

"Okay!" Jacob picked up half of the gooey grilled cheese sandwich and took an enthusiastic bite.

With a final wave, Wally stepped out of the room and continued down the hall, renewed energy and motivation surging through him. Witnessing even one child's spirit and optimism in the face of daunting circumstances was profoundly moving. It served as a reminder of why this work mattered so deeply.

Wally wanted to protect that optimism and give every child the chance for a full, joyful recovery. His bandages could make an incredible difference, not just physically but emotionally. Seeing the light return to a child's eyes when they realized their suffering was ending - that was what made all the secrecy and long hours worthwhile.**Scene #8:** Juggling the demands of his business and the need for secrecy, Wally manages to fit his visits to the hospitals into his busy schedule. Although tiring, these visits are crucial for staying connected with the progress and impact of his work, and they provide immeasurable emotional rewards.

There would be challenges ahead, Wally knew. More trials, regulatory hurdles, and tough decisions about how to ethically distribute the technology. But he chose to focus on the Jacob's of the world rather than the obstacles. If his mission could restore their hope and resilience, it would all be worth it.

Wally stepped outside into the sunshine, reflecting on the encounter that had reignited his passion. He pulled out his phone and navigated to the encrypted folder containing his DNX-109 research. There was more work to be done. More refinements to the formula, more testing with Dr. Sanchez, and more young lives to restore.

Filled with renewed purpose, Wally set off to prepare for the next phase of trials. Jacob's smile stayed with him, a reminder of the light that could return to the eyes of suffering children through this medical breakthrough.

WALLY PULLED INTO THE parking garage of Houston Children's Hospital, finding his usual spot on the third floor. As he stepped out of his car, he felt the familiar mix of excitement and trepidation that came with these visits. While rewarding, seeing the young patients always reminded Wally of the immense responsibility that came with his creation.

Making his way through the lobby, Wally stopped by the gift shop and picked up a bag of small toys and coloring books. The staff knew him well by now, greeting him warmly as he made his way to the pediatric burn unit.

"Hey Wally, glad you could make it today!" said Claire, one of the nurses. She was in her late 20s, with a bubbly personality that brightened the ward.

"I brought some new toys for the kids," Wally said, holding up the gift shop bag. Claire's face lit up.

"You're the best, you know that? The kids will be thrilled."

Wally smiled, happy to contribute something positive during such difficult times for these families. He followed Claire, glancing in each room as they walked down the hall.

In one room, a boy no older than five proudly showed his mother a coloring page while a FlexiBandage covered his arm. The skin underneath was healing remarkably fast, the bandage's work nearly complete. The boy's contagious smile warmed Wally's heart.

In the next room, a teenage girl sat up in her bed, texting on her phone, a FlexiBandage wrapped around her leg. Though her expression was nonchalant, Wally could see the relief in her eyes, knowing the worst was behind her.

As he walked, Wally recalled the countless hours in his laboratory, the meticulous experiments and modifications, all leading to this - helping children rebuild their lives. The sacrifices and secrecy required were all worth it for these moments.

"Jacob's been asking about you," Claire said as they arrived at his room. Jacob was eight years old, a lively kid even while recovering from second degree burns on his shoulder. He was obsessed with dinosaurs, his room filled with drawings.

"Wally, you're here!" Jacob shouted. Wally high-fived the enthusiastic boy.

"I got some new coloring books and toys for you," Wally said, placing the gift shop bag on the tray table. Jacob rifled through it eagerly.

"Awesome! Look at these dinosaur stickers!"

Wally smiled as Jacob examined his haul. Claire mouthed a thank you before slipping out to continue her rounds.

"So, how's your shoulder feeling today?" Wally asked.

"It's a lot better. The bandage makes it stop hurting. And look!" Jacob pulled back his hospital gown, revealing smooth new skin under the bandage. "It's almost all better now."

Wally examined the healing skin, amazed by how rapidly the FlexiBandage was restoring Jacob's shoulder. "That's great progress buddy! You'll be out of here racing dinosaurs in no time."

Jacob laughed. "Yeah, then I can go to the zoo and see the real ones!" His enthusiasm was contagious.

Wally spent the next half hour chatting with Jacob about dinosaurs, superheroes and his favorite cartoons. For a moment, Wally could forget the weight of responsibility on his shoulders and simply enjoy connecting with this remarkable kid.

But then his phone buzzed in his pocket. Glancing down, Wally saw a message from Dr. Sanchez. Time to get back to real life.

"Alright Jacob, I've gotta head out. But I'll come visit again soon okay?"

Jacob's face fell briefly but then he smiled. "Okay! I'll make you a dinosaur drawing for next time."

Wally said his goodbyes and left the room, Jacob's innocent optimism lifting his spirits. He made his way back down the hall, saying goodbye to Claire and the other nurses. Each time he visited, he was reminded why he worked so tirelessly - for the chance to give kids like Jacob hope.

Back in his car, Wally checked Dr. Sanchez's message. It was time for their weekly check-in about FlexiBandage distribution and production. As rewarding as his visits to the hospital were, the secrecy required was mentally draining.

Wally started his car, he turned on some upbeat music, trying to shift his mindset after the emotional visit. He had to compartmentalize - focus just on the task at hand, not the big picture. Otherwise the pressure was crushing.

At a stop light, Wally's phone buzzed again. It was a calendar reminder for an upcoming trip to Bird Island to check on equipment. Wally took a deep breath, juggling all the demands in his head. He truly loved the hands-on, technical work. But it required time and focus, which was hard to come by these days.

Wally arrived downtown, parked in his company's lot and took the elevator up to his office. He grabbed an energy drink from the communal fridge before sitting down at his desk. As he booted up his computer, he thought about delegating some of his current projects to his team. But there were certain things he had to oversee himself.

Opening his encrypted files, Wally reviewed the latest production numbers for FlexiBandages. Everything looked on track.

He scrubbed the data, closing the files just as Ronnie popped his head in.

"Hey man, how'd it go at the hospital today?" Ronnie asked.

"Really good actually. The kids are recovering well, it's amazing to see."

Ronnie smiled. "That's awesome." He knew how much the visits meant to Wally. "Well when you get a chance, take a look at the R&D proposal and let me know what you think."

"Will do," Wally said. Ronnie headed back to his own office as Wally's calendar dinged again. Time for the call with Dr. Sanchez. He took a long sip of his energy drink, shifting gears once again. Just another day in his compartmentalized world.

The video call connected and Dr. Sanchez appeared on screen. "Hello Wally. How are you holding up?"

"Hey Doc. I'm alright, keeping all the plates spinning," Wally said with a tired smile. "How's the latest trial batch looking?"

As they reviewed the latest FlexiBandage details, Wally felt the familiar tension of leading this clandestine operation. But he focused on the task at hand, committed to ensuring production and distribution went smoothly.

The hospital visit reminded him what made it all worthwhile. The costs were heavy, but helping kids like Jacob heal made it possible to keep carrying the load, secret by secret.

DR. SANCHEZ STOOD BEFORE her team, her eyes filled with determination. "We cannot rest on our laurels," she said, her voice firm and resolute. "The success of this bandage treatment is not an end in itself, but a beginning. We must continue to improve and refine our methods, to ensure that we are providing the highest possible standard of care for our patients."

She paused, looking around the room at each member of her team. "Vigilant monitoring is also crucial," she continued. "We must be constantly aware of any potential issues or complications that may arise, and be prepared to address them swiftly and effectively."

Wally nodded in agreement, his mind already racing with ideas for further improvements to the bandage technology. He knew that Dr. Sanchez was right – their work was far from over, and they needed to stay focused and committed if they wanted to make a real difference in the lives of burn victims around the world.

As the trials progressed, Wally and Dr. Sanchez worked tirelessly to refine their bandage treatment, making small but significant adjustments based on feedback from patients and medical professionals alike. They were determined to create a product that was not only effective but also comfortable and easy to use – a true game-changer in the field of burn care.

One day, as they sat together in Dr. Sanchez's office going over the latest trial results, Wally couldn't help but feel a sense of pride at what they had accomplished so far. The data was overwhelmingly positive – patients were healing faster than ever before, with minimal scarring and no adverse side effects reported. But he also knew that there was still so much more they could do to improve the treatment further.

"What do you think we should focus on next?" Dr. Sanchez asked him, her eyes sparkling with curiosity and excitement. Wally thought for a moment before responding. "I think we should look into developing a way to customize the bandages for different types of burns," he said finally. "That way, we can ensure that each patient receives the most effective treatment possible based on the specific nature of their injury."

Dr. Sanchez nodded in agreement, clearly impressed by Wally's insightful suggestion. She jotted down some notes on a nearby whiteboard before turning back to him with a smile on her face.

"That's an excellent idea," she said warmly. "Let's get started on it right away."

Over the next few weeks, Wally and Dr. Sanchez poured all their energy into developing a new system for customizing their bandages based on different types of burns – everything from superficial first-degree burns all the way up to deep third-degree burns with extensive tissue damage. They experimented with various materials and formulations until they found the perfect combination that would allow them to create bandages tailored specifically for each patient's unique needs.

As they worked tirelessly on this new project, Wally couldn't help but feel an immense sense of satisfaction at being able to contribute so directly to such an important cause – one that had touched his own life so deeply many years ago when he had suffered his own devastating burn injuries as a child growing up in Texas' Gulf Coast region during Hurricane Carla in 1961 when he was just eight years old...

WALLY SAT IN HIS HOME office, reviewing the latest trial data on the FlexiBandages. The results continued to astonish him - accelerated healing, minimized scarring, and improved mobility. He leaned back in his chair, feeling a swell of pride at what he and Dr. Sanchez had accomplished.

Despite the breakthroughs, Wally grappled with frustration. Their production capacity remained limited, restricting how many children could benefit from the bandages. If only they had more resources, he thought, they could help so many more.

Wally's phone rang, jolting him from his contemplation. It was Dr. Sanchez. Her voice brimmed with excitement.

"Wally, you're not going to believe this," she said. "I just got off the phone with the Houston Children's Hospital administrator. An anonymous donor gave a massive contribution earmarked specifically for purchasing our bandages!"

Wally bolted upright. "Wait, what? How massive are we talking?"

"Five million dollars!" Dr. Sanchez exclaimed. "Can you believe it? With this funding, we'll be able to supply bandages for every pediatric burn patient at Houston Children's. It's going to change so many lives."

Wally's mind reeled. This anonymous act of generosity was the answer to their production woes. Who could possibly have that kind of money to give?

"Did they give any hint to their identity?" he asked.

"None," said Dr. Sanchez. "The administrator said the donor wished to remain completely anonymous. We just received a cashier's check in the mail with a letter specifying the donation's purpose."

"That's incredible," murmured Wally. His excitement then gave way to a realization. "But with our current production capacity, we can't fulfill an order that large. We'd need to dramatically scale up."

"I know," said Dr. Sanchez. "But perhaps we could use a portion of the funds to expand our manufacturing. I have some trusted contacts we could bring on board."

Wally nodded slowly. "That could work. We'd have to vet them thoroughly first."

"Of course," said Dr. Sanchez. "I'll develop a plan for ramping up production and run it by you. This changes everything, Wally. Just think - now we can help every child who needs it, not just a select few."

Wally smiled, envisioning hospital rooms filled with children whose severe burns rapidly healed to nothing more than faint scars. It seemed almost too good to be true.

"You're right," he said. "This takes our work to a whole new level. Keep me posted on the production expansion plan. I can't wait to see the look on those kids' faces when they realize their pain will be over so much faster."

They ended the call, and Wally sat motionless, processing it all. Five million dollars. From an anonymous giver. It was astonishing.

Who could possibly have access to that kind of money yet want no recognition? Wally pondered the possibilities. An eccentric billionaire? A foundation dedicated to healthcare? The mystery nagged at him.

But one thing was certain - this changed everything. With proper manufacturing, they could distribute the bandages across children's hospitals nationwide. Wally imagined a future where no child suffered prolonged burns ever again.

The very thought of it made the years of research and trials all worth it. He could not wait to get started, to build a production line robust enough to deliver their innovation at the scale it deserved.

Wally spent the next two weeks working closely with Dr. Sanchez to refine their manufacturing process. They vetted suppliers and specialists, assembling a team they could trust. By the end of the month, their new facility was operational.

The first large-scale batch rolled off the production line - bandages by the thousands ready for shipment. Wally inspected them, heart swelling. This was only the beginning.

At Houston Children's Hospital, staff gathered for the arrival of the massive FlexiBandage shipment. Wally and Dr. Sanchez stood to the side, watching the unveiling. As the boxes were opened, audible gasps filled the room.

Nurses lovingly picked up the bandages, adorned with colorful designs. The administrator shook Wally and Dr. Sanchez's hands firmly. "You've outdone yourselves," he said. "These will change so many lives here."

They toured the pediatric wing, meeting young patients. One girl, Madison, had suffered third-degree burns on her leg. As Dr. Sanchez gently wrapped the FlexiBandage around her wound, Madison grinned. "It doesn't even hurt," she said, eyes wide.

Later, Wally asked Madison's mother how she felt about her daughter receiving the new treatment. She dissolved into tears.

"You can't imagine what this means to us," she said. "The thought of Madison being in pain for months was so hard. But now..." She gestured to where Madison sat coloring, leg wrapped in a bright bandage. "Now we have hope."

Wally had to turn away, swallowing the lump in his throat. This - this was exactly why he engineered the microbes. Why he undertook years of secretive research.

It was all worth it to give families like Madison's what they desperately needed - hope. A chance at a normal childhood, unencumbered by prolonged suffering.

As Wally departed the hospital, he felt as though he were walking on air. The bandages were already changing lives, just as he had dreamed. And this was only the beginning.

He thought again of their mysterious benefactor. Whoever they were, Wally wished he could shake their hand. Their selfless gift had catapulted FlexiBandages into the spotlight, positioning them to help untold numbers of children.

Wally could hardly fathom the magnitude of it. With production scaled up, they could distribute nationwide. Partner with hospitals across the country. Offer the bandages to pediatric burn units everywhere.

The possibilities were endless. Wally's heart swelled thinking of all the children that could now be helped - children just like Madison. Their lives irrevocably changed for the better.

This breakthrough was the culmination of years of work. Of late nights in the lab and secretive testing. Wally had persevered through all the challenges, never losing sight of his goal. And now his creation was poised to change the world, one healed child at a time.

As he drove home, Wally made a silent vow. He would not forget the gift he had been given - the ability to revolutionize pediatric burn treatment through his scientific knowledge. It was a gift he would not take lightly.

Wally would continue his tireless efforts to perfect the FlexiBandages, ensuring they realized their full, world-changing potential. Every batch produced would be done so with meticulous care and quality control. He owed that much to the suffering children and families who so desperately needed this medical breakthrough.

Most of all, Wally owed it to the anonymous donor who selflessly shared his vision. The one who catapulted FlexiBandages into the spotlight so they could finally, after all this time, help the multitudes of children waiting in hope.

For that mystery person's generosity, Wally would be forever grateful. And he would strive the rest of his days to prove that their faith in him - and in his creation - had not been misplaced. The future was brighter than ever, and Wally could not wait to forge ahead into it.

THE PEDIATRIC BURN unit at Houston Medical Center was bustling with activity. Nurses in colorful scrubs tended to young patients while parents kept watchful eyes over their recovering children. Laughter and chatter filled the halls as the kids played games and watched movies, providing a sense of normalcy amid challenging circumstances.

In room 417, an 8-year-old girl named Sophie smiled brightly as a nurse carefully removed her bandages. "Look mommy, it's getting better!" she exclaimed, craning her neck to examine the healing skin on her arm and torso. Just weeks prior, Sophie had suffered second and third-degree burns after a backyard accident. With the experimental bandages provided by Dr. Sanchez, her recovery so far had outpaced all expectations.

The nurse, Diane, nodded encouragingly even as her brow furrowed. She had never seen burns heal so quickly. Glancing at Sophie's chart, she noted that the child was due to be discharged tomorrow after just a 3-week stay. Diane had seen similar injuries require months of specialized treatment and skin grafts. She made a mental note to ask Dr. Sanchez about the new bandages later.

Down the hall, investigative journalist Daniel Brooks waited to interview Dr. Mark Simmons, head of pediatric care at the hospital. Daniel was researching a story on recent advances in burn treatment. He planned to highlight an innovative spray-on skin product that was reducing healing times.

Dr. Simmons entered the waiting room, smiling warmly as he approached Daniel. "Thanks for coming today," he said, shaking Daniel's hand. "Why don't we chat in my office?"

Once settled inside the office, Daniel started his recording device. "So doctor, I understand you've been using some new treatments for burn victims with promising results. Can you tell me about that?"

Dr. Simmons nodded. "Yes, we are very excited about a new spray-on biosynthetic skin substitute developed by Sanex Pharmaceuticals. It's been a game-changer for reducing healing times and improving outcomes."

The doctor proceeded to provide details that Daniel took notes on. After some time, Daniel paused. "Have you implemented any other new treatments lately? I've heard rumors of patients being discharged exceptionally quickly."

Dr. Simmons hesitated briefly. "Well, we always seek to utilize the latest evidence-based treatments. But no, there is nothing else new and significant that I can report on currently." He glanced at his watch. "Now if you'll excuse me, I'm due for patient rounds."

Daniel frowned slightly as Dr. Simmons ushered him out. Something seemed off. He decided to probe further.

Wandering the pediatric wing, Daniel looked for anything out of the ordinary. He noticed one room with a large handmade "Welcome Home!" banner hung across the door. Glancing at the chart outside, Daniel saw the patient was an 8-year old boy who had been admitted just shy of 3 weeks ago with severe electrical burns to his torso and arms. Daniel's eyes widened in surprise. That recovery time seemed implausibly fast.

Just then, a nurse exited the room. Daniel approached her. "Excuse me, I couldn't help but notice how quickly that boy recovered from some very serious burns. Is that typical here?"

The nurse, Diane, hesitated before responding. "Well, we have an excellent pediatric burn team. But honestly, yes, that was unusually fast. We've had a few cases like that lately." She lowered her voice. "Rumor is it's some experimental new bandages, but I haven't gotten any official word."

Daniel's ears perked up. This could be a major medical story in the making. He thanked the nurse and headed for the exit, his mind racing. He needed to look into this further, maybe get access to patient records and recovery stats. If word of seemingly miraculous healing got out, it could cause a storm. Daniel wondered if someone was trying to keep things under wraps. Either way, he was going to get to the bottom of this.

Across town, Dr. Elena Sanchez was just wrapping up patient visits at the Houston Medical Center adult burn unit. Her phone buzzed with an urgent message from Dr. Simmons requesting she call immediately. Stepping into a quiet hallway, Elena dialed the number.

"Elena, I think we may have a situation," Dr. Simmons said without preamble. He explained the unexpected questions from the journalist that seemed a little too probing.

Elena felt her stomach drop. This could threaten everything. "Did he seem to know specifics? Or was he fishing for information?" she asked.

"Hard to say. He didn't mention the bandages directly. But he clearly picked up on something unusual happening here."

Elena thanked the doctor and hung up. She quickly called Wally Eastwood, arranging an emergency meeting at his lab. This required immediate discussion.

Thirty minutes later, Elena arrived at the nondescript warehouse that served as Wally's discreet research facility. She filled him in on the conversation with Dr. Simmons.

Wally's expression darkened with concern. "Do you think our cover could be blown?" he asked.

Elena sighed, crossing her arms. "I'm not sure. This journalist seems to just have vague suspicions right now. But he could eventually uncover the truth if he keeps digging."

"We need to get ahead of this," Wally said. He began pacing, his mind sorting through various contingency plans. "Maybe we should consider moving up the timeline for public disclosure. Get out ahead and control the narrative."

"Perhaps," Elena said slowly. "Though I worry we're not ready for that. Our production capacity is still limited. And we haven't completed long-term studies." She shook her head. "A premature reveal could be disastrous."

Wally nodded grimly. "You're right. We need to be meticulous." He sat down, thinking hard. "For now, let's intensify security. I'll work on anonymizing any data that could point to the bandages. You coordinate with the hospitals - emphasize discretion without raising too much alarm."

"Agreed." Elena checked her watch. "I better get back to Medical Center before I'm missed. We'll keep each other updated on any developments." She turned to leave, feeling the weight of their predicament. A single misstep could have far-reaching consequences. They needed to stay vigilant.

Wally saw her out, then got to work. There was much to do to cover their tracks. But he remained confident in their careful approach. With dedication and care, they would guide their innovation to change lives without allowing its immense power to spiral out of control. For now, they just needed to keep the genie in the bottle a little longer.

WALLY STEPPED OUT INTO the warm Houston night, the door to FFOne closing behind him with a heavy thud. He took a deep breath, letting the muggy air fill his lungs as he looked up at the few stars visible beyond the city lights. It had been another long day at the office, full of meetings and mundane tasks, but now his real work could begin.

Sliding behind the wheel of his car, Wally reached into the glove compartment to retrieve a small metal case. He popped it open, revealing two round pills, speckled blue like robin eggs. Tossing them back, he swallowed and started the engine, feeling the familiar tingle spreading through his limbs as the pills took effect. Energy and focus heightened, Wally pulled out of the parking lot and merged onto the freeway.

The city blurred past as he made his way to the outskirts of town. Here, the bright lights and bustle faded away, replaced by dark country roads winding through shadowy forest. Wally followed the familiar turns off the main road until he reached the gated driveway that led to his secluded property.

Parked in the garage, Wally entered a code on a keypad nestled behind a loose brick in the wall. A concealed door swung open, revealing a staircase descending into the earth below the house. As Wally climbed down, motion-sensor lights flickered on, illuminating the windowless passage.

At the bottom, he entered another code to open the heavy steel door protecting his underground laboratory. Stepping inside, Wally was greeted by the hum of equipment and glow of monitor screens. This was where he did his real work, hidden from prying eyes.

Moving to a refrigerated storage unit, Wally withdrew a tray of small glass vials filled with a faintly shimmering silver liquid - his regenerative formula DNX-109. Carefully, he loaded the vials into a padded case along with sterile syringes and bandages. Tonight, he would bring his creation to those who needed it most.

Dressed in dark clothing with the case secured in his backpack, Wally drove across the city once more. The neighborhoods grew rougher as he neared his destination: Houston Medical Center's burn unit. Slipping in through a side entrance, Wally followed little-used hallways until he reached a supply closet near the pediatric ward.

Inside the closet, he quickly changed into hospital scrubs and grabbed a clipboard. Now disguised as an orderly, Wally calmly walked the halls, nodding politely to nurses and doctors as he passed. In his pocket, the vials of DNX-109 felt heavy, both a burden and a gift.

Checking room numbers against a crumpled paper, Wally entered the room of a young boy named Danny. The child's small body was swathed in bandages, but his eyes brightened when he saw Wally. "Hi, are you my new nurse?" Danny asked.

Wally smiled warmly. "I'm here to help you feel better," he said, then got to work changing the dressings, discreetly applying DNX-109 to the worst burns. Danny winced at first but soon relaxed as the solution soothed the pain. After securing fresh bandages, Wally offered a little toy car from his pocket to cheer Danny up.

Over the next two hours, Wally visited a dozen rooms, using DNX-109 to secretly treat children's burns. With each smiling, hopeful face, his heart swelled even as exhaustion set in. He lived for these small moments that made the whole struggle worthwhile.

Near dawn, Wally returned to the supply closet to change back into his civilian clothes before slipping out to his car, the case of remaining vials once more hidden in his backpack. As he drove home through the breaking light, weariness weighed on him but so did a deep sense of fulfillment.

Back in the underground lab, Wally secured the DNX-109 next to its formula locked inside a heavy safe. He meticulously cleaned his equipment and destroyed any trash that could link him to the night's activities. Though risky, this was his solemn duty - to use his gift to quietly help others from the shadows.

Upstairs, Wally showered and changed into fresh clothes before brewing a strong pot of coffee. He had to be at the office again in just a couple hours. Sipping the hot, bitter drink, Wally reviewed the latest reports from Dr. Sanchez regarding their official bandage trials. Their success was growing, but Wally remained cautious and tight-lipped, even with those closest to him.

Arriving at FFOne, Wally grabbed a doughnut from the breakroom and exchanged idle chatter with coworkers about sports and office gossip. He smiled and laughed, playing the part of an ordinary man with an ordinary job. But behind his cheerful facade, the weight of his knowledge hung heavy.

From his desk, Wally responded to emails and calls, coordinating shipments and payments for his tech company's latest projects. It was the public face he showed the world, hiding his true work conducted in secret late at night.

During lunch, Wally joined some colleagues at a nearby cafe, keeping the conversation light. Walking back, they passed a newspaper stand. On the front page, a headline declared "Miracle Burn Treatment - But Who's Behind It?" Wally's pulse quickened, but he said nothing, hiding his reaction.

Back at his desk, an email from Dr. Sanchez confirmed Wally's fears. Rumors about the pediatric burn patients' rapid healing were spreading. They would need to be even more cautious with security and supplies of DNX-109. Wally typed a short reply, his stomach in knots.

Leaving the office that evening, Wally felt the weight of his secrets pressing down. He longed to tell someone, anyone, about what he had created and the lives he had changed. But he knew the stakes were too high, the balance too fragile. For now, his fulfillment would have to come from silent deeds rather than acclaim.

Wally stopped to pick up flowers on his way to the hospital, then changed into scrubs in the supply closet. Tonight, he would focus on the good work, leaving the burdens outside... at least for now. With the vials ready in his pocket, Wally stepped into the first child's room, smiling.

MURMURS AND SPECULATIONS started to percolate through medical circles, hinting at a "miracle" treatment that had been aiding the remarkable recoveries of young burn victims. While no one could pinpoint the source, the buzz grew as clinicians and researchers alike strived to learn more.

Dr. Alicia Chen, a pediatrician at Houston Medical Center, flipped through the chart of her latest patient, 12-year old Sophie. Sophie had suffered second and third degree burns over 30% of her body from a house fire. Yet just three weeks after being admitted, her wounds were nearly healed. Dr. Chen traced her finger over the girl's barely visible scars, marveling at the speed of her recovery. In two decades of practicing medicine, she had never seen anything like it.

She closed the chart and headed to the nurse's station, hoping to glean some insight from the nursing staff. Claire, the head nurse, was updating a whiteboard with patient information when Dr. Chen approached.

"Claire, got a minute?" Dr. Chen asked.

"For you? Always." Claire smiled. She could tell from the doctor's furrowed brow that she had a puzzle she was trying to solve.

"What can you tell me about Sophie Evans' treatment regimen? Her chart lists the standard interventions, but her healing process seems...accelerated."

Claire nodded knowingly. "We were all amazed by it. That special bandaging they used made a huge difference."

"Special bandaging?" Dr. Chen's interest was piqued.

"Mmhmm. Some experimental dressing that the company donated. It promoted rapid re-epithelialization while preventing infection. I've never seen anything like it."

"Do you remember the name of the company?" Dr. Chen pressed.

Claire shook her head apologetically. "No, they didn't provide any info. But maybe Dr. Simmons knows more. She coordinated the donation."

Dr. Chen's mind raced as she headed to Dr. Simmons' office. This mystery bandaging could be groundbreaking if they could figure out who created it. She rapped sharply on the door.

"Come in," Dr. Simmons called out. She looked up from her computer screen, removing her reading glasses as Dr. Chen entered.

"Sorry to bother you, but I had a question about a patient's treatment," Dr. Chen began. She relayed the details of Sophie's rapid healing process.

Dr. Simmons nodded thoughtfully. "The experimental bandages. Yes, they've been remarkably effective for our burn victims."

"Do you know anything about who provided them? I'd love to learn more about how they work."

Dr. Simmons hesitated. "I'm afraid I can't disclose much. The donors requested confidentiality."

Seeing Dr. Chen's disappointed look, she added gently, "But I assure you, this technology is like nothing I've ever encountered. Our patients' recoveries speak for themselves."

Dr. Chen left the office more determined than ever to uncover the mystery. If word got out about these revolutionary bandages, it would be a game changer for burn treatment everywhere.

She decided to start digging through the hospital's acquisition records. Several hours later, bleary-eyed from combing through endless files and databases, she finally unearthed a shipping manifest.

"Eureka!" she whispered triumphantly. The bandages had been supplied by something called the Phoenix Foundation. She had never heard of them, but it was a start.

Typing rapidly, she searched for any information on the Phoenix Foundation. All she could find was a generic website listing it as a medical nonprofit. No names, no contact info. Another dead end.

Who were these people? And what exactly was in these bandages that made them so effective? She was more perplexed than ever.

Over the next few weeks, Dr. Chen noticed more and more rapid burn recoveries. The news of the experimental treatment seemed to be spreading amongst the staff, though no one knew any concrete details.

Intrigued researchers started reaching out to pick her brain.

"Chen, what's going on over there with your burn patients? I'm hearing crazy recovery times," her colleague Dr. Bradford asked over the phone.

"I wish I knew," she admitted. "Some mystery benefactor supplied these bandages that seem to work miracles. But I can't figure out who's behind it all."

"Well don't stop digging. This could be Nobel-worthy research if we can get to the bottom of it!" he encouraged her.

At the weekly Morbidity and Mortality conference, all the doctors were abuzz with chatter about the bandages and their seemingly magical properties. No one had answers, only more questions.

Dr. Chen silenced the room. "I know we're all curious about this treatment that's been making the rounds. But we have patients to care for. I'm sure in time we'll learn more. For now, let's focus on what we do know - it's helping people heal. That's what matters most."

The doctors murmured in agreement and turned their discussion back to reviewing cases. But the allure of a medical miracle captivated them all.

Later at home, Dr. Chen sipped a glass of wine, contemplating her next move. Whoever had created this technology clearly valued discretion. She would have to be smart and tread carefully.

Logging in to her computer, she posted on a medical research forum:

"Seeking information about experimental bandaging for rapid burn healing. Please contact Dr. Alicia Chen at Houston Medical with any relevant information. Discretion assured."

She hoped casting a wide net might turn up a new lead. Someone out there must know something. She was determined to unravel this mystery - not for personal gain, but to help burn patients everywhere benefit from this revolutionary treatment.

Until then, she would keep observing her patients' recoveries, gathering data to better understand the effects. With meticulous documentation, she aimed to prove the bandages' efficacy beyond a doubt.

Satisfied with her plan, she shut down her computer and went to bed, hoping to dream up fresh ideas. The answer was out there somewhere. She just had to find it.

WALLY SAT QUIETLY IN the corner of the pediatric burn unit's brightly colored playroom, watching as young patients engaged in therapeutic activities designed to aid their recovery. Though their injuries varied in severity, each child bore the unmistakable marks of trauma, both physical and emotional. Bandages swathed limbs and torsos, some dotted with spots of blood that had seeped through. Even with pain medication, many winced or favored their wounds as they moved.

But as Wally observed, he also saw incredible resilience in the face of such adversity. A young boy, no more than six or seven, gingerly held a crayon in his bandaged hand as he focused intently on coloring a picture. A teenage girl absently rubbed her arm, crisscrossed with healing burns, while laughing with another patient. Two siblings built a block tower together, though one wore a headwrap that covered extensive injuries. The children carried on, finding moments of joy and normalcy amidst their struggles.

Wally felt a swell of purpose and protectiveness rise within him. These brave children had no idea that the unassuming man in the corner was responsible for the bandages aiding their recovery in ways they couldn't imagine. The regenerative powers of DNX-109 remained Wally's closely guarded secret, shared only with his most trusted allies. Still, seeing the impact firsthand filled him with a sense of fulfillment that no personal acclaim could provide.

He was drawn from his thoughts as a nurse approached. "Mr. Eastwood, thank you again for the generous toy donations," she said warmly. "It means the world to our patients. Especially with the holidays coming up, this will help lift their spirits."

Wally smiled. "It's my pleasure, Claire. I'm just glad I can help in a small way."

Claire nodded towards a boy sitting alone, intently working on a Lego model. "Jacob's having a rough day. His last skin graft didn't take as well as we'd hoped. I know he'd love it if you stopped by to chat with him for a bit."

"I'd be happy to," Wally replied. He crossed the room and sat down next to Jacob, who barely glanced up from his Legos. "That's shaping up to be an impressive spaceship," Wally observed. "How's it going?"

Jacob shrugged. "Okay, I guess." He winced slightly as he stretched to grab another block.

Wally's heart ached for the boy, but he kept his voice upbeat. "Mind if I help? I've got some experience building cool spacecrafts."

A flicker of interest crossed Jacob's face. "Like what kind?"

"Well, let's just say I've worked on some top-secret projects," Wally said with a wink.

Soon they were immersed in constructing the ship, Jacob visibly cheering up as they worked. Wally asked questions and listened intently as the boy opened up about his interests. He learned Jacob's dream was to be an astronaut, and Wally assured him he was well on his way with such impressive skills.

As their time drew to a close, Wally stood up. "Thanks for letting me help out, Jacob. This is by far the best spaceship I've ever worked on." He held out his fist. "You keep working hard, and you can do anything you set your mind to. We'll finish this next time I visit, deal?"

Jacob grinned and bumped Wally's fist with his own. "Deal!"

Wally said his goodbyes and left the playroom, reflecting on the encounter. It was interactions like that which fueled his drive and made the pressures of secrecy worthwhile. Knowing he could ease some small bit of suffering for just a moment made all the difference.

He was stopped by Claire as he headed towards the exit. "Thank you for spending time with Jacob," she said warmly. "He really looks up to you. You have a wonderful way with the children."

Wally smiled modestly. "They're the amazing ones. I'm happy to help any way I can."

Claire nodded. "Well, it means more than you know. With the holidays coming, things can be especially tough on our long-term patients. Your visits make a real difference in their spirits."

"I'll be sure to stop by again soon," Wally assured her.

As he stepped outside into the brisk winter air, Wally pulled his coat tighter against the chill. Despite the cold, he felt a renewed sense of warmth and purpose following the visit. Hard as it was to see the children suffering, those moments of connection made him more determined than ever to continue his clandestine efforts.

The world saw Wally as nothing more than a modestly successful tech businessman. Even those who knew of his involvement with Dr. Sanchez's regenerative bandages were unaware of his integral role in their creation and distribution. Only his closest allies understood the full extent of his discoveries and sacrifices. But Wally asked for no acclaim or recognition. The chance to quietly change lives was reward enough.

There would be challenges ahead. Production limitations, security risks, ethical dilemmas - Wally knew the road was long. But witnessing firsthand the impact on these children fueled his unwavering dedication. He would press on, leveraging his discoveries to transform lives and acting as an invisible guardian.

As he arrived home, Wally headed straight for his basement lab. There was always more work to be done. Improvements to trial, new delivery mechanisms to refine, and increased production goals to meet. He would steal a few hours of sleep later on. But for now, Wally turned his focus to the task at hand, re-energized by the knowledge that each small breakthrough brought him one step closer to helping more children heal.

Chapter 9

Wally sat at his desk, surrounded by stacks of medical textbooks and scientific journals. His eyes scanned the pages intently, absorbing every detail on the intricacies of Alzheimer's disease. For hours he pored over the material, fueled by a sense of purpose. This was no idle academic pursuit, but a mission to comprehend the complex mechanisms of a ruthless illness and unlock its secrets.

The statistics were sobering. Over 50 million people worldwide afflicted. A progressive deterioration of memory, thinking and behavior that eventually destroyed a person's very identity. No cure. Minimal treatments to temporarily slow an inexorable decline. The enormity of the suffering wrought by Alzheimer's weighed heavily on Wally as he studied.

He turned to a journal article detailing the latest research on amyloid plaques and tau tangles, the protein abnormalities that were hallmarks of Alzheimer's. Wally's mind ignited with insight as he analyzed a proposed pathway for plaque accumulation and nerve cell death. Equations and chemical formulas spun through his thoughts. Here was a puzzle to be solved, a biological lock awaiting the right key.

Wally's eyes narrowed with determination. He would apply the full force of his intellectual gifts to conquer this disease. His scientific prowess could be used for more than financial gain or acclaim - it could restore hope where despair reigned. As he envisioned a future free from the ravages of Alzheimer's, Wally's spirit soared.

A photo in a textbook captured his attention: an elderly woman's eyes, once bright with life, now clouded with confusion. Wally's breath caught in his throat. This was the human toll that called him to action. To sit idly by while millions suffered such a fate would be unthinkable. He would answer the call.

Turning to his computer, Wally pulled up the latest research on ketones and coconut oil. A radical new approach, yet the initial results were promising. Wally's sharp mind fused connections as he took notes. Adjust the compound here, introduce a catalyst there - a medley of ideas swirled through his thoughts.

The sheer complexity of the challenge only seemed to sharpen Wally's focus. He lived for unraveling intricate problems and innovating beyond the status quo. And with stakes this high, his motivation ran deeper than any intellectual puzzle. Lives hung in the balance. Suffering begged to be relieved. Hope awaited discovery.

Wally glanced at the clock - 3:17 AM. He had been reading for over six hours straight, but his energy remained undimmed. This work ignited him like nothing else. The volumes around him contained merely a fraction of the knowledge needed to defeat Alzheimer's, but Wally was up for the task. One step at a time, one insight leading to the next, he would dismantle this terrible disease.

For now, his eyes required a break, even if his mind raced on. Wally rose and stretched his arms overhead, joints cracking. He blinked hard, then splashed cold water on his face from the bathroom sink. The shock of the water jolted his senses awake. He took a deep breath and stared at his reflection in the mirror. The face staring back at him was weary but resolute. Wally knew the long hours and tireless efforts this endeavor would require, but he would not waver. Too much was at stake.

Wally returned to his desk with a fresh cup of coffee. The hot liquid delivered a welcome rush of caffeine to keep his brain energized. He added a vial of AXI-218 to the coffee - a microbial supplement to enhance auditory perception. With his hearing augmented, Wally could detect the subtle background noises that would normally distract his focus. Instead, he simply tuned them out, creating an ideal environment for intense concentration.

The first rays of dawn peeked through the window. Wally turned his attention to cutting-edge research on the microbiome. An avalanche of recent studies pointed to the influential role of gut bacteria on brain function. Could microbes be manipulated to prevent plaque formation and protect cognitive abilities? The prospect fascinated Wally as he took notes.

His phone buzzed with a reminder - time for his morning regenerative formula. Wally retrieved the vial of DNX-109 from the biometric safe. He scanned his fingerprint, heard the click of the lock disengaging, and removed the vial. After meticulously measuring out the proper dosage, he drank the tangy liquid. Wally trusted the benefits of this creation, but respected its power. He would handle it only with the utmost care.

After returning the vial to the safe, Wally prepared for the day ahead. A long road lay before him, full of complex challenges, but he would follow it relentlessly. For today, the next step was clear - continue learning all he could about the intricacies of Alzheimer's disease. The suffering it inflicted demanded nothing less than his absolute best efforts.

Wally sat down amidst the stacks of materials once more. He flipped open a reference book on the latest pharmacological approaches. As he dove back into the dense text, the familiar thrill of intellectual pursuit mingled with the weight of humanity's need. This was no mere puzzle for his personal satisfaction. Lives were at stake. And he would unlock the secrets to save them.

WALLY WORKED METICULOUSLY, his hands moving with practiced precision as he assembled the components of his latest creation. Laying on the table before him was an array of beakers, pipettes, vials, and medical devices, all perfectly organized to aid in his groundbreaking work. At the center of it all was a small capsule, no larger than a vitamin pill, that contained Wally's hopes for the future.

The human brain is an energy-intensive organ, accounting for about 20% of the body's energy expenditure despite only making up about 2% of the body's weight. It typically relies on glucose as its primary source of energy. Glucose from carbohydrates that are consumed is circulated through the bloodstream and across the blood-brain barrier to fuel neural activity. This energy is crucial for processes such as neurotransmission, maintaining cellular health, and supporting cognitive functions.

However, in some situations, the brain may become starved of glucose. Conditions such as Alzheimer's disease, other forms of dementia, or even after prolonged periods of fasting, the brain's ability to utilize glucose can be compromised. In Alzheimer's disease, for example, the brain cells lose their ability to efficiently take up and use glucose due to insulin resistance and other metabolic deficiencies, leading to cognitive decline and neuron damage.

When the brain cannot access enough glucose, it can adapt to using an alternate source of fuel—ketones. Ketones are produced by the liver during periods of low carbohydrate intake, fasting, or intense exercise. They are made when fatty acids are broken down. These compounds can cross the blood-brain barrier and be used by brain cells for energy. The three primary ketone bodies produced in the body are beta-hydroxybutyrate, acetoacetate, and acetone, with beta-hydroxybutyrate being the most abundant and stable form.

Studies have suggested that ketones can provide a more efficient and cleaner-burning fuel than glucose, potentially offering neuroprotective benefits. For individuals with compromised glucose metabolism, a diet that induces the production of ketones, such as the ketogenic diet, can help provide an alternative energy source to maintain brain function. Moreover, certain ketone supplements can deliver ketone bodies directly to the brain, bypassing the need for dietary changes.

The brain's ability to switch to ketone metabolism is an example of metabolic flexibility, and this process may help to protect and support brain cells under conditions of metabolic stress or in neurodegenerative diseases. However, extensive research is ongoing to fully understand how ketone bodies affect the brain in both healthy individuals and those with cognitive impairments.

Carefully, Wally filled the outer shell of the capsule with a viscous, amber-colored liquid. This was a unique ketone body solution he had formulated to provide alternative brain fuel and support cognitive function. As the fluid flowed into the capsule, Wally's mind wandered to his friend Ronnie and others suffering from neurological diseases like Alzheimer's. He pictured their struggles and imagined this invention being a lifeline for them.

With the ketone solution loaded, Wally turned his focus to the inner core of the capsule. Using a pair of tweezers, he lifted a miniscule square of material dotted with tiny pores. This was a time-release fabric he had engineered to slowly diffuse the contents of the capsule over a 12-hour period. Sliding it into place, Wally encased the precious ketone solution.

Meticulously, Wally fused the two halves of the capsule together using a dental laser. A barely perceptible seam formed, sealing the contents safely inside. Wally held the capsule up and inspected it, satisfied with the clean construction. He placed it under a microscope and zoomed in, ensuring the integrity of the bonds. A moment of quiet pride washed over him as he stared at the fruition of months of research and experimentation.

But the work was not yet complete. Wally reached for a glass vial containing a faintly blue liquid. This was a culture of genetically modified microorganisms he had designed to deliver targeted nutrients to the brain. With a steady hand, he extracted a precise amount using a glass syringe. Moving slowly and deliberately, he injected the microbes into a port on the exterior of the capsule. They now swam inside a micro-chamber, ready to be released along with the ketones.

After wiping down the exterior with an alcohol swab, Wally submerged the capsule in a sterile saline bath and sonicated it to remove any residual contaminants. He then placed the capsule in a vacuum chamber to remove all moisture before depositing it in a glass jar and sealing the lid.

Wally held up the jar and gazed at its contents. Years of tireless research had led to this moment, the creation of this ingenious delivery system that would bring both immediate and sustained benefits for cognitive health. He imagined the microbes spreading through the body, nourishing neurons and neural pathways. The ketones would fuel the brain's energy needs, providing an alternative to glucose. It was a revolutionary development, and Wally felt the weight of what it could mean for sufferers of Alzheimer's, dementia, and other neurological diseases.

But Wally also carried the burden of responsibility. He alone knew the capsule's true origin and potential. How could he ensure it got into the right hands while keeping its secrets safe? His mind turned to the risks - the possibility of misuse, exploitation, or unintended effects. With a technology this powerful, Wally understood there would be no turning back once it was unleashed into the world.

A knock at the lab door jarred Wally from his contemplation. It was his research partner, Dr. Elena Sanchez, arriving for a scheduled meeting. Wally carefully placed the glass jar containing the capsule into a concealed safe. He would discuss next steps with Dr. Sanchez, but the technology itself would remain protected for now. There was much more testing to be done, and many questions still to answer.

Wally let Dr. Sanchez into the lab and they sat down to review the latest trial data. Her insights would prove invaluable, as always, in guiding the responsible development of this advance. As they delved into the analysis, Wally's mind flickered back to the unassuming capsule and all it represented - both the awe-inspiring potential and the weighty responsibility that now rested on his shoulders. He had vowed to help those suffering from neurological decline, to be the guardian of this technology and steward its development for the good of mankind.

The road ahead would not be easy, Wally knew. There would be setbacks and hard choices. But with steadfast purpose, an ethical compass, and trusted allies like Dr. Sanchez by his side, Wally felt confident he could navigate the winding path towards bringing this invention from his carefully controlled lab out into the wider world. Where it would go from there, only time would tell. But Wally would proceed cautiously, staying true to his principles.

For today, celebrations were premature. There was much work yet to be done. Patience and discretion must remain Wally's guiding virtues. He and Dr. Sanchez continued their studious review late into the night, speaking in hushed tones, their voices barely audible amidst the gentle hum of machinery. Tomorrow they would plan the next phase of trials. For now, Wally's creation would remain a well-kept secret, hidden away like buried treasure, its powers still largely unknown. After Dr. Sanchez had left, Wally placed the jar containing the capsule into a cryogenic freezer for safekeeping. Though tempted to immediately share his breakthrough, wisdom guided his hands, not pride. Step by step, he would slowly unveil his creation.

THE STERILE HUM OF the lab served as a backdrop to the earnest consultation between Dr. Sanchez and Wally. They pored over charts and data, discussing the revolutionary possibilities encapsulated within FlexMend-111. Could this be the key to unlocking a new future for Alzheimer's patients?

Wally's eyes scanned the latest trial results, hope and trepidation warring within him. The data showed promise, with FlexMend-111 demonstrating enhanced synaptic plasticity and neurogenesis in animal models. But scaling up to human trials brought a host of new variables and risks that left Wally uneasy.

"The hippocampal regeneration is remarkable," Dr. Sanchez said, tapping her pen on an image of a mouse brain slice. "If we can replicate even a fraction of this in patients, it would be groundbreaking."

Wally nodded, rubbing his chin pensively. "No doubt about the potential impact. But we have to be absolutely certain of safety before proceeding. I don't want to repeat the same mistakes as others who rushed experimental treatments to market."

Dr. Sanchez's expression grew solemn. They had both witnessed the tragic consequences of well-intentioned but recklessly accelerated drug trials. Lives ruined, trust shattered.

"You're right to urge caution," she said. "We'll take this one step at a time. Vet every protocol, triple check the formulations. I don't want to lose sight of the big picture, but we can't overlook the details either."

Wally appreciated Dr. Sanchez's meticulous approach. It mirrored his own tendency to dive deep into the particulars without losing perspective. They made a good team, balancing one another's strengths.

"I think we need to re-examine the delivery mechanism," Wally said. "The lipid nanoparticles performed well in the animal models, but the pharmacokinetics may differ in an aged human blood-brain barrier."

Dr. Sanchez nodded, jotting a note. "Agreed. And we should investigate alternative routes of administration too. Intranasal, intravenous, even intraventricular if warranted."

They debated options for another hour, delving into the minutiae of pharmacology and drug design. It was mentally taxing work, but exhilarating too. The tantalizing prospect of undoing the neuronal damage wrought by Alzheimer's fueled their stamina.

A knock at the lab door interrupted their focus. Dr. Sanchez's research assistant entered, looking harried.

"Sorry to bother you, doctors, but the suppliers are on the phone about the peptide order. They're saying the batch purity is below spec."

Dr. Sanchez sighed, removing her glasses to rub the bridge of her nose. "I'll handle it. Thank you, Nina."

After the assistant left, Dr. Sanchez turned to Wally with an apologetic look. "Duty calls. We'll have to pick this up later."

Wally waved off her concern. "No problem, these things happen. I should get back to Ronnie soon anyway."

Dr. Sanchez departed to deal with the supplier headache, while Wally tidied up their notes and research materials. His gaze lingered on an image of amyloid plaques marring a diseased brain. So much devastation wrought by misfolded proteins. But perhaps their work could undo some of that damage. Help families ravaged by this cruel disease.

After locking up the lab, Wally headed out to his car. But his mind remained back in the lab, turning over ideas. He had learned not to force solutions; often they arose spontaneously, precipitating out of the saturated solution of his subconscious. Sleep, exercise, music—these activities precipitated insight.

Wally turned the radio up as he drove, letting the melody and rhythm of jazz perfuse his thoughts. By the time he arrived home, the seed of an idea had begun to sprout. A possible way to improve FlexMend's specificity using dendrimer-conjugated aptamers...

Ronnie looked up from the stove as Wally entered. "Hey, bro! How'd it go today?"

Wally smiled, embracing his friend. "Really good. We're making progress on something big."

He left it at that. Only a few people in the world knew about FlexMend, and for now, that was safest. Ronnie knew Wally worked on important medical research, but not the details. Someday, hopefully, FlexMend's benefits could be available to all. But they had to walk before they could run.

Over dinner, Wally decompressed as Ronnie recounted office mishaps and funny customer stories. Ronnie had a gift for finding humor in everyday things, and Wally appreciated the moments of levity. Still, part of his mind continued working on the obstacles facing FlexMend. Delivery, dosage, stability...so many challenges to solve.

After clearing up dinner, the two friends headed out to shoot some hoops at a nearby court. The familiar ritual helped Wally unwind further. Here in the invigorating chill of the night air, worries seemed to slip from his shoulders. All that existed was the thump of the ball, the scrape of shoes on asphalt, Ronnie's good-natured trash talk.

Later at home, Wally felt recharged. He bid Ronnie goodnight and then headed to his home office/personal lab. Pulling up digital molecular models, he began experimenting with new dendrimer linker designs. It was hard to restrain his eagerness; he had to constantly remind himself to be meticulous. No rushing this process.

In the early hours of the morning, Wally finally forced himself to step away from the computer. He prepared some chamomile tea and then headed upstairs to his bedroom. Slipping under the covers, he let his mind drift...

Wally stands on a stage, looking out over a sea of faces. He clears his throat and begins: "When I started this work over a decade ago, many dismissed it as impossible, or worse, irresponsible..." A montage plays behind him - failed trials, protests, warnings about "playing God."

"But we persevered. We refined and rethought, never losing sight of our duty to patients. And today..." Wally gestures as a new image lights up the screen. "Today, we celebrate the approval of FlexMend for the treatment of Alzheimer's disease!"

The audience erupts into applause. Wally spots familiar faces - Dr. Sanchez, Ronnie, his mentors and colleagues - all beaming with joy. Parents embrace children, spouses hold each other, patients cheer.

"Of course, our work has just begun," Wally continues, waiting for the applause to subside. "We will continuously improve on this technology, expanding its application while remaining vigilant about its responsible use. But for now, let us recognize this milestone, made possible by the tireless work of so many. Let us celebrate hope!"

More applause thunders through the auditorium. Wally's heart swells, eyes growing moist. After so many late nights, so much uncertainty, this moment makes it all worthwhile. To see such joy, such relief, knowing his life's work is finally fulfilling its purpose...no words can fully capture this feeling.

Wally opens his mouth to continue, but a buzz from his nightstand cuts short the speech. Groggy, he reaches for his phone. A text from Dr. Sanchez: "Conference call with General Matthews at 1100 hours."

The auditorium vanishes as waking reality sets in. Wally sits up, rubbing his eyes. So it was just a dream. The approval and celebration lies ahead, someday. With diligence and care, it can become real.

Wally smiles, rising from bed with renewed vigor. Time for morning coffee. Back to the lab soon. The future awaits.

THE LABORATORY WAS quiet except for the soft hum of machines and the scratch of pen on paper as Dr. Sanchez recorded her observations. She studied the monitor closely, watching for any changes in the neural activity of the rat after being administered a small dose of FlexMend-111. So far, the results were promising.

The patterns on the screen were beginning to normalize, suggesting the compound was having a positive effect on the impaired pathways. Dr. Sanchez allowed herself a small smile. After years of painstaking research, it seemed they may have finally created a substance with the potential to reverse the ravages of Alzheimer's disease.

She made a note on her clipboard then walked over to check on the rat in its enclosure. It was moving about normally, showing no ill effects from the dose. She gave it some food and water then returned to observe the monitor.

Wally entered the lab, looking eager. "How's it going so far?" he asked.

Dr. Sanchez gave him an encouraging nod. "So far, so good. See for yourself."

Wally studied the monitor, his brow furrowing in concentration. Then his eyes widened. "The neural patterns are definitely improving. This is really promising!"

"It's still early, but yes, FlexMend-111 seems to be doing what we hoped it would. We'll need to run more trials of course, but this first one is going well."

Wally grinned, his excitement palpable. "I can't believe we might finally have a real shot at beating this disease. All the late nights and dead ends will have been worth it if this pans out."

"I know. I can hardly believe it myself," Dr. Sanchez replied. "But we have to stay cautious and methodical. No cutting corners."

Wally nodded. "Of course. We'll follow every protocol and then some. But I have a really good feeling about this substance, Elena. It's like we unlocked something here."

Dr. Sanchez smiled warmly at his enthusiasm. "I hope you're right. Now, let's get the next trial started..."

Over the next several hours, they conducted three more trials, administering small doses of FlexMend-111 to rats with induced Alzheimer's-like conditions. The results continued to show improved neural activity and no adverse effects.

As the day stretched into evening, Dr. Sanchez and Wally reviewed pages of notes and monitor printouts with growing excitement. The data was clear - their new compound appeared to be reversing the neural degeneration they had worked so hard to induce in the lab animals.

"I can't wait to try this on an actual Alzheimer's brain sample," Dr. Sanchez said, her eyes bright with anticipation. "If we can replicate these results, we'll know for sure we have something extraordinary on our hands."

Wally nodded. "I already have some cell cultures prepped. We could start first thing tomorrow."

"Perfect. Though I confess I'm tempted to get started tonight!" Dr. Sanchez said with a laugh.

Wally chuckled. "I know the feeling. This is the most promising result we've ever gotten. It's hard not to get ahead of ourselves."

Dr. Sanchez gave him an affectionate pat on the back. "You're right, we need to stay grounded. But for today, let's celebrate this success. All your hard work has paid off - you should feel proud."

Wally smiled, looking both exhilarated and contemplative. "I do feel proud that we might help so many people...but it's sobering too. The responsibility of wielding this kind of knowledge."

"I know. But we'll proceed with the utmost care at every step," Dr. Sanchez said reassuringly.

Wally nodded, his expression serious. "We have to. The world is depending on us."

They gathered up the day's results and locked them safely away. After a quick cleaning and equipment check, they donned their coats and prepared to leave the lab for the night.

Dr. Sanchez put a hand on Wally's shoulder. "Try not to worry too much. You've created something incredible. Just remember your own advice - stay hopeful."

Wally gave her a small smile. "You're right. Thanks, Elena. See you in the morning?"

She nodded. "Bright and early. Sweet dreams!"

They parted ways in the parking lot, each filled with a mix of pride, hope, and trepidation about what the future held. As Wally drove home, his mind spun with possibilities. If FlexMend-111 continued to show promise, it could revolutionize Alzheimer's treatment and prevent countless families from suffering. He tried to temper his enthusiasm with patience. There was still a long road ahead. But today was a very promising start down that road.

THE FLICKER OF A FLUORESCENT light illuminates Wally and Dr. Sanchez as they draft the necessary documentation to secure ethical clearance. Alzheimer's patient trials loom ahead, each signature a step closer to the precipice of clinical discovery.

Wally scratches his head, staring at the complex consent form in front of him. He knows the exhaustive paperwork is a necessary part of conducting ethical human trials, but the technical legalese seems almost designed to confuse rather than inform. Glancing across the table, he notices Dr. Sanchez equally engrossed, her brow slightly furrowed in concentration.

"This section on potential side effects needs more detail," Dr. Sanchez remarks, not looking up from the document. She picks up a pen and begins writing in the margins. Wally nods in agreement, impressed by her diligence.

For over an hour, they meticulously go through each section, ensuring nothing is missed or misconstrued. As lead researcher, Dr. Sanchez bears the ultimate responsibility for the trial's adherence to ethical guidelines. Her reputation and career are on the line.

Wally's role as co-researcher is less public, his involvement known only to Dr. Sanchez and a few select members of the research team. This veil of secrecy allows him to operate in the shadows, developing his regenerative solutions without the scrutiny of the mainstream science community. Still, he shares Dr. Sanchez's sense of duty and obligation to 'do no harm.'

"I think this covers the key points," Dr. Sanchez says, putting down her pen and flexing her fingers. She takes off her reading glasses and rubs the bridge of her nose. "Now we just need to get it approved by the ethics review board."

Wally nods, gathering up the scattered pages into a neat stack. He slides them into a folder and places it into his briefcase. "I know the team has been working hard to get all the supporting documents together as well. Let me know if you need anything else from me."

"Your input has been invaluable," Dr. Sanchez replies. "It's not often one gets to collaborate with a genius in regenerative solutions." She smiles warmly.

Wally feels a flush of gratitude at her acknowledgement. "I'm just glad I can use my knowledge to help people. It's not every day you get the chance to be part of something so meaningful."

Dr. Sanchez regards him thoughtfully. "It's a tremendous opportunity, but not without its challenges and responsibilities. We're venturing into uncharted territory here. If this trial is successful, it will change countless lives. But we must proceed cautiously."

Wally absorbs her words. The weight of what they are undertaking settles upon him. "I know. This is just the first step. We'll take it one day at a time."

"Agreed. Well, I won't keep you any longer." Dr. Sanchez gathers her things and stands up. "I'll be in touch as soon as I hear back from the review board. Hopefully we'll get their approval quickly."

"Sounds good. Have a good night, Dr. Sanchez." Wally picks up his briefcase and heads for the door.

"Please, call me Elena," she replies warmly.

Wally smiles. "Good night then, Elena."

He exits the research building into the muggy night air. The parking lot is mostly deserted, just a few cars scattered under the halo of the streetlights. He gets into his sedan and begins the drive home, reflecting on the day's progress.

Gaining ethical approval for human trials is a major undertaking, but a necessary step for responsible scientific research. Wally feels the weight of their work settling on his shoulders, but also a growing sense of optimism. This could be the breakthrough discovery he has spent years working towards.

Still, excitement is tempered with caution. Wally knows he and Elena must tread carefully. As the saying goes, 'With great power comes great responsibility.' The power to regenerate human cells and tissues is immensely valuable, but also dangerous if mishandled. Strict protocols and oversight will be critical.

The miles pass smoothly beneath his tires as he traverses the quiet streets. He pulls into the driveway of his modest suburban home and heads inside. After changing into comfortable clothes, he goes to his laboratory.

Rows of plants under grow lights greet him, lush and verdant. Wally examines them closely, taking notes on each specimen's development. These plants are infused with custom regenerative compounds, undergoing testing to gauge efficacy and refine delivery mechanisms.

Satisfied with their progress, Wally moves to a bench littered with notes, vials, and scientific equipment. Here is where he performs the painstaking work of honing his regenerative formulas. It is a delicate, complex process requiring equal parts creativity and precision.

He preps a new set of tissue samples and gets to work, losing himself in the familiar rhythms of experimentation. The hours pass unnoticed as he strives to perfect his techniques.

At some point, exhaustion begins to set in. Wally caps the last vial and cleans his workspace, getting things in order for tomorrow's efforts. He lock up the lab/ on stiff legs, suddenly feeling the lateness of the hour.

After a quick frozen dinner, he slips into bed. As his head sinks into the pillow, his mind continues to turn over ideas and possibilities. But eventually, the comforting darkness of sleep embraces him.

The work ahead will require all his energy and concentration. But for now, he can rest. The answers he seeks are waiting to be uncovered, one methodical step at a time. As he drifts off, Wally feels a renewed sense of hope and purpose. The future is uncertain, but he knows he won't face it alone. The journey has only just begun.

WALLY STEPPED OUT OF the nondescript office building into the humid Houston air, blinking against the bright sunlight after hours under artificial lights. He paused on the sidewalk, gathering his thoughts after the intense meeting with the review board concerning the upcoming clinical trial protocol.

Though the board members had seemed skeptical of the experimental treatment at first, their demeanor shifted after reviewing the preclinical data and proposed trial plan. In the end, they agreed the potential benefits justified moving forward, albeit with numerous safeguards and oversight measures.

Wally felt the weight of responsibility settle over him once more. So much depended on getting this right. Countless lives hung in the balance.

"Dr. Eastwood?" a voice spoke from behind him.

Wally turned to see a man approaching with an outstretched hand. He appeared to be in his early forties, with close-cropped salt-and-pepper hair and wire-rimmed glasses.

"I'm Dr. Neil Camden," the man introduced himself as they shook hands. "I was in the observation room during your presentation."

"Oh, of course," Wally replied, vaguely recalling the man sitting towards the back of the room. "What can I do for you?"

"I wanted to let you know I'm fully in support of moving forward with your trial," Dr. Camden said. "In fact, I'd be interested in collaborating, if you're open to it."

Wally raised an eyebrow, intrigued but cautious. "What did you have in mind?"

"Well, I'm a neurologist, and I specialize in researching progressive cognitive diseases like Alzheimer's," Dr. Camden explained. "When I heard about your proposed treatment, I was fascinated by the potential."

Wally nodded slowly, weighing how much to reveal. Dr. Sanchez had emphasized the need for discretion. But an expert neurologist could prove invaluable...

"To be honest, we could use someone with your background on the team," Wally admitted. "The treatment is...unconventional. We've seen incredible preclinical results, but scaling up to human trials is a massive undertaking."

Dr. Camden's eyes lit up behind his glasses. "I suspected as much. The data you presented is too remarkable for an ordinary therapy. You're on to something big here."

Wally held up a hand. "It's early days still. Nothing is guaranteed."

"Of course," Dr. Camden agreed. "But the possibility is thrilling. I'd love to offer my expertise in any way possible. My knowledge of the brain could complement your treatment nicely."

Wally considered for a moment. "I'd need to discuss this with my colleague, Dr. Sanchez. She's been integral to the work so far."

Dr. Camden nodded. "Of course, just let me know. Here's my card."

Wally pocketed the business card. "I'll be in touch soon. But for now, discretion is paramount. The treatment is highly...sensitive."

"I understand completely," Dr. Camden assured. "Patient confidentiality is my top priority."

They parted ways, and Wally headed to his car, mulling over the unexpected encounter. The man's background could prove invaluable, bringing a new dimension to their research. But letting in an unknown quantity also carried risk.

Wally resolved to thoroughly vet Dr. Camden before proceeding. If he checked out, the collaboration could pay dividends. But only with the utmost care and oversight.

Wally met Dr. Sanchez at their discreet research facility, eager to share the news of Dr. Camden. As expected, she reacted with equal parts intrigue and wariness.

"He certainly seems qualified," Dr. Sanchez mused, reviewing the neurologist's credentials. "And an expert on Alzheimer's would align well with our goals..."

"That's what I thought," Wally said. "But I wanted to discuss with you first."

Dr. Sanchez nodded. "I appreciate that. I think we should proceed, but with the usual precautions. Thorough background checks, legal safeguards, limited disclosure..."

"My thoughts exactly," Wally agreed.

Over the next few weeks, they conducted an exhaustive review of Dr. Camden's history and references, turning up nothing amiss. Finally, the two colleagues brought him to the facility for a preliminary meeting.

After a non-disclosure agreement was signed, they provided a high-level overview of the treatment, emphasizing the need-to-know nature of their project. Dr. Camden absorbed the information eagerly.

"This is more revolutionary than I could have imagined," he remarked. "The potential impact on Alzheimer's and dementia is astronomical."

"It's early still, but we're cautiously optimistic," Dr. Sanchez replied.

They delved into the technical details of the formula, its method of action, and the results observed so far. Dr. Camden asked thoughtful questions and provided insightful feedback.

By the meeting's end, both Wally and Dr. Sanchez felt reassured by engaging with the neurologist's expertise. Perhaps this new ally would provide the x-factor they needed.

In subsequent weeks, Dr. Camden consulted on the clinical trial protocols, emphasizing neurological assessments and brain imaging metrics. His fresh perspective shed light on nuances of the treatment they had overlooked.

Meanwhile, Wally and Dr. Sanchez focused on shoring up the drug manufacturing process and security measures. The last thing they needed was a breach of any kind.

Finally, the day came to commence the landmark clinical trial. Volunteers with early stage Alzheimer's arrived at the discreet facility, eager for a chance at slowing the disease's progression.

Wally, Dr. Sanchez and Dr. Camden observed the first treatment administration through a one-way mirror. It was a humbling moment, the culmination of years of research and preparation.

Whatever the outcome, they had achieved something remarkable in joining together—a neurologist, a biochemist and an engineer. Each brought something invaluable to their shared quest.

As the trial volunteers departed, the three colleagues shared a look heavy with meaning. Their work had just begun, but its impact could ripple through countless lives. They would proceed with utmost care and consideration at every step.

Too much depended on getting this right. Failure was not an option.

Wally extended his hand, and Dr. Sanchez and Dr. Camden each grasped it in turn. A simple handshake sealed their partnership and the promise of their continued efforts.

THE STERILE WHITE WALLS and antiseptic smell of the clinic did little to diminish the energy in the room. Dr. Camden watched with keen interest as his patient, 72-year-old Margaret, worked through a series of cognitive tests. Her responses were faster, her recall sharper than he had seen before. Though the changes were subtle, Dr. Camden sensed the unmistakable glow of progress.

He finished jotting a note and looked up. "Excellent work today, Margaret. How are you feeling overall?"

"I feel good, doctor," Margaret said, a touch of surprise in her voice. "My mind feels less foggy lately. I don't know how to explain it."

Dr. Camden nodded. "That's wonderful to hear. We'll want to keep monitoring your progress closely." He helped her up from her chair. As he escorted her out of the exam room, his eyes met Dr. Sanchez's. The two doctors exchanged a knowing look.

In a conference room down the hall, Drs. Camden and Sanchez debriefed with Wally Eastwood. As lead research scientist for the clinical trial, Wally had been observing the sessions from behind a one-way mirror.

"The preliminary data is very encouraging," Dr. Camden said, shuffling through his notes. "Two weeks into the trial, we're seeing improved cognition, reaction times, recall. The compound appears to be having a measurable effect."

Wally nodded, trying to contain his excitement. "Let's not get ahead of ourselves. We need more time and more participants before drawing conclusions." He glanced at Dr. Sanchez. "But I agree, the initial indicators are promising."

The doctors spent the next hour reviewing each patient's test results in detail, looking for patterns and anomalies. Though the sample size was small, just five patients so far, the subtle improvements across cognitive and memory tasks were remarkably consistent.

As the meeting adjourned, Dr. Camden pulled Wally aside. "I know you want to remain cautious, but I've been in this field for thirty years. What you've developed here is extraordinary. It's going to change everything." He gripped Wally's shoulder firmly before walking away.

Alone in the room, Wally allowed himself a moment to process the weight of what they had accomplished. After years of research and failed trials, his compound FlexMend-111 was demonstrating real potential as an Alzheimer's therapy. But Dr. Camden's words echoed in his mind. This was only the beginning. There were still so many unknowns, so many ways it could all go wrong. Wally straightened his shoulders, exhaled slowly, and went to prepare for the next patient.

Over the ensuing weeks, the trial expanded to 20 participants. In controlled, double-blind conditions, half received a placebo while the other half received varying doses of FlexMend-111. As the doctors closely tracked their progress, the improvements in the treatment group became increasingly obvious.

By week eight, there was no longer any doubt. FlexMend-111 was exhibiting measurable, sustained benefits for Alzheimer's patients. Even Wally had to admit it as he compiled the latest data. This was no statistical anomaly or wishful thinking. His creation was working.

At the next data review, the doctors could hardly contain their excitement as they discussed the trial's successful first phase. For the first time, they allowed themselves to envision the future impact this drug could have.

"We need to be prepared for increased scrutiny when we submit the data," Dr. Sanchez said. "We'll face questions, demands to share more details. But we expected that." She glanced around the room. "I think we're ready for the next phase." The others nodded, smiles spreading.

As the meeting adjourned, Dr. Camden pulled Wally aside again. "This is your moment, son. Your creation is going to change the world. I know you'll face this with wisdom." He gripped Wally's shoulder. "But remember to celebrate too. What you've accomplished is extraordinary."

That evening, Wally sat alone watching the sun set over the marsh behind his house. Dr. Camden was right, he thought. He had been so focused on the work ahead that he hadn't paused to appreciate how far FlexMend-111 had come. From his home laboratory, to tightly controlled trials, to now demonstrating real promise for Alzheimer's patients.

Wally thought of his grandmother. How different her last years could have been if a therapy like this had existed. Her bewildered fear haunted him, fueled his research. Maybe soon that pain could be spared for others.

Wally raised his glass in a silent toast as the sun dipped below the horizon. There was still so much to do, so much responsibility ahead. But for now, he let himself enjoy this moment, this glowing ember of hope.

Chapter 10

Wally gazed out the window of his home office, watching the sunrise cast its warm glow over the neighborhood. He sipped his coffee, contemplating the monumental task that lay ahead. After years of painstaking research and testing, FlexMend-111 was showing incredible promise in human trials for treating Alzheimer's disease. The potential to restore cognitive function and radically improve people's quality of life was beyond anything he had imagined when he first began tinkering with experimental compounds in his makeshift home laboratory.

Yet with each new discovery came an immense weight of responsibility. Wally understood the power he held in his hands, and the need to proceed with the utmost caution. He turned from the window and opened the locked drawer of his desk, removing a single capsule of FlexMend-111. Holding it up, he marveled at how something so small could change the world. The sound of his phone ringing shook him from his thoughts.

"Good morning, Dr. Sanchez," Wally answered. "I was just thinking about the trial. How are the patients responding?"

Dr. Sanchez's voice came through the phone, unable to contain her enthusiasm. "Wally, Margaret showed measurable improvement in her cognitive assessment this morning. At 72 years old, she was struggling with basic tasks last week. But today, she completed the exercises with flying colors. I even spotted her reading a book, something I haven't witnessed in months."

Wally felt a swell of pride, quickly tempered by caution. "That's incredible news. But we have to remain measured in our optimism. There's still so much we don't know."

"You're absolutely right," Dr. Sanchez replied. "We're seeing real progress, but we must keep our euphoria in check. There are still countless variables at play."

Wally nodded. "Have you spoken to Dr. Camden? I know he was observing participants closely for any adverse effects."

"I'm meeting him after rounds," she responded. "So far, his reports have been encouraging. No noticeable side effects. But we'll continue to monitor closely."

"Good. Let's take things one step at a time," Wally said. "I know it's hard not to get swept up in the excitement. But we have to remain hyper-vigilant."

He thought for a moment before continuing. "The board will want a full briefing soon. We should start preparing our most comprehensive data. They'll have a litany of questions, and we need to demonstrate that every precaution has been taken."

"You're right. I know some will question whether we should even proceed further given the risks," Dr. Sanchez replied.

Wally understood her concern. The medical community would be divided on the ethics of testing an experimental drug on vulnerable patients. "We'll help them see our commitment to the wellbeing of every participant," he assured. "I'll work on our protocols for safeguarding the patients throughout the remainder of the trial."

After finalizing their plan, Wally ended the call, his mind already racing ahead. Every detail mattered, from the controlled storage of the drug to the psychological evaluations of each patient. He would need to strengthen security measures and work closely with the nursing staff to ensure the participants were closely monitored.

His phone buzzed again, this time with a text from Ronnie. "I have a good feeling about today! Meet you on the court in 20?" Wally felt a pang of guilt, realizing he had been consumed by his work lately, neglecting his best friend. He knew a game of basketball would provide a welcome distraction.

"Be there in 10," he responded. As he grabbed his gym bag, his eyes returned to the single pill on his desk. He carefully locked it away before heading out the door.

On the court, Wally felt the tension in his shoulders release as he ran back and forth, the familiar motions taking over. Ronnie's energy was infectious, and Wally found himself laughing freely. For a brief time, he could let go of the immense responsibility that weighed on him and simply enjoy the game.

Afterward, as they gulped water on the sidelines, Ronnie turned to him with a serious expression. "So what's been going on with you lately? You've seemed preoccupied."

Wally hesitated. He hated keeping secrets from his friend, but knew he couldn't reveal anything about the drug trial. "Just busy with work," he answered vaguely.

Ronnie nodded, though his eyes revealed he wasn't fully convinced. Wally felt compelled to share at least a glimmer of the truth. "I'm involved in an important project that could really change lives. But it's confidential. I wish I could tell you more."

"No need," Ronnie replied supportively. "I trust you're doing something meaningful in that big brain of yours." He clapped Wally on the back. "Just don't forget about your friends, okay?"

Wally smiled, feeling grateful. "Never."

Back home, Wally headed straight for his small basement lab. He carefully prepared a new batch of FlexMend-111, triple-checking his work. His phone buzzed with a message from Dr. Camden requesting an urgent meeting about one of the trial participants. Wally felt his chest tighten anxiously. Had something gone wrong?

Sitting in Dr. Camden's office an hour later, Wally listened intently as the neurologist described the situation. "Greg Thompson's wife reported him becoming agitated and confused this morning. His cognitive scores have also declined the past two days. I'm concerned it may be related to the trial."

Wally's mind raced, considering the implications. "What steps have you taken?"

"I've suspended his dosage and scheduled additional neurological exams," Dr. Camden replied. "I thought it best we meet to discuss our options."

Wally nodded. He knew this moment would come eventually, the first signs of potential side effects. "Thank you for letting me know right away. Please keep me updated on his status. In the meantime, let's review our protocols again for responding to adverse reactions."

The two physicians talked through the contingency plans, considering ways to enhance their safety procedures. Wally also requested Dr. Camden share his recommendations for improving the medication's formula to minimize risks. They discussed the delicate balance required in shepherding the drug's development.

That evening, Wally video-conferenced with Dr. Sanchez, updating her on Greg's situation. She shared his concern, and they spent hours reviewing trial data and strengthening their patient monitoring system.

"We need to ensure the board has a complete picture of both the successes and potential complications," Dr. Sanchez said. Wally concurred, aware they needed full transparency.

As he finally climbed into bed, Wally's mind continued dissecting each minute detail of the trial. The weight of responsibility felt heavy, but it was buoyed by the incredible good the drug could achieve. He had to believe that with proper precautions, they could navigate the ethical maze. Lives depended on it. As he drifted off,

Wally resolved to follow the path ahead with care, caution and compassion. The way forward would be challenging, but he knew the journey was worth it.

WALLY STEPPED BACK from the microscope and rubbed his eyes. He had been peering into its lenses for hours, meticulously analyzing the latest batch of DNX-109 bandages. The data was promising, showing enhanced tissue regeneration in the lab samples. But something still nagged at Wally. There was more work to be done to perfect the formula.

He glanced at his watch. It was already past midnight. Wally sighed, realizing he had once again lost track of time in the lab. His demanding pursuit of medical innovations required long hours and laser focus. But it was all worth it for the chance to make a difference.

Wally's phone buzzed, jolting him from his thoughts. It was a text from Dr. Sanchez. "We need to meet ASAP. Call me when you get this." Wally felt a knot form in his stomach. Her message implied something serious. He quickly gathered his things, locked up the lab, and dialed her number during the short drive home.

"Wally, I'm glad you called back so quickly," Dr. Sanchez answered on the first ring. Her voice was strained. "We have a situation with the DNX-109 trial. I just received word that the FDA has suspended our approval due to concerns over the bandages' rapid tissue regeneration rate."

Wally gripped the steering wheel tightly as she explained the details. Because their wound healing technology was so advanced, the regulators feared it could have unintended consequences. They wanted to halt the trial until exhaustive additional safety studies were conducted.

"This could set us back years," Dr. Sanchez said grimly. "I have a meeting with the FDA administrators first thing tomorrow to plead our case. But I'm not optimistic we can convince them to reverse course."

Wally's mind raced. All their momentum and progress helping soldiers and burn victims could grind to a halt.

"Don't worry, we're going to figure this out," he reassured her with more confidence than he felt. They agreed to meet in the morning to strategize before her FDA meeting.

Wally barely slept, consumed with how to navigate this obstacle. At dawn, he downed a cup of coffee laced with a unique brain-boosting microorganism to sharpen his mental acuity. If anyone could find a solution, he could.

He arrived at the discreet DNX-109 production facility and found Dr. Sanchez already hard at work. She had covered a whiteboard with notes and diagrams, mapping out an approach for the FDA discussions.

Wally reviewed her ideas, and then added his own. They debated and refined their strategy until they had crafted a compelling case. Though daunting, this was not an insurmountable challenge. Together they would logically and ethically make their position clear.

After finalizing their game plan, Dr. Sanchez departed for the FDA offices. Wally busied himself optimizing the next round of bandage production. But it was difficult to focus; his thoughts kept drifting to how the pivotal meeting might unfold.

Several tense hours passed before his phone finally rang. "Wally, it's a mixed bag, but overall I think it went as well as we could hope," Dr. Sanchez reported. She had convinced the regulators to allow the trial to resume in a limited capacity while additional safety studies were conducted. It was not an ideal compromise, but far better than a complete stoppage.

Over the next week, they worked nonstop to satisfy the FDA requirements. Every day brought new bureaucratic hurdles, from paperwork filings to facility inspections. But Wally and Dr. Sanchez persevered, tackling each challenge as an essential step toward their goal.

Late one night, Wally was once again hunched over a microscope, assessing the latest bandage sample. His phone rang, jolting him from his intense focus. It was Dr. Sanchez, and he could hear the smile in her voice. "Wally, we did it! The FDA just approved the restart of the full clinical trial."

Relief and joy washed over him. Their tireless efforts navigating regulatory red tape had paid off. The obstacles had only strengthened their steadfast commitment to seeing this through. There would be more roadblocks ahead. But tonight, a major victory. Tomorrow, back to work.

Wally congratulated Dr. Sanchez, then tidied up his lab before heading home. In the car, his mind drifted to those they aimed to help - the soldiers, the children. This was all for them. The image of young Jacob's smile, colored green for Wally's Seawings, flashed into his mind. Wally's grip tightened on the wheel with renewed purpose. Obstacles be damned, he and Dr. Sanchez would press on.

NIGHT FALLS BUT THE lights in the lab remain ablaze. Wally makes incremental changes to the FlexMend-111 formula, a delicate dance of chemistry and hope. Each adjustment is a whisper of possibility, a chance to enhance the future.

Wally stands motionless at the lab counter, eyes fixed on the array of vials and beakers before him. The gentle hum of the ventilation system and the rhythmic drip of a leaking faucet mark the passage of time in the otherwise silent room. He reaches for a pipette, drawing up a precise amount of clear liquid. With a steady hand, he releases a single drop into a swirling mixture contained within a Erlenmeyer flask. The droplet sends ripples across the surface, blending seamlessly into the solution.

Watching intently, Wally waits and hopes for the desired reaction. A faint glow begins to emanate from the flask, bathing his tired but determined face in a warm light. A slight smile crosses his lips. Another whisper of possibility, another step in the delicate dance.

He records the proportions and effects in a leather-bound journal filled with countless iterations of the formula. Each page signifies untold hours of research, hypothesizing, and experimenting. A chronicle of his unwavering pursuit of a treatment for the disease that took his beloved grandmother.

Wally replaces the flask in the fume hood and straightens up to stretch his weary muscles. He glances at his watch - nearly midnight. But sleep can wait. The formula still requires refinement, and enhancements. His mind churns with potential tweaks and modifications. Crossing to a whiteboard covered in chemical equations and molecular diagrams, he picks up a marker and begins scribbling new formulas.

The shrill ring of his cell phone pierces the silence. Wally fishes it out of his pocket and glances at the name on the screen. Dr. Elena Sanchez. His trusted collaborator and voice of reason when his obsessive nature takes over. He slides his finger across the screen to answer.

"Elena. I'm surprised you're still awake," he says by way of greeting. Her warm laugh echoes through the phone.

"I could say the same to you, my friend. Burning the midnight oil again?" she asks knowingly. Wally smiles ruefully. She knows him too well.

"You know me - once I start tinkering there's no stopping. I think I'm on the verge of a breakthrough with FlexMend-111," he admits. He can sense her hesitation through the silence that follows.

"Just...remember to pace yourself. We knew this would be a marathon, not a sprint," she reminds him gently. He nods, even though she can't see him.

"Of course. Slow and steady wins the race. But I just can't silence that voice urging me to keep trying, to never stop looking for the answer," he replies earnestly. She hums in understanding.

"I know. And your dedication will change lives, I have no doubt. Just don't forget to change out of your lab coat and get some rest too," she says. He smiles.

"I will. Thanks for keeping me accountable. Enjoy the rest of your night," he tells her.

"You too. Good luck with the formula tweaking," she says warmly before ending the call.

Wally sets down the phone and turns his eyes back to the lab bench. Elena's words echo in his mind. Slow and steady. With renewed patience, he approaches the equipment. There's no need to rush this delicate process. Each step must be undertaken with care and consideration.

He thinks of his grandmother again. Her kind smile and sparkling eyes, the way her laugh could fill a room. He remembers the light fading from her gaze as the disease progressed. His hands clench with determination. Failure is not an option. He will refine this formula and find a way to restore that light.

Wally measures and mixes, observes and records late into the night. The lights in the lab remain ablaze as he works with singular focus. The dance continues, steps flawlessly executed from muscle memory honed over years of meticulous research.

As dawn's first light filters through the windows, Wally straightens up and surveys the array of vials and beakers before him.

Each contains a slightly altered version of the formula, brimming with untapped potential. He removes his gloves and runs a hand through his unruly hair. It's time for a break, a chance to clear his mind before the next round of trials.

Wally steps outside into the crisp morning air, taking a deep breath to reinvigorate his tired mind and body. The possibilities swirl within him, but he knows not to get ahead of himself. There will be setbacks and frustrations amidst the hope. But he is prepared for the marathon ahead.

As the sun rises on a new day, he gazes at its light with renewed energy and purpose. The future remains unwritten, each coming moment a chance to enhance it through dedication and care. Wally is ready to continue the dance, one graceful step at a time.

THE MORNING SUN STREAMED in through the slatted blinds of the Houston Medical Center's small conference room, casting lines of light across the serious faces seated around the oval table. Dr. Elena Sanchez sat with her hands folded, gazing down at the manila folder in front of her as if it contained precious secrets. Across from her, Dr. Camden slowly turned the pages of the trial report, his brow furrowed in concentration.

At the head of the table, Wally Eastwood leaned back in his chair, fingers laced behind his head. Though his posture conveyed ease, there was an undercurrent of tightly coiled energy about him. His eyes continuously scanned the room, taking in each minute movement and expression.

After what seemed an interminable silence, Dr. Camden closed the folder with a definitive thump. He removed his reading glasses and looked to Dr. Sanchez. "The data is clear. This is...groundbreaking."

Dr. Sanchez released a slow exhale, as if she had been holding her breath this entire time. "Yes. It's extremely promising for Alzheimer's patients in the early to moderate stages. FlexMend-111 appears both safe and effective based on this initial trial."

Wally dropped his hands to the table, leaning forward intently. "But we need to see long-term results. And test for any potential side effects with continued use."

Dr. Camden nodded. "Absolutely. We must proceed with an abundance of caution. But..." A smile teased the corners of his mouth. "I believe congratulations are in order."

Dr. Sanchez's serious expression finally melted into a smile. "It's a major milestone. One I wasn't sure we'd reach after all the setbacks." She shook her head wonderingly. "To think our work might give Alzheimer's patients and their families new hope..."

"This is only the beginning," Wally reminded them, even as a look of satisfaction settled on his features. After years of obsessive research in his home laboratory, the promise of this breakthrough was the payoff he had relentlessly pursued.

Dr. Camden stood, raising the glass of water that had been provided for each of them. "A toast then - to perseverance, to the scientific process, and to the patients and families who inspire our work each day."

Dr. Sanchez and Wally rose, lifting their glasses. The crystal rang out musically as they touched them together.

"To the future," Dr. Sanchez added softly. They sipped the cool water, eyes bright.

In this moment, there were no bureaucratic hurdles to navigate nor reports to compile. There was simply quiet celebration of work that mattered. Work that would change lives.

Wally set his glass down. "I know there are miles to go before FlexMend-111 is available to patients. But I believe this is the beginning of something life-altering."

Dr. Camden clapped him on the back. "Well said. Our work continues." He gestured to the door with a smile. "Shall we?"

The three filed out of the conference room, chatting lightly about informational sessions to schedule with medical staff and finalizing the Phase II trial protocol. As they walked down the bustling hallway, Wally felt a lightness buoying his steps. The positive trial results were the culmination of years of intense research. He had vowed never to give up, determined to honor those who had suffered from the ravages of Alzheimer's - like his beloved grandmother.

Now, with the promising data in hand, the future seemed bright with possibility. FlexMend-111 would need refinement and larger trials, but its potential was real. Wally imagined an army of researchers building on these results, leading to improved treatments and one day, perhaps even a cure.

The group rounded the corner toward the burn unit, falling silent as they passed wide-eyed children peering from doorways. Though not involved in the Alzheimer's trial, Dr. Sanchez still felt a pull toward these small patients that relied on the bandages she and Wally had developed. Their work here was far from over either.

Wally gave a little wave to a boy with an IV stand, eliciting a gap-toothed grin. The child's eyes were bright with resilience, his small hand wrapped in a FlexiBrandie bandage. Wally felt that buoying sensation again. With the FlexiBrandies and now FlexMend-111, they were writing new futures for those who needed them most.

As they passed the nurse's station, Dr. Sanchez paused, turning to Wally. "Will you notify the team at Phoenix Pharmaceuticals about the results? I know they've been eager for an update on a project they felt was...risky."

Wally nodded. "Of course. I'll stop by their office today." The shadow company had invested significant funds in FlexMend-111's development, providing the resources needed for the exhaustive research required. While demanding results, they had largely given Dr. Sanchez and Wally the freedom to direct the project.

Dr. Camden bid them goodbye as he peeled off toward the neurology wing. Dr. Sanchez lingered, resting a hand on Wally's forearm. "Thank you for sticking with me...and with this. I know the road was long and full of obstacles. But we're doing something meaningful here. Something that matters."

Wally covered her hand with his own. "We're in it for the long haul. Today was just the first step."

Dr. Sanchez gave his arm a final squeeze. As she walked away, Wally marveled at how far they had come. The first tentative trials had been housed in his home laboratory, with a seemingly impossible goal. Now, they stood on the cusp of a real breakthrough.

Wally pushed through the hospital's heavy double doors into the parking lot, the brilliant sunlight temporarily blinding him. He lifted a hand to shade his eyes, gazing upward. Somewhere his grandmother was looking down, guiding him still.

"This is for you, Grandma," he whispered. The results of today's trial were the first fruits of a promise made long ago, over her hospital bed. A promise to turn his abilities to the service of others.

Wally crossed the lot with a spring in his step, new ideas already churning. There was so much yet to do. But for today, he would celebrate how far science had brought them - and how much further it could still take them.

AS DAWN STREAKED THE sky with pink and orange, Dr. Sanchez, Dr. Camden, and Wally gathered in the conference room to begin planning for a larger, double-blind study of FlexMend-111. Numbers and theories collided as the symphonic arrangement of science and strategy took shape, poised to peel back the layers of uncertainty surrounding the treatment.

Dr. Sanchez stood at the whiteboard, marker in hand, as she outlined the proposed study design. "Based on the remarkable results we saw in the open-label trial, I think we should aim for at least 100 participants this time, with a 1:1 randomization between drug and placebo."

Dr. Camden nodded, glancing over the neatly organized stacks of paper in front of him. "Agreed. And we'll need to recruit across multiple sites to reach that number quickly."

"Exactly," replied Dr. Sanchez. "I suggest we bring Houston Medical Center, George St. Marry's, and Memorial Walker on board to start. We can see about adding more centers later if needed."

The doctors delved into the intricacies of the protocol - inclusion and exclusion criteria, dosage schedules, primary and secondary endpoints. Wally listened intently, chiming in occasionally with a clarifying question or suggestion drawn from his deep knowledge of the drug's pharmacology.

As the sunrise spilled through the windows, the conversation turned to the challenges of executing a large, multi-site trial with a complex experimental medication. Strict oversight would be needed to prevent any protocol deviations or lapses in quality control. Extensive monitoring plans were outlined, along with provisions for audits and site inspections. Wally took diligent notes, cognizant of his pivotal role in producing and supplying FlexMend-111.

"Of course, before we can proceed, we'll need IRB approval," said Dr. Camden. "I suggest we submit the package for initial review next week. That should give us time to incorporate any feedback and still stay on track for a Q3 start."

"Agreed," said Dr. Sanchez. "I know the team at Houston Medical's IRB, and I'm happy to take the lead on navigating the review process."

Talk then turned to statistical analysis plans, with Dr. Camden walking through the power calculations and sample size justification. "Based on the effect size we saw previously, 100 participants should give us at least 90% power to detect a significant difference between groups at the 5% level," he explained, scribbling equations on the whiteboard.

Wally's mind churned with ideas as the intricacies took shape. This symphonic arrangement of science and strategy would need to be executed with meticulous precision. The layers of uncertainty required peeling back systematically, note by note. Wally envisioned himself as the conductor, guiding each component harmoniously towards a crescendo of clarity and truth.

The meeting concluded on a hopeful note, with plans set in motion to launch the landmark trial. As the doctors gathered their belongings, Wally felt both the weight and thrill of what lay ahead. This double-blind study marked a pivotal moment, poised to elevate FlexMend-111 from a promising compound to a proven treatment.

Wally stayed behind in the quiet conference room as the others departed, taking a moment to gather his thoughts before the intensity of the day pulled him in further. He closed his eyes, picturing his grandmother and her struggle with Alzheimer's that had first sparked this journey. "We're getting closer, Grandma," he whispered. "Just hold on a little longer."

With a renewed sense of purpose, Wally gathered his things and headed out to begin the day's tasks. There was much to do - securing trial sites, navigating regulatory requirements, and meticulously preparing each dose of the precious medication. It would require persistence, patience, and care.

As Wally drove to the lab, the city waking around him, he contemplated the immense responsibility that he and his colleagues now bore. This drug had the potential to restore lives and renew hope for millions affected by this devastating disease. That possibility both invigorated Wally and grounded him in the importance of getting it right, guided not just by science but by compassion.

He arrived at the lab ready to delve into his work, fueled by possibility. With meticulous focus, he prepared the first experimental batches of FlexMend-111, envisioning the day they might reach waiting patients. Wally worked through the morning, stopping only when his phone rang. Dr. Sanchez's number flashed on the screen.

"Wally, it's Elena. I have an update on the IRB submission..."

IN THE DIM LIGHT OF his home laboratory, Wally pored over the molecular formula for FlexMend-111, the groundbreaking Alzheimer's drug he had developed. The soft glow of his desk lamp illuminated the pages of notes spread out before him, each one covered in his tidy scrawl detailing the intricate composition of the drug. FlexMend-111 represented the culmination of years of obsessive research, testing, and refinement, driven by Wally's fierce determination to find an effective treatment ever since his beloved grandmother had suffered from the devastating disease.

Now, on the cusp of a major clinical trial that could validate the drug's potential, Wally was plagued by worries over protecting his discovery from those who might try to steal or misuse it. The formula possessed immense value, both monetary and humanitarian, which made it highly vulnerable to unscrupulous individuals or corporations looking to profit from his work. Wally understood the need to proceed with the utmost caution in order to safeguard FlexMend-111.

As he reviewed the molecular makeup of the drug once again, a notification sounded from his computer, indicating an incoming video call. Wally leaned over and accepted the call, the screen lighting up with the face of his trusted collaborator Dr. Elena Sanchez. Her expression was serious, mirroring the apprehension Wally felt over their project.

"Burning the midnight oil again I see," she remarked. "How's it coming along?"

Wally sighed, rubbing his eyes. "I've gone over the formula a dozen times. I'm confident this represents the optimal version for large-scale production while preserving efficacy. But..."

"You're worried about keeping it secure," Dr. Sanchez finished. She nodded knowingly, her dark hair shifting against her lab coat. "Believe me Wally, I share the same concerns. A discovery like this, it would be invaluable to any pharmaceutical company. And we know they play dirty."

The two scientists had built a strong working relationship rooted in trust, but they had also witnessed unscrupulous corporate tactics in the past when groundbreaking research was at stake. The profits to be made from FlexMend-111 were too tempting for certain entities to resist.

"We'll need to be extremely judicious in who we disclose the details to," Wally said gravely. "This formula cannot become public knowledge. I can't let it fall into the wrong hands."

"I agree completely," Dr. Sanchez replied. She hesitated a moment. "But we also can't let secrecy prevent us from getting FlexMend through clinical trials. It has too much potential to languish indefinitely in the shadows. We need to find the right balance."

Wally nodded slowly, contemplating her words. It was a delicate line to walk. Exposing too little risked halting their progress due to lack of data and approval. But exposing too much placed the precious formula in jeopardy.

"Perhaps we should explore options like patenting a modified version of the formula - something close but not quite identical to the true composition," Wally proposed after some thought. "It would provide some protection and allow us to proceed, while still keeping the genuine formula concealed."

"That could work," Dr. Sanchez said, looking intrigued by the suggestion. "We'd have to be very careful about the differences. But it would give us an added layer of security."

She glanced down, shuffling some papers offscreen. "In the meantime, I think we should minimize digital copies of the formula. Keep the master version locked away somewhere ultra secure. My safe at the research facility has biometric access controls - we could store it there."

"Good idea," Wally agreed. He thought for a moment. "I should make a physical copy as well, in case something happens to the digital one. We can split them between two different locations."

Dr. Sanchez nodded approvingly. "Redundancy is key. The more decoys and physical barriers we can put up, the better."

Despite their concerns, Wally felt reassured by Dr. Sanchez's input and strategic thinking. With her guidance, he was confident they could usher FlexMend-111 through the next crucial phase of testing while protecting it from those who would misuse its immense power. The two scientists had devoted themselves completely to this mission of combatting Alzheimer's, unwilling to compromise on their ideals.

"We'll get through this, Wally," Dr. Sanchez said gently, as if reading his thoughts. "It's a difficult road ahead, but think of all the good we can do. Your grandmother would be so proud."

Wally smiled softly, a bittersweet pang in his heart as he pictured his grandmother's kind face. She had endured Alzheimer's with grace and dignity, never losing her spark. His work honored her memory.

"You're right," he replied. "We just need to stay cautious. And follow our moral compass."

Dr. Sanchez nodded firmly. "Exactly. Our mission is to help people, not pursue profits or prestige. As long as we stay true to that, we'll make the right choices."

Buoyed by her encouragement, Wally felt a renewed sense of purpose. They would move ahead with the clinical trial, taking every precaution. There would be challenges, but the potential payoff was monumental.

"I should get some rest," Wally said, glancing at the time. "We'll need to be at our sharpest for the planning meeting tomorrow."

"Yes, I'll let you get to bed," Dr. Sanchez agreed. "See you in the morning. And remember - stay positive."

"I will," Wally said. "Goodnight, Elena."

The call ended, and Wally began tidying up his notes. FlexMend-111 represented a beacon of hope, cutting through the darkness of Alzheimer's. Wally would protect it at all costs, driven by his desire to honor his grandmother and help countless others. As he turned off the desk lamp and headed upstairs, Wally carried that spark of hope in his heart.

WALLY STEPPED OUT ONTO the back patio, gazing up at the dusky evening sky. A few faint stars had begun peeking through as the sun slipped below the horizon, bathing the clouds in hues of orange and pink. A light breeze ruffled his hair as he took a deep breath, letting the fresh air fill his lungs.

It had been a long day in the lab, full of meticulous trial preparations, but Wally's mind was already leaping ahead to what lay on the horizon. More trials with the Alzheimer's drug FlexMend-111 were slated to begin soon, this time with an expanded participant group. Wally felt the nervous anticipation that always accompanied the start of a new trial, that trembling moment between possibility and certainty.

There was still so much work to be done, an endless array of tests and tweaks before FlexMend could be deemed safe and effective enough for the general population. But the initial trial had shown such promise, with noticeable improvements in multiple participants after just a few weeks on the drug. Wally allowed himself to envision a future where FlexMend offered real help, a future where his grandmother and so many others would have a chance to reclaim their memories and selves.

Wally thought of his grandmother often these days, recalling her kind smile and warm hugs from his childhood. He could still picture her sitting in the rocking chair on her front porch, inviting him to join her for a glass of lemonade after playing outside all afternoon. She had been the one to teach him chess, patiently explaining each move as they whiled away hours on lazy summer days.

When she had started forgetting things, misplacing her glasses and struggling to remember familiar faces, the light in her eyes had gradually dimmed. The disease had stolen so much, not just memories but her very personality, erasing the vibrant woman Wally had known and loved. He was determined to change that fate for others, driven by the chance to restore what Alzheimer's so cruelly took away.

There was so much still unknown about FlexMend's effects, particularly long-term. Wally and Dr. Sanchez had gone back and forth about dosage levels, delivery mechanisms, potential side effects. It was a delicate balance, tweaking the formula and trial parameters just right to maximize benefits while minimizing risks. Wally knew there would be setbacks, adjustments required as new data emerged. But the drug's restorative potential fueled him through each painstaking modification.

Wally thought of the trial participants, how some had broken down in tears when their test results showed improved cognition and memory. He pictured the disbelief and joy on their faces, that spark of renewed hope in their eyes. Those moments were the ones that made all the late nights and stress worthwhile, that reminded Wally why he had started down this path so many years ago.

His mind drifted back to that fateful discovery, the regenerative microbe he had first stumbled upon and cultivated in his home laboratory. It had set off a chain of events beyond anything he could have predicted at the time, leading him to found Flexagon with Dr. Sanchez and pursue treatments for Alzheimer's, burns, and injuries. Wally marveled at how one serendipitous finding had opened up a world of possibility.

There was still so much potential to uncover in that microbe's unique properties, Wally mused. His research with Dr. Sanchez had only scratched the surface of possible applications. But they had decided to stay laser-focused for now on developing FlexMend for Alzheimer's, wanting to ensure it was thoroughly tested and proven before expanding into other areas. Wally knew the temptation to move too quickly was always there, but they had to remain disciplined and vigilant.

As the first stars began to glow brighter overhead, Wally's mind wandered to the children recovering from burns because of the bandages he and Dr. Sanchez had developed. He pictured their smiles when nurses changed their dressings to reveal smooth new skin underneath, free of scars. The joy in those kids' eyes was the greatest gift, confirmation that all the secrecy and long hours were worth it. Wally hoped to bring that same joy to Alzheimer's patients and their families soon.

There were still so many questions and unknowns, as there always were on the winding path of scientific discovery. But Wally allowed himself to envision a future illuminated by the possibilities before him, a future where FlexMend offered Alzheimer's patients their lives back. There would be more trials, more tweaks and late nights in the lab - but there would also be more breakthroughs, more glimpses of hope.

Wally knew there were those who would seek to exploit his discoveries for profit or power, just as there were still smugglers and spies trying to steal secrets from Bird Island. He would need to remain vigilant against those threats. But he also had allies like Dr. Sanchez he could count on, partners who shared his vision of helping others. Together they would navigate the challenges ahead.

As the sunset faded into twilight, Wally felt a sense of peace and purpose settle over him. The road ahead would not be easy, but he was ready for whatever it held. For tonight, he allowed himself to enjoy this quiet moment and all that it promised. Change was coming, healing was on the horizon. And he would do everything in his power to meet it when it arrived.

Wally took one last look at the darkening sky, smiling softly. Then he turned and headed back inside, his mind already racing with plans for the trials, innovations, and lives soon to be transformed.

Chapter 11

Wally sat by his mother's bedside, holding her frail hand in his. She had always been so strong, the backbone of their family, but now the cruel progression of Alzheimer's was stealing her away bit by bit. Her once bright eyes had a distant, vacant look that broke Wally's heart.

"Mom, it's me...Wally," he said gently. "Do you know who I am?"

She stared at him blankly for a moment before a flicker of recognition crossed her face. "Wally," she repeated softly. A faint smile tugged at her lips.

Wally smiled back, blinking away the tears that welled up. "That's right, Mom. I'm so glad you remember me today."

Some days she knew him, other days he was a stranger. Each time she failed to recognize her only son, it felt like a knife twisting in his chest.

Wally spent the next hour keeping his mother company, talking about happy memories from the past. She drifted in and out, sometimes lucid, sometimes lost. He fed her lunch, wiping away the bits that dribbled down her chin. His strong, self-sufficient mother was now fully dependent on others for her basic needs.

As he left her room, Wally took a deep, shaky breath. Seeing his mother this way and knowing her future held only further decline filled him with sorrow and anger. He wanted to scream at the unfairness of it all. Instead, he channeled those feelings into an iron resolve.

Wally would find a way to stop this cruel disease if it was the last thing he did. His work in the lab took on a new urgency now that Alzheimer's had invaded his own family. He would keep fighting on his mother's behalf and for all those suffering. The battle was personal now, and he was determined to win it. Wally would never give up hope.

WALLY SAT BY HIS MOTHER'S bedside, watching her chest slowly rise and fall with each labored breath. The toll that Alzheimer's had taken on her over the past few years was evident in every line on her face and each vacant look in her eyes. Some days she still recognized him, lighting up with a smile and calling him by name. But more often than not, she gazed at him with a detached confusion, this woman who had once known him better than anyone in the world now struggling to recall his face.

It was agonizing for Wally to witness the cruel erosion of his mother's memories and personality. She had raised him on her own, working tirelessly to provide everything he needed. Now, he helplessly watched as the disease robbed her of her essence, one cherished memory at a time.

Wally tenderly clutched her frail hand, wishing he could infuse her with his own vitality. As he sat keeping vigil, his thoughts turned to the vial of FlexMend-111 secured in the breast pocket of his shirt. The experimental compound represented years of obsessive work aimed at reversing the ravages of Alzheimer's. Early trial results had been promising beyond his wildest hopes. But testing it now, on his own mother, felt like an unfathomable leap.

The scientist in Wally understood the importance of rigorous clinical trials. Letting emotion dictate medical decisions could lead to catastrophic outcomes. But the grieving son could not bear to watch his mother slip further away, not when a possible cure was within his grasp. He grappled with the weighty dilemma, uncertain which path was the ethical one.

A soft knock at the door pulled Wally from his contemplations. Dr. Elena Sanchez, his most trusted colleague, entered the room. One look at Wally's anguished expression told her everything she needed to know. She laid a sympathetic hand on his shoulder.

"How is she today?" Elena asked gently. Wally just shook his head, a lump forming in his throat.

"I want to try the compound," he confessed finally. "I know we should wait for the next trial phase, but..." His voice broke.

Elena's face reflected the struggle within her. She believed deeply in the scientific process they had committed to. But she also knew the depth of Wally's pain.

"This is your decision," she said at last. "I can't tell you what to do. But I trust you, Wally. I know you'll choose out of love."

Wally looked down at the vial in his hand, rolling it between his fingers. His mother's life, the culmination of his work, the ethics of medicine - it felt like an impossible choice.

DR. SANCHEZ SAT ACROSS from Wally in her modest office, sunlight filtering through the blinds to cast a gridded pattern on the wall behind her. She studied Wally's face, seeing the deep lines of exhaustion and worry that had settled there in recent weeks. His mother's steady decline weighed heavily on him.

"I know you only want what's best for her," Dr. Sanchez began gently. "But we have to consider all the risks before proceeding with an untested treatment, even if it's motivated by love."

Wally nodded, his eyes downcast. He understood her caution all too well. The experimental compound he had created, while promising, was still an unknown entity. But his mother faded more each day, her memories and personality slipping away in the grip of Alzheimer's. Time was running short to make a difference.

"Believe me, I wish there was a simple solution," Dr. Sanchez continued, her voice kind but firm. "But giving an untested drug, even to a consenting patient, opens the door to consequences we can't predict. We have a duty to uphold the highest ethical standards."

She let the statement hang in the air between them. The ticking second hand of the clock on her bookshelf punctuated the silence.

"But I also understand the depth of your hope," she added, her tone softening. "And your intentions are admirable. If it were my own mother..."

She trailed off, but the unspoken words echoed in Wally's mind. If their roles were reversed, she too would move heaven and earth to offer a chance, however slim, at restored life and memory. He looked up to meet her eyes, reading the empathy and conflict there.

"Why don't we revisit the idea in a few weeks, once we've completed the next phase of trials?" Dr. Sanchez suggested. "That will give us more data on any potential side effects. I know it's difficult to wait when time is of the essence. But a few more weeks of observation could make all the difference in ensuring your mother's safety."

Wally considered this, knowing she had a point. Rushing ahead without adequate safeguards could put his mother at greater risk. But the visceral urge to act now warred with his scientific mind. Each passing day made it less likely his compound could reverse the damage already done.

"I'll take the time to think it over," he finally replied. Dr. Sanchez gave an approving nod. She understood the impossible dilemma he faced, balanced between hope and precaution. In her eyes, Wally saw empathy mingling with duty, a mirror of the conflict raging within himself.

"You know I'm always here if you need to talk through the options," Dr. Sanchez said. "We'll continue gathering data, and reassess in a few weeks. Just remember - patience now doesn't mean surrendering hope for the future."

Wally managed a small, grateful smile. However difficult the wait would be, he knew Dr. Sanchez cared deeply about his mother's well-being. Her guidance stemmed from both medical experience and compassion. With a heavy heart, he rose to take his leave, the two scientists united in their shared mission of discovery and healing. The path forward remained unclear, but Dr. Sanchez's wisdom would light the way.

WALLY SAT BY HIS MOTHER'S bedside, holding her frail hand in his. Though her body was weak, her eyes were as lively and warm as he remembered from his childhood. She smiled at him, radiating a sense of peace despite her declining condition.

"Are you sure about this, Mom?" Wally asked, his voice quivering. "We can wait until more trial results come in. There's no need to rush."

She patted his hand reassuringly. "I'm sure, dear. My time is running out, but this could give us more of it together. I trust you."

Wally nodded, tears welling up in his eyes. He took a deep breath to steady himself before carefully administering the IV infusion of FlexMend-111 into his mother's arm. As he watched the experimental treatment drip slowly into her veins, Wally said a silent prayer, hoping against hope that this would restore some of what the cruel disease had stolen from her mind.

The sterile scent of the hospital room mingled with the earthy aroma of the flowers Wally had brought. He focused on the steady beep of the heart monitor, finding odd comfort in its rhythmic reminder of life. His mother hummed softly, like she used to do while making cookies in their little kitchen.

Wally stayed by her side as the IV bag emptied, watching closely for any reaction. But she seemed peaceful, occasionally squeezing his hand or murmuring about memories from his childhood. He clung to each precious word and touch, every interaction more meaningful now.

After an hour, the bag was empty. Wally carefully removed the IV, bandaged his mother's arm, and helped her get comfortable in the hospital bed. She was growing tired, so he simply sat with her in silence until her eyes drifted closed. Even in sleep, she held his hand.

Wally's own eyes were heavy with exhaustion and emotion. It had been a long and difficult journey to get to this point, from the first inklings of his mother's decline to the late nights developing an experimental treatment. Now, in this moment, all he could do was wait and hope.

Leaning down, Wally kissed his mother's forehead as she slept. "I love you, Mom," he whispered. Whatever happened next, they would face it together.

Wally stayed by her side as the night stretched on, keeping vigil over her fitful sleep. Nurses came and went, checking vitals and adjusting medications. His mother would stir briefly at the interruptions before sinking back into slumber.

In the still of the early morning hours, Wally dozed in the chair, jerking awake frequently to check on his mother. As dawn approached, golden light filtering in through the blinds, her sleep seemed to grow more restful. Her face appeared relaxed, her breathing deep and even.

Wally blinked bleary eyes, shaking off the clutches of sleep. He rose and stretched, joints stiff from the night in the chair. Moving quietly to avoid disturbing his mother's slumber, he slipped out to splash some cold water on his face and get a cup of bitter hospital coffee.

The hot liquid helped clear the cobwebs as Wally mentally prepared for what this day might bring. So much hope was riding on this experimental treatment. But there were no guarantees, he knew. All he could do was take it moment by moment.

Wally returned to the room just as his mother was waking. She looked at him and smiled. "Good morning, dear," she said, her voice stronger than he'd heard in weeks.

Wally rushed to her side, hardly daring to hope. "Mom, do you...do you know who I am?" he asked tentatively.

She expressed iteration at his question. "Of course I do, Wally. You're my son."

Wally's eyes welled with tears. It was the first time in months she had recognized him without hesitation. Unable to speak past the lump in his throat, he simply hugged her gently, conveying all his love and relief in that embrace.

They sat like that for several minutes, mother and son reunited if only for a fragile moment. Eventually Wally pulled back, wiping his eyes and composing himself. There were battery of cognitive tests ahead to determine if this treatment had truly worked. But just this brief respite felt like a miracle.

The day passed in a blur of tests administered by Dr. Camden, who could hardly contain his excitement at the early results. Wally's mother tired easily but remained lucid and aware all day. She even recalled snippets of conversation from the previous day.

Cautious optimism reigned as Wally shared the promising updates with Dr. Sanchez. But they knew the real test would be whether these effects lasted or if it was just a temporary surge. Wally tamped down on his soaring hopes, not allowing himself to fully celebrate just yet.

Still, as he kissed his mother goodnight and promised to return in the morning, Wally felt a lightness he hadn't known in years. For the first time since this nightmare had begun, he had hope. It was fragile and tentative, but it was hope. And for now, that was enough.

Wally practically floated down the hospital corridor, the events of the day playing over and over in his mind. His feet carried him automatically out the doors and into the parking garage as his thoughts swirled. It was only when he reached his car that Wally realized he had one more stop to make tonight.

The nearly full moon illuminated the quiet path as Wally walked slowly through the cemetery. The peaceful setting soothed his soul. He paused before a simple gravestone marked Hannah Eastwood, laying a hand on the cool granite.

"We're one step closer, Grandma," Wally said softly. "I wish you could have met Mom today. Just for a little while, I had her back."

He stayed for a while, telling his grandmother about the events of the past day and all the work left ahead. But he knew she would be proud. She had inspired him to fight this disease every day since her own decline. And he would keep fighting, for her, for his mother, and for everyone else still suffering.

Wally laid a single white lily on the gravestone. Then he stood, squared his shoulders, and walked steadily back down the path. The night was dark, but there were glimmers of light ahead.

IN THE ENSUING DAYS, Wally's vigil by his mother's side was a portrait of the son's love entwined with the scientist's scrutiny. Each slight return of lucidity in his mother's eyes was a glimmer in the dimming twilight of her disease.

Wally sat in the armchair next to his mother's bed, observing her closely as she slept. The beeping monitors and the hiss of oxygen filled the quiet room. He studied her face, noting the deepening creases on her forehead and the slackness of her jaw. Even in sleep, the toll of the Alzheimer's was evident.

His mother's stirring broke Wally's concentration. Her eyelids fluttered open, blinking against the sunlight streaming in through the window.

"Morning, Mom," Wally said softly. "Did you sleep okay?"

She turned her head toward him, eyes cloudy. "Who are you?" she asked, her voice raspy.

Wally swallowed down the lump in his throat. "It's me, Mom. It's Wally, your son."

He reached for her hand resting atop the blanket, giving it a gentle squeeze. Her fingers remained limp in his grasp.

After a long moment, a flicker of recognition crossed her face. "Wally," she repeated slowly. The fog in her eyes cleared just a little.

Wally's heart swelled at that single word. "That's right, I'm Wally. Your son."

She gave him a faint smile. "You look tired, dear."

"I'm okay, Mom. Don't you worry about me."

He brushed a strand of silver hair back from her face, cherishing this fragile thread of connection. Her periods of lucidity were growing shorter, but he clung to them desperately.

A nurse entered then, greeting them both cheerfully. She checked the monitors and IV drips, making notes on a clipboard. Wally observed her movements closely, ever the scientist studying a subject.

"Everything looks good, Mrs. Eastwood," the nurse said. "Let me know if you need anything. Just press the call button."

After she left, Wally's mother drifted back into a fitful sleep. He kept hold of her hand, maintaining that physical link. His thoughts turned to the experimental compound hidden away in his lab.

Perhaps it could bring back more than just fleeting moments of clarity.

But Dr. Sanchez's cautionary words echoed in his mind. The treatment was untested, the effects unknown. He had sworn to uphold ethical standards, to proceed with care.

Wally noticed his mother's breathing growing more labored. Her chest rose and fell rapidly beneath the thin hospital gown. He recognized the signs - she was having a nightmare.

Gently, he squeezed her hand again. "It's okay, Mom, I'm right here," he soothed. He stroked her forehead until her breathing slowed. Mercifully, she did not wake.

Wally released a heavy sigh, the weight of helplessness pressing down. Watching his mother deteriorate was agony. He would move heaven and earth to restore her, but the limitations of science bound him cruelly.

There were still tests to be run, data to be analyzed. Perhaps in time the compound could halt or even reverse the progression. But time was the one thing slipping away.

His mother's stirring ended Wally's brooding. She blinked several times before focusing on him.

"Wally?" she said.

"I'm here, Mom," he replied, relief washing over him.

Her brow furrowed. "You look so tired, dear."

Wally smiled sadly. "I'm okay."

The nurse entered again to check vitals and administer medication. Wally observed the procedures, ever the diligent scientist. His mother drifted back to sleep soon after.

Alone again, Wally considered his options. He could continue testing the experimental compound, hoping to gather enough data to ethically administer it to a human subject. Or he could take a leap of faith, driven by love instead of logic.

His mother's hand lay limp once more in his own. He studied the papery skin stretched over pronounced veins and knuckles swollen with arthritis. Hands that had soothed and nurtured him all his life.

Whatever time she had left, he wanted her mind intact. For her moments of lucidity to outnumber the foggy lapses. Most of all, he wanted her to truly know her son in what time remained.

His decision was made, Wally pressed a kiss to his mother's cool forehead. The scientist in him railed against what he was about to do, but the son would not be deterred.

"I love you, Mom," he whispered. "Just hold on a little longer."

Wally stood, taking one last look at his mother's sleeping form. Then he slipped quietly out the door, a man on a mission.

The automatic doors of the hospital whooshed closed behind him. He strode purposefully to his car, mind racing ahead to the vial waiting in his laboratory. A compound untested on humans, but infused with hope.

Wally turned the key in the ignition. Whatever the outcome, he would face it with courage. For now, he clung to the possibility of even one more moment of true recognition in his mother's eyes.

It was all he had left to hope for. And he would grasp at even the faintest glimmer in the gathering darkness.

The engine rumbled to life. Wally pulled out of the parking lot, and towards home. Towards a future he could not predict, but which held a promise long overdue.

Come what may, he would remain by his mother's side. Her son, her caregiver, her tireless champion. He drove onward through the bright morning light.

AS HIS MOTHER'S FAMILIAR yet faded eyes attempted to focus, Wally braced against the surging tides of hope and trepidation.

His heart fluttered with every sign of her potential recovery, the data collected meticulously chronicled yet emotionally charged.

He held his breath as she turned towards the sound of his voice, recognition slowly dawning across her features. "Wally?" she croaked, uncertainty mingling with a glimmer of awareness in her gaze.

"I'm here, Mom," he replied gently, taking her frail hand in his. A single tear traced down his cheek as her bony fingers curled around his in response. It was the first flicker of connection they'd shared in weeks of decline.

Meticulously documenting her responses, Wally continued his one-sided conversation, heart swelling at each fleeting sign of lucidity. Her eyes tracked his movements, her brow furrowing in concentration as she struggled to comprehend his words. Every clipped sentence, every faint nod was a monumental breakthrough.

"Your vitals are stabilizing, neurological responses improving," he murmured, equal parts scientist and caregiver. "Just need to monitor any side effects closely." His clinical analysis helped temper the rising tide of desperate hope.

Her lips moved soundlessly, like a marionette whose strings had been cut. Wally paused, leaning in as she strained to form words.

"Not...gone," she rasped at last. "Still here."

The declaration winded him, words he'd longed to hear for so long. His hand trembled around hers.

"I know, Mom. I'm going to do everything I can to keep you here," he promised vehemently.

She regarded him with sudden clarity. "My Wally. Always trying to fix things." The fondness in her tone pierced his heart.

He squeezed her hand, unable to speak past the lump in his throat. To hear his name on her lips, the warmth of her love and recognition in her eyes...it was more than he'd dared hope for.

As the day progressed, the fleeting moments of lucidity came and went like clouds passing over the sun. But their frequency steadily increased, the fog of confusion receding bit by bit.

Wally meticulously tracked her responses, vital signs, and any adverse reactions. So far, she remained stable. The initial indicators were promising, but he knew better than to let hope eclipse caution.

When fatigue finally claimed her, he tucked her in with a kiss on the forehead. "Sleep well, Mom. I'll be right here when you wake." Shutting off the light, he retreated to the adjoining room to analyze the data.

It was all there in stark black and white - elevated neurotransmitter levels, improved neural conductivity, decreased amyloid plaque formation. The compound was working, restoring and regenerating her failing synapses.

Wally leaned back, exhaling sharply. After months of tireless work, he held the key to reversing his mother's decline in his hands. But the gravity of what he'd done tempered his exhilaration.

He thought of Dr. Sanchez's ethical warnings, his own nagging doubts. He'd allowed desperation to eclipse reason, administering an untested treatment to his own unsuspecting mother. Was it an act of love or selfishness?

The debate raged in his mind, guilt and conviction colliding. He thought of the countless others suffering as she had, prisoners in their own fading minds. If her improvement continued, if the results held...countless lives could be transformed. It was a staggering possibility.

But first, he had to ensure her safety and well-being above all else. Resolved to proceed with utmost caution, he prepared for the critical days ahead. Her needs would dictate their course, not his desire for answers.

When she woke the next morning, the cloud of confusion remained partially lifted. She greeted him by name, clear-eyed and present.

Over breakfast, she haltingly shared snippets of memories - his graduation, his father's laughter, a long-ago camping trip. Each rediscovered fragment was a gift, proof of her emerging from the fog.

But by midday, she grew increasingly agitated and confused. Her vitals spiked, hands plucking anxiously at her clothes. "Who are you?" she demanded in panic, shrinking away from his touch. "Where am I?"

Wally's heart clenched, but he maintained a calm demeanor. "It's alright, Mom. I know you're frightened, but you're safe. I'm taking care of you."

He administered a mild sedative, hating to stifle her consciousness but unable to bear her distress. As the drug took effect, her breathing slowed, her limbs grew heavy and her eyes clouding. But she continued mumbling incoherently, lost in shadowy visions only she could see.

Wally stayed by her side, monitoring her closely. When she finally succumbed to sleep, he retreated to the adjoining room with a heavy heart. This was his worst fear realized - unintended side effects and volatile reactions. She deserved better than to be an unknowing test subject.

He thought of Dr. Sanchez's stern but compassionate wisdom. His colleague had been right to urge caution and restraint. Wally knew then he should have waited, no matter how desperately he wanted to help his mother.

How long he sat there staring at her slumbering form, he didn't know. But seeing her so peaceful in repose helped calm his inner turmoil. She was still here, still fighting - and so was he.

He wouldn't give up on her. But from here on out, her wellbeing and dignity would remain paramount. There were no shortcuts on the path ahead. All he could do was proceed with care, honor her humanity, and hope love would light the way.

Resolved, Wally returned to her room. He took her hand gently in his own. "I'm here, Mom," he whispered. "We'll take this one day at a time."

Her eyelids fluttered at the sound of his voice but did not open. Still, she gave his hand a faint, reassuring squeeze. It was enough.

Chapter 12

Against the backdrop of monitoring equipment, Wally and Dr. Sanchez become scribes of progress. Each cognitive flicker and behavioral nuance fuels their belief in FlexMend-111's capabilities. The evidence compiled is bearing witness to a medical marvel unfolding.

Wally stands in the observation room adjacent to the clinical trial ward, fixated on the monitors tracking vital signs and neural activity. Beside him, Dr. Sanchez reviews a clipboard filled with observational data, pausing to make notes or murmur affirmations. The two work in sync united in their meticulous documentation of the landmark Alzheimer's drug trial.

On the screens, EEG readings dance with spikes of activity as a patient works through cognitive tests. In the background, nurses ensure participant comfort, their presence fading into the periphery as Wally and Dr. Sanchez narrow their focus. For them, the sterile examination room becomes a theater where neurological transformation unfolds one improved test result at a time.

Their gazes flit between monitors, faces filled with concentration. Wally tracks EEG frequency changes, calling them out to Dr. Sanchez who translates the readings into concise clinical notes. Each scribble on her clipboard captures a moment where lost cognition flickers back to life.

When a trial participant laughs at a joke, the sound makes them lift their eyes in unison to glimpse the human behind the data. Dr. Sanchez's face warms with a smile even as her pen swiftly marks the occurrence of spontaneous positive affect. Their celebration is silent but shared in that lingering look.

Later, when a participant's forehead crinkles in momentary confusion, Wally is quick to identify an abnormality in the EEG. Dr. Sanchez frowns, records it, then suggests adjusting the medication dose. He nods, trusting her clinical wisdom. For them, each data point matters.

As afternoon stretches into evening, their focus remains steady. Wally brings Dr. Sanchez coffee, exchanging few words in their shared language of science and diligence. Side by side, they bear witness to the drug's effects, filling legal pads with details.

When a participant's EEG normalizes for a full hour, Wally highlights the achievement with a tap on Dr. Sanchez's shoulder. She circles the finding, then squeezes his hand in acknowledgment. They share a look of awe at the milestone.

Their documentation paints a mosaic of changes reflecting neurons reawakening. Dr. Sanchez tallies quantitative markers like reaction times while Wally notes the qualitative human impacts. Together, they capture the full scope of the drug's restorative influence.

As the day's observations come to an end, Dr. Sanchez neatens her piles of completed assessment forms ready for digital entry. Wally organizes his handwritten logs by participant number, ensuring each change is attributed correctly. Their desks become twin shrines to the science of noticing.

Finally, they gather by the one-way glass for a last visual check. Participants relax in recliners as nurses administer medications. Some doze, others watch TV, but all are undergoing a metamorphosis invisible to the naked eye. Wally and Dr. Sanchez see past the surface to the cellular regeneration happening underneath.

With weary satisfaction, they make their way to the parking lot, debriefing on the day's promising developments. Their words come rapid-fire, two minds in sync. Reaching her car, Dr. Sanchez promises to have the initial data analysis ready to review after the weekend. Wally tells her to get some rest first. Their diligence never falters but their humanity remains.

As Wally drives home, his mind replays the day's observations. He feels the weight and privilege of bearing witness to the trial. Each data point flashes in his mind like embers of hope. He holds onto that image during the quiet evening ahead.

On Monday, Wally enters the facility rejuvenated. Participants are led through assessments, their focus palpably sharper than weeks prior. Dr. Sanchez greets Wally with a knowing smile. Side by side, they resume their watch.

The week unfolds in rigorous documentation. EEG readings continue normalizing, cognition improves, and life seeps back into once dull eyes. Dr. Sanchez tracks every sign of neural regeneration while Wally notes the human impacts. Each Post-it note stuck to their growing data wall marks a small miracle.

There are moments of uncertainty too. Periodic confusion, fatigue, and test score declines have Wally on alert for potential side effects. Dr. Sanchez adjusts medication and increases monitoring. Together, they balance celebration with vigilance, always putting the participants first.

By week's end, the data pool holds a hundred shining examples of improvement contrasted by a few dim outliers. Dr. Sanchez spends the weekend analyzing, scrutinizing, and interpreting while Wally plans protocol tweaks to minimize side effects. Their work continues well beyond the confines of the clinical trial room.

Monday morning brings new energy and a refined approach. Dr. Sanchez implements medication changes while Wally modifies assessment parameters. Their coordination is seamless, with two scientists on a mission.

On it goes, their days an unbroken chain of observation, interpretation, and optimization. Each data point adds to the mosaic, filling in the picture of a treatment on the cusp of something great. Wally and Dr. Sanchez's dedication becomes the binding force moving it forward.

Where the story goes from here depends on the outcome of their efforts. But regardless of what comes next, their work in this room will be remembered as an undertaking fueled by science and humanism in equal measure. The data on their desks pays tribute to those lost to Alzheimer's while offering a lifeline to those still clinging to precious memories.

For Wally and Dr. Sanchez, this trial is the culmination of tireless work and personal loss. Each small win within these walls sustains their hope. They understand the gravity of this pursuit and honor it through their diligence.

Their reward is bearing witness to lives transformed firsthand. The knowledge that their observations will one day improve countless more is the momentum propelling them forward. Wally and Dr. Sanchez remain devoted to this pursuit, scribes of a medical breakthrough still unfolding.

WALLY SAT BY HIS MOTHER'S bedside, holding her frail hand in his. Her once bright eyes now stared vacantly ahead, clouded by the haze of Alzheimer's that had steadily consumed her mind over the past few years. At times, she would stir slightly, mumbling incoherently as if trapped in a dream. Wally would squeeze her hand gently, hoping to tether her to this moment, but she would soon drift away again into the maze of her fading memories.

He studied her face, lined with age but still so familiar, and wondered if today might bring one of those rare moments of lucidity that seemed to come and go without warning. There was no telling when the fog might lift, however briefly, and allow his mother to truly see him again, to know him as her son. He clung to those flickers of recognition like a drowning man grasping at strands of light piercing through dark waters. So he kept vigil, waiting.

As the morning stretched on, his mother grew increasingly restless, her mumbling rising in urgency. Wally stood and leaned over her, stroking her forehead. "It's okay, Mom. I'm right here," he soothed. She tossed her head fretfully, then her eyes suddenly focused on his face hovering above her.

"Wally?" she whispered hoarsely. "Is that you?"

Wally's breath caught in his throat. "Yes, Mom, it's me," he replied gently.

A look of confusion creased her brow. "What are you doing here? Don't you have school today?"

School. She thought he was still a young boy. Wally hesitated, unsure whether to correct her or play along. He decided on the latter. "No, no school today. I wanted to spend the day with you."

His mother's eyes softened with affection. "My sweet boy. Come here." She patted the bed weakly beside her.

Wally sat down and took her hand again. "Mom, do you remember when I was ten, and Dad helped me build that treehouse in the big oak in our backyard? I was so proud of that treehouse. You even let me eat dinner up there once, remember?"

She stared past him as if seeing something far away. Then a faint smile lifted the corners of her mouth. "Yes, I remember. Your father put a little window in it so you could look out at the birds." Her voice was growing stronger now. "Oh, how you loved sitting up there watching those birds. You even wanted to sleep out there once until I convinced you our house was better."

She chuckled softly at the memory. The sound, so rare these days, resonated through Wally's core.

"I'd draw pictures of the birds and show them to you," he prompted gently.

"That's right! You got very good at those drawings. I kept so many of them. My little artist." She gave his hand an affectionate squeeze.

Wally felt a swell of emotion rising in his chest. In this moment, she truly saw him, knew him. He didn't want it to end.

"I remember how you would pack a little picnic lunch for me to eat up in the treehouse," he continued. "Peanut butter and jelly sandwiches, apple slices, and always a special treat - those chocolate chip cookies you used to bake just for me."

"Oh yes, your favorite!" Her eyes lit up at the memory. "You could never get enough of those. Always wanted me to bake extra so you could have more."

"They were so good. I can still picture them fresh from the oven, the chips still gooey and melting. I would sneak one as soon as they cooled just a little, even though it burned my mouth. You would swat me away, telling me I had to wait until after lunch."

His mother giggled, a youthful, girlish sound. "That's right, you were such a little scamp about those cookies! I knew you'd spoil your lunch, but you were so happy. My sweet boy." She reached up and stroked his cheek tenderly.

Wally covered her frail hand with his, tears stinging his eyes. To sit here with her, immersed in memories long buried but now vibrant and alive again, seemed a miracle. He held onto this moment fiercely, engraving every word, every sensation into his mind.

The light in her eyes was starting to dim again as she grew tired. "You're a good son," she murmured. "A good..." Her voice trailed off as she started to withdraw back into the fog.

"I love you, Mom," Wally whispered. He kissed her forehead softly. Her eyes were closed now, her chest rising and falling steadily with sleep.

Wally stayed a while longer, keeping a silent vigil and replaying their conversation in his mind. He had learned over time to accept these brief interludes for the gifts they were, not knowing if or when the light might shine through again. For now, this was enough.

Finally he rose, taking one more long look at his sleeping mother. He felt both joy and sorrow - joy for the precious memories relived, sorrow knowing the darkness was already moving back in, inexorable as the tide. But he would keep coming back here as long as needed, for as long as she needed him.

With a heavy heart full of love, he turned and left the room.

HOVERING OVER CHARTS and reports, the implications of broader trials are dissected. Dr. Sanchez, Dr. Camden, and Wally pore over the data from the initial FlexMend-111 Alzheimer's trial, analyzing the results down to minute details. As lead researcher, Dr. Sanchez focuses on scrutinizing the cognitive test results, looking for any anomalies or concerning patterns among the participants. Dr. Camden provides his clinical expertise, interpreting how the quantitative data correlates to observable patient improvements or declines.

Wally takes a big picture view, considering how the drug impacted inflammatory biomarkers and neural regeneration. He runs simulations to model how an increased sample size could affect key metrics in a larger trial. The team works late into the evening, fueled by coffee and their shared commitment to ensure this breakthrough is rigorously validated. Their excitement about FlexMend-111's potential is tempered by an acute awareness of the responsibility inherent in developing a treatment for such a cruel, devastating disease.

Around midnight, Dr. Sanchez stretches and suggests they call it a night. "We've made excellent progress evaluating the data from the first trial." She notices Wally seems lost in thought, his gaze distant. "Is everything okay, Wally?"

He blinks, returning to the moment. "Oh, yes. Just thinking about the next steps. You're right, it's late. We should pick this up tomorrow." He begins gathering the scattered papers, eager to escape into the solitude of his drive home.

After parting ways outside the research building, Wally gets in his car but doesn't start the engine right away. He just sits there, head in hands, as a profound wave of sadness washes over him. His mother's face appears in his mind's eye, her warm smile fading to confusion. Wally is no stranger to melancholy, but tonight it feels like a vise around his chest.

Starting the car, he begins the 45-minute drive home on autopilot, mentally and emotionally exhausted. His work analyzing FlexMend's trial data has been a welcome distraction from his mother's worsening condition, but now, alone with his thoughts, that reprieve disappears. Wally grips the steering wheel tightly, overcome with anger at the cruelty of such a merciless disease. Anger at the helplessness he feels watching the woman who raised him slip away bit by bit each day.

Pulling into his driveway, Wally drags himself from the car and heads inside, craving the oblivion of sleep. But after going through his nightly routine, he lies awake, thoughts drifting to his mother's care facility nearby. On impulse, he gets dressed again and drives over, seeking some solace in this late-night visit. The night nurse smiles sympathetically as she lets him into his mother's room.

Wally sits by her bedside, watching the steady rise and fall of her chest as she sleeps. The ache inside him threatens to rupture into sobs, but he just breathes deeply, keeping vigil over her. He thinks about the endless hours spent by her side in this very room, looking for glimpses of the mother he knows buried somewhere within the dementia's cruel grip. The visits where she lights up with recognition, showering him with love. But also the devastating days where she lashes out in confusion, accusing this stranger of hiding her real son.

Wally closes his eyes, transported back to his childhood when the world seemed simple and safe in her comforting embrace. He would give anything to see her brilliant mind restored, her memories returned to her. Opening his eyes, Wally leans in and gently squeezes her hand. "I'm going to fix this, Mom," he whispers. "Just hold on a little longer."

Driving home as dawn breaks, Wally's sadness has been replaced by a simmering determination. The FlexMend trial data consumes his thoughts now, its potential and limitations analyzed from every angle. He decides he will request the team immediately start preparations for an expanded Phase II trial. The steep challenges of executing a large-scale study are pushed from Wally's mind by visions of his mother whole again, recognizing him, laughing together as they did when he was young.

After a quick shower and change of clothes, Wally gulps down coffee and a nutritional supplement to sharpen his mental acuity. The lack of sleep tugs at his body, but anticipation of the day ahead overpowers any fatigue. He heads to the lab, energized by this renewed sense of purpose.

Upon arriving, Wally dives right in to start developing a proposal for the larger FlexMend trial. He is so focused on his work that he doesn't notice Dr. Sanchez enter until she touches his shoulder. "You're here early! Did you even go home last night?" she asks, noticing his worn appearance.

Wally smiles sheepishly. "I couldn't turn my brain off after we met, so I figured I might as well put it to good use." He shows her the trial proposal draft. "We need to move quickly while the initial data is still fresh. I think we should aim to start Phase II in six months, enroll at least 300 patients across six sites."

Dr. Sanchez's eyes widen at the accelerated timeline and expanded scope. But she knows Wally is driven by more than ambition. FlexMend's success has become personal for him. "That's incredibly aggressive," she says, "but if we bring Dr. Camden on board, we can make it happen. Let's plan to meet later today to discuss logistics."

Wally's excitement is palpable. "This is exactly the breakthrough we've been working towards. All the late nights and setbacks will be worth it if we can make this a reality." He turns to Dr. Sanchez, his expression serious. "I want to dedicate this trial to my mother. We have to do this for her and everyone else fighting this battle."

Dr. Sanchez puts a hand on his shoulder. "We will, Wally," she says resolutely. "We're going to beat this disease together."

WALLY ENTERED HIS MOTHER'S room quietly, not wanting to startle her. She was sitting in her favorite armchair by the window, gazing out at the gardens below. He studied her face, noticing the deep lines that had formed over the past few years, etched by the steady erosion of her memories. Even now, he could see the confusion in her eyes as she struggled to place her surroundings.

Wally pulled up a chair beside her. "Good morning, Mom," he said gently. "It's a beautiful day outside. How are you feeling?"

She turned to him, and for a moment there was a spark of recognition. "Wally? Is that you?"

His breath caught. It had been over a week since she had called him by name. "Yes, Mom, it's me," he replied, taking her hand.

"You look different," she murmured, peering at him intently. "Older, I think."

Wally nodded. "It's been a few years since I was a kid."

His mother frowned, gazing out the window again. "Time goes so quickly," she whispered. Wally stayed quiet, letting her gather her thoughts. There were good days and bad days lately. He cherished these moments of lucidity, ephemeral as they were.

After a few minutes, she turned to him again, eyes brightening. "Wally, when did you get here? It's so nice to see you!"

He smiled. "Just got here. I wanted to spend some time with you today."

She beamed back at him. "What a wonderful surprise!" Her delight was childlike in its purity.

They chatted for a while, his mother reminiscing happily about Wally's childhood antics. He lost himself in her stories, forgetting for a moment the toll that Alzheimer's had taken.

A nurse entered with a tray of food. "Time for breakfast, Diane," she said briskly. Wally's mother looked at the food in confusion, then back at him.

"Wally, what's happening? Where am I?" Her voice shook.

He kept his tone soothing. "You're in an assisted living facility, remember? For the past two years now. This is Marie, one of the nurses who takes good care of you."

Diane stared at him, distress mounting. "Two years? No, that can't be right. Just yesterday I was home, making you pancakes before school..." She trailed off as tears filled her eyes.

Wally's heart broke. He explained again, keeping his voice steady through long practice. After some time, she grew calmer and began eating breakfast. But the light had gone from her eyes.

Over the next few hours, they drifted in and out of lucidity. Sometimes his mother thought he was still a child, marveling at how much he'd grown. Other times she asked for his father, who had passed away years before.

Wally weathered each transition patiently. He knew tomorrow might be a day where she didn't recognize him at all. For now, he cherished every glimpse of the woman she had been.

Later, they sat in the gardens together. Diane smiled softly, face turned up towards the sun. "It's so beautiful here. Peaceful. I think I could stay forever."

Wally swallowed down tears. "I'm glad you're happy, Mom."

She looked at him tenderly. "Of course I'm happy. My son is here." She squeezed his hand.

They sat in silence for a while, watching birds flit from tree to tree. His mother's eyes were clear, her expression serene.

Wally's phone buzzed - an update from Dr. Sanchez about the latest trial results. He felt a flicker of hope. Each step brought them closer to a treatment that would slow the cruel progression of this disease.

His mother turned to him. "Is everything okay?"

He smiled. "Couldn't be better."

She nodded, gazing out over the gardens again. "Such a lovely place to spend the afternoon together," she murmured.

"Yes it is, Mom." Wally blinked back tears, focusing on this moment - her hand in his, the gardens blooming around them. For now, she was still here with him. Wherever this journey led, he would walk it with her until the end.

WALLY SAT BESIDE HIS mother's bed, watching her chest rise and fall with each shallow breath. The beeping of the heart monitor marked the passage of time in the otherwise still room. He studied her face, peaceful for the moment, though he knew that could change in an instant. The ups and downs of her condition left him constantly on edge.

One minute she would be lucid, recognizing him and conversing normally. The next, she would spiral into confusion, speaking to people who weren't there, lost in memories real and imagined. Wally lived for those fleeting minutes when the haze would lift and his mother would return, however briefly.

In those moments, he would cling to her, sharing news, reminiscing, simply sitting in companionable silence. He treasured every second, never knowing which would be the last before she slipped away again into the grasping fog of Alzheimer's.

Wally glanced at his watch. Nearly time for her next dose of the experimental FlexMend-111 formula he had created. He carefully measured out the viscous, amber liquid, filling the syringe. Taking her limp arm gently, he found the vein and slid the needle in, pressing the plunger down slowly.

He watched her face, looking for any reaction. After a few minutes, she began to stir, blinking heavily as she emerged from the depths of sleep. Wally leaned forward, hope rising in his chest.

"Mom? Can you hear me?" he asked softly.

She turned toward him, eyes focusing. "Wally? Is that you?"

Relief washed over him at the sound of recognition in her voice. "Yes, Mom, it's me. How are you feeling?"

"Oh, I'm alright I suppose," she replied, her voice gravelly from disuse. "My mind feels a little less foggy today."

Wally's breath caught. This was the clearest she had been in over a week. A smile broke across his face.

"That's wonderful. I'm so glad to hear that." He squeezed her hand gently. "I've missed talking with you like this."

She returned the squeeze, though hers was weak. "Me too. Sometimes it feels like I'm lost at sea, adrift. But right now, my mind feels almost clear. What day is it anyway?"

"It's Tuesday, May 15th," Wally replied.

"May already? Goodness, how time flies." She paused, brow furrowing. "How long have I been in this place?"

Wally hesitated. "A few weeks now. Since early April."

"Weeks? Has it really been that long?" She looked troubled.

He nodded solemnly. "You've had some rough spells. But you're doing a bit better today it seems."

"Well, I suppose that's something to be grateful for then." She shifted slightly, wincing.

Wally adjusted her pillows, easing her discomfort. They sat without speaking for a few minutes, the silence intimate rather than awkward.

Eventually she broke it, asking, "Have you spoken to your father lately?"

Wally froze. How to answer? Her memory was still hit or miss if she could forget weeks in the care home but recall his father as if still living. He chose his words carefully.

"I haven't spoken to him recently. But I'm sure he'd be happy to see you doing better today."

She nodded vaguely, seeming to accept this. Wally internally sighed with relief at the dodge.

A nurse entered then to check vitals and administer medication. Wally stepped aside, watching closely. So far his surreptitious FlexMend doses seemed to be helping, but he took nothing for granted. His mother's moments of lucidity were hard-won, the result of endless adjustments to the formula.

Each tweak was an agonizing gamble. Too little, and there was no improvement. Too much, and negative side effects emerged. Wally tread the razor's edge, guided only by intuition and love. He had to believe that the answer was out there, somewhere in the intricate dance of proteins, enzymes, and neurotransmitters.

After the nurse departed, Wally resumed his bedside post. His mother gave him a searching look.

"You seem tired, Wally. Are you sleeping alright?"

He huffed a weary laugh. "I'm okay, Mom. Just been busy with work is all."

It was partly true. His regular job kept him occupied during the day, but nights were consumed with researching supplements and poring over his mother's test results. He managed a few hours of sleep when exhaustion forced him under.

She tutted disapprovingly. "You need to take care of yourself. Don't spend all your time worrying about me."

Wally's throat tightened. Even now, lost in the wilderness of her own mind, she was still trying to mother him.

"I'll be alright," he assured her. "It's you I'm focused on right now."

She opened her mouth to respond but was interrupted by a violent bout of coughing. Wally helped her sit up, gently patting her back until the fit subsided. She slumped back against the pillows, spent.

"Sorry about that," she murmured, eyes already drifting closed. "Just...need to rest..."

"It's okay, Mom," Wally soothed. "You rest. I'll be right here if you need anything."

But she was already gone, claimed by the creeping oblivion once more. Wally watched helplessly as her breaths grew deep and regular again. The brief moment of connection was over.

Rising slowly, he gathered his things. Time to get back to the lab. The dose had been too low today; he would have to increase it incrementally for next time. His notes from the past weeks swam through his mind, a mosaic of variables and responses.

There was a pattern there somewhere amidst the noise. He just had to filter it out, synthesize each data point into an optimal formulation. Wally shouldered his bag and cast one last look back at his mother's slumbering form.

"I'll figure this out," he whispered. "Just hold on a little longer."

Whether she heard him or not, he couldn't say. But it didn't matter. He would repeat the promise as many times as necessary until he made it reality. For her sake, he had to.

Wally stepped out into the hall, the monitored door closing firmly behind him. The lights seemed overly bright after the dimness of his mother's room. He blinked, adjusting. Time to get to work. The answer was out there somewhere, and he would find it. Failure was not an option.

As he exited the care facility, the setting sun washed the sky in hues of orange and pink. Wally paused for a moment, letting the fresh air revive him. Somewhere birds chirped. Life went on.

With renewed purpose, Wally headed for his car. The day's dose may not have been optimal, but tomorrow's could be. He would run more tests tonight, recheck his calculations. No giving up now.

Wally drove away, focused on the work ahead. His mother was counting on him. He would find a way to navigate her out of the darkness. One adjustment at a time.

WALLY SAT BY HIS MOTHER'S bedside, as he had done countless times before. Her Alzheimer's had steadily eroded her memories and cognition over the past few years, despite his tireless efforts to find a treatment. On most days now, she hardly recognized him, slipping in and out of lucidity amidst a fog of confusion.

But today felt different. Wally noticed a new alertness in his mother's eyes as he entered her room. She tracked his movement in a way she hadn't done for months.

"Hi Mom, it's me...Wally," he said gently.

To his surprise, she smiled. "Wally...my son."

Wally's heart leapt. It had been over a year since she had called him by name. He grasped her hand, which felt less frail than before.

"How are you feeling today?" he asked, keeping his voice steady despite the emotion welling up inside.

"I'm alright dear. A little tired but my mind feels...clearer." She paused, seeming to search for the right words.

Wally could hardly believe what he was hearing. His latest experimental treatment must have had an effect. But he dared not get his hopes up just yet. Her moments of lucidity never lasted long these days.

His mother looked thoughtful. "You know, I had the strangest dream last night. I dreamt I was young again, back when your father was still alive. We were dancing at our wedding."

Wally squeezed her hand. That wedding photo still hung in the hallway outside, though she hadn't recognized it in years.

"It was so real," she continued. "I could vividly see the flowers, hear the music playing. And your father..." Her voice caught with emotion. "He was as handsome as the day I first saw him."

Wally sat transfixed, hanging onto her every word. She hadn't spoken this much, let alone with such clarity, in longer than he could remember.

Over the next half hour, she shared more memories that surfaced in her dream - raising two young boys, family vacations to the beach, Sunday dinners with grandparents. Every recollection was a small miracle to Wally.

When her energy began to flag, he helped prop her up with pillows. "It's okay Mom, you just rest now. We can talk more later."

She nodded drowsily but managed a smile. "Thank you for visiting Wally. It's been...good to remember."

As she drifted off, Wally stepped out of the room, exhilarated by the visit. His experimental compound, FlexMend-111, had produced the cognitive leap he'd been waiting for. The fog had lifted, at least temporarily, to reveal the mother he knew and loved.

Wally hurried to analyze the latest data, eager to understand the mechanisms behind the breakthrough. In his home laboratory, he pored over brain scans, bloodwork results, and observational notes. After hours of study, he determined that a recent tweak to the dosage and delivery method had likely caused the spike in lucidity and recall.

For the first time in over a year, his mother had emerged from the haze of Alzheimer's. She had recognized her only son and shared treasured memories. It was the confirmation Wally needed - proof that his tireless research could restore faded minds.

He continued fine-tuning the FlexMend formula late into the night, energized by the promise of this development. There was still a long road ahead; one day of clarity did not mean a cure. But it gave him hope.

Over the next two weeks, Wally kept a close watch over his mother's cognition. To his relief, she continued to have periods of improved alertness and memory. They were able to have real, meaningful exchanges - something he had sorely missed. She delighted in recounting stories from his childhood that he thought lost forever.

During a visit, his mother turned to him. "Wally, have I been ill?"

He hesitated. How much should he say? "You've been struggling with memory problems lately. But we've been working hard to help you get better."

She considered this quietly. "Well whatever you've been doing seems to be working. I feel more like myself." She gave his hand an affectionate squeeze.

Wally had to blink back tears. It was working. All the years of research were paying off. He still had much to do, but his mother had been returned to him, if only in glimpses.

He spent as much time with her as he could, embracing every precious moment of clarity. They took short walks around the care facility gardens, basking in the fresh air and familiarity of being mother and son again.

One morning, she turned to him with a knowing look. "You're going to conquer this, Wally. I can see the determination in your eyes."

Her faith in him filled Wally with purpose. He would keep fighting this disease with every resource he had until Alzheimer's took no more memories. His mother's brief respite from its grasp showed him it was possible.

Wally increased FlexMend-111 dosing under careful supervision. Every step brought them closer to restoring his mother's cognition long-term. There were setbacks, but he persisted. Her smile when a memory surfaced made every sleepless night in the lab worthwhile.

The day came when she greeted him by name three visits in a row. For hours at a time, her mind remained clear. Wally knew then that they had turned a corner. The woman he loved was coming back to him.

There was still much work ahead. But as he embraced his mother, for the first time in years her memories intact, Wally allowed himself to celebrate this victory. With steadfast purpose, fueled by love, he had brought her back from the brink. For now, that was enough.

WALLY SAT BESIDE HIS mother at the small table in her room, watching intently as her delicate fingers moved purposefully over the fragmented image. Piece by piece, she assembled the jigsaw puzzle with a look of contented focus, carefully inspecting each part before connecting it to the whole.

The act was simple, yet deeply symbolic. Just weeks ago, those same hands had tremored uncontrollably, barely able to grasp a spoon or cup. Now they deftly manipulated the small cardboard shapes, guided steadily by a mind emerging from the shadows.

Wally could hardly believe the transformation in his mother since he had begun administering the experimental FlexMend-111 treatment. Her once vacant eyes now shone with awareness, and her confused ramblings had given way to coherent conversation. Like the fragmented puzzle taking form before them, her scattered faculties were coming back together.

His mother paused, studying the remaining pieces intently. "This one goes here," she murmured decisively, sliding a piece depicting part of a tree branch into place. Wally smiled, marveling at how she discerned the proper fit based on color and pattern alone. Her spatial reasoning abilities, so badly eroded by Alzheimer's, were rebuilding.

"You're getting really good at these puzzles, Mom," Wally said encouragingly. She looked up at him, eyes crinkling in a smile.

"Well, I have my son to thank for that." She patted his hand tenderly. "I don't know what you did, Wally, but I feel like myself again. The fog is lifting."

Wally nodded, swallowing the lump in his throat. In truth, he could hardly believe FlexMend-111's efficacy himself. After years of obsessive research and testing, his creation was reversing the cruel damage Alzheimer's had inflicted on his mother's mind. But Wally also knew the treatment was still experimental, with more testing required before it could be deemed safe and effective.

"I'm so glad you're feeling better, Mom," he replied. "We'll keep working together to help you get even stronger."

She smiled again before returning her attention to the puzzle. A comfortable silence descended as she focused intently on assembling the image—a photograph of a moonlit forest that she had always loved.

Wally studied his mother's face, noting the clarity in her hazel eyes. The distant, bewildered look that had resided there for so long had been replaced with awareness and recognition when she looked at him. It filled his heart with hope.

After weeks of witnessing her steady decline, barely able to recall his name or her own, Wally had begun to lose faith that she could come back from the brink. But here she was, her nimble mind piecing together reality once again.

With a satisfied sigh, his mother placed the final puzzle piece, completing the serene night scene. She leaned back and observed the finished product, then turned to Wally with a proud smile.

"Your father bought me this puzzle a long time ago. I remember us staying up late to finish it, with hot cocoa and Frank Sinatra playing in the background." Her eyes took on a wistful look. "It's one of my favorite memories."

Wally felt a catch in his throat. "I'm glad you remembered that, Mom," he said hoarsely. For so long, he had watched helplessly as Alzheimer's stripped away her precious memories. Now, piece by piece, they were coming back to her.

His mother reached across and grasped his hand, her touch warm and steady. "I'm so thankful you've been here through this journey, Wally. I know it hasn't been easy." Her eyes glistened with emotion. "But having you by my side has meant everything."

Wally had to turn away for a moment, composing himself. His mother had always been his anchor and inspiration. Seeing her so diminished had shaken him to his core. But now she was emerging from the fog, her light steadily returning.

He squeezed her hand gently. "I'll always be here, Mom. Whatever you need."

She patted his cheek affectionately. "I know you will. You're my guardian angel."

They sat in tranquil silence for a few moments, the completed puzzle between them. His mother ran her fingers over the image, as though committing every detail to memory once again.

Wally considered the long road still ahead. FlexMend-111 would need much more testing and refinement before it could be deemed a cure for Alzheimer's. There would surely be challenges and setbacks to overcome. But right now, none of that seemed to matter. What mattered was this moment—his mother coming back to him.

"Would you like to do another one?" he asked, gesturing to the stack of puzzle boxes on her dresser.

Her face lit up. "I'd love to. Let's do the lighthouse one next. That was always so calming."

As Wally rose to retrieve the box, his heart swelled with love and pride for his mother's resilience. Her light had refused to be extinguished, even when the darkness of Alzheimer's tried relentlessly to snuff it out.

And now, like the fragmented pieces of a puzzle, she was putting herself back together again, one memory at a time. For Wally, it was all the confirmation he needed that his life's work truly meant something. He had given his mother back her life.

WALLY SAT BESIDE HIS mother in the living room, watching her work intently on a 1000-piece jigsaw puzzle of a meadow scene. Her brow furrowed in concentration as she searched for the right piece, fingers tracing over the cardboard edges methodically. Ever so gently, she clicked a piece into place, beaming as the image came together.

"That one was tricky," Wally said. "But you got it."

His mother smiled, her eyes lighting up. "This puzzle is really challenging. But I'm determined to finish it."

Wally nodded, heart swelling. Just weeks ago, she could barely hold a coherent conversation. But his experimental treatment,

FlexMend-111, had begun restoring her cognition and memories. Each day brought more glimpses of the mother he knew and loved.

"We make a pretty good team," he said.

She chuckled. "We always did. Ever since you were little, helping me in the kitchen." Her expression became wistful. "You were such a serious little helper, following every direction precisely."

Wally grinned, recalling their times baking together. "I loved learning from you. Your snickerdoodle recipe is still my favorite."

His mother's eyes misted over. "I remember us baking those cookies every Christmas." She squeezed his hand. "It's so wonderful to look back on those memories together."

Wally blinked back tears, overcome with gratitude. "It really is, Mom."

Just then, the front door opened, and Wally's father came in carrying grocery bags.

"Need any help, Dad?" Wally asked, standing up.

"No need, I've got it." His father set the bags on the counter, then came over to the puzzle table. "This is looking great! You're making excellent progress."

Wally's mother smiled up at her husband. "Wally's been helping me. We make a pretty good team."

Wally's father squeezed his wife's shoulder affectionately. "That you do." He gazed at her with pride and tenderness.

Wally felt his heart swell watching his parents share this moment. After so many months of his mother's confusion and distance, his father's quiet joy at having her back was palpable.

"Dinner will be ready soon," Wally's father said. "I'm making your favorite - pot roast."

"Mmm, I can't wait." His mother turned to Wally. "Will you stay and eat with us?"

"I'd love to," Wally replied.

"Wonderful! Why don't you boys set the table?" She began sorting through the puzzle pieces again.

Wally and his father went into the kitchen, gathering dishes and silverware. As they set places at the table, his father shook his head in amazement.

"I can hardly believe it's really her again," he murmured. "Your mother, clear as day."

Wally nodded. "She's made so much progress. I think the treatment is finally dialed in."

His father's eyes glistened. "Getting moments like these back - it means the world. You gave us a miracle, son." He pulled Wally into a fierce embrace.

They held the hug for a long moment before his father pulled away, composing himself. "Come on, let's get this food on the table before your mother's stomach starts growling!"

Wally laughed. "She did always get hangry waiting for dinner."

They dished up generously ladled pot roast, buttery mashed potatoes, and steamed vegetables. Carrying the platters into the dining room, they called for Wally's mother to join them.

She dutifully added a few more puzzle pieces, then made her way to the table. "My boys know how to cook a delicious meal," she said, sitting down.

They all bowed their heads as Wally's father said a brief blessing. Then they dug in, the clink of silverware and hums of enjoyment filling the air.

Between bites, Wally's mother said, "The pot roast is perfect. Takes me back to all our family dinners over the years."

"All those nights around this table are such special memories," his father replied, smiling tenderly at his wife.

Wally cherished this moment, watching his parents reconnect over a shared meal. It seemed to embody everything he had hoped for when he first administered the experimental Alzheimer's treatment to his mother.

After dinner, they cleared the table together, then sat down for coffee and dessert. His father brought out a tray of snickerdoodles, eliciting a gasp of delight from Wally's mother.

"My favorite!" she exclaimed, taking a cookie and biting into it blissfully. "Mmm...just like I remember. The cinnamon, the soft dough." She shook her head in wonderment. "Absolutely perfect."

"Wally used your recipe," his father explained with a wink.

She turned to beam at her son. "You've always had a gift for baking, Wally. Just like your mother."

They continued chatting over dessert, reminiscing about Wally's childhood and his father's various DIY mishaps around the house. Laughter rang out often, the conversation punctuated by warm smiles and pats on the back.

As the evening wound down, Wally hugged his parents tightly at the front door. His father clapped him on the back. "Thank you for this gift, son. Your mother back again - it means everything."

Wally's mother held his face in her hands. "You've always made us so proud, Wally. I feel so blessed to really remember that now."

Wally left their home with his heart full. Despite the challenges ahead, this evening had been a profound reminder of what truly mattered. Each shared memory, each rediscovered connection was a triumph. He would move forward cautiously but hopefully, treasuring every precious moment with those he loved. For now, Wally allowed himself to savor the joy of having his mother back and their family made whole once more.

Chapter 13

S everal motion alarms had been tripped on Bird Island late
yesterday evening. Wally was at the burn hospital at the time and
could not immediately leave to investigate. He had spent the
afternoon visiting young patients and their families, bringing toys
and words of encouragement. Though it filled him with joy to see the
children recovering with the help of his bandages, he could not fully
relax knowing that the island's security had been breached.

It had been weeks since Wally's last encounter with Marco. After
their previous run-ins, he thought the smuggler had given up on
gaining access to the island's hidden treasures. Marco was as
persistent as he was cunning, and Wally realized he could never fully
let his guard down. The latest alarm was surely Marco's doing. Wally's
mind raced with concern about what the man could be after this
time, and what new tactics he might employ.

At first light, Wally pulled into his parking spot at the FFOne
facility to pick up a FlexiCommander Suit. He had asked Ronnie
to prepare one for him, knowing he would need its protective
enhancements for whatever awaited him on the island. As Wally
walked briskly through the building, Ronnie emerged to hand him a
discreet case containing the suit.

"Be safe out there," Ronnie said, giving his friend a pat on the
back. Though he wished he could join Wally on the adventure, his
leg injury still prevented him from such rigorous activities.

Wally nodded, his expression serious. "I'll scope out the situation
and report back. With any luck, it's just a false alarm." But his gut
told him otherwise.

Within minutes, Wally was airborne in his seaplane Seawings, headed for Bird Island with the case securely stowed onboard. As he flew over the bay's shimmering waters, he mentally prepared for the challenges ahead. Marco was smart and determined, but Wally had the advantage of the island's terrain and his own tactical skills. He would do whatever it took to protect the island's secrets.

FROM A DISTANCE, WALLY circled Bird Island, scanning the horizon for any signs of human activity. His heart raced as he spotted three boats anchored on the northwest tip of the island. He knew that Marco and his crew were up to no good, and he couldn't let them get their hands on the secrets hidden within his underground lab.

Wally set Seawings down on the very opposite tip of Bird Island and secured her to a live oak tree on shore. He unpacked a cookie pack from his backpack and bit into each, feeling the microorganisms begin to infuse his body with superhuman abilities. With renewed strength and speed, he prepared for what lay ahead.

Stashing his backpack in a clump of cordgrass, Wally began to break out his protective suit. He knew that Marco and his crew were dangerous, and he needed all the protection he could get. As he slipped into the suit, Wally felt a sense of confidence wash over him. He was ready for whatever came his way.

WITH HIS VISION GREATLY enhanced by the VAM-365 infused cookie, tracking was a given, he could see by their footprints that they had found the northwest most entrance but had not entered the bunker.

This was one of the most secure entrances to the bunker due to its massive size and strength, it would take them a while to gain entrance if they had tools otherwise this would not be breached soon.

The men, 17 in all, were busy unloading supplies in preparations to setting up camp. They had picked a spot almost in the same location that Jack, Harry, and the Russian had picked years ago. This was good for Wally, some distance from the bunker and their boats, making it hard to watch all at the same time.

Wally hoped to discourage them, scare them off, make them uncomfortable, not confront them, to stay out of sight adding to the mystery and confusion, even if it took days to do so.

Keeping his distance, Wally observed the smugglers establish their camp. He noted the locations of their tents, supply crates, and perimeter markers. With his enhanced vision, he could make out details from afar - the men's weapons, the contents of opened crates, even whispers between those on watch.

Wally's seaplane was well hidden on the opposite side of the island. He had landed in a sheltered cove, concealing the aircraft with camouflaging netting. Before trekking to spy on the smugglers, he had consumed one of the special cookies containing VAM-365. Its effects were already apparent, with his vision sharper and hearing more acute. He anticipated these would be critical assets for his covert operation.

As dusk fell over the island, Wally put his plan into motion. He silently approached the smugglers' camp, moving stealthily between trees and boulders. At the edge of their site, he applied a malodorous paste to a few branches. It contained sulfur compounds that would waft through the camp, creating an unpleasant stench.

Next, Wally crept towards the supply crates. He carefully opened one filled with food and water. Reaching into his pack, he retrieved a small vial of liquid laxative, which he proceeded to inject into the jugs of drinking water. Satisfied with his work, Wally slipped away undetected into the growing darkness.

Over the next few hours, Wally continued his campaign of subtle sabotage and psychological tactics. He rigged fishing lines with bells that would create eerie sounds around the smugglers' tents as the wind blew. Using luminescent algae, he painted phantom-like figures on trees. He even released a swarm of insects he had gathered, sending the biting midges to plague the unwelcome visitors.

As Wally observed, his efforts were already taking effect. The smugglers swatted at the air, complained of odd smells, and made more frequent trips to relieve themselves in the woods. He could see their frustration and apprehension mounting. Still, Wally knew driving them off the island might require days of carefully orchestrated incidents.

The next day, the smugglers awoke irritated, exhausted, and on edge. They had passed an unsettling night, disturbed by strange noises, smells, and creatures. As they emerged from their tents, an ominous fog now shrouded their camp.

Wally watched from a bluff as the men argued about what to do next. He had created the mist by dispersing water through a network of pipes hidden among the rocks. The man called Marco shouted that they should continue their mission, while others insisted on leaving this cursed place.

As the smugglers debated their next move, Wally maintained his concealed position. He was cautious not to take actions that could reveal his presence on the island. Marco eventually declared they would stay one more night.

Wally realized he needed to escalate his scare tactics for the coming night. As the smugglers reluctantly continued preparations for their operation, Wally withdrew to gather more supplies and plan his next moves. Night would fall again soon, and with it, his chance to implement the next phase of his plan.

Under the cover of darkness, Wally made his way back toward the smugglers' camp. He had prepared a variety of new tricks and traps to unleash, all designed to prey on their superstitions and fray their nerves. Approaching stealthily, he could already hear the agitated voices of Marco's men.

Wally began by triggering loud cracking sounds around the perimeter. He then activated a device which emitted low-frequency vibrations that induced uneasiness.

As the night wore on, even Marco's stubborn resolve showed signs of weakening. The strange events continued, including eerie music that seemed to come from everywhere and nowhere. Wally even used the cover of darkness to slip into a supply tent and remove the batteries from their electronics.

THE SMUGGLERS' BOATS, three formidable vessels bobbing placidly in the island's secluded bay, were momentarily forgotten by their owners. The men were too preoccupied with the enticing enigma of the southeast bunker entrance, their curiosity whetted by the unyielding steel door and the secrets it held. Wally watched from his hidden vantage point, taking advantage of their distraction.

With stealth that belied his bulky frame, Wally made his way towards the boats. The moonlight was a double-edged sword; it provided just enough illumination for him to navigate the terrain without alerting the smugglers. He was a phantom in the night, blending into the dense vegetation that fringed the shoreline.

Wally approached the first boat, a sizable craft capable of ferrying half of Marco's crew. With deft hands and a focused mind, he disabled its motor. A small victory smirk played on his lips as he moved to the next one, a slightly smaller but equally sturdy vessel.

Once again, his hands worked with practiced efficiency, leaving the boat as useless as a fish out of water.

Of the three boats, only the smallest remained operational - an intentional choice by Wally. He could already envision the ensuing chaos; seventeen burly men crammed onto a boat meant for eight, struggling to maintain balance and ward off capsizing.

Back in his hidden perch, Wally turned his attention to Marco and Javier. They were hunched over by the bunker entrance, trying to break its lock with rocks and anything else they could find in their desperate quest for access. Their persistent attempts stirred a swirl of questions in Wally's mind - why had they returned? Were they here to smuggle or pilfer hidden secrets?

A rustling sound drew his attention away from the scene. A nutria scurried through cordgrass nearby, triggering a memory. Wally recalled the Microorganism #10, a remarkable formula that granted the ability to comprehend and communicate with certain animals. He had only used it once, an experiment to understand the symphony of bird calls in his backyard.

Now, he realized, it might serve a greater purpose. He fished out a cookie from his backpack, its dough imbued with Microorganism #10. He nibbled at it, the sweet taste belying the potent change it would trigger within him.

The effect was immediate and staggering. The cacophony of nighttime sounds morphed into distinct voices. He could hear the chirping crickets discussing their next meal, the rustling leaves whispering tales of the wind, and more importantly, the low grunts of the nutria nearby.

Wally reached out mentally to the nutria, asking for its help. The creature paused in its scurrying, its tiny eyes looking up at Wally in understanding. With newfound allies and heightened senses, Wally prepared to unravel the smugglers' plans and protect his beloved Bird Island.

UNDER THE DIM TWILIGHT, Bird Island appeared more mysterious than ever. Its rugged shoreline and dense vegetation were a dark silhouette against the evening sky. Among its many secrets, the island housed the two smugglers, Marco and Javier, as they hunkered down in their makeshift base at the bunker entrance labeled "M1". They were oblivious to the extraordinary spectacle about to unfold.

At Wally's command, nutria, a local rodent species known for their keen sense of direction and adaptability, emerged from the shadows. They moved in unison like an organized army. Their eyes glinted in the low light as they scampered toward the M1 entrance where Marco and Javier were engrossed in their devious planning.

The sound of hundreds of tiny feet rustling through the undergrowth echoed through the night. Startled by the noise, Marco and Javier spun around to face a surreal sight. A swarm of nutria stood at the entrance, their bodies silhouetted against the moonlight.

As if choreographed, every single nutria turned towards Marco and Javier. For a moment, they held their gaze steady on the two men who looked back in bewilderment. Then, as if obeying some invisible command, all the nutria bowed synchronously before vanishing into the darkness.

The spectacle left Marco and Javier spooked. Their hearts pounded in their chests as they exchanged nervous glances. Without uttering a word, they sprinted towards their boats moored on the shoreline. Their hurried footfalls echoed through the silence of Bird Island as they made a desperate dash for escape.

However, when they reached their boats, they found them disabled beyond repair. Oars were missing; engines were sabotaged; fuel was drained. Their eyes widened in shock as they realized they were stranded on Bird Island - alone and helpless.

Their initial panic gave way to an eerie silence as they processed their situation. Their escape plan had been thwarted, their illicit activities disrupted. The men found themselves at the mercy of Bird Island and its mysterious guardian, their dreams of establishing a covert drug smuggling base shattered.

As they stood on the shoreline, their breaths ragged and hearts still pounding, they felt the weight of their isolation. The darkness around them seemed to close in, making the island appear even more daunting.

Wally, from his vantage point, watched as Marco and Javier grappled with their predicament. He had successfully used the nutria to spook the smugglers and had sabotaged their only means of escape. His actions had thrown a wrench in their illicit operations and left them stranded on Bird Island.

His heart pounded with a sense of victory. But he knew this was just the beginning. He had managed to disrupt their operations for now, but Marco and Javier were cunning and ruthless. They wouldn't give up easily.

Wally gazed at the island he had vowed to protect. The battle was far from over. As he prepared for what lay ahead, his resolve hardened. He would stop at nothing to protect Bird Island from those who threatened its tranquility.

Meanwhile, Marco and Javier huddled together on the beach, staring out at the dark expanse of water that separated them from mainland Texas. They were stranded on an island with no means of escape and an unseen enemy who had successfully outmaneuvered them at every turn.

The events of the night replayed in their minds - the swarm of nutria bowing in unison, their sabotaged boats - all pointing towards an adversary who was both cunning and resourceful. Their clandestine operation had been upended in ways they hadn't anticipated.

For now, they were prisoners on Bird Island - an ironic twist to their initial plan of using it as a covert base for their smuggling operations. They were alone, stranded, and helpless, left to face the mysteries of Bird Island and its unseen guardian.

THE SEAGULLS FLUTTERED about the shoreline, their raucous calls echoing across the expanse of Bird Island. Wally Eastwood approached one of the birds with an air of purpose. His hazel eyes were filled with determination, a contrast to the usual softness they held. He communicated with the bird, a bond formed through Microorganism #10.

The gull squawked, cocking its head at him before spreading its wings and disappearing into the distance. The sky turned into a flurry of white feathers and squawking cries as dozens of other gulls appeared, creating an aerial spectacle that had a hypnotic rhythm to it.

Not far away, Marco Alvarez and Javier Rodriguez stood transfixed, their faces reflecting confusion and apprehension. Their roughened hands clutched at each other, their breath hitching in their throats as the birds swooped closer. The wind carried the sharp cries of the gulls to them, filling their ears with a disconcerting cacophony.

Suddenly, like an orchestrated dance routine, the swarm descended upon them. Their cries grew louder, a symphony of chaos that sent shivers down the men's spines. The men tried to swat them away, but there were too many.

Their rough voices filled with fear echoed across the island as they turned to run. Their boots slipped on the damp soil, sending splatters of mud flying behind them. Their eyes were wide with panic as they ran blindly into the dense cordgrass.

The gulls pursued relentlessly, their caws growing louder and more aggressive. Javier stumbled first, his broad-shouldered frame crashing into the tall grasses. Marco wasn't far behind, his dark eyes wide with fear as he tripped over his partner's fallen body.

Lying on their backs in the cordgrass field, they could do nothing but shield their faces from the flurry of feathers and claws. The gulls swooped down on them, their caws filling the air with a deafening sound. Exhausted and overwhelmed, the two men could do nothing but lay there, hoping for an end to this aerial onslaught.

Wally watched from a distance, his face stoic. His heart pounded in his chest, but he felt a strange sense of calm wash over him. He had communicated with the birds, used them as allies to defend Bird Island from the smugglers.

As the gulls eventually dispersed, leaving behind two worn-out men lying amidst the cordgrass, Wally knew he had managed to send a clear message to the intruders. His island was not to be trifled with. The two smugglers, their bodies bruised and battered, looked around in dazed confusion. The echo of the gulls' cries still hung in the air, a stark reminder of what they had just endured.

The sun began its descent in the sky, casting long shadows across Bird Island. Wally watched as Marco and Javier slowly picked themselves up from the ground. Their bodies were stiff from their ordeal, their faces etched with confusion and fear.

He knew they wouldn't forget this day anytime soon. The island had defended itself, through its guardian and his avian allies. As night began to fall on Bird Island, Wally retreated back into his solitude, leaving behind two men forever marked by their encounter with nature's defenders.

As Marco and Javier stumbled back towards their remaining boat, their minds raced with questions and fears. They had come here seeking refuge for their illicit activities, only to be met with an island that fought back. Their initial plan had been foiled, leaving them unsure of what to do next.

As they drifted, pushed by the wind, away from Bird Island under the cover of darkness, they couldn't shake off the feeling of unease that settled deep within them. The echo of squawking gulls still rang in their ears, a haunting reminder of the island's defenses.

Meanwhile, Wally stood on the shoreline, watching the boat disappear into the distance. The island was quiet once again, its tranquility restored.

UNDER THE GLARING MIDDAY sun, Bird Island had returned to its natural state. Wally had painstakingly erased all signs of human disturbance, leaving only footprints that would soon be washed away by the tide. The flora and fauna were once again the island's sole inhabitants, and an air of tranquility had been restored.

He had tucked away the FlexiCommander Suit with practiced efficiency, folding it into a compact bundle that belied its immense protective capabilities. His fingers traced over the material, lingering for a moment on the TitanThread-X10 boots he'd crafted with such precision. As he secured the suit in its protective case, he cast one last look over the serene landscape of Bird Island.

Aboard Seawings, his reliable ICON A5 aircraft, Wally performed a pre-flight check with meticulous attention to detail. Satisfied with the aircraft's condition, he climbed into the cockpit and adjusted his headset. As he started up the engine, Seawings came alive beneath him. He took a deep breath, relishing in the familiar vibration that resonated through his seat.

He gently guided Seawings off the choppy bay and into the sky. Below him, Bird Island grew smaller until it was just a green speck surrounded by a sea of blue. Setting his heading northeast, he allowed himself a brief moment of satisfaction before focusing on the journey ahead.

Upon landing back home, Wally dedicated himself to maintaining his beloved aircraft. With practiced hands, he wiped down Seawings' exterior, ensuring no trace of saltwater or sand remained. Each stroke was an act of care and respect for the machine that had faithfully carried him through countless journeys.

His next stop was FFOne—the facility now under Ronnie's capable management—where he securely stored away the FlexiCommander Suit. It was nestled among other remarkable inventions—each one a testament to their shared commitment to protect and preserve.

Inside the bustling plant, Ronnie greeted him with a firm handshake and a warm smile. The two friends caught up on recent developments, their conversation punctuated by the rhythmic hum of machinery. Ronnie updated Wally on the facility's operations, his voice carrying the familiar tones of responsibility and dedication.

Just as he was about to leave, a familiar face appeared from behind a row of workstations. Richie—Wally's childhood friend and co-discoverer of the Bird Island bunker—emerged, wiping his hands on a grease-stained rag. Seeing Wally, his eyes lit up, and he approached with a wide grin.

The two old friends exchanged greetings, reminiscing about their teenage years spent exploring the island's hidden secrets. Despite the passage of time, their shared memories of Bird Island remained vivid—a testament to the bond forged in the bunker's shadows.

As the day drew to a close, Wally headed home, his mind filled with thoughts of Bird Island's defense and his ongoing projects at FFOne. He knew that each day brought new challenges but also fresh opportunities to make a difference. Guided by his dedication to safeguarding Bird Island and furthering scientific advancements, he looked forward to what tomorrow would bring.

THE WEIGHT OF THE PAST months had carved a certain fondness in Wally's heart for Dr. Sanchez. Their shared professional respect had morphed into a friendship, subtly laced with a sense of affection that was hard to ignore. Wally was aware of this transformation, and maybe it was time he let her into a piece of his world that had always remained secluded.

With that thought in mind, he reached for his phone, the number to Dr. Sanchez already saved on speed dial. His heart drummed against his chest as he heard the line connect, and soon enough, her voice echoed from the other end.

"Hello, Wally," Dr. Sanchez's voice came through the phone, professional yet warm.

"Hello, Elena," Wally responded, "I was thinking about something..."

His words trailed off for a moment before he gathered his thoughts. "You know about Bird Island, right? I was wondering if you'd like to see it first hand this weekend."

Silence stretched between them as he awaited her response. It wasn't every day that he invited someone to Bird Island. The place held secrets and memories only known to him.

Dr. Sanchez's laughter tinkled through the silence, breaking it apart with its warmth. "I'd love to see Bird Island," she said. Her words carried an undercurrent of excitement that made Wally's heart leap.

They spent the next few minutes discussing logistics before hanging up. The anticipation of sharing Bird Island with Dr. Sanchez stirred something inside him. He felt a certain lightness that had been missing for quite some time.

As the weekend neared, Wally prepared himself for their expedition to Bird Island. He checked the conditions of his ICON

A5 aircraft and stocked it with necessities. He imagined showing Dr. Sanchez the beautiful landscapes and secret hideouts of Bird Island - his own personal haven.

The day finally arrived when he would be sharing a piece of his world with someone he cared for. The morning was bright, and the wind was gentle - perfect for their trip. He met Dr. Sanchez at the local airport, and they both embarked on the journey to Bird Island.

As they soared above the clouds, Wally couldn't help but steal glances at Dr. Sanchez. Her eyes were wide with awe, and her lips curled into a smile as she took in the beauty of the sky.

Once they landed on Bird Island, Wally led her around, showing her the places that held a special place in his heart - the old military bunker, the streaks of chalky clay, and the occasional sandy beach area.

They spent the day exploring the island, sharing laughter and stories. Wally felt an indescribable joy in showing Dr. Sanchez around Bird Island. For once, he wasn't alone on this piece of land that had witnessed so many of his solitary moments.

As the sun started to set, they settled down on a sandy patch, watching as the golden rays of sunlight danced on the water surface.

The day had been more than what Wally had hoped for. Sharing Bird Island with Dr. Sanchez was like unveiling a part of himself that he had kept hidden for so long.

As they sat there in comfortable silence, Wally looked over at Dr. Sanchez. Her face was lit up by the soft glow of sunset, and she seemed lost in thought. It was in that moment that Wally realized just how much he cherished her presence in his life.

Bird Island had never felt more alive than it did in that moment. With Dr. Sanchez by his side, Wally felt an unusual sense of contentment wash over him - one that he hadn't experienced before.

With their day on Bird Island coming to an end, Wally felt grateful for this shared experience with Dr. Sanchez. As they prepared to head back, he hoped that this was just the beginning of many more shared moments between them. Little did he know, his life was about to take an unexpected turn.

WALLY EXPERTLY PILOTED the seaplane back towards the mainland as the sun began to dip below the horizon, casting a warm golden glow across the sky. He and Dr. Sanchez sat in a comfortable silence, both reflecting on the day's events.

The trip to Bird Island had been enlightening for both of them. For Dr. Sanchez, it was an opportunity to see firsthand a place that clearly held great meaning for her trusted colleague. She was honored that Wally had chosen to share the island's secrets with her, and it deepened her respect for the man beside her.

As for Wally, bringing Dr. Sanchez to Bird Island had felt natural, despite its status as his own private sanctuary. Her intellect and ethical principles had earned his admiration long ago, but today he realized that his feelings ran deeper. Her delight in exploring the island was infectious, and he found himself noticing little details - the way she brushed her hair from her face, how her eyes lit up at a discovery.

Wally had always valued keeping his work and personal life separate. Bird Island was the one place where his scientific mind could rest, where he was simply himself. Yet being here with Dr. Sanchez, he realized that compartmentalizing his life in this way was perhaps an unnecessary burden. As the boundaries softened, he felt a sense of peace and wholeness.

The seaplane landed smoothly, and Wally taxied it expertly up beside his hangar. He secured the aircraft then helped Dr. Sanchez collect her belongings before disembarking. Making their way up to the hangar, neither was in a rush for this day to end.

Wally unlocked the side door to the hangar office and flipped on the lights. The space was meticulously organized, with various aviation charts and maps hanging neatly on the walls. He offered Dr. Sanchez a seat while he quickly filed his flight plan.

"Thank you again for today, Wally," Dr. Sanchez said. "Bird Island is really quite remarkable. I appreciate you welcoming me into your world."

Wally smiled warmly. "Of course. I'm glad you enjoyed the visit. It's a special place for me, but sharing it with you somehow made it even better."

A touch of pink colored Dr. Sanchez's cheeks, and she averted her gaze for a moment before meeting his eyes again. "Well, it's been a wonderful day. But I should probably let you get home to your family."

Wally nodded, though he felt a pang of reluctance. "Let me walk you to your car," he offered.

The sun had now slipped below the horizon, and a few stars were just visible in the violet sky. Cicadas hummed in the trees around the airfield, greeting the night. Wally and Dr. Sanchez made their way slowly across the tarmac, neither quite ready to say goodbye.

They reached her car, and Dr. Sanchez placed her bag on the passenger seat. Turning back to Wally, she suddenly stepped forward and embraced him. Wally wrapped his arms around her, savoring the warmth of the moment.

As they parted, Dr. Sanchez reached up and gently kissed Wally on the cheek. "Thank you," she said softly. "For everything."

Wally's cheek tingled where her lips had been. He reached for her hand and gave it a squeeze. "Elena, I..." His voice trailed off, uncertain of the right words.

Dr. Sanchez's dark eyes were tender. "I know," she said. "Let's talk soon."

Wally nodded, his heart brimming. He stepped back and watched as Dr. Sanchez started her car and pulled away, giving him a small wave before turning onto the road leading back to the city.

Alone under the emerging stars, Wally replayed the day's events in his mind. Visiting Bird Island with Dr. Sanchez had awakened something in him, though he couldn't yet give it a name. All he knew for certain was that he wanted to see where this new path might lead.

Wally returned to the hangar, tidied up his office, and locked the door. Getting into his own car, he drove home through the darkened countryside, windows down and radio off. His thoughts were filled with images of Bird Island and quiet moments shared with Dr. Sanchez.

Wally awoke before sunrise, the events of yesterday still fresh in his mind. The aroma of coffee wafted through the quiet house as he brewed a pot, eager to begin the new day. Settling into his favorite armchair, he cradled the warm mug in his hands and allowed his thoughts to drift back to Bird Island. More specifically, back to Dr. Sanchez.

Elena. Her name echoed in his mind, conjuring up vivid memories from their day together. The way she leaned in close to examine a specimen, her unabashed curiosity and keen intellect lighting up her features. The feeling of her hand resting gently on his arm as they navigated the rugged terrain. Her radiant smile when he showed her the hidden grove of rare orchids. He recalled it all in perfect detail, like scenes from a treasured film.

Wally shook his head, chuckling softly at himself. He couldn't remember the last time he had been so preoccupied with another person. But there was something about Elena that had awoken feelings and desires that he'd long kept dormant and focused on his work. For the first time in years, he felt the stirrings of possibility, of a new path unfolding.

Glancing at the clock, Wally was surprised to find it was nearly 10 AM. The morning had slipped by in a reverie of contemplation about yesterday and anticipation of what lay ahead. Swallowing the last sip of coffee, now lukewarm, Wally headed to his small home office and sat down at the orderly desk. He opened his planner, scanning the upcoming weeks. A smile spread across his face as an idea began to form.

Picking up the phone, Wally dialed the number he knew by heart. It rang three times before a familiar voice answered. "Dr. Sanchez speaking." Hearing Elena's voice sent a little flutter through Wally's chest. "Good morning Elena, it's Wally Eastwood." "Wally! It's wonderful to hear from you. How are you today?" Elena sounded genuinely glad to hear from him. Wally hoped he wasn't calling too soon. "I'm doing very well, thank you. Listen, I wanted to ask if you were free next weekend. There are some parts of the Bird Island bunker I've yet to fully explore, and I thought you might like to join me on another expedition."

There was a pause on the line, and Wally felt a twinge of nervousness creep in. "I'd love to!" Elena finally replied enthusiastically. "I've been thinking a lot about our trip to the island. I'd really enjoy helping uncover more of its secrets." Wally exhaled in relief. "That's great news. I'm looking forward to it too." They discussed dates and travel plans, Wally jotting down notes. As they were about to end the call, Elena spoke again, her voice warm. "Thank you for thinking of me, Wally. Bird Island is such a special place - I can't wait to discover more of its wonders together."

Wally's heart swelled at her words. "Me too, Elena. I'll call you with more details soon. Have a great rest of your day." After exchanging goodbyes, Wally carefully replaced the handset, scarcely able to contain his excitement. An entire weekend of adventure and discovery awaited them on Bird Island. But more importantly, more time to deepen his connection with this extraordinary woman who had captivated him, mind and spirit. The days couldn't pass quickly enough.

Wally leaned back in his chair, gazing out the window with a renewed sense of anticipation. The future, once defined solely by his work, now held the promise of so much more. And he had Dr. Elena Sanchez to thank for awakening that realization within him. Wally smiled to himself, his thoughts returning to the island getaway and the joy of her company. For now, that was enough to sustain him. The rest could wait until they were exploring the bunker together, secrets revealed in more ways than one.

WALLY, HUNCHED OVER his workbench, was engrossed in the final inspection of a freshly assembled FlexiCommander Suit. The hum of his well-lit lab was his sole companion, its white noise a comforting soundtrack to his work. He reveled in the isolation, his thoughts ricocheting between the intricacies of the suit's construction and the imminent arrival of Dr. Elena Sanchez.

The weekend had dissolved into a blur of prototypes and blueprints, with Wally's mind unable to stray far from Elena. She had a way of seeping into his thoughts, a warm presence that anchored him amidst the flurry of his work. But it wasn't until midweek that someone noticed the subtle change in him.

During a routine visit to FFOne, Ronnie had paused mid-conversation, eyeing Wally with a discerning gaze. "Wally, somehow you seem different, everything ok?" he asked, curiosity tinting his voice.

Wally turned away from the FlexiCommander Suit he was inspecting and met Ronnie's gaze. His eyes twinkled with an unspoken excitement as he replied, "Ronnie, things are more than ok." He gave Ronnie a reassuring pat on the shoulder before diving back into their latest batch of suits.

As Friday loomed closer, Wally found himself in an unfamiliar territory. Anticipation twisted knots in his stomach as he pictured Elena stepping off Commuter Air's plane at Austin Executive Airport. He imagined her professional demeanor giving way to surprise as she took in the cityscape from above.

His heart pounded as he envisioned her exit from the plane, hair windblown and eyes sparkling with curiosity. He could see her scanning the tarmac for him amongst the bustle of baggage handlers and ground crew members.

With each passing moment, his eagerness grew until it became an insistent thrum beneath his skin. Wally found himself checking the clock more often than necessary, the hands seeming to crawl at an agonizing pace. He found it difficult to concentrate on his work, his mind continuously wandering back to Elena.

His usual routine seemed to drag on endlessly. He found himself pausing frequently, lost in daydreams of Elena's arrival. Each tick of the clock brought him closer to the moment he would pick her up from the airport, a thought that sent waves of anticipation coursing through him.

Finally, Friday arrived, bringing with it a crispness that hinted at the onset of fall. Wally could hardly contain his excitement as he prepared for Elena's arrival. He set aside his work early, spending extra time grooming himself and choosing a suitable outfit for their reunion.

As he finally set off for the airport, Wally could hardly believe how quickly the week had passed. He was a bundle of nerves and excitement as he navigated the familiar route, each mile bringing him closer to Elena.

The hum of his car's engine did little to drown out his thoughts. His heart pounded in time with the rhythm of the road, every beat echoing Elena's name. His palms were sweaty against the steering wheel, a testament to his mounting anticipation.

As he neared the airport, Wally could hardly wait to see Elena again. The anticipation had built up over the past week, and now it threatened to consume him. His heart pounded in his chest as he parked his car and made his way towards the terminal.

Every second felt like an eternity as he waited for her plane to land. He paced nervously, casting anxious glances towards the runway every few seconds. His heart skipped a beat every time a plane came into view, only to resume its frantic pounding when he realized it wasn't hers.

Despite his anxiety, Wally couldn't help but smile at his predicament. He was about to reunite with Elena and nothing else mattered. He knew the wait would be worth it, and he couldn't wait to see her again. As he stood there, lost in his thoughts, Wally was filled with a sense of contentment. He was exactly where he wanted to be, waiting for the one person who made him feel complete.

Chapter 14

Bird Island appeared on the horizon, a jewel of greenery in the endless expanse of blue. As Wally maneuvered the ICON A5 aircraft, aptly named Seawings, toward the island, his eyes flickered with anticipation. Dr. Elena Sanchez sat beside him, her sharp gaze taking in the approaching landmass with a mixture of curiosity and wonder.

In the cockpit, the drone of the Rotax 912 engine was a steady backdrop to their conversation. They exchanged ideas about what they might discover on Bird Island, their voices laced with excitement and an underlying current of tension. This wasn't just a weekend getaway; it was a chance to further explore their shared passion for science and innovation.

As Seawings touched down gently at the southeast tip of Bird Island, a sense of adventure swept over them. The aircraft bobbed lightly on the water as Wally cut off the engine. The sudden silence was replaced by the soothing sound of waves lapping against the hull and distant bird calls echoing from within the island.

They unloaded their gear: extra clothes, food and water supplies, and bedrolls for their stay. Among these essentials was a container filled with special cookies—Wally's secret weapon against potential threats or unexpected situations. His past experiences had taught him to always be prepared for anything on Bird Island.

Stepping out onto one of Seawings' planing wingtips, Wally jumped down into the warm water. The shallow water around Bird Island was a clear turquoise hue that allowed him to see his feet sinking into the sandy bottom. Elena followed suit, her practical nature overtaking any apprehension about wading ashore.

Their journey to shore was slow and deliberate, each step measured to avoid disturbing any marine life that might be lurking underfoot. It was a surreal experience, wading from sea to land on an island brimming with mystery and history. The whispering cordgrass seemed to greet them as they finally set foot on dry land, their clothes damp but spirits undeterred.

Wally's heart pounded with a mix of exhilaration and nostalgia. For him, Bird Island was more than just a place—it was a part of his identity. The old military bunker, the WWII structures, the low ridge that ran the length of the island—all were familiar landmarks etched in his memory.

Beside him, Elena was a study in fascination. Her eyes roamed over the island's features, her scientist's mind cataloging details and making mental notes. This was her second time on Bird Island, but her eager curiosity made it seem as if she was reuniting with an old friend.

The first day on Bird Island drew to a close with a stunning sunset that bathed everything in a warm, golden glow. As Wally and Elena set up camp for the night, they exchanged stories and laughter under the star-studded sky. Despite the lingering anticipation of what lay ahead, they found comfort in their shared passion and companionship.

Bird Island held many secrets—some known only to Wally, others yet to be discovered. As the pair settled into their bedrolls for the night, they were unaware of the exciting discoveries and challenges that awaited them. Yet, for now, all was peaceful under the protective cover of night on Bird Island.

ELENA AND WALLY HAD both drifted off to sleep early last night. It had been a long week for both of them, and each needed a good rest. They had found it on Bird Island, quiet and peaceful. Wally hoped it would stay that way.

Wally woke first and, building a small campfire, put on a pot of coffee. Elena, smelling the brew, was soon up and waiting on her first cup of the day.

Donning military-style clothing more suitable for exploration, they prepared to enter the bunker shortly after a quick breakfast.

It was not yet 5 AM, but the bunker did not care. It was dark day or night.

They approached entrance "E3," Wally's favorite entrance, and went inside.

Wally switched on his headlamp, casting a bright beam down the concrete corridor. He glanced back at Elena, her face shadowed and serious in the dim light. "This way," he said, leading her down the passage.

Their footsteps echoed off the walls as they descended farther into the earth. The air grew cooler and drier, with a musty undertone. Wally inhaled deeply, comforted by the familiar scent.

After several turns, they arrived at a heavy steel door. Wally spun the wheel lock and heaved it open with a resonant creak. Beyond lay a cavernous chamber, empty save for dust and shadows. Elena followed him inside, sweeping her light over crumbling control panels and equipment racks.

"What was this place?" she asked, voice hushed in the oppressive stillness.

"Some kind of operations center, from the look of it," Wally replied. He crossed to a bank of cracked monitors. "Most of this tech is ancient, but a few systems might still work."

He pressed a button, and lights flickered on with a hum. Elena blinked in the sudden glare, taking in details she had missed before.

Diagrams and maps covered the walls, interspersed with gauges and screens. She peered at a schematic showing the island and surrounding waters.

"This must have been a surveillance station of some kind," she mused.

Wally nodded. "My guess is military, back in the Cold War days. There are other clues deeper in that suggest..."

A scraping sound cut him off. They both froze, ears straining. After a tense moment, Wally gestured for quiet and drew his flashlight. He swept the beam over the room methodically, finding nothing. Elena watched the dark doorways, pulse racing.

Wally touched her shoulder and pointed to a vent high on the wall. The cover hung askew, and scratches marred the metal surface around the screws.

Elena let out a shaky breath. "Just an animal. Nothing to worry about."

Wally gave a tight smile. "Probably right. Still, we should keep alert down here. Never know what we might run into."

They moved on, checking offices and storage bays. Most were empty, aside from useless debris and thick layers of dirt. In one room, heavy scuff marks disturbed the grime on the floor. Elena spotted them first, waving Wally over.

"Could be from explorers like us," he said after inspecting them. "Or maybe kids looking for trouble."

Elena frowned. "Seems awfully remote for bored teenagers."

"You'd be surprised. I've caught a few over the years trying to sneak onto the island." Wally's expression turned serious. "Usually they just want to poke around, prove how tough they are. But every now and then..."

He trailed off, gaze distant. Elena studied him for a moment. "You're worried they're not just kids."

Wally focused on her again. "I've dealt with certain...unscrupulous people in the past. Smugglers, mercenaries. This bunker has things they'd kill to get their hands on."

"What kinds of things?"

"Old tech, mostly. Experimental weapons, stealth systems. There's a prototype submersible down on level three that..." Wally hesitated, seeming to catch himself. "Well, let's just say the less people know, the better."

Elena nodded slowly. She had suspected there were secrets here that Wally kept even from her. Glancing around the decrepit room, she wondered what purpose it had all once served. What clandestine plans had taken shape in this buried maze, hidden from the world above?

She shook away the thoughts. Whatever its past, the bunker's mission had ended long ago. They pressed deeper into the complex, finding a medical bay with examination tables and glass-fronted cabinets. Elena's gaze fixed on one containing rows of vials and syringes.

"Any idea what they were testing?" she asked.

Wally scanned a chart on the wall. "Hard to say. Could be vaccines, experimental treatments. Maybe even..."

He hesitated, and Elena gave him a sharp look. "Maybe even what?"

Sighing, Wally met her eyes. "I probably should have told you sooner. There's evidence they were studying ways to enhance human abilities. Higher strength, senses, intelligence."

Elena's brow furrowed. "How?"

"A variety of methods. Special diets, mental conditioning, biochemicals. Some of it ties into very advanced research on..." He faltered, seeming to catch himself again.

Elena stepped closer. "Research on what, Wally?" she pressed.

He held her gaze for a long moment. "Microorganisms," he said finally. "There are certain organisms on this island with...unexpected effects."

Elena's eyes widened. Wally had hinted about unique organisms before, but always in vague, cryptic terms. Her mind spun with the implications.

Before she could respond, a sharp crack split the air. They whirled toward the sound as more cracks followed, echoing through the bunker. It took Elena's adrenaline-spiked brain a moment to identify them as gunshots.

Wally was already moving, taking her hand and pulling her toward a side passage. She ran with him, heart pounding wildly. The gunshots continued, along with shouting voices drawing closer. Elena's only thought was reaching safety, though she knew nowhere was truly safe with armed intruders in the bunker.

They sprinted down utility tunnels, the staccato bangs ringing from behind. Suddenly Wally pulled up short, throwing out an arm to stop Elena. Flashlight beams danced ahead where the tunnel ended at a larger passage. The voices filtered from that direction, along with crisp bootfalls.

Trapped between the searchers ahead and the gunmen behind, they pressed into the shadows of a maintenance alcove. The beams drew steadily nearer, probing the tunnel. Elena held her breath, willing herself invisible.

Beside her, Wally shifted. Before she could react, he hurled something down the tunnel toward the bobbing lights. A moment later a concussive blast rocked the passageway, sending Elena's ears ringing. Choking smoke billowed up, and the flashlight beams whipped wildly.

Wally yanked her back the way they had come. They ran hard, lungs burning from smoke and fear. Elena's mind reeled with questions, but survival eclipsed all else. The gunshots had ceased, yet she knew the threat remained.

They reached a heavy steel door and slipped through into a small chamber. Wally secured the door, then sagged against the wall, chest heaving. Elena tried to slow her own gasping breaths. Her limbs trembled with adrenaline aftereffects.

"What...what was that?" she managed between gulps of air.

Wally's face was grim. "Trouble I hoped we'd never see again. Come on, we need to get somewhere safe."

Pushing off the wall, he crossed to a locker. Elena watched numbly as he retrieved a small duffel bag and a utility belt holding a holstered pistol. He checked the gun expertly, glancing up at her.

"I know you have questions. I promise I'll explain everything, but right now we need to focus on getting out of here." His tone brooked no argument.

Elena nodded mutely. Wally handed her a flashlight and small backpack. "There's an emergency exit through the ventilation system. We'll have to squeeze through some tight spaces. You okay with that?"

"Lead the way," Elena replied, surprised at the steadiness of her own voice.

Wally gave a terse smile. "That's my girl." He pulled open a vent cover. "Stay close. No matter what happens, we survive this together."

SOON ELENA IN TOW BEHIND Wally exits the bunker via an emergency escape hatch "Observation Point Egress". Wally pauses, and extracts from his backpack a strip of cookies, red, blue, orange, and violet. He turns to Elena and says, "I need you to trust me. Eat these cookies and you'll gain abilities that will help us get through this."

Though perplexed, Elena trusted Wally completely. She took the strip of cookies and examined the different colors curiously. Wally broke each cookie in half and handed her the halves. "The red ones will give you immense stamina, the blue ones enhance your memory, the orange provides tracking abilities, and the violet allows you to hear at extreme frequencies," Wally explained.

Elena consumed the cookies without hesitation, chewing slowly to savor the flavors. At first she felt no different, but then a tingling sensation spread throughout her body. Her senses became sharper, her mind clearer. She could hear the rustling of animals far in the distance and zeroed in on a conversation happening a mile away.

"Your abilities are activating," Wally said, noticing the shift in Elena's demeanor. "Stay close behind me. We need to get back in there."

Elena nodded, feeling energized and ready for whatever lay ahead. She followed Wally closely as he led her back into the bunker through the hidden escape hatch. Now with her enhanced senses, she noticed details she had missed before - markings on the walls, hollow spaces behind panels, the sound of scurrying mice.

As they walked through the corridors, Elena could hear two men talking in a room up ahead. She signaled this to Wally using hand signs she instinctively knew from her military training. Wally's face told her he heard them too. They approached cautiously, hugging the wall just outside the room.

Elena felt no fatigue despite their extended physical exertion. Her mind was sharp, her vision precise enough to detect the slightest motion. When a rat darted across the hall ahead of them, she tracked its path effortlessly in the darkness.

Wally held up a fist, indicating for them to pause. Through the doorway, two armed men in fatigues were examining crates of artifacts. "These old experiments could be worth millions to the right buyer," one said.

Wally turned and whispered almost silently to Elena, "Military smugglers. They must have followed us. We need to lay low."

Elena nodded in agreement, impressed by how clearly she could hear Wally despite his volume. She noticed a ventilation shaft 20 feet back and tapped Wally, signaling toward it.

They silently maneuvered closer to the shaft until they were directly underneath it. Wally formed a stirrup with his hands to give Elena a boost up. She placed one foot in his hands and, with his help, reached up and pulled herself into the metal shaft. Despite using only her upper body strength, she felt no strain.

Once inside, she reached down and helped Wally up. They crawled through the narrow space, careful not to make a sound. Elena tracked the movements of the smugglers, listening to make sure they weren't followed.

After some time, Wally stopped at a grate that opened into a small storage room. He slowly unscrewed the grate, setting it aside before hoisting himself down. Elena dropped down beside him, landing lightly in a crouch. They appeared to be in an old munitions supply room, lined with dusty crates and barrels.

Wally cracked open a crate and sifted through straw padding, uncovering glass vials. "More experimental serums," he murmured. "We need to keep these from the smugglers."

He opened his pack and gently placed several vials inside before closing the crate again. Elena kept her senses tuned for any approaching threat. Her hearing and vision remained sharply enhanced.

Wally led the way to a corner of the room where a large cabinet stood. He moved it aside, revealing a hidden trap door in the floor. "This should take us outside," he told Elena.

The trap door opened to reveal a ladder descending into darkness. Wally climbed down first. Elena followed, closing the door above them. At the bottom was a tunnel sloping upward. They followed it until fresh air flowed in.

Emerging from brush, they found themselves outside the bunker's perimeter. Elena scanned the surroundings, spotting the smugglers' camp hidden in the trees.

"The coast looks clear," she told Wally. "But they can't be far."

Wally nodded. "Let's move quietly and get to my plane. Stay sharp."

They set off through the dense cordgrass, retracing their steps from earlier. Elena's energy and focus remained steady thanks to the cookies' lasting effects. She monitored for any indication of the smugglers as morning sunlight streamed down through the canopy.

They were nearly to the southern tip of the island where Wally had left his seaplane concealed. He turned and gave Elena an impressed smile. "You're a natural with those new abilities. We make a good team."

Elena smiled back, feeling closer to Wally than ever. She was grateful for his trust in sharing such a monumental secret with her. Together, they would ensure it did not fall into the wrong hands.

WALLY TURNED TO ELENA, his face etched with concern. "Elena, you can outrun, outswim, stay underwater for minutes with those special cookies, but you can't stop a bullet. Please stay here, I have to stop these men."

Elena started to protest, but Wally was already moving swiftly towards the southeast bunker entrance labeled E3, the closest to his hidden laboratory. She watched his retreating figure until he disappeared from view.

Wally entered the bunker, senses heightened. He made his way carefully through the dim passages, following the faint sounds of the intruders shuffling around, searching the chambers. Gripping his bag of vapor grenades, he crept steadily closer.

Rounding a corner, Wally could make out two figures up ahead rummaging through storage crates. He paused, considering his options. The men seemed unaware of his presence. Keeping to the shadows, Wally selected one of the non-lethal grenades. He pulled the pin and rolled it towards the men, then swiftly retreated a safe distance.

A loud bang resounded in the enclosed space, followed by surprised shouts and coughing. Wally peered around the corner to observe the results. The men stumbled around in a disoriented state before collapsing unconscious on the floor.

IN THE HUSHED SILENCE of the bunker, Wally moved like a shadow. He drew upon his knowledge of the labyrinthine layout, turning it into an advantage. The dormant chambers echoed with a history that now served his purpose, concealing his movements as he set up a snare for the smugglers.

He pulled from his pocket an assortment of grenades, their sleek forms holding a promise of chaos. A quick check confirmed their readiness - pull the pin, and havoc would follow. With practiced ease, he attached them to thin, nearly invisible wires and began rigging them at each exit point. The result was an invisible web of devastation waiting to be triggered.

Wally's eyes, hardened by years of strategic warfare and high-risk operations, swept over his work. The once-secure exits now held a lethal surprise for anyone attempting to leave. Each step could be their last; each breath could trigger an explosion that would disorient and incapacitate them.

With the trap set, Wally retreated into the bunker's depths. His plan was simple yet effective - force the men to endure the grenade effects repeatedly as they tried to escape. And if that failed? Well, he had a contingency plan.

Wally reached into his pocket again, this time pulling out a small device resembling a remote control. With a flick of a switch, the bunker was plunged into darkness. He knew the layout like the back of his hand; every twist and turn etched into his memory. But for the smugglers? They would be like blind mice in a maze.

A sinister smile crossed Wally's face as he retreated further into the shadows. The thought of Jack and Harry stumbling around in the dark brought him a sense of satisfaction he hadn't felt in a while. This was their game now; their survival hinged on navigating through a dark maze rigged with explosive surprises.

Back in the main chamber where Marco and Javier lay unconscious, the silence was deafening. The bunker seemed to hold its breath, waiting for the inevitable chaos to ensue. As Wally watched from his concealed position, his heart pounded with anticipation.

He knew this was just the beginning of a long night. He was ready to defend Bird Island at all costs. His plans were in motion, and there was no turning back. It was a game of survival now - a game he intended to win.

But even as he reveled in his preparations, Wally's mind wandered to Elena. He remembered her eyes widening in surprise as she took her first bite of the special cookie, the look of awe on her face as she discovered her enhanced abilities. Her courage and determination had left him impressed.

For a moment, he allowed himself a brief respite from his strategic mindset, indulging in the memory of Elena's smile. But as quickly as it came, the moment passed. He shook off the distraction, refocusing on the task at hand.

This was not a time for distractions; it was a time for action. And so, armed with a plan and determination forged in the fires of conflict and adversity, Wally waited for Marco and Javier to awaken.

Their fate lay within the darkened corridors of the bunker - corridors filled with disorientation, fear, and an unyielding guardian who would stop at nothing to protect his island. The stage was set for a confrontation that would test their mettle against his resolve.

The darkness seemed to grow thicker with each passing second as anticipation hung heavy in the air. The only sounds were the occasional drips of water from somewhere deep within the bunker and Wally's steady breathing.

And so began a dangerous game of cat and mouse within the confines of Bird Island's forgotten relic - a game that would determine who held dominion over this secluded haven.

WALLY EXITED THE SOUTHEAST bunker entrance labeled "E3", carefully closing the heavy steel door behind him. He blinked a few times, adjusting to the bright midday sun after being in the dimly lit underground corridors. Glancing around, he saw no immediate signs of activity or intruders in the dense foliage surrounding the entrance. Wally moved swiftly but silently through the brush, making his way along the familiar forested path to the rendezvous point he had set with Elena earlier.

As he walked, his mind raced over the events that had just unfolded in the bunker. He had managed to incapacitate the group of smugglers who had broken in using non-lethal vapor grenades. They would be unconscious for some time, giving Wally a window to further secure the bunker and destroy any evidence that might reveal its secrets. He was relieved his countermeasures had been effective, but knew the threat was far from neutralized. Marco and his crew were persistent and would be back. Wally would need to be ready.

He spotted Elena up ahead, waiting anxiously near a copse of trees that hid their makeshift campsite. Her face flooded with relief when she saw him emerge unharmed from the forest. Wally quickly crossed the remaining distance and gave her a reassuring hug.

"It's done, they've been handled for now," Wally said, keeping his voice low. He rapidly updated Elena on what had transpired in the bunker, including the smugglers' infiltration and his use of vapor grenades. "They'll be out long enough for us to cover our tracks and get off the island safely," he told her.

Elena listened intently, her scientific curiosity mingling with her concern for Wally's safety. "Will they return?" she asked pointedly. Wally nodded grimly.

"Almost certainly, but I have a plan to discourage them from further smuggling activity here," he replied. There was much more to discuss, but their first priority was clearing any trace of their presence on the island.

Wally led Elena to the clump of trees that concealed their small campsite. They had only been on the island for two days, but had already accumulated an array of supplies and equipment. Wally swiftly gathered up their tents, sleeping bags, cooking gear, and other belongings, packing them efficiently into a large duffel bag.

"Grab anything we might have left behind," he instructed Elena. She did a quick sweep, collecting stray items like flashlights, insect repellant, and a first aid kit. Soon, their campsite showed no signs of recent human habitation.

Wally lugged the heavy duffel bag containing all their gear down to the shoreline. With a mighty heave, he launched it into the gentle surf where it floated just offshore, bobbing up and down with the waves. "That should keep our stuff safe until we can collect it later," he said. He had anchored the bag so it would not drift far.

The only trace of their camp that Wally left behind was a water canteen, which he carefully placed in the center of the former campsite. Tipping the canteen to his lips, he quickly gulped down the remaining water and refilled it from a bottle of magnesium citrate laxative mix he had brought along. Wally shook the canteen, mixing in the laxative, and loosened the lid so some would spill out.

"Now it looks like someone dropped this as they hurriedly left with the rest of the gear," Wally remarked with satisfaction. He and Elena retreated deeper into the brush, finding a concealed vantage point where they could observe if anyone approached their former campsite.

They did not have to wait long. Within fifteen minutes, they heard the sounds of people tramping clumsily through the forest, cursing and coughing—clear signs the smugglers had regained consciousness and exited the bunker as Wally had anticipated. He tensed, ready to act if needed, as the voices drew nearer.

Through a screen of leaves, Wally and Elena watched as two smugglers emerged into the clearing, Marco and his right-hand man Javier. "Looks like someone was just here!" Javier exclaimed, rushing over to pick up the water canteen. He guzzled thirstily from it as Marco looked around in confusion.

"Spread out and search for any sign of who was here!" Marco ordered the others. But soon their search was interrupted by the effects of the doctored water beginning to set in. One by one, the smugglers rushed back into the forest to relieve themselves, leaving Marco and Javier alone and perplexed at the abandoned campsite.

Wally allowed himself a small smile of satisfaction. The laxative had worked perfectly. He and Elena remained hidden, listening as Marco and Javier debated what to do next. They clearly did not understand what had happened to their crew. Wally's knowledge of the island had allowed him to turn its resources into an effective deterrent.

Soon the sounds of the searching smugglers grew fainter as they retreated back to the beach, too sick and disoriented to keep looking. Wally knew he and Elena would need to move quickly, before the men could regroup and cause further damage. The island's secrets had been preserved for now, but at a cost. The sanctuary he had known since boyhood was now marked by this conflict.

WALLY'S MIND RACED as he recalled the ingenious traps he had built years ago to protect Bird Island from intruders. Harry had been relentless in his pursuit of the island's secrets, forcing Wally's hand. Now, new trespassers threatened Wally's sanctuary once again.

It was time to put his skills to use. Wally set to work gathering materials from around the bunker - old wires, sturdy wooden planks, rusted spikes and screws. His hands moved with precision and purpose as he assembled tripwire snares designed to incapacitate, not kill. Seven traps in all, each one nestled cleverly into the landscape across paths and trails leading to and from the bunker.

Wally stepped back, visually scanning the area. The traps were undetectable, seamlessly blending into the surroundings. He was satisfied knowing any trespasser would trigger them, immediately immobilized by the spring-loaded arm swinging out to strike their legs. Escape or further access would be impossible. The island's secrets would remain secure.

Elena watched Wally work, marveling at his ingenuity. She too wanted to protect this sanctuary from the smugglers who sought to exploit it. Together, they took up position hidden among the trees, waiting and listening for signs of intrusion. The morning sun rose higher as the day progressed uneventfully. But they remained vigilant, patiently keeping watch over the island they both cherished.

As dusk fell, Wally's acute hearing picked up sounds coming from the northwest shore. He motioned to Elena - someone was approaching by boat. Adrenaline flooded their bodies as they swiftly moved into position, their eyes and ears trained on the bunker's entrance. This time, the threat was real. Now it was time to see if their preparations would be enough to defend Bird Island once more.

UNDER THE HUSHED VEIL of night, Wally and Elena crouched behind a cluster of dense bushes, their eyes locked on the shadowy figures inching closer to the bunker. Each step the intruders took was an intrusion, a violation of the island's serene solitude. Wally's fingers twitched at his side, itching to spring into action. Beside him, Elena's sharp gaze never wavered from the approaching trespassers.

Among them was Javier, his hulking form recognizable even in the dim light. His eyes scanned the terrain, missing nothing but understanding little. Unbeknownst to him, he was mere steps away from a hidden sentinel. With a blind faith in his brute strength and misplaced confidence, Javier marched forward and triggered the trap.

In an instant, the quiet of Bird Island shattered. The trap sprung to life with an alarming speed and precision. The spring-loaded arm, a mechanical viper in hiding, lashed out, striking Javier just below the kneecap. A gasp ripped through his lips as he was unceremoniously swept off his feet and thrown onto the ground.

Panic erupted among the group like a startled flock of birds. They scattered in all directions, their composure crumbling under the weight of unexpected assault. But amidst this chaos, an unexpected ally emerged from Bird Island's quiet inhabitants.

A rustling in the underbrush announced their arrival before they came into view - nutria. Dozens of them scurried forth, their beady eyes gleaming in the moonlight and sharp teeth bared. To the uninitiated eye, they were harmless creatures; to those standing on foreign soil with guilt lining their hearts, they were an unforeseen threat.

Like a living wave of fur and claws, they washed over the invaders' boots and gnawed at their heels. Their sudden onslaught added fuel to the fire of confusion, transforming it into a bonfire of fear. The smugglers stumbled and retreated, their shouts echoing through the island's silent expanse.

In the chaos, Wally and Elena remained as still as the age-old trees surrounding them. There was no gloating in their victory, no triumphant grins exchanged. Only the understanding that they had managed to protect Bird Island for one more night. Their gaze followed the retreating figures until they disappeared into the darkness, swallowed by the same shadows that had spit them out.

With the imminent threat dispelled, the nutria retreated back to their burrows, leaving behind a battlefield marked by trampled grass and disturbed earth. Wally and Elena emerged from their hiding place, their faces illuminated by the moonlight that filtered through the dense canopy above.

There was still much to be done - traps to be reset, defenses to be reinforced - but for that moment, they allowed themselves a pause. They stood amidst the silent symphony of nature, taking in the untouched beauty of Bird Island. It was a fleeting moment of peace, a quiet victory before another day's battle. And with the rising sun, they would be ready to defend it once more.

WALLY'S EYES BLINKED open, his mind awash in the gentle haze of the predawn hours. The question of whether he had slept at all was an elusive one, lost somewhere in the folds of the previous night's events. A fine layer of perspiration clung to his skin, evidence of the heightened state induced by the infused cookies he had consumed.

Normally, such a whirlwind of activity would have taken its toll on him, grinding him down until he waved the white flag in surrender. But these were not normal circumstances, and the cookies were not ordinary baked goods. Each bite had released a rush of energy into his bloodstream, giving him a stamina that defied human limits.

The taste of those cookies still lingered on his tongue—rich chocolate mingled with a hint of something indefinable, an ingredient that took a simple confection and transformed it into a source of superhuman endurance. They had fueled both him and Elena through the long night on Bird Island.

Elena—her name brought a smile to Wally's face as it always did. She had been an equal partner in their nocturnal escapades, matching him step for step with an energy that was astounding. The same fortified cookies had infused her with a boundless vitality that never seemed to wane. Together, they had turned what could have been a grueling ordeal into an unforgettable adventure.

The memories of their shared night on Bird Island glowed warm in Wally's mind. He replayed each moment, from their daring defense against intruders to their mutual triumph when they succeeded in driving them away. The image of Elena standing beside him, fierce and determined under the moonlit sky, was one he would cherish forever.

The night gradually receded, giving way to the subtle lightening of dawn. With it came a new day on Bird Island—an island that held more significance now than ever before. Wally and Elena had defended it together, creating a bond that neither of them would forget.

Rising to greet the day, they made quick work of their breakfast, a simple meal that tasted like victory. The sun had barely broken the horizon when they decided to bathe in the island's shallow waters. The cool touch of the sea was a welcome contrast to the tropical heat, washing away the grime and fatigue of the previous night.

They stepped into the water, allowing it to envelop them in its embrace. The gentle lapping of waves against their skin served as a soothing balm, healing the scrapes and bruises they had incurred during their adventure. As they bathed in the early morning light, Bird Island bore silent witness to their shared triumph—a testament to their courage and determination.

The rising sun painted streaks of gold across the sky, heralding the start of a new day. It was a beautiful scene, yet its beauty paled in comparison to the sight of Elena emerging from the water, her skin glistening under the golden light. For Wally, it was a sight more breathtaking than any sunrise.

Their laughter echoed through the island as they splashed water at each other, a playful exchange that further cemented their bond. Their shared night on Bird Island had been one of danger and excitement, but also one filled with moments of joy and camaraderie. It was a night they would always remember—a night that had transformed Bird Island from a mere location into something far more meaningful.

The sun continued its ascent in the sky, casting long shadows across Bird Island. As Wally and Elena stepped out of the water, their eyes met in silent understanding. They had faced adversity together and emerged victorious. They were no longer just visitors on Bird Island—they were its protectors.

As they began another day on this island paradise, Wally knew that whatever challenges lay ahead, he and Elena would face them together. After all, they had already proven that they were a formidable team, capable of overcoming even the most daunting obstacles.

The island basked in the warm glow of the morning sun, a silent sentinel to the bond forged between Wally and Elena. It was more than just an island now—it was a testament to their shared experiences, a symbol of their resilience, and a beacon of hope for future challenges.

With the memories of their unforgettable night still fresh in their minds, they welcomed the new day on Bird Island. Despite the trials they had faced, they found joy in their shared victory and anticipation for what lay ahead. As they faced the rising sun, their smiles mirrored the golden light, reflecting a shared resolve to protect Bird Island at all costs.

ELENA CURIOUSLY ASKED, "Wally, how long does this effect last?"

Wally replied, "Sometimes four or five days, on average maybe 3, until it's completely out of your system."

"Interesting," she replied.

Wally and Elena packed up their camp, removing all traces of activity. They checked their gear and entered the bunker.

Wally believed they needed to use hallway HW-900 to find the submarine. He and Elena were excited about what they could find within the mysterious vessel. They easily navigated the dark bunker, their vision still enhanced from the special cookies.

Soon the submarine came into sight. Its sleek blue form beckoned them closer, promising secrets yet to be discovered. Wally ran his hand along the smooth exterior, marveling at the advanced craftsmanship. Elena examined the conning tower instruments, amazed by the sophisticated technology.

Wally opened the hatch and they climbed inside. The interior was compact yet efficient, built for function over comfort. Elena investigated storage lockers while Wally inspected the controls. "This is incredible," Elena murmured, engrossed in examining logbooks and artifacts.

Suddenly a loud bang reverberated through the hull. Wally and Elena exchanged startled looks. "What was that?" Elena whispered. Wally held up a hand, listening intently. Then came the unmistakable sound of voices.

"Smugglers," Wally mouthed. Moving swiftly, he took Elena's hand and led her toward the aft compartment. They had to hide before the intruders discovered them. Wally's mind raced, focused on protecting Elena and the submarine's precious secrets. This unexpected development would require quick thinking and resolute action. For now, stealth was their ally as they silently slipped into the shadows.

WALLY AND ELENA CROUCHED silently in the shadows, hidden behind a large piece of equipment as the loud bang echoed through the expansive submarine bay. Peering around the edge, they spotted two smugglers entering the area, glancing around shiftily as they discussed their plans in hushed voices.

Wally's eyes narrowed as he focused his enhanced hearing, picking up the smugglers' conversation.

"This old sub is perfect for moving major product," one smuggler said. "No one even knows it's down here. We can load it up, head out to the rendezvous point, and be back before anyone's the wiser."

The other smuggler nodded. "Good thing the boss sent us down here to scope out the situation after those other idiots failed. This place is a goldmine!"

Wally tensed, realization dawning about the scale of their plans. This was no small-time operation - they aimed to use this historical submarine and the secrecy of the bunker to run a massive smuggling route right under the noses of the authorities. He exchanged a look with Elena, seeing his own steely resolve reflected in her eyes. They had to stop this, no matter the cost.

As the smugglers approached the submarine, Wally held his breath, hoping his modifications would do their work. He had rigged the hatch to trigger a disabling vapor when opened, buying him time to deal with intruders without harming them.

Sure enough, the hatch released a burst of hazy gas as soon as one smuggler pulled it open. Coughing and wheezing, the men staggered back, collapsing onto the floor as the non-lethal formula quickly incapacitated them. Wally felt a swell of satisfaction - the traps had served their purpose.

After the effects wore off, the groggy smugglers picked themselves off the floor. "Let's get out of here - this place is bad news!" one declared. They hurried from the submarine bay, disoriented and shaken by the strange experience.

Wally and Elena emerged from hiding, relieved that the criminals had fled - for now. But they knew the operation was larger than these two men.

As the pair quickly exited the submarine bay, heading down a narrow passage, they suddenly heard shouts and curses behind them. The smugglers must have inadvertently triggered another vapor trap that Wally had set up! He grabbed Elena's hand and they rushed onward, weaving through the maze-like tunnels.

They turned a corner and Wally spotted a rusted ladder heading up to a stone hatch - a possible escape route! He helped Elena climb up before following, pushing open the hatch to reveal a small, hidden alcove with an exit to the island through a camouflaged doorway.

"This must have been an emergency exit from the submarine bay," Wally whispered. After making sure the passage was clear, they slipped outside into the moonlit night, putting distance between themselves and the underground tunnels.

Wally took a deep breath of the fresh sea air, relieved to have escaped the close call unscathed. He turned to Elena, who gave him a smile of gratitude.

"That was close, but we got what we needed - information," she said. "Now we can take steps to prevent them from misusing that submarine."

Wally nodded. "We have the advantage of knowing their plans. We'd better get back to camp - we have lots of planning to do."

They set off together under the stars, a new sense of purpose fueling their steps. The serenity of the island at night contrasted with the chaos they had just encountered. But Wally knew that tranquility was an illusion - there was much work ahead to safeguard the bunker's secrets and protect his beloved Bird Island. With Elena by his side, he felt ready to take on any challenge.

The next morning, as golden light filtered into the tent, Wally outlined his ideas to sabotage the smuggling operation.

"If we damage the contraband, they won't transport it," he explained. "I can rig a timed explosive to go off after they load their contraband. It will destroy the goods without harming anyone."

Elena considered this. "That could work. But we should also set up surveillance to identify the players involved. That way we can completely dismantle the organization."

Wally smiled. "I like the way you think! We can place hidden cameras around the shoreline where they dock their boats. Let's gather some supplies from the bunker and get to work."

Soon they were fully engrossed in their mission. Wally programmed the detonator while Elena set up the discreet cameras, camouflaging them skillfully with vegetation. At dusk, they finished their preparations.

Sitting by the fire, they ate a simple meal, needing no words. A newfound understanding existed between them, forged by their harrowing experiences over the past few days. Wally felt Elena's steady presence reassuring, giving him renewed vigor.

As the days passed, they vigilantly monitored the surveillance feeds. Sure enough, a pattern emerged - the smugglers arrived on a rotation to load up the submarine with illegal cargo. Wally and Elena allowed this to continue, biding their time.

Finally, the day came when the submarine was fully loaded. Under the cover of darkness, Wally slipped into the bunker and set the timed explosive, praying their plan would work. Then he joined Elena outside to watch the surveillance feeds.

At dawn, the smugglers arrived to transport their precious cargo. As they prepared to depart, a massive explosion suddenly split the air, erupting from the bunker's hidden depths. The criminals shouted in shock and anger as their entire shipment went up in flames.

From their vantage point, Wally and Elena observed the disarray. "It worked!" Elena said. "Now let's get out of here before they come looking."

They raced to the plane and took off swiftly, leaving the criminals to deal with the charred remains of their operation. As they flew over the island, Wally was filled with bittersweet relief. Though not yet safe, Bird Island had survived another threat thanks to their efforts.

He reached over and squeezed Elena's hand affectionately. Together, they would continue the fight to protect this sanctuary and its secrets - no matter the cost.

WALLY PILOTED THE ICON A5 expertly over the coastal waters as he and Dr. Sanchez made their way back from Bird Island. The early morning sun glinted off the wings of the seaplane as it cruised smoothly through the sky.

Dr. Sanchez sat in the co-pilot's seat, gazing out at the scenic view below. "It's so beautiful up here," she remarked. "I can see why you love to fly."

Wally smiled. "There's nothing quite like it. The freedom, the views...it's incredible."

He glanced over at his passenger. "Thanks for coming out to the island with me. It was really special to share that place with you."

Dr. Sanchez returned his smile warmly. "I'm glad I could see it. You've protected something very special there."

Wally cleared his throat, suddenly feeling shy. "So, I was wondering...would you like to meet my parents when we land? I've told them a lot about you and I think they'd love to have you over for dinner."

Dr. Sanchez looked surprised but pleased. "I'd love to meet them," she replied.

Wally grinned, thrilled that she had accepted. As they approached the landing strip, he expertly guided the seaplane down, its pontoons lightly kissing the water's surface.

After securing the aircraft in its hangar, Wally led Dr. Sanchez over to his Hyundai Santa Fe. He held the passenger door open for her before climbing into the driver's seat. Soon they were cruising down the country roads leading to his childhood home.

Pulling up the gravel driveway, Wally took a deep breath. Dr. Sanchez gave his arm a reassuring squeeze.

As they entered the cozy house, the smell of roast chicken wafted through the air. "Mom, Dad, we're here!" Wally called out.

His mother, Nell, came bustling into the room, her face lighting up when she saw them. "Wally, so good to see you!" She gave him a big hug before turning to Dr. Sanchez with a warm smile. "And you must be Elena! I'm so happy to finally meet you."

Wally's father, William, followed close behind, shaking Wally's hand firmly before greeting Dr. Sanchez. "We're glad you could join us for dinner," he said sincerely.

The four of them soon sat down to eat, chatting comfortably as if they had known each other for years. Nell kept their plates full of delicious food while William asked thoughtful questions, wanting to learn more about their work together.

After dinner, Nell packed up generous leftovers for Wally to take home. "You're welcome here anytime, Elena," she said fondly. Dr. Sanchez was touched by the genuine warmth and care she had received.

Saying their goodbyes, Wally and Dr. Sanchez got back into the SUV for the drive home. "Thank you for inviting me, that meant a lot," said Dr. Sanchez. Wally just smiled, happy she had connected so well with his parents.

Wally faces Elena and asks, "Would you remain overnight?"

Elena responds, "Wally, I would be delighted to."

As the Santa Fe disappeared down the road, the sleek submarine waits patiently in its hidden underwater bay on Bird Island, ready for its Guardian's return.

Epilogue

As Wally, Elena, and Robert stood united on Bird Island, their living fortress thriving around them, they reflected on the extraordinary journey that had brought them to this point. Their story was one of innovation, courage, and the unyielding pursuit of knowledge - a tale that had begun with a simple yet revolutionary discovery.

In the first book of the series, **"Powders to Microorganisms,"** Wally Eastwood, a brilliant young scientist, had stumbled upon a groundbreaking find on Bird Island. Hidden within the island's unique ecosystem were microorganisms with unparalleled potential - microscopic wonders capable of enhancing human abilities in ways never before imagined. Alongside his childhood friends, Pug and Richie, Wally had embarked on a quest to unravel the secrets of these extraordinary organisms.

Their adventures had led them to the second installment, **"Powders to FlexiCommander,"** where Wally's ingenuity had given birth to a revolutionary piece of technology - the FlexiCommander Suit. Powered by the island's microorganisms, this cutting-edge armor had become a symbol of their commitment to harnessing innovation for the greater good. As they navigated the challenges of bringing this creation to life, Wally and his team had grown not only as scientists but also as guardians of the island's secrets.

Here, in **"Powders to BandAids,"** we find ourselves at the beginning of a new chapter, where the seeds of discovery sown in the island's soil have blossomed into a revolution in the realm of medicine. The microorganisms that once granted enhanced